MELODIES OF THE DAMNED

CROWNS OF GODS AND MONSTERS
∽∾ BOOK 1 ∾∽

NAKITA KIRWAN

MELODIES OF THE DAMNED

© February 2026 by Nakita Kirwan

Ebook ASIN: B0G528CWJN

Paperback ISBN: 978-0-646-73331-9

First Edition

Self-Published

Cover Design & Formatting: Ivy @ Hawthorn & Aster (www.hawthornandaster.com)

Editing: Twinflower Manuscript Services

*I ONCE THOUGHT THE ABSENCE OF LOVE
CREATED EVIL.*

I WAS WRONG.

IT WAS BETRAYAL.

CONTENT WARNING

Melodies of the damned is a dark fantasy romance intended for 18+. Reader discretion is advised.
Dark themes and sexual content are present in this novel.
While this book is a work of fiction, your mental health is important to me.
Please check the trigger warnings before you step into the dark.
Happy reading

Trigger warnings

- Violence
- Abuse
- Explicit sexual content
- Death
- Drowning
- Mention of rape
- Torture
- PTSD
- Panic attacks
- Suicidal ideation
- Self-harm
- Psychological trauma
- Abuse of trust
- Panic attacks
- Dubious consent
- Possessive behaviour
- Captivity/ Captor romance
- Sacrificing
- Blood play
- Loss of self

For the people worried about what the world will think.
Stop hiding.
If the world can't handle you...
Find the monster who'd burn the world with you,
and fuck you senseless in the ashes.

ONE
THE BROKEN PRINCESS

My heels clicked against the polished marble like a countdown I couldn't escape. Each step echoed like a cry for help that no one would answer. After all, broken things were not worth saving. The guards tracked my every movement, following each restless pace of the corridor. The sound of my dress hissing against the ground behind me only made my blood rush faster through my veins. Everything would change tonight, and I knew they were waiting for me to run. *Again.*

I spun on my heel, circling away from the staircase that yawned like a mouth, waiting to swallow me into the ball below.

Tonight, the court would raise their glasses in celebration. Their princess was finally serving a purpose. My hand in marriage would strengthen my father's alliance with the south, but I did not share the Kingdom's excitement. Nor did I care for political gain. Honestly, I'd be thrilled if Father's Kingdom crumbled, burying him and his precious priest along with it. But a princess does as she is told. Being the pliable, delicate thing they wanted me to be was the only way to escape. So, I took deep breaths. But it was cut short by the corset I had been shoved into against my will. I tugged at the blue silk cinched too tightly around my ribs, as if loosening it might free me from my birthright. If only it were that easy.

Run. Run. Run.

I stilled. The whispers bled from the empty corridor, clawing through my mind with a chill that tore gooseflesh from my skin.

"I will when the time is right," I muttered, turning to grip the cold iron bars of the window separating me from freedom.

"What was that, Princess?"

I peered over my shoulder at the burly guard wearing my father's armour. He crossed his arms over Stonebriar's emblem: two swords clashing over a crown. Funny how every man longed for a crown, yet most seemed too weak to wield it. My father was far from weak, which was why he had held the crown for thirty years, a record in the history of our Kingdom.

"You were speaking to thin air again," the guard said, glaring at me as if my madness was contagious.

"Perhaps it is *you* who is hearing things," I replied sweetly, turning back towards the window.

"Crazy bitch," he said in a hushed tone to the other guard, who stifled a laugh.

I bit my tongue, fighting the urge to scream at them. No, I needed to bide my time. To smile politely and be a good little puppet.

Once, I had read that love makes a person whole, and in its absence, evil grows. Perhaps that was why darkness churned beneath my skin like the tides battering the cliffs below.

The Dead Sea thrashed against the snowcapped cliffs in the dying light, pulling a longing ache from my chest. It was like the sea had hooked its claws beneath my skin and squeezed.

In mere hours, that cliff would hold the sacred rite of Ascension. Not that I was allowed to attend. I'd been kept inside my gilded cage since I was twelve, after I had run away from my guards, pulled by the waters' allure, and touched the Dead Sea.

To touch the Dead Sea outside Ascension was to die. It was the god's curse. For a thousand years our Kingdom had carried that curse. But I didn't die. Father had the guard who witnessed it hung. I was to never talk of it again.

"You look perfect, Lyra." Aldric appeared in the reflection of the frost-kissed windowpane.

I startled, dropping my hands from the bars of my prison to greet my brother.

His dark blond hair was neatly combed back, and his brown eyes held mine with quiet concern before flicking away. He adjusted one of his cufflinks, shifting uncomfortably. Aldric was the perfect prince, not one thing out of place. His suit was a flawless cage of starched fabric that he enjoyed wearing.

I forced the delicate, hollow curve of my lips that never reached my eyes. The soft smile seemed to make me more palatable, hiding the monster they tried to bleed from me.

"It is time for you to join us, dear sister. Your betrothed has arrived."

Reluctantly, I dragged my eyes from the sea to take my brother's outstretched arm.

Aldric's grip tightened as we walked towards the staircase, a gesture I assumed was meant to ease my nerves. It didn't.

"Please behave, Lyra. Just for one night," he murmured, his voice barely audible above the music and chatter that grew louder with each step. "We need this alliance."

I wanted to scoff.

But no, a princess *behaves*. Or more scars would blemish my skin.

"No, Aldric. It's every night for the rest of my life," I said, my voice laced with venom.

He sighed, leading me down the wide marble steps.

The ballroom spread out like a golden wound below us, bleeding wealth and glittering with false promises. Candlelight shimmered in crystal chandeliers, catching on the wine-stained lips of southerners and the sharpened smiles of northern nobility. A rare sight, but they were not here just to witness my forced engagement.

No, this was the Ascension Ball. Everyone was here to celebrate before the sacrifices began at midnight. Sacrifices to Gods who had turned their back on us.

Laughter threaded through the string ensemble like poison as eyes tracked my descent. Whispers slithered from below, hissing of the mad, silver-haired princess. I wondered if they were real or from my own unravelling mind. It was hard to tell at times.

"Smile," Aldric whispered through clenched teeth.

The practised mask slipped over my face as I focused on one step after another.

King Vaylor waited at the base of the stairs; his greying hair gleamed beneath a golden crown with points as sharp as the judgment in his eyes. He was the ruler the Mortal Kingdom feared, but the father I feared more.

The man beside him was handsome in the way most royalty was. His brown hair was sleeked back, framing an angular face with high cheekbones and a strong jaw. He almost looked like a prince from a fairytale. It was a fleeting thought; his eyes crawled over me like groping hands and his teeth flashed in a serpentine smile. I could *feel* his ambition; it oozed off him like perfume. His eyes flicked to my father every few seconds, and I knew I was nothing more than an alliance to the crown.

I paused on the bottom step, looking down at the man who was to be my husband. My mask slipped and venom pooled in my eyes.

Tear the flesh from his bones.

I smirked, wondering if he would whimper while his skin tore like wet parchment.

"Daughter," King Vaylor warned, his gaze searching for defiance.

The silk of my dress rippled as I curtsied, casting my gaze at the feet of the powerful men who expected me to be weak. *Submissive. Always submissive.*

"Viscount Barden, I present Princess Lyra Meridian, your betrothed."

My father's words shuddered through me like nails dragging against stone. I didn't want this.

"Her eyes are a little unsettling, but the rest of her is exquisite." The viscounts voice grated against my nerves, objectifying me. But how could he not when I was forced on a pedestal of perfection? He circled me like a vulture, assessing me as if I were a prized animal.

I longed to claw his eyes out.

"I assume her purity has been preserved for our union?" The viscount asked.

Aldric tensed beside our Father, shifting uncomfortably. He knew the truth about the guards I lured into my bed. Not for love, not even for pleasure, but to reclaim something that had been stolen from me.

Control.

In his quiet way of protecting me, he made them disappear so rumours could not spread, keeping father in the dark. I didn't care about them anyway, not anymore. I had fallen in love once, and I thought he loved me too, but clearly, I was naïve.

My father inclined his head with a single, decisive nod, sealing my fate with a gesture. "Wonderful," my future husband leered, dragging a finger down my cheek.

I flinched, a small movement that I knew would cost me.

He made a disapproving noise, then leant in with a smile that promised pain. "Careful," he whispered against my ear, the stench of wine curling off his breath. "You will treat me with the respect I deserve, or I will have you punished."

Anger seared beneath my skin while I fought to keep the docile mask that needed to stay in place to avoid my father's attention.

Aldric's pleading eyes caught mine over the viscount's shoulder, mouthing one word: *behave.*

My betrothed stepped back with a satisfied smile and raised his voice. "I'll be expecting a dance, Princess Lyra."

I curtsied to the man who thought he would soon hold my leash. "Of course, Viscount."

I dropped my gaze, giving him the same submissive show my father always enjoyed. I was going to use that leash to strangle him if he got too close. My show seemed to please them both, and he bowed before disappearing into the swirling ball gowns.

Aldric re-took my arm before Father could speak.

"Lyra is feeling out of sorts. I shall escort her to the musicians to calm her nerves."

I hated being spoken about like a crazed woman, but he was right.

My father nodded reluctantly, letting Aldric steer me through the crowd of curious stares.

I hummed with the strings of the orchestra, letting the melody press like balm against my frayed nerves.

"Maybe not tonight, Lyra." Aldric eyed my body swaying to the music.

"Brother, balls are for dancing." I grinned at him as I gathered my skirts in my hands.

"Yes, with men who Father tells you to dance with, not by yourself," he chastised. "It is improper."

His shoulders tensed as I floated amongst the partnered dancers, twirling through the notes like a ghost revelling in her own funeral.

The strings curved through the air, breathing life into my veins. Weightless, I moved like a predator seducing its prey, dazed eyes following as though I'd cast a spell. It was the same reason I was forbidden to sing; people became enthralled far too easily.

My spin halted mid-step as I caught the golden embroidery of my father's jacket glinting in the candlelight. He stalked towards the marble dais in the centre of the ballroom, shooting me a disapproving glare before climbing the steps and perching on his throne of twisted metal. A small flick of his fingers signalled Aldric, pulling the leash of obedience that was shackled to both of us.

"Come," my brother murmured, lacing his arm with mine and leading me through the crowd.

I knew better than to protest. The dancers stopped and parted for us with hushed curiosity as my father raised his arms, signalling the crowd to be quiet.

Aldric took his seat in the smaller throne beside him, while I remained standing. Alone.

There was no throne for me. I was an ornament, meant to gleam, not to speak.

My Kingdom forged crowns for powerful men and celebrated their sons, but left their daughters to rot beneath the weight of *perfection*.

This was only a reminder of my place, as if I needed one. The scars etched into my skin beneath my dress were an effective enough reminder of what happens when I do not listen.

"Tonight," King Vaylor declared, "we celebrate the sacred Rite of Ascension. Every seven years, we offer our own to the Gods to be blessed with power to protect our people or be chosen for sacrifice."

The crowd erupted in applause, cheering for the impending deaths in the name of our estranged Gods. "We need these initiates into the Iron Guard more than ever. The Commander of Death has returned."

Gasps rippled through the crowd; the name alone had the ability to evoke fear even into the most powerful men. Gooseflesh tore across my skin as a shiver ran up my spine. I had heard his name whispered in the halls. He was the monster my Kingdom feared the most. A legendary weapon that left nothing but destruction in his path.

"Anyone brave enough is encouraged to take the leap."

Whispers slithered through my mind, clawing over each other in an unsettling crescendo.

No one will save you, they hissed.

They were right, but perhaps I could save myself. I knew Ascension would certainly promise death. But live or die, I would rewrite my fate. And if I lived, perhaps the darkness I carried would finally have a purpose. My lips parted before I could think.

"I wish to Ascend, Father."

My voice was quiet and weak, but I may as well have screamed. The air grew thick as mutters rippled through the crowd at my boldness. My father slowly turned. His face was carved in perfect serenity, except for his eyes, which held enough anger to burn.

"My daughter wishes to Ascend," he repeated, voice light with mock amusement. Laughter scattered through the room like broken glass.

"No, the *Gods* have a plan for you already. It is my pleasure to announce princesses Lyra's engagement to viscount Barden," he said with a smile, raising his goblet as my skin burned with shame. "May their union tether the Northern and Southern territories to prevail against the Fae."

The crowd made sounds of approval, cheering for a union that I would do anything to stop.

"But tonight, we honour the Gods," my father continued, his voice rising, "and pray they grant us warriors strong enough to kill the nightmare that has returned."

Everyone raised their goblets in a toast.

Except me. I wasn't allowed wine. Not since the night I dared use the goblet as a weapon. The hall echoed with cheers. Then the crowd returned to their dancing, spinning like painted marionettes.

My father's mask dropped as he turned to me and the weight of his fury was smothering.

"What have I told you about speaking when not spoken to, girl?" Spittle sprayed from his lips.

"I'm sorry, Father, I—"

"Ten lashes."

The words landed like a punch, and my muscles turned rigid in anticipation.

Aldric turned away, eyes fixed on the dancers. He always turned away.

"I'll present to the priest," I said, swallowing against the bile rising in my throat.

"No." My father waved a hand as if flicking away a fly.

"Your disobedience will not ruin such a sacred night for the Priest. You will dance with your future husband, then retire. First light, you report for punishment." My heart rate galloped as I curtsied, the thing inside me screeching at the thought of being whipped again.

"As you wish, my king."

I descended the steps as if walking to my execution, each footfall a drumbeat of dread. The whispers returned. This time they sung that same damned song I'd heard since childhood.

A melody in my blood.

It's not real, I told myself, yet I was unable to stop from humming along to the tune floating only to my ears.

Viscount Barden grinned as though I were already his as I curtsied, barely masking the revulsion curling in my gut.

"You requested a dance, viscount."

"Princess," he replied, seizing my hand before I could offer it. His fingers were clammy as he led me to the centre of the dance floor, curious eyes clinging to our every movement. He pulled me against his body, hand splayed far too low on my back. I willed my body to conform against a man I did not want to touch. I tried not to glare at him, moving in sync perfectly to the music like I had done a thousand times before. He guided me through the dance with grace, and for a moment, I let myself pretend he would offer me love and protect me from my father and the priest.

"What occupies your spare time, Viscount?" I asked politely.

"That will not be necessary."

I gritted my teeth, counting five slow breaths before I responded to ensure I did not snap at him. "Excuse me?"

"We do not need to get to know each other. Accepting this marriage is a last resort to protect my people against the Commander of Death and his legions. Other than that, you will be a warm place to put my cock and a womb to sow my seed. Nothing more."

My hand tightened on his shoulder, causing him to grin darkly.

"Are you going to fight me on our wedding night?" he asked. "Because that would make you far more interesting."

Make him bleed, the thing inside me demanded. The room spun, and nausea clawed up my throat. The melody haunting me rose, clashing with the string orchestra in a way that gritted against my nerves.

My vision darkened, and I *squeezed.* Hard enough that my fingernails dug into his shoulders and made him hiss. He shoved me backwards with a force that made me stumble.

"You stupid cunt!"

A shiver ran through me. The darkness inside me had answered. Perhaps one day it would take over me completely.

Aldric was suddenly at my side, taking my hand and giving Barden a polite smile that didn't reach his eyes.

"The princess must retire now, before the Ascension begins."

The viscount gave me one last leer. "We'll finish that dance soon, won't we, my bride?"

I leant in close, just enough that only he could hear me. "I will never let you have me."

His grin only deepened at my promise as Aldric led me away.

With each step that took me away from my betrothed, the voices grew louder, burrowing themselves into my mind.

Save yourself. Run. Kill.

Torches flickered along the stone walls, their flames casting long shadows that danced like ghosts just out of reach against the tapestries.

"Why can't you just behave, Lyra?" Aldric's voice was soft, as though he feared the walls might listen. "Just for once, not get yourself in trouble with Father."

I exhaled, weary to my bones. "I do try, Al." My words trailed off like a dying breath. He didn't reply. Just walked beside me with tense shoulders and hands that curled into fists then loosened again. The only sound between us was the hush of my ball gown against the floor.

"Are you still hearing them?" he asked eventually, barely louder than a whisper. "The voices. The songs." He slid his hands into his pockets, a motion so casual it stung. As if my mind, my madness, were an inconvenience to be politely tucked away.

"No," I lied, too quickly.

"You can trust me, Lyra."

A bitter laugh slipped past my lips, my heart aching. My gaze flicked to the iron bars across the nearest window, as if blaming him for their existence. They'd been added after I'd shattered the glass to sit on the ledge.

He had seen his haunted sister singing into the darkness in a nightgown, dangerously close to a fall that would have been fatal.

They had thought I was trying to jump. But no. I'd only wanted to feel closer to the sea. Its song had woken me from sleep, luring me there.

"Like last year?" I hissed. "You told Father about the window, who increased my blood lettings to every second day. The priest gets even more time with me locked in the dungeon as his little plaything thanks to *me* trusting *you*."

He flinched as if my words had hurt him. Regret flickered across his face, but he said nothing. Just looked away like he always did. "You could have died Lyra. I worry about you," he muttered.

"Don't." My voice was sharper than I intended. "The bloodlettings hurt, but they are helping," I lied.

The truth was it barely dulled the whispers and melodies that plagued my mind, but at least I didn't see the dead anymore.

We walked through the dimly lit corridors in silence. I ignored the artwork and revolting displays of riches. My father loved collecting rare things while our Kingdom starved. But I did notice the lack of guards pacing the hallways. I stopped at the threshold of my chambers, fingers resting on the carved wood of the door.

"If you'll excuse me," I said, summoning the ghost of a smile, "I need to rest. I've got an early morning lashing to prepare for." I didn't wait for his reply, closing the door in his face and pressing my back against it as the latch clicked into place. For a moment, I simply stood there, alone in the quiet, where no one could see the cracks beneath the surface.

I gathered my skirts and rushed to the barred window, gripping the cold iron. A fire flickered in the darkness atop the jutting cliffs where Ascension would be held in mere hours.

Not one part of me believed I'd survive, but I was already drowning slowly, in a life that didn't feel like mine. I sang absently, smirking down at the dark waves below.

Tonight is Ascension night, and I will change my fate, or I will die trying.

Two

Escaping the Gilded Cage

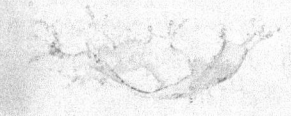

A smile tugged at my mouth at the distant bonfire flickering like a beacon in the night. A beacon of danger but my only hope at freedom. It was too dark to see the sea beyond it, but I knew it was there, looming like a giant pit in the moonless night waiting for the sacrifices to begin.

I ripped off my ball gown and rushed to open my armoire. Rifling through the dresses, looking for something light, something that wouldn't weigh me down in the water. No, they were all too heavy and would drag me to my death faster.

I glanced at my pile of slips, each nothing more than a thin piece of silk to wear beneath a dress. I couldn't help but smile as I slid one of the silver undergarments over my head. It skimmed my thighs and exposed far too much skin.

How improper indeed. I wrapped a thick black cloak around me to keep the never-ending winter from biting into my exposed flesh. I expected to die tonight but, if I survived, my soul would belong to the Gods, and I would be given a gift strong enough to kill a Fae. I wouldn't just be free of my father, I would be *stronger* than him, and that blow to his pride may very well kill him for me.

I wove my long, silver hair into a tight braid, hiding it beneath my hood to not give me away.

By dawn, I would either rise as something more, or drown, forgotten, like the countless others who had offered themselves for judgment. Either way, I would no longer be my father's possession or a plaything for the priest.

Wrapped tightly in my cloak, I eased open the heavy wooden door to my bedchamber. Seeing there were no guards, I slipped quietly into the torchlit corridor beyond.

I took slow and steady steps while shadows danced like watching figures against the walls. The faint echo of guards' boots drifted towards me, each step a reminder of the danger I was putting myself in.

If they caught me outside of my room, the punishment would be worse than the lashings that already awaited me in the morning. It would be weeks chained underground, left to rot in the dark. Being left in the hands of the priest scared me more than sacrificing myself to the Gods.

I walked quickly, silently praying to Gods who didn't listen that they would not hear me. Every scuff of my slippers against the marble floor seemed too loud in the suffocating silence. *Could they hear me too?*

A guard rounded the corner ahead of me and I pushed myself against the wall, begging the shadows to hide me. Without pausing, he continued walking straight ahead, not bothering to turn down this part of the corridor. I placed my hand on my chest, urging my heart to calm. *Keep moving before he comes back.* Stepping out of the shadows, I rushed down the open hallway. My brother's room and the library were the only other rooms in this wing of the castle. I just needed to make it to the small door the servants used to-

A flare of torchlight caught the edge of my cloak.

Gods damn it. Another guard rounded the corner, and I pressed myself behind a pillar, muscles locked and burning as I flattened against the icy stone. I heard his footsteps come to a halt and my mouth went dry. I could almost feel his gaze sweeping too close.

For a heartbeat, time stopped.

And then he passed. His steps faded into the distance, leaving behind only silence—sharp, suffocating silence. I let go of the breath I didn't realise I was holding and moved again, faster this time. I was so close to the servant's hallways and since guards didn't bother to patrol them, I would be safer there.

"Stop." The word scraped across my soul from behind me. "Remove your hood," the guard instructed.

Tears pricked at the corners of my eyes as the sinking feeling in my stomach threatened to pull me under. *Kill him and run,* the dark voice whispered in my mind.

I ignored it, like I always did, and reached for my hood with trembling hands. As soon as my silver braid was freed, I heard the guard's quick intake of breath.

"Princess Lyra, I shall escort you back to your room. My king does not have to know."

I turned, recognising the voice.

"No," I replied.

"I promised Orin I would look out for you when I could." I set my shoulders and raised my chin. I hated hearing his name. Orin was the only person I had ever had feelings for. Until he promised to help me then left me behind.

"Too bad. If you want to drag me back, you will have to kill me, Fredrick."

He sighed, but I could see the sweat beading on his forehead.

"What if I promise that I will return after I am satisfied?" I paused, walking towards him with a sway to my hips until I could peer up through my lashes at his blushing face. "Unless you have finally decided *you* want me."

He opened his mouth to say something but closed it before letting out a flustered sigh. After Orin left, Fredrick had checked on me and showed me nothing but kindness. He was Orin's best friend, and I had tried to sleep with him to satisfy the dark, hurting part of me. But he was too loyal to give me the satisfaction.

"That's what I thought." I shrugged, taking a step away from him. "I'm meeting a kitchen hand. Wait here if you please, but I may be awhile." I swallowed hard, wondering if he could see through my lies.

"You get one hour. I'll wait here and escort you back to your room myself. If you don't come back in that time, Lyra, I will have to alert your father."

I winked at him and opened the door to the servant's corridor. *In less than an hour I would be either dead, or on the shores of the barracks.*

The door closed behind me and I pressed my hand against my chest, taking a deep breath through my nose and out of my mouth. If it had been any other guard, I would be in chains right now.

The hidden servant tunnels wound through the castle like veins. I'd memorised every path, every turn, every chance at freedom. Not that it had ever helped me. My fingers brushed the stone wall as I passed, grounding myself against the rising tide of unease in my stomach. These hallways were empty. Vast and cold. But I liked them better than the grand displays of *riches* that decorated every other part of Stonebriar.

The corridor finally gave way to the kitchens, and I pressed my ear against the door, listening for signs of life. But none came. There was no clatter of knives, no voices, just the sound of my own thundering heart.

The door creaked on heavy hinges as I walked into the stale air of the kitchens to find it empty. *Thank the Gods*. It seemed everyone was at the Ascension, even the servants.

I hurried past the pots and knives stacked on the benches, eyes locked on the back door.

"Who's there?"

I froze.

A kitchen hand stood in the doorway, a sack of flour slung over one shoulder, eyes narrowing on my face.

"I was hungry," I said with a practiced shrug, feigning innocence.

Suspicion flickered across his face, and I knew he didn't believe me. His gaze slid towards the small brass bell on the counter, meant for summoning the guards.

"I'll send food to your chambers, Princess," he began, turning away from me to grab the bell. "The guards will help—"

His words cut off in a wet gurgle.

Crimson sprayed across the counter and painted my hand with sudden warmth.

My fingers slipped from the knife's handle, a knife I didn't remember grabbing, as his body hit the floor with a dull, final thud, the sack of flour spilling open next to him. The darkness inside me stirred, a quiet, eager pulse, as if savouring the kill.

"I'm sorry," I whispered to the dead man, kneeling next

to him as his blood began to pool on the ground. "It's just trying to protect me. It couldn't let you call the guards."

My fingers slid across his eyelids, closing them for the final time. "It was you or me," I explained to his unhearing ears, trying to justify my guilt. But it wasn't *me* who picked up that knife. No one should find the body until morning because of the ritual, and by then, I'd be dead or free. It wasn't the first time the darkness had taken over and someone had gotten hurt. Between bloodlettings, it was growing stronger, and I feared I would lose myself to it. *Perhaps sacrificing myself in the name of the Gods would be a mercy.*

THREE
ASCENSION

I opened the door and stepped into the night, leaving the metallic scent of blood behind.

Snow lashed against my face like needles of cold biting into my skin. It had been so long since I had felt fresh air that despite its harshness, I welcomed it.

Stonebriar Castle loomed behind me, silent and watching. Or perhaps that feeling was the weight of the life I had just taken. Either way, I was glad to run away from it.

My teeth chatted as the damp snow soaked into my slippers with every hurried step, the salty smell of brine creeping closer with every inhale.

I stuck close to the walls of the courtyard, moving fast and keeping low. It seemed most of the guards were at the Ascension, but I didn't want to take any chances. After making it this far, there was no chance in the Seven Hells I was going back now.

The wrought-iron gates of the courtyard squeaked against the night, making me cringe at their noise. I veered into the woods, seeking the cover of the trees. The main path would be quicker, but it wound through the village outskirts, and I couldn't risk wandering eyes. Not yet. I tore through the canopy of dead trees, stumbling over splintered branches with my palms outstretched to feel the way. The dark was so complete, I could scarcely make out the shape of my own fingers, and the trees punished me with every blind step.

The sound of drumbeats growing closer were the only thing that proved I was running in the right direction.

I glimpsed the ritual fire flickering between the trees, and I picked up my pace. Each rapid inhale of cold air burned my lungs as my feet pushed through the fresh snow.

I paused at the edge of the clearing, staying out of sight while I braced my hand against the rough bark of a tree, taking deep steady breaths to calm my racing heart. I was not used to running. There wasn't room to do that on a pedestal of broken expectations.

People twirled and stumbled around the fire in a frenzy to the uneven pounding of drums while flames danced against the starless night. I watched them for a moment, mesmerised by their freedom, and a pang of envy shot through my stomach while my breathing steadied.

You will never be happy. The voice floated to me on the breeze. Maybe it was right. But perhaps the afterlife would be kinder.

My father stood at the foot of his dais closer to the tree line, speaking to viscount Barden with Aldric at his side. The sacred fire sat between them and the cliff face.

I set my shoulders and stepped into the clearing, heading for the opposite side of the fire, closer to the dead sea, and further away from the men who would drag me back to my gilded cage. My fists clenched against the folds of my cloak, trying to clean my hands of the servant's blood while I weaved between people. Hopefully they were all too drunk to notice.

The scent of smoke and wine lingered in the air, mixing with the sharp tanginess of sea salt and primal beating of the drums. That, combined with the anticipation of the sacrifices felt intoxicating enough.

I kept my eyes trained on the ground, trying to ignore the rise and fall of drunken laughter, the clink of goblets and the gazes that felt too close. I welcomed the warmth of the bonfire latching onto my skin through the oppressive cold, bodies dancing around me to the wild beat of the music. I longed to join in. But my fear of being discovered kept my body from moving to the heady rhythm. I pushed through the crowd of commoners and nobles towards the cliff's edge, where the music faded and the air grew heavy. No one danced there. No one laughed. Fear twisted some faces. Others were frighteningly still, as if they had already died. Some were praying to Gods who didn't listen. *Sacrifices.* I stared at the churned snow beneath my slippers and took my place among them.

"Sacrifices!" A loud voice boomed from one of my father's guards clad in grey winter armour. "Line up against the cliff!" Cheers from the crowd broke out from around me, spiced liquor spilling onto the snow as they raised their glasses and stomped their feet.

I swallowed my fear, joining the line of people that had begun to form against the edge of the cliff. There were at least two hundred of us. Dark, angry waves smashed against the sheer jagged rockface, each one a violent promise of a brutal death. I hadn't realised how high we truly were until now. From here, we would be able to see the other Sacrifices make their leap into the waiting mouth of the sea.

The sea's roar, tangled with the crowd's fevered

murmuring, grated against my uneasy nerves. The person in front of me moved, and I shuffled forward, keeping my eyes trained on the angry waves. My foot slipped, the ground vanishing beneath me in an instant.

A jolt of terror shot through my chest.

My arms flailed for a moment before I crashed onto my back. The wind whooshed out of my lungs and my hood fell from my head. I sat quickly and tore the hood back over my hair, tucking my braid firmly back in place. The frozen slush seeped through my cloak and the thin material of my slip, dragging a violent shiver from my body. *Gods, did someone see me?*

A pair of sturdy boots stepped into my vision, and I forced my gaze up to meet a pair of assessing brown eyes.

I waited for her to shout for the guards, fear sinking in my stomach. But instead, she tilted her head at me. Whatever desperation she saw was enough for her to hesitate.

A small, knowing smile curved her lips as she extended a graceful, brown hand. Her black curls sprung from the two braids that hung over her shoulders, refusing to be tamed.

"Silk does not fare well against ice." She looked down at my slippers as I considered her hand. "Don't worry though, they have real shoes at the barracks."

I reached for her hand hesitantly and let her help me to a standing position, embarrassment flushing my cheeks. I offered her a small smile before tucking my hood further over my head.

"Thank you," I said softly. If she recognised my face, she clearly did not care.

My eyes drifted back to the Dead Sea's black waters; it was boiling with a hunger born from a hundred years of curses and grief. A graveyard of broken souls.

It was a living testament to the wrath of the Gods who had loved the Sirens and mourned their extinction with such fury that they cursed the seas they died in. Father said the Sirens deserved to die, that they held too much power and fed off men, Fae and Mortal alike. But it was the Fae who slaughtered them after finding a way to steal their magic.

"It's intimidating being this close, isn't it?" The dark-haired woman said, watching the sea next to me.

"Yes, though I find myself enthralled," I answered honestly.

"Well, I guess we are all a bit crazy for volunteering to do this," she stated idly. My back stiffened at the word, but she didn't seem to notice, lowering her voice and leaning towards me. "Whatever your reason is for running. Make it worth it. Run far and do not look back." Before I could respond, a tall man with dishevelled brown hair pushed in front of me, earning a shove from another initiate. "Fancy meeting you here on such a fine evening, Dreya." The man looked at the woman who had helped me, a mischievous smile lighting up his face. "Go to Hells Riven," she glared at him, and he chuckled. I stood frozen, unable to look away from him. He was devilishly handsome, but that was not why my gaze clung to him. His grey eyes met mine, and my breath stuttered to a stop. There was something so familiar about those eyes. I dipped my head quickly, letting the hood swallow my face. Before I could be sure if he saw my face, the drums surged. Deep and primal, like a heartbeat before a kill. The crowd fell into silence as a priestess stepped to the stone basin at the cliff's edge, the bonfire behind her throwing her grey robes into ripples of firelight. But it was the man walking next to her that turned my stomach.

The architect of my scars. The emissary to our estranged Gods.

The priest.

But how could they favour him when I knew how his eyes darkened with hunger every time that he fastened my chains? I knew how hard his cock got every time he cut open my skin. His blonde hair was cropped shorter at the sides and sleeked back neatly at the top. Robes of deep grey surrounded his strong build. Others found him handsome. *Charming.* But I knew the truth. My breath turned shallow, shoulders hunched against the memories. My skin crawling with the need to run. The priest hid his vulgarity behind the mask of divine righteousness, abusing me in the name of our Gods. I swallowed the bile clawing up my throat and kept my gaze low. But rage sparked behind my eyes, hot and trembling. *Spill his blood,* the whispers carried to me on the breeze. *Kill him.* My vision blurred. Not from tears. But from sheer, bone-deep rage. I *wanted* to give in to the voice. To let my darkness take over and make him suffer. But I couldn't give in completely. If I did, there was a chance I wouldn't remember it. And I *wanted* to remember every second of his death. They stopped before a large stone basin, arms raised to the blackened sky.

The wind died and the music dulled to a pulsing thrum, and it felt as though the entire crowd held their breath.

The surface of the water rippled as if something beneath stirred. Something waiting.

The priestess began to chant, her voice high and shrill. The priest echoing her, a harmony that made my stomach churn with bile. His voice was silken, each word slithering over my skin like the blade he had held to me so many times. Their eyes began to glow. My fists clenched beneath the cloak, imagining carving screams from the same mouth that had whispered prayers against my bleeding skin.

"Tonight, we sacrifice to the Gods!" The priest's voice echoed unnaturally across the clearing, burrowing beneath my skin like an infection. "Our beloved Gods, hear our prayer!" He looked up at the dark sky, speaking to the heavens. To Gods who had turned their backs on us long ago. "We beg your judgment. We offer our blood. May you find worthy souls to Ascend, or may you find pleasure in feasting on their souls." The shiver that curled up my spine had nothing to do with the cold.

"We vow to use the power you bless us with to avenge the Sirens and spill the blood of the Fae." The Priest lowered his arms, the crowd watching with rapt attention. "Sea Goddess, we mourn you. Moon God, shine on us once more. Goddess of Love, find us in your heart again. And our beloved Sun God, *rise*! Come back to us and end this eternal winter you blight us with."

The waters below reacted violently to his words, darker shadows stirred beneath the waves, monstrous creatures rising in preparation to feast for our estranged Gods. The priest pressed his sacred knife into the hand of the priestess. I knew without looking that symbols where carved into its hilt: I had stared at them many times while it sliced into my skin.

"In the waters of the Dead Sea, the Gods will weigh your soul. If you are strong enough, they will allow you to swim to the shores of the barracks where you will become *more*."

I squinted into the distance, a flickering bonfire marking our target on the shores of the small island off the continent of the Mortal Kingdom. It was impossibly far away; I wasn't even sure if I could swim. I tried to swallow the laugh that almost bubbled out of me, wondering how exactly I was going to die. Would I simply drown? Or would a monster would eat me?

"This is binding by blood. If you are not worthy," she said, tilting her head as her glowing eyes swept over the Sacrifices, "you will die."

Her eyes seemed to settle on me, and I checked that my hair was firmly hidden with trembling hands.

"Let the Ascension begin!"

I heard my father's cheer rise above the onslaught of noise that erupted in anticipation.

Good. He'd soon watch the daughter he caged choose her own fate. An unbidden smile tugged at my lips, because tonight, I would be the one to hurt *them*. All of them. A young man stepped to the edge of the cliff, arms hanging limply at his sides as he took one unsure step after another towards the priest and priestess.

He grabbed the knife from her with trembling hands, the wind whipping his blonde hair in his face.

"State your name," the priestess invited.

"Jerome Blankley." His voice cracked as he spoke, with either nerves or the timbre of adolescence. I wondered if he was too young to survive. The Gods favoured initiates between seventeen and twenty-seven years old. Any age could sacrifice themselves, but they were always killed.

He sliced the blade of the dagger across his hand, grimacing as red blood dripped into the bowl. Glancing back over his shoulder at the crowd with tear-filled eyes, he turned. Running and leaping into the frozen abyss.

The crowd erupted in cheers, swallowing the boy's scream. I held my breath while I watched the water, waiting for him to break through the waves. His head surfaced against the whitewash of the tide, and I exhaled an unsteady breath.

He made it.

His arms cut through the water frantically, swimming to the distant shores of the barracks. The waves seemed to still for an unsettling moment, the water rippling around him in an unnatural pulse.

That was the only warning that came before water exploded around him. A monstrous maw rose from the depths, snatching his body from the water and dragging him into the darkness of the Dead Sea.

A pained scream violated my ears, cutting through the cheers like a blade through flesh.

A woman with the same shade of brown hair sobbed hysterically, thrashing against a male's arms and trying to run to the edge of the cliff.

My pulse thrummed like a hummingbird's wings trying to take flight as I stared at the hysterical mother crying for her son. *Would anyone cry over the death of their mad princess?* I suppose I would never know, but I doubted it. I didn't know what it was to be loved.

The priest and priestess were completely unfazed. The crowd only cheered louder at the slaughter, drowning out the mother's cries.

"Move forward." The priestess gestured to the next initiate with a curve of her lips that looked more intimidating than reassuring.

I focused on the glistening snow. The coldness sinking into my silk slippers made my feet feel painfully numb. But it grounded me, and in an odd way, the pain gave me comfort.

I tried not to listen to the names of the Sacrifices or the screams that sometimes followed, shuffling closer to my demise.

"Jump or die!" a general shouted from the sidelines.

"Come on!" someone from the crowd screamed and an onslaught of angry jeers followed. Reluctantly I pulled my gaze to a woman with dark brown hair and frantic eyes crying at the edge of the cliff.

"Please! I don't want to die," the woman begged.

"This one is going to be messy," the man who had pushed in front of me, Riven, muttered under his breath. He turned towards me with a grimace, pushing his brown waves off his forehead. But I couldn't look away. Blood curdling screams ripped from her throat as her knees crashed into the snow.

Riven leant down into my line of sight with a sly grin, dimples flashing, his voice low and amused.

"I enjoy a woman's screams, but usually I'm the one causing it."

My eyes shot to his, meeting a striking grey filled with mischief. If he hadn't seen my face before, he certainly had now.

"You are disgusting," Dreya said from behind me.

The woman's screams rose to a feverish pitch. Her skin was turning a dark grey. Lifeless. Sinking in on itself as though it were rotting.

Riven turned back for a moment, his face darkening as he caught sight of the army generals dragging the twisted, lifeless body to throw into the Dead Sea.

I could feel my breathing become shallow. *It's nearly my turn.*

"Hey, you. Eyes here." He snapped his fingers in my

face dragging my attention yet again. His easy-going smirk returned, crooked and full of reckless charm.

"Don't worry, Princess, I'll give you something inspiring to watch." He grinned and turned towards the priestess, walking with a confidence I envied.

He bowed at the alter, though the gesture seemed more mocking then genuine.

He sliced his hand with a flourish, tossing the knife back onto the alter. "Riven Ashford," his voice boomed through the clearing.

With no hesitation, he launched himself off the cliff backwards, his body flipping in a wide arc before disappearing into the mist below.

Gasps followed his fall until he resurfaced, his laugh echoing over the sound of the waves before being swallowed by the crowd's cheers. He swam into the darkness, disappearing.

"Step forward," the priestess beckoned me, her eyes glowing with barely contained curiosity. The air felt heavier with every breath, suffocating me as I stepped onto the alter.

I took the sacrificial dagger from the priestess; it felt heavy in my hand.

The wind howled around me, pulling at my cloak as my pulse roared, but I didn't hesitate. Gripping the hilt tightly, I glanced towards the throne.

My father sat rigidly upon the edge, watching me with an anger hotter than the crackling fire. His gaze burned into mine, filled with fury, confusion and something else... Fear.

I pulled my hood back, silver hair catching the firelight.

Shock rippled through the crowd, but I kept my eyes locked on his. For the first time in my life, I didn't flinch.

I smiled.

"Lyra Meridian," I yelled over the crowd's uproar.

I raised my hand over the bowl, dragging the blade across my palm. I didn't flinch; I was used to blades. But the electric feeling that radiated into my soul made me shift uncomfortably. Blood welled dark and thick in my hand, ready to set me free.

"Lyra!" my father roared with anger.

My brother stood from his throne, jumping off the dais into the crowd. "Please!" He yelled, "Lyra don't do this!"

My heart clenched at the rawness in his voice. Aldric never lost control. Yet there he was, shoving through the crowd, his hair falling loose from its careful styling. His polished facade splintered further with each frantic step. The perfect prince was gone; only my brother remained, undone by fear.

But I held my ground. I tipped my hand as he pushed his way through the crowd that seemed to part for him. A figure broke the formation of the line and crashed into Aldric.

Dreya grappled with my brother, the prince, in the damp, ash-covered snow.

Her dark eyes burned with fury as her slender frame held his struggling form to the ground.

My blood splashed into the bowl, almost black against the cursed water's red gleam. The moment it touched, a violent shock tore through my veins.

As though ice and fire raged a war inside me, the ancient power sank its claws into my very soul.

"Come now, Princess, I will convince the Gods you made a mistake," the priest coaxed in a soothing voice. But venom lurked beneath it, I could see it for the poison it was.

I stared at the hand he offered, the same hand that carved symbols into my skin with a blade, the same hand that touched me against my will.

I fluttered my eyelashes at him before widening them to make myself looked frightened. "You would do that for me, my priest?"

"I would," he said gently. "The Gods speak through me, and they will show you mercy. They know you are only a broken girl. Come now."

My teeth clenched, and I gripped the ceremonial dagger with purpose, letting him come closer.

They called me broken. Perhaps they were right—but broken glass cuts the deepest.

I drove the knife into his chest. His flesh split with a sickening squelch as the dagger sunk into his flesh. He sucked in a fractured breath as I forced the blade deeper, my knuckles hitting skin. His eyes widened in disbelief, lips parting in a soundless scream.

I grinned, the dark thing inside of me drinking in the bloodshed, begging me to make him suffer. I twisted the knife, and he finally found his voice.

The sound of my torturer screaming was beautiful, like a lullaby crafted just for me.

For a heartbeat, everything else disappeared. The wind, the crowd, even the roaring sea as I watched him fall to his knees.

"Jump!" Dreya shouted, cutting through my enchantment.

Aldric sobbed my name, choked and broken. It cut straight through my heart. Perhaps he did love me, but I knew he would never love me enough to save me from Father.

I did not look back.

Sprinting towards the cliff's edge with my heart lodged in my throat, I shed the cloak like a second skin, spread my arms, and dove into the waiting dark. My vision tilted.

The cliff.

The sea.

The world.

The air bit at my skin, sharp and cold as it whooshed past me, stealing the air from my lungs.

For a single, blinding moment, I was weightless.

I was free.

FOUR

DROWNING

The Dead Sea seized me in its cold, suffocating embrace as I crashed through the surface and plummeted into its depths.

Everything was dark and soothingly quiet. Almost peaceful. I let go and allowed my limbs to go heavy. My body surrendered to the water as I sank. There was no fear left. No desire for the Gods to save me. The only certainty I had was that this was how it ended. The salt burned against my skin. A sharp, crawling heat that prickled along every nerve. I wanted it to flood me. To break me open and end this ache from the inside out. But my stupid body wouldn't obey. My lungs began to tighten. It started as pressure. Rising to a dull ache that bloomed beneath my ribs. As though my chest were slowly being crushed. I let myself sink further. Forcing myself not to move. Not to reach for the surface. Not to beg for air. The water pressed against my mouth and nose, patient and absolute. Whispers of a melody drifted to me on the current. The same one that had haunted me since I was twelve. But it had never felt like this before. Never this close. Never this alive.

Even in death, madness followed me.

The ache sharpened. My chest spasmed, greedy for air and for life that I did not want. My throat burned as my body demanded breath with a violence. I clenched my jaw, trying to deny it, but panic seeped in anyway. Cold, invasive panic. Shapes moved in the black water around me. Monstrous forms circling me in the depths, staying far enough away that I could not truly see them. *Would I see one before it sunk its teeth into me?* I found myself hoping for it to come. Anything to stop the fire in my lungs. Anything to make the end arrive faster. Another spasm rocked through my lungs. My body finally gave in, gasping violently. Salt and agony rushed into my mouth, ripping through my throat and filling me. My chest heaved again, harder this time. The water filled me until I ceased to exist as something separate. It invaded every hollow, fragile space. Erasing the shape of me from the inside out. I did not know where my body ended and the sea began. I was being unmade. My body arched against the pure agony that tore through me.

Find the pieces.

The voice slid through the melody, familiar and wrong. It wrapped around my thoughts, urgent and insistent. My body shook. Another violent spasm tore through my chest, dragging more water down into lungs that no longer knew the difference between air and pain. My limbs jerked weakly, hands clawing at nothing. I hated the way my body fought me. Hated the instinct that refused to accept the end I had chosen.

Find the pieces. Find the pieces. Find the pieces.

Bubbles spilled from my mouth as the phrase echoed again, louder. Piling over itself inside my head. My limbs grew heavier. Each movement slower than the last. The thrashing dulled into sluggish, desperate motions as my strength bled away. My vision blurred at the edges. Darkness crept inward, pulsing in time with the slowing beat of my heart. My consciousness began to fray, thoughts slipping loose, the melody winding tighter around what remained of me. I was floating. I was sinking. I was drowning. I felt it before I saw it. A deep sense of power radiating through my bones, forcing me to cling to consciousness. The water shifted, a deep, unnatural pull that tugged at my body from beneath, as if the sea itself had begun to inhale. Vast and patient, the monster unfurled from the black like a continent waking. The current bent and curled around it, drawn inward as though answering a summons older than the sea itself. My mind screamed hallucination, clung to it desperately, but the shape kept coming. Obsidian scales slid into view one by one, catching what little light remained and swallowing it whole. They rippled as the creature rose, each movement slow and deliberate. Its eyes fixed on me, pale as drowned moons and I realised it wasn't a monster. It was the Serpent. The priest had told me the story of how the Gods left the Serpent behind to watch us suffer until we atoned. The current moved me away from its watchful gaze, like unseen hands gripping my body. Water rushed around me, moving unnaturally fast. Then everything stopped. The burning in my chest eased, and the water stilled.

For a moment, the Dead Sea felt like something it had not been known for in over one thousand years: calm.

The water cradled me, pushing me upwards as I fought the battle with consciousness. My lifeless body drifted without fight. It could have been moments. Hours. I couldn't tell. I was weightless and unfeeling. *Dead.* Rocks scraped against my feet, snapping me out of my tranquilised state.

My legs searched for stability, finding footing on slippery black rocks. Confusion sank its claws into my oxygen-deprived mind. My head burst from the water, my chest seizing before I gasped violently, dragging down breaths of air that felt like liquid fire.

I staggered through the shallows like a deer with new legs, water splashing at each clumsy step. My chest heaved, each breath a rasp that felt almost foreign. *How am I breathing?* The world seemed to tilt. I was certain I had drowned. I should be dead. I looked down at myself, silver hair unbound and clinging to my almost translucent slip of clothing. *Very much alive.* Then I saw them.

Curious stares bore down on me. Surviving initiates and armour-clad officers all faced me with the same shock marrying their faces. Perhaps it was the unnatural calm of the waters at my back. Or it was because I was their princess, stumbling ashore, half-clothed and a survivor of Asenction. Stonebriar's army barracks loomed over the dark pebbled shore; its stone towers were capped in snow and reaching into the dark night.

I took another step, but my foot caught on a jagged stone, and I crashed back into the cursed water. My body trembled violently as I crawled, coughing. Water scorched the back of my throat and dribbled down my chin.

Perhaps I'd hallucinated the Serpent, and the tide had washed me ashore by mistake. Or the Gods found it a cruel joke to spare me.

Find the pieces! The voice was so clear it was as though someone had yelled it in my ear.

A strange and broken sound tore from my mouth, the memory of drowning fresh in my mind. While I doubted many things, I knew that I had drowned. I had felt the water claw down my throat and fill my lungs. Even now, I could still taste the salt on my tongue. I would have called surviving luck if I had not *wanted* to die. A ragged laugh clawed from my chest—half elation and half madness as I dragged myself onto the dark, icy pebbles. I was alive and I had killed the priest. But I was still hearing voices. Realisation crawled beneath my skin, shooting ice through my veins. I was free from my father and his monster, but I would never be free from my darkness. From *myself*.

I kneeled in the shallows, the cursed waters lapping at my skin as I tilted my head back. Looking up towards the dark, oppressive clouds—towards the heavens and the Gods who had turned away. The laughter died in my throat. "Fuck you all."

A blue-robed priestess standing on the rocks gasped, her hands flying to her mouth at my blasphemy. Her eerily glowing eyes piercing me with judgment as she stared down at me. I bared my teeth in an unfriendly smile. She raised her pointer and middle finger to her forehead in a religious gesture, muttering a prayer I couldn't understand.

"Siren," she whispered and took a step back, eerie eyes filled with hatred. I brushed off the insult; the priestesses labelled a woman a *Siren* when they thought they were improper.

"State your name," an Iron Guard demanded from next to her, quill and scroll at the ready.

I stood, pushing the wet tendrils of hair away from my face and raising my chin. "Lyra Meridian," my voice carried across the silent beach, the only sound coming from the soft waves and the crackling fire.

His quill slipped from his hands as he looked at me with wide eyes. The beach was so deathly quiet, you could hear it clatter against the pebbles.

A figure pushed through the crowd, fast footsteps

crunching against the stones. A rough hand closed around my upper arm and yanked me to the side.

"Tell me my eyes are playing tricks on me, Lyra," a familiar voice growled.

I looked up, locking onto pale green eyes filled with fury.

Hair the colour of darkly spilled blood, cropped short against his tanned skin, shadowed a face I didn't think I would see again.

His hand lingered on my skin for a fraction of a second before he let me go, as if touching me burnt him.

"Orin," I whispered. My hands shook at my sides, with the need to either slap him or embrace him, I wasn't sure.

The last time I had seen him played in my mind countless times. When he had kissed me on the forehead before leaving my bed, he had obviously known he was leaving. I was only eighteen, but it was the closest thing I had ever felt to love.

"You *knew* you were going to Ascend!" I shoved my icy hands against his muscular chest. He grabbed them and held them together; I struggled in his grip.

"You can't be here," he gritted through clenched teeth.

My gaze swept over the crowd with wide, innocent eyes, then down the length of my exposed body before cutting back to him with a slow, deliberate smile. "It's a bit fucking late for that."

His face softened, as he dropped my hands and wrapped his arms around my frozen body. I stilled for a moment before letting myself melt into his embrace. The scent of leather and steel overtook my senses, his heart beating against my ear. I nestled in closer.

"Gods help me, Lyra, this is no place for a Princess." His voice was low, edged with something dangerously close to desperation. Pulling away from me, he levelled a glare at the onlookers, who turned back towards the fire. The sound of talking filled the beach as they all returned to their conversations. Obviously Orin held some sort of power here.

"Lucky for me, I am not a princess anymore. I am an initiate," I whispered, giving him a small smile.

He shook his head, eyes softening as he looked down at me, but I could see the truth in them.

Hurt filled me, but I squared my shoulders. I pierced him with my gaze, willing the tears to clear from my vision.

"A lot has changed since you left me—"

"Left you?" His voice cracked as he interrupted me, eyebrows rising. He looked away, jaw tight, as if the sight of me was more than he could bear.

Before I could respond, a loud yell pulled my attention back to the Dead Sea.

Angry waves swirled and crashed, aggressively pulling at the initiate trying to make his way through the shallows.

Riven waded onto the shore with grace, slamming his fist in the air.

"Fuck yes!" he exclaimed.

Riven's thick eyebrows raised in question, studying me like a riddle he wanted to solve. His gaze flicked back over his shoulder to the cliffs rising in the distance, as if measuring the impossible path I must have taken to reach the shore before him. He gave his name to the Iron Guard before walking over to me.

"How *did* you get here before me, princess?" Riven ran a hand through his brown, unruly hair, pushing back the damp strands plastered to his forehead. "Actually, it doesn't matter. Did you like my flip?"

Riven grinned with light-hearted mischief, slinging an

arm around my shoulders as if we had known each other for years.

He barely had time to steer me a few steps away before Orin's hand slashed out, ripping Riven's arm off me and twisting it behind his back.

"You do not touch the princess," Orin snarled, his grip tightening.

Riven winced theatrically under Orin's grip.

"Strong grip, soldier. Do you practice on your own?" Riven hissed through his teeth with pain but widened his smirk.

Orin's grip tightened, drawing a low, deliberate groan from Riven. He shot me a wink, and he leant into Orin's body.

"How'd you know I like it rough?"

"Shut up," Orin grunted, pushing a laughing Riven away with disgust.

I pursed my lips and shook my head, turning towards the bonfire. I was alive, and if I was going to stay alive long enough to find out why the Gods spared me, I needed warmth. Not to watch a match of testosterone. "Wait," Orin said, shrugging out of his jacket and extending it to me.

I stared at it as if it had teeth. "I don't *want* your help," I said before turning away from him.

"I take it you have some history there," Riven said as he followed me, shaking out his arm dramatically and flexing his fingers.

I glanced over my shoulder at Orin, who watched me intently.

"Something like that," I replied.

We pushed through the throng of drenched initiates crowding the fire, a sigh of relief escaping me as its warmth soaked into my numb skin.

"And honestly, the backflip was an unnecessary risk to take. You could have easily died smashing into the rock face."

"Princess, I happen to be good at taking unnecessary risks. You on the other hand..." He chuckled. "We both know you're not here with the king's blessing. I'm assuming you've run away."

He dipped his head so I could see the amusement playing in his grey eyes.

I cast my gaze down, expecting him to deliver the same blow Orin did, that I was too weak. Instead, he started slow clapping. He smirked and I couldn't help but return his grin.

"So, she swaps gowns with swords to protect her beloved Kingdom herself." He shook his head in wonder.

I stifled a startled laugh. I wasn't here for any noble reason. The only thing I had sought was the finality of death.

"Dreya!" Riven called past me, and I turned to see the woman who tackled Aldric walking towards us, arms wrapped around herself.

Slowly, my skin began to thaw. I drowned out Riven and Dreya's conversation and ignored the cheers as more initiates stumbled ashore. My skin may no longer be numb. But I was.

"Initiates!" A commanding voice cut through the excited chatter, rising above the roar of the waves.

I'd seen this man speaking with my father before, and the memory made me instantly wary.

Commander Earl Kragthorne stood atop a large rock, radiating authority.

Behind him, the rockface opened like a maw leading to the barracks while the bonfire flared at our backs. His eyes were piercing and unnerving through his war hardened face, his grey armour baring the mark of the Iron Guard on his chest plate.

"Formation!" he bellowed, the sneer twisting his grey-streaked beard.

Iron Guard soldiers closed in from the edges of the clearing, some with orange or yellow bands strapped tight around their biceps.

They barked orders and shoved initiates into place, driving us into harsh, orderly rows.

"The Gods have deemed you worthy of Ascension!" his voiced echoed, and the initiates around me clapped and cheered.

"Don't celebrate too soon. The Gods chose you, but I haven't yet. Weakness festers. It's my job to cut it out before it spreads. If your Sanctum does not reveal itself in the first two weeks, I will sacrifice you to the Gods myself." Muttering broke out around us.

"Quiet!" his voice boomed across the clearing, and silence followed.

"Seventy-five of you survived out of the two hundred that jumped. A record high. You will be divided into squads; a sergeant and a corporal will help you acclimate. Welcome to the Iron Guard, where fear is forged into obedience, and mercy dies."

One-hundred and twenty-five innocent lives lost to feed Gods who don't care about us.

"What a morbid speech," Riven muttered under his breath.

Commander Kragthorne unrolled a parchment, his gauntleted fingers scraping against the brittle edges.

He called each name like a demand, the sound carrying over the crash of the waves. At every summons, a ranking

Iron Guard stepped forward to claim the initiate, pulling them into squads of seven, the bands on their biceps catching the firelight. It seemed that the sergeants wore a yellow band and the corporals had orange.

"Lyra Meridian." I looked up to see Commander Kragthornes eyebrows bunch together as he stared at me with shock.

I swallowed hard and stepped forward, the feeling of everyone's eyes crushing down on me made me feel naked.

"First Squad."

I was ushered towards two initiates that stood to the side of the clearing, two higher-ranking officers standing behind them. I inwardly groaned when I saw that Orin was one of them. Two more initiates joined us, and I breathed a sigh of relief to have Riven and Dreya in my squad.

"You will answer to your sergeant. If they tell you to do something and you disobey, they have my blessing to kill you themselves. Now, get out of my sight, training begins at dawn."

I could feel the weight of Orin's presence behind me, and I inwardly cursed the Gods. Whoever had put me in this squad wanted me to suffer.

FIVE
WELCOME TO THE IRON GUARD

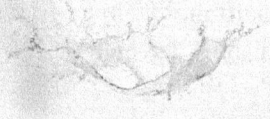

We were led through a narrow passage in the rockface. The line narrowing as we climbed over the rocks and into a large courtyard. Torches flickered against stone pillars, illuminating a large fenced-off area.

"Those are the fighting pits," Orin said as we walked past.

Other squads moved in tight formations around us, their chatter blending into the steady thud of boots scuffing the ground.

The barracks loomed over the fighting pits; large steps led to double iron doors that were jarred open.

We followed him inside, and the scent of steel and smoke from the torches clung to the air. I had only walked up two steps when a shiver crawled up my spine.

I looked over my shoulder at the large pillars that seemed to be the entrance to the fighting pits.

"Why does it feel like death there? What are those pillars used for?" I asked, pointing at the large beam joining the two pillars. The others gave me an odd look, stopping as Orin raised an eyebrow at me.

"Sacrificing the weak and disobedient," he said before continuing to walk up the stairs and through the doors.

The cold pressed deeper, threading beneath my skin, clinging like something unseen had taken notice. Or perhaps I was just exhausted.

"Ah, the charm of military life. The ever-present smell of crushed dreams and the threat of death." Riven spread his arms out wide, looking around the dimly lit foyer. If it weren't filled with initiates right now, it would be scarcely empty.

"You don't take anything seriously, do you?" Orin said, shooting him a sharp look.

"Of course I do. I'm going to take being a pain in your ass very seriously."

Orin exhaled through his nose and a man with sandy blond hair tied into a bun placed his hand on his shoulder. I eyed the orange band on his bicep; he must be our corporal.

"Making friends already Riven?" Dreya asked mockingly, glancing back over her shoulder at him.

Riven gave her a wink. "Don't worry, I think he likes me."

"I'd think I would prefer the company of a Fae," Orin scoffed.

Riven clutched his chest in mock hurt, but Orin ignored him, leading us further into the barracks as the crowd began to clear.

"That's the auditorium. You will have theoretical class there. Mess hall is down that way, but we will show you that tomorrow."

We stood at the base of a large spiralling staircase, Orin pointing down a long high vaulted hallway. I had thought

Stonebriar castle felt cold, but the barracks made it feel like a cozy cottage in comparison.

I found myself walking next to Dreya on the steps, Orin and our lieutenant in front of us. I hesitated, unsure how to even begin, then finally spoke.

"Thank you." She arched a strong brow at me, as if questioning my appreciation.

"For tackling my brother, *the prince*, to the ground and, for not yelling for the guards when you saw my face. Honestly, I wasn't sure if they were going to let you Ascend after you did that."

"They figured the Gods would kill me for my transgression, and I figured you were running from something bad." She leant in and lowered her voice. "Though I do have questions about why you stabbed the priest.

"I don't know how to repay you," I replied, ignoring her question.

"Just survive."

Somehow that statement felt easier said than done, I hadn't really considered what surviving would entail.

Find the pieces.

The whisper wracked through me; I stumbled on the step and my breath caught. Dreya shot me a questioning look as I gripped the wrought iron railing, but she didn't say anything. I was grateful for that.

By the time we reached the fifth floor, my legs felt unsteady, and my heartbeat seemed to pound in my ears.

We followed Orin into a wide hallway that seemed to breathe darkness. Arched wooden doors carved into the stone on both sides. The torches sputtered as though choking on their own smoke, their frail light birthing shadows that writhed along the walls like starving fingers reaching for flesh.

Tingling stretched over my neck as though I was being watched.

My eyes were pulled to the winding staircase looming above me that seemed to vanish into darkness so thick that I couldn't see through it.

Faint voices drifted through the inky void from below. The darkness shifted, and I struggled to focus, as though something unseen had just moved.

"Are you coming?"

I jumped at Dreya's voice, not realising the rest of my squad had gone further down the hallway.

"Yes," I muttered and followed her.

Orin opened the first door on the right and stood aside, gesturing us to enter.

"Welcome to your new home," he said dryly.

"All of us?" a flaxen-haired woman who stood two feet taller than me questioned.

"Shared bunks build camaraderie," Orin replied in a clipped tone. I didn't remember him being this clipped. But, if anyone understood how time could change someone, it was me. Casting one last glance at the spiral staircase, I followed the others into the room. But something, or some-one, was watching me.

A large, windowless room greeted me, seven beds evenly spaced apart.

The air was thick with mildew and woodsmoke from a dim fire flickering in the open hearth.

The sheets looked rough and threadbare, the walls veiled in cobwebs, and a wooden door set into the stone led to what I assumed was a shared washroom.

I had expected luxury, but standing in the dim light, surrounded by such stark simplicity, a quiet shame crept over me.

I had been wrapped in comfort my whole life and this was a stark comparison to what I was used to.

"This is Bohdi. First Squad's corporal, my second in command."

The man with dark-blond hair loosely tied back with a few strands escaping to frame his sun-kissed face who had walked with us. His eyes were a deep blue; the colour I imagined the sky would be beneath the clouds that cursed our skies. I wouldn't know though, because I had never seen it. He felt bright and warm, his soft smile radiated compassion as he lifted his hand in a small wave.

"Welcome to First Squad. It is my job to look after you, help you survive the first year. After that, you will be incorporated into the Army of Iron. I know how hard the adjustment can be to military life, so if any of you need to talk, I am here for you."

A strange feeling of peace washed through me, tension dripping from my shoulders like wax from a melting candle.

"Stop using your Sanctum on them!" Orin snapped, hitting Bohdi across the shoulder with the back of his hand.

The peaceful feeling eroded as quickly as it had settled on me, the hard reality of fear, uncertainty and the weight of my decisions came crashing back with such vengeance it took my breath away.

"You're an empath?" Riven beamed. "I bet you get lucky with that little trick all the time."

"Enough." Orin rubbed his jaw in frustration before sitting on the bed closest to the door. "We are expected to train in only a few hours."

"You will find towels already hung for each of you and clean clothes folded on the benches. I know how new this all feels, but I promise you will settle in." Bohdi's warmness radiated into me, and I wondered if he was using his

Sanctum again or if he naturally oozed kindness. The bathing chamber was damp with the scent of old stone, and the six exposed showerheads that lined the walls offered no privacy.

The flaxen-haired woman shed her sodden clothes with ease, unbothered. A man with tanned skin and a crooked nose from too many fights followed, lining his boots neatly against the wall.

I hesitated, dripping and cold with Riven and Dreya at my back.

"What's wrong, Princess?" the woman with flaxen hair seethed. "This is the world your family built for us. Honestly, I hope you suffer in it as much as we have." Her words hit harder than I expected, the room shrinking, the air thickening.

"I have suffered," I said softly. Who was she to judge me? The woman laughed mockingly, anger swirling through my veins.

Dreya cut in, unimpressed. "Shut it, Hadley."

Hadley rolled her eyes, still chuckling as she stepped under the spray of water.

Drown her.

The whisper slithered through me, and for a heartbeat, my vision darkened. The water seemed to bend towards me, begging to be commanded.

I tore my gaze away and said nothing, ignoring the voice and the strange sensation buzzing beneath my skin.

Riven stretched his arms behind his head with a lazy grin, shamelessly watching Hadley's naked form. "Thank the Gods for camaraderie."

Dreya punched him in the shoulder, the easy familiarity between them catching me off guard. She noticed my stare and only shrugged. "We are both from the slums. My mother gave him shelter this year's snowstorms in exchange for his thieving skills. Hadley is from the slums as well."

"It's a shame I won't have to steal anymore, really. I was a damn good thief." Though, I hardly heard his words, the room narrowing around him. He pulled his shirt over his head slowly. Deliberately. As if the act itself were an invitation to look. Compact muscle revealed inch by inch, openly on display. He did not rush, letting the moment linger. I suddenly understood his confidence. His gaze flicked to mine, just long enough to confirm I was watching, and a slow, knowing satisfaction settled into his posture. A silver mark seared into the side of his ribs, shaped like a flickering flame. Something cold slid down my spine.

I knew that shape. It was the same as the curse nestled between my breasts. Riven noticed my gaze but said nothing.

"Like what you see, Princess?" He winked at me, unbuckling his belt.

I said nothing, I didn't need to. The flush of my skin answered him enough. Did he hear things that were not real, like me?

"I'm going to wash the scent of death ritual off. Try not to stare at my ass," he grinned and walked towards one of the free showers. "Or do." Dreya scoffed and rolled her eyes.

With a sharp breath, I peeled off my slip, the fabric clinging stubbornly before landing on the ground with a wet thud.

The dim light and rising steam blurred the edges of my form, offering little coverage. But I hoped it was enough to hide my scars from the others.

The hot water struck my skin like a cleansing tide, unravelling the tension coiled tight in my shoulders. I did it.

I was free. The priest was dead, and my father no longer controlled me. Tears burned at the corners of my eyes, but I made no sound as they fell, dissolving into the water as if they had never existed. I reached for the bottled soap, but something caught my eye. A mirror stood just beyond the edge of the steam.

I tried to turn away before I could see my reflection, but a chill slid down my spine despite the heat of the shower. It burrowed deep in my bones, as if something unseen had coiled around me, watching...waiting.

Movement flickered at the edge of my vision. My gaze snapped up, locking onto the mirror. Teal eyes stared back, haunted and rimmed with exhaustion.

I barely recognized the girl looking at me. My silver hair clung to my shoulders, trailing over the scars that marked every inch of my back.

Beyond the reflection, shapes bled into the drifting haze. Wisps coiling through the steam, stretching into figures that drifted unnaturally.

My breath caught. I knew this feeling: the cold hush, the invisible pull, the sense that even the world itself was holding its breath. Ghosts.

Find the pieces. Find the pieces. Find the pieces.

The whispers slithered through me, and before I could stop myself my lips parted.

A single note escaped, threading into a soft, haunting melody.

The dead stilled.

They are not real. I reminded myself as I sung.

Yet the steam shivered at my voice, and one by one the figures unravelled, edges fraying into nothing as the song wrapped around them.

The chill broke. The haze went still.

I pressed my palm to the cool tile, swallowing hard as my song died in my throat.

Behind me, the other initiates had quieted. They always did when I sang, captivated by notes they didn't understand. That was why Father forbade it. Why he called my voice a curse.

I cut the song off sharply. The silence seemed louder than the melody as I wrapped a towel around myself. I kept my eyes trained on the ground as I walked through the steam, the weight of their eyes pressing down on me.

SIX

SWORDS AND TENSION

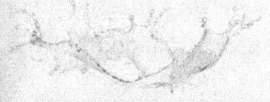

Rough blankets were torn off me, and the embrace of the early morning air enveloped my body. I tried to grab them and yank them back over me, but my fingers came up empty. I groaned, struggling to open my eyes against the haze of sleep.

"Rise and shine, initiates!"

My eyes snapped open to the dim torchlight.

Orin paced the length of the barracks, all sharp angles and severity, while the others laced boots and buckled themselves into grey uniforms.

His gaze softened when it landed on me, just for a breath, and it made my chest ache with the memory of before. But the warmth vanished as quickly as it came, his face shuttering into the cold mask of a sergeant. The mask of a stranger.

"Welcome to your first day in the Iron Guard. Get dressed, initiate." I glared up at him, not used to hearing him speak to me with such bite in his voice.

"I can't wait," I said, voice seething with sarcasm and

snatching the folded uniform from my nightstand. Why would the Gods spare me from drowning for *this?*

Kragthorne had said the Iron Guard was where fear is forged into obedience. I hated being told what to do.

I slid the stiff material of my pants on under my night-gown, stopping to frown at a band of material that sat on top of my tunic.

I was used to getting dressed by maids, shoved into corsets, silks, and jewels. Made to gleam for the court. Not whatever *this* was.

I cast a glance over my shoulder. Dreya was tying her boots on the bunk next to me, indifferent.

With one swift movement, I yanked the fabric over my head, hugging it to my chest.

The angry silver lines of punishments were laid bare beneath the dim torchlight.

I picked up the long piece of fabric and tried to wrap it around my breasts, fumbling with the material. I cursed under my breath as the material slipped.

"Here. Lift your arms." Dreya's voice came from behind me and I stilled. My eyes slammed shut against the panic. This close, she would be able to see every echo of pain etched into me. *Please don't ask about my scars.*

Hesitantly, I lifted my arms. Her fingers moved with practiced ease, binding me in firm, even pulls. It wasn't cruel like a corset. It felt purposeful. Strong.

She pulled harder and I gasped, adjusting to the way it squeezed air from my lungs. Dreya huffed a laugh.

"Lyra?"

The sound of my name spoken softly turned me rigid. Riven stood a few paces away, grey eyes churning like storm clouds as they traced the scars across my skin. He looked haunted.

Cold sweat prickled down my spine. My stomach knotted. I clutched the tunic to my chest as dizziness threatened to pull me under. *No. No. No.*

"What happened to you?"

The air thinned. A dull ringing swallowed the world. My chest seized against the binder as memories coiled around me like inescapable chains, ready to drag me under the surface of sanity.

"Shut up," Dreya muttered to him, but she sounded far away. The priest's voice slithered through my memories, haunting me from beyond the grave.

You're evil. I'm doing this to fix you. My cherished. Let me fix you.

"None of your fucking business," I snapped towards Riven, my voice too sharp. Too frayed. I kept my eyes fixed on the ground, but it did nothing to dull the pressure of his gaze pressing into me as I shouldered past him. My hands curled at my sides, fingers tightening until my nails bit into my palms. The image of them closing around his throat flashing through my mind. The urge spiked, sudden and ugly.

Run.

The voice echoed through my head, low and insistent. Not the priest. But the one that belonged to my curse. My darkness.

Run. Run. Run.

My jaw clenched. My vision tunnelled. For a heartbeat, I wanted blood on my hands. I wanted to give in to the primal urge I had to end an innocent's life. Riven's life.

Slit his throat and drown him in the blood that spills from his body.

"Stop!" I shouted, the word tearing out of me as I shoved my hands through my hair. I gripped the strands as though I could rip the voices free along with it. My pulse thundered. My muscles coiled, ready to lash out. I turned before I could act, shoving past Riven and the stunned stares of the squad. I yanked the door open and slammed it behind me, the impact rattling the frame as I staggered into the empty hallway, breath coming hard and fast. The stone was cold against my back as I pressed myself into it, fingers re-tangling in my hair. The ringing in my ears drowned out the world, leaving me alone with the darkness in my heart. My hands trembled as I forced myself upright, counting my breaths to calm my racing heart.

The door creaked open and Orin's large build filled the doorway. His arms were crossed, and his gaze cut into me with warning, but there was a softness there. Reminding me of the man who was once mine.

"You can't do that here, Lyra, they kill things they can't control."

"Good," I sighed, leaning my head back against the wall and closing my eyes. Death is all that was left for me.

He was suddenly close enough to me that I could feel the heat of his body, his face inches away from mine.

"Not good, Princess. I'd be the one who'd have to kill you, and the rules are something I will not bend. Even for you."

His hands wrapped around my shoulders, holding me in place as he leant his forehead against mine. For a quiet moment, I let myself melt against his touch.

"Do it then," I begged quietly, opening my eyes to meet irises as green as the forests the Gods stole from us, before they froze them bare and left only ruin behind.

"No," he whispered, pushing my hair behind my ear with a tender brush of his fingers. "Promise me you will try to stay in line."

The door to our quarters opened. The hallway filled with initiates as the other doors slammed open. Orin stepped away, putting distance between us, and I breathed out in relief. At least I didn't have to lie to him. The cold claimed the space he left behind, and my chest tightened with a longing I could not afford.

I followed my squad, and the truth sank deeper into my stomach. I had swapped one cage for another. Dawn was little more than a bruise behind the thick, oppressive clouds that never cleared as we walked into the training pits. My breath misted in front of my face as I kept my eyes down, not wanting to see the judgment in the gazes I could feel on me. No one spoke. The only sound was boots crunching against iced cobblestone and the comforting roar of waves. The Dead Sea battered the rocks nearby, each hollow crash of the waves echoing up the cliff from the beach where we had washed ashore last night. A hand rested on my shoulder, and I jumped.

Bohdi smiled down at me, his eyes an endless blue filled with nothing but kindness. A look I was not used to seeing.

"The past can only touch you if you let it," he said. The words slipped past my defences like salt in an open wound, stinging and soothing all at once. My throat tightened, but no sound came. I only stared up at him, afraid that if I spoke, the cracks would show.

Orin shoved Bohdi aside, breaking his contact with my shoulder and asserting himself next to me.

"Don't make our squad look weak out there today," Orin addressed everyone, but his eyes stayed on me.

"You will be assessed from the moment training begins. And you are a reflection on Orin now, which is why he is so uptight," Bohdi said with a smile that Orin glared at.

"Initiates!" Commander Kragthorne enhanced his voice

to boom as though he was yelling directly into each of our ears. Orin and Bohdi walked towards the other Iron Guards lining the edge of the pits.

"Welcome to the first day of training. Some of you won't make it out of the pits, but that is the Gods' grace. The weak will be broken."

A steely-looking woman with a greying dark braid and frown lines stepped up beside Commander Kragthorne. No one dared to speak.

"I am Captain Bronwyn. It is my job to turn you pathetic initiates into Iron Guards," she barked. "You will grow faster, stronger and grow your Sanctum by *my* training. Now run! Laps around the barracks until I say stop."

For one suspended heartbeat, the world held still. Then the first initiates stumbled into motion, their boots crunching over ice. The sound jolted me, and my body obeyed before my mind could, legs moving and heart beginning to pound.

Cold air scorched my throat with every breath as we ran out of the training pit. The moment I stepped off the cobblestone, I inwardly groaned. My boots sunk through slush that seemed to swallow my feet whole. I hated the snow. The cold. Everything about the never-ending winter of the Mortal Kingdom. The wind lashed needles against my face, each step dragging and slowing me down.

"Sorry for upsetting you," Riven said easily beside me, not winded in the slightest. "Your scars are none of my business... it just took me by surprise."

I stumbled, almost falling into the snow. Apologies were something I was not used to hearing. The kindness coiled like guilt in my chest. It was a foreign feeling that made my words lodge in my throat.

"It's fine," I managed between laboured breaths. We

both knew he could run much faster, but he kept pace with me. For a heartbeat, the quiet loyalty only worsened the guilt. I had wanted to hurt him less than an hour ago. We rounded the corner of the barracks, where the island expanded into dense trees. Somehow, I could sense the ocean was further away in that direction, like an inner compass. The blackened limbs of the trees rustled from a breeze I couldn't feel, and snow dusted towards the ground. An unnatural stillness prickled over my sweat-soaked skin.

Find it. My steps faltered.

It's here. A piece. Find the pieces.

The voice rasped through the branches, a chorus of whispers scraping against my bones. The shadows seemed to pulse, drawing me towards them.

"Lyra?" Riven's voice sliced through the trance.

"It's nothing," I said quickly, shaking my head and forcing my body back into motion. We had fallen behind. But the voices followed, threading through my skull, impossible to shake.

"You sure?" Riven pressed, eyes narrowing as if he could see straight through my lie.

I gave him a tight-lipped smile and ran faster. He chuckled from behind, keeping pace with infuriating ease. By the time they called us to halt, my muscles were trembling so violently I could barely stand. We jogged towards the group of initiates who looked like they may have stopped running a while ago.

I doubled over, hands on my knees, thankful that they hadn't fed us breakfast before training because I was sure it would be spilled in the snow by now.

Riven nudged his shoulder against mine, his body heat pressing into me. His grey eyes bore into mine, holding me captive for a moment.

"You did well for a princess," he said, his half smile causing a dimple in his cheek.

"I guess I'm used to running," I murmured, tilting my head up to look at him. I hadn't realised how tall he was. Or the rust-coloured flecks bursting around his iris, like a hint of golden sunlight through storm clouds.

"Arm yourselves!" Captain Bronwyn's voice startled me, and my eyes broke from Riven's as a stack of swords got dumped into the snow in front of us.

My fingers felt numb as I picked one up, nearly dropping it. It was heavier than it looked, the cold metal biting into my palms.

Lieutenants and corporals bled into the pits from the viewing benches, joining their squads.

Orin paced in front of our squad, Bohdi standing behind him with his arms crossed over his chest.

"Hold your swords in an attack position," Orin commanded. I almost laughed; I had no idea what that was. I glanced around and the others held their swords with two hands, braced in front of them with a wide stance, ready to strike at moment's notice. Clearly, they had done this before.

I struggled to mimic the stance. The sword wobbled as my balance threatened to give way.

Hadley seemed to be having difficulty as well, the tip of her sword dipping towards the ground. Her hands slipped and her sword dropped into the snow with a wet thud.

Bohdi walked over, picking up her sword and placing it in her hands with a warm smile.

"Let's try that again," he told her gently. She nodded and followed his directions.

"This is not a toy," Orin said, voice low and cold. "It's

not for show. When your Sanctum burns out, your weapon is the only thing between you and death."

He walked down the line, assessing grips and stances, stopping short when he reached me. His jaw flexed, a sigh escaping him as if he'd expected no less than to see me struggling.

"Your grip is too tight," he muttered.

He nudged my boot with his, forcing my stance to open. The heat of his body pressed into my back as he walked behind me. Large hands closed over mine, prying my white-knuckled grip loose before adjusting my hold on the hilt.

His familiar scent of leather and steel washed over me, rich and steady, tugging me back to memories of being in his arms.

It was a smell I had missed for seven years, though so much had changed since then. I was not quite the fragile princess Orin had left behind.

"Keep your shoulders down," he murmured, voice rougher now. "That's it." He was close enough that his breath stirred the hair at my temple. A flush crept up my neck. When he finally stepped away, the place where his hands had been felt cold. My stance felt steadier somehow, the sword no longer so heavy in my palms.

He walked in front of me, assessing me before nodding in approval. He continued walking down the rest of the line.

"Riven and Roman," he called, voice rising just enough to carry, "you two have the strongest stances. Let's see what you've got."

Roman stepped forward first, rolling his shoulders. His dark skin gleamed with a fine sheen of sweat despite the cold, and the muscles in his arms flexed as he gripped his sword. A thin, eager smile curved his lips, and there was something unsettling in the way his eyes glittered, like he was hoping this would be more than a drill.

Riven sauntered to meet him, grey eyes bright with mischief. A lock of wavy brown hair fell across his forehead as he tilted his head, assessing Roman like he was trying to gauge his skill. He spun the blunted blade once in his palm, casually as if he were about to toss it aside.

"Try not to cry when you lose," Riven said lightly, his grin sharp.

Roman only bared his teeth in a humourless smile and lunged. Their swords met with a metallic clash that rang in my ears, and I let my own sword drop to my side.

Roman drove forward, each strike heavy and precise, forcing Riven to retreat step by step across the packed snow. But Riven's grin never wavered. He moved with an easy, fluid grace, letting each of Roman's attacks glance off his blade as though he'd been born with a sword in his hand.

Roman grunted, pivoting into a downward strike meant to end it, but Riven twisted aside at the last instant. His blade flashed up. There was a blur of movement, Roman's sword spun from his grip, clattering across the ground.

Riven ducked and swooped his leg under Roman's, who landed flat on his back with a grunt.

Riven stood over him, not even breathless. He tapped Roman's chest lightly with the tip of his sword, smirk curling his mouth.

Roman's jaw clenched as he glared up at him, but Riven just offered a mocking bow before sauntering back to stand beside the others. As though he hadn't just humiliated one of the strongest in the group.

"Clearly you both have experience with swords. Where have you trained?" Orin asked.

"I have been in the Southern Army since I was sixteen,"

Roman answered with a slight Southern drawl, standing and straightening his uniform.

I raised my eyebrows. The Northern and Southern Kingdoms both had armies who fought between each other over food and land. Something my marriage was meant to fix. The one thing both Armies had in common was their resentment for the Iron Guard for never intervening in their squabbles. Never picking a side. No, the only thing the Iron Guard did was protect the Mortal Kingdom from the Fae.

Orin raised his eyebrows at Riven, expecting an answer.

"I'm just naturally talented at everything," Riven almost purred, clearly trying to get under Orin's skin.

"I'm sure you will still learn a thing or two," Orin replied, tension on his face.

"Doubtful. I could probably teach *you* some things," Riven drawled.

Orin stepped closer to him, the toes of their boots almost touching. Riven looked down at him with a smirk.

"Laps. Now!" Orin yelled.

"Don't get your panties in a knot," Riven drawled. "My legs could use another stretch anyway." He winked, then turned and broke into a run. With how quickly he moved through the trodden snow, it was obvious he had been holding back when he ran with me. I watched him disappear around the barracks, his pace effortlessly controlled. Too controlled. My thoughts slipped to the showers. To the silver mark I had seen nestled against his muscular torso. Not exactly the same as mine. But close enough to leave a hollow feeling in my chest that I could not explain. Apart from his absurd confidence and cockiness, he hadn't once seemed *unhinged*. Unlike me. If we were anything alike, then it was clear he knew how to control it. How to keep it leashed.

SEVEN
PURPOSE

After what felt like an eternity, a break was called. Orin and Bohdi had run us through various drills with our swords. Repetitively. Until my limbs felt like jelly and my hair clung to my sweat-soaked face. Despite my fatigue, it felt good to hold the sword in my hands. I liked holding a weapon. The darkness inside me liked it even more. Steel drums littered what seemed to be a common area between the barracks and the training pits, alight with flames. My squad trudged towards one of the rusted steel drums as Bohdi handed us each a brown packet. I unwrapped it reluctantly, the paper crunching beneath my fingertips. Rations of stale bread and jerky stared back at me, dry and unappetising. Food was an issue in our Kingdom, one that was marginally better in the castle. It was impossible to grow anything in a frozen wasteland, but I was used to tender meats, root vegetables and rich sauces. But I didn't want them to think me a spoilt princess, so I grabbed the jerky without hesitation and brought it to my mouth. I hid my grimace; it was as dry as I thought it was going to be.

No one spoke at first, everyone eating in uncomfortable

silence. Well, it felt uncomfortable to me. I was not used to being around so many people. Dreya lifted her chin, her voice sounding almost forced like she needed to break the silence for her own sanity. "Why'd you all Ascend?"

"For the glory, obviously. And the women. But mostly the glory." Riven grinned, sending a wink in my direction that spread heat across my cheeks.

Orin gave him a look of withering disdain.

"My little sister used to look up to the Iron Guards. I wasn't strong enough to save her then." Bohdi looked into the flickering flames. "But now, maybe, I can save someone else."

A silence fell. Orin's hand clasped Bohdi's shoulder, giving it a light squeeze.

Dreya's voice was quiet. "I'm here for family as well. We live in the slums of Talloport. With me here, they'll never starve again. And if I'd died...one less mouth to feed."

Hadley snorted. "I couldn't stand that place a moment longer. After my father died, it was this or whoring."

Roman's eyes were hard as flint. "I'm here to kill Fae. The more of those bastards I gut, the better."

One by one, their gazes found me over the flames, as if it were my turn to share.

I picked at the dense bread in my hands. "I couldn't handle it anymore." I shrugged, picking a close enough truth.

Hadley barked a humourless laugh. "I've heard the rumours. They say you're insane. But I didn't think you were *stupid*."

"You don't know anything about me," I said, venom lacing my voice.

"Oh, you poor spoilt, little thing, it must have been hard living in a beautiful castle, being fed every night and having a warm bed to sleep in. You wouldn't have lasted a day in the slums below your pampered fucking feet, people kill over food scraps and freeze on the street!"

The darkness hit like a fever, flooding my veins, tearing through every restraint I had left.

My vision split, everything sharpening, humming. I didn't remember moving, only the sound of Hadley's breath catching as my hand wrapped around her throat. My fingers squeezed against her windpipe and her face reddened, her mouth open in a soundless scream. I could feel a strange pull coming from inside of her. It almost felt like water, vibrating beneath her skin and waiting for me to control it.

"Let go of your squad mate, initiate," Orin said from behind me. But I couldn't. I needed to hurt her. No. I wanted to *drown* her. I reached for the water in her body with my mind. I could feel every single molecule. I tugged at it. Hadley's hazel eyes bulged, her body shaking as she scratched furiously at my hand.

"Lyra, I can feel your anger. I'm going to help you calm down. Okay?" Bohdi's voice cut through my haze. But Hadley's body began to slump, the fight dying from her eyes. Her skin turned a beautiful shade of purple, red splotches blooming on her throat around my hands. Bohdi stood behind me, gripping my shoulders. I could feel him pushing against my mind, offering me calmness. I pushed against it, slamming a wall of water over my mind. Bohdi cursed under his breath and drew his hands back as if they were burnt.

"Orin, I can't," Bohdi said, shocked.

"Let go now, Lyra!" Orin yelled. But I didn't care. I pulled at those little water threads harder, pushing them towards her lungs. My hand squeezed tighter against the frantic pulse fluttering at my fingertips.

Drown.

A hand wrapped around my forearm. Gentle. Tentative.

"Eyes on me, Princess." My head snapped up. Grey eyes, with dancing flecks of amber filled my vision. Like the sun breaking through a storm. I gasped, fingers loosening slightly.

"Good girl. Now, please let go of Hadley," Riven urged. I don't know why I listened, or how he cut through the darkness, but my fingers went slack. Hadley choked on a ragged breath, crumpling forward, coughing and spluttering. The haze over my vision lifted, leaving only the terrible clarity of what I'd done. I let my hands fall to my sides.

Roman and Bohdi were already there, hauling her upright by the elbows. Orin pressed his thumb to his brow, muttering a curse that burned more than if he'd shouted.

"Let's get her to the infirmary," he ordered, then his sharp gaze cut to me. "I'll deal with you later."

I took a stumbling step back, my eyes fixed on the purple bruises blooming across Hadley's throat, perfect imprints of my fingers.

"It's alright, Lyra." Riven's voice slipped through my daze, steady where mine had fled. Orin led Hadley towards the barracks, his expression unreadable. I could only stare, words lodged behind the tightness in my chest. I should feel remorse. Guilt for hurting someone. Shame for letting the darkness take over. But all I felt was anger. Anger at myself. The Gods for willing me to live against my will.

Riven slipped an arm around my shoulders. I flinched at the contact, but didn't pull away.

"Come on," he murmured, leading me to the cliff we had climbed through the night before. Dreya walked quietly next to us, the curious stares of the other squads following us. Their gazes felt like a physical weight, suffocating me. The wind clawed at my flushed cheeks as we reached the cliff's edge. The Dead Sea writhed below, its waves shattering against the black-pebbled shore like a thousand furious hearts beating out of time.

I took a deep breath, the salt sinking into my lungs and tingling through my veins soothingly.

"I don't think she will bother you again after that," Dreya said hesitantly, picking up a rock and throwing it into the waves. She eyed me with a mix of curiosity and wariness, as if she expected me to lash out at any moment.

"I didn't mean to lose control like that," I muttered, arms wrapping tightly around myself. My body could still feel the heat of Hadley's pulse beneath my fingers, the way it faltered when I'd squeezed too hard. The way I had liked it. I *hated* that I liked it.

Dreya picked up another rock, studying it in her hands. "It's this place. We went into the Dead Sea and lived. It unmade us. Our bodies are changing. Becoming stronger. Faster. Soon, we will have our Sanctum. I think a temper tantrum here and there is allowed."

I watched her rock disappear, claimed by the violent waves. But that wasn't the first time I had touched the sea and craved more. Even after drowning during Ascension, I longed to go back.

"Did the sea drown you?" I murmured absently. Perhaps it happened to everyone.

"Drown?" Riven asked. "It was hard to swim against the swell. But no, clearly none of us drowned, Princess, or we wouldn't be standing here." They both stared at me as though I was broken. I sighed. I had drowned, and since then the voices had never been so loud. The urges so close to the surface.

Something inside me felt awake in a way it never had before. It scared me how natural it felt. I had spent my life fighting it, fearing it. Now it lurked just beneath my skin, patient and volatile.

"What happened to you in the water, Lyra?" Dreya asked with careful wariness, studying as if I were an animal about to lash out. "Did *you* drown?"

"Nothing happened," I said too quickly. The words tasted wrong even as they left my mouth. I shoved the unease aside as it tightened in my stomach, willing it not to show.

"You can't be serious, Dreya," Riven scoffed, his attention flicking to her before returning to me. "You know those myths are just stories."

"Those myths are all we have left of our Gods! It is our duty to—"

"To believe every little bedtime story?" Riven cut in. His grin came effortlessly, and he punctuated it with a wink towards me, as though Dreya's worry meant nothing. Before I could ask what story they were talking about, Captain Bronwyn's voice boomed from the training pits. "Break's over, initiates!"

Captain Bronwyn's boots struck the floor in a steady, merciless rhythm, echoing through the amphitheatre like the pulse of a war drum as she walked down the steps. We were herded from the barracks into a vast hall opposite the dining room, the theory hall. Rows of iron chairs descended towards an empty stage, silent and expectant. I sat in between Riven and Dreya, watching the shadows dance against the stone walls as the flames of the torches flickered. Roman sat next to Riven, he had returned without Hadley. A part of me wanted to ask if she was okay, the other part hoped she wasn't.

"Forget what you know about our history. About our purpose as Iron Guards," Captain Bronwyn's voice echoed as she stopped in front of a large chalkboard.

"Now that the Commander of Death has resurfaced, they will be unpredictable and ruthless." She paused, the silence as taut as a wire. "We are preparing for bloodshed."

Riven's leg brushed mine. Light, accidental even, yet heat bled through the fabric and into my skin. I stared at the place we touched. I told myself to move. To pull away. Not to be curious about the steadiness his touch offered. But I couldn't. I didn't want to.

Bronwyn's cold voice carried across the amphitheatre. "It is because of this that the war games are being brought forwards. They are designed to awaken your *Sanctums*. The squad with the highest number of victories by year's end earns leadership within the Iron Guard." She paused, letting the weight of her words settle. "They will be more brutal than ever to ensure we are as strong as we can be." A ripple of murmurs spread through the amphitheatre. My pulse quickened, a drumbeat of equal dread and excitement at the thought of more bloodshed, more death. Maybe the Gods will change their minds and take me as a sacrifice after all.

"Now," she said, turning towards the slate board, "let's begin. It's time you learn the *true purpose* of the Iron Guard."

Captain Bronwyn's gaze swept over us, sharp as drawn steel. She seemed the sort of person who had forgotten how to smile long ago.

"Before the Gods left us, the Sirens didn't just rule the sea," she began. "Their queen ruled over us *all,* Fae and Mortal alike. Until the Fae slaughtered them."

She walked along the stage slowly, hands clasped. "Does anyone know why the Sirens were killed?"

Hands shot up around the room, Captain Bronwyn pointed at an initiate in the front.

"Their blood held magical properties, drinking it gave you powers, *strength*." My skin prickled. Perhaps I had something in common with the Sirens, they had also been drained of their blood against their will.

"Correct. But what commoners don't know is that the Sea Goddess herself was their queen. She turned her back on our beloved Gods, because she fell in love with a Mortal. The Gods were furious with her. And because it was a Mortal that she fell for, our Gods turned their back on *us*. They stole her Mortal lover and turned him into a monster and cursed our lands. As you already know, the Fae led the final battle," Bronwyn continued. "They slaughtered the Sirens and the Sea Goddess for the Gods, staying in their favour. It is because of her we are cursed."

She turned towards the slate board, drawing three sharp lines across it with a piece of chalk.

"But before she died, the Sea Goddess shattered her own soul, splitting it into three Relics scattered across the realms. The Soul Relics."

Bronwyn faced us again, her eyes hard. "Our duty, the true purpose of the Iron Guard, is to find these Relics and destroy them before the prophecy is fulfilled. This is not knowledge shared beyond this island." Her voice dropped to a near-whisper, though it carried like a threat. "The prophecy says the Sea Goddess will rise again, that she will drown the world for killing her Sirens and kill the Gods themselves for taking her lover. We exist to make certain that never happens, and if we destroy the Relics, the Gods may shine on us again. And that, initiates, is why anyone who manifests a water Sanctum is deemed too dangerous to live."

Captain Bronwyn kept talking, but I couldn't hear her over the pounding of my own heart. My stomach dropped; the air felt too thin. I'd moved the water in Hadley's body, hadn't I? No. That couldn't mean... My hand gripped Riven's thigh, and I sat rigid on the edge of my seat. I'd done it. I had moved the water in her body. It had sung to me. No. I was confused. I was just angry. Caught up in the moment.

"Uh, Princess?" Riven shifted beneath my touch.

I blinked, pulling my hand away. "Sorry."

"Oh, it's more than fine," he murmured, that stupid, lopsided grin tugging at his mouth. "Just... maybe not in public."

Heat rushed to my cheeks, and I shuffled away as Dreya leant forward with an irritated sigh.

"Can you two be quiet?" she hissed, snapping her book shut.

Riven only rolled his eyes, slinging his arm across the back of my chair. But the seed of worry had already taken root in my stomach. I'd felt my Sanctum awaken, and it was something forbidden.

EIGHT
WAR GAMES

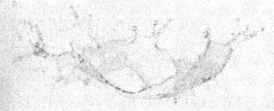

Riven and I rounded the stairs and stepped into the dim corridor leading to our rooms. After being dismissed by Captain Bronwyn, we were instructed to return to our rooms. Riven hadn't said a word to me, but the occasional brush of his arm against mine felt almost reassuring. My steps faltered. Roman and Dreya's conversation died off from behind us as Orin came into view. He leant against the wall beside our door, arms crossed, the hard lines of his face and body radiating tension.

"You look grumpy, fearless leader," Riven drawled, voice dripping with mockery.

He pushed off the wall, closing the distance between them and shoving Riven. "Shut your Gods-damned mouth, initiate."

Riven grinned in his face, squaring his shoulders. "Do it again. I dare you."

"Riven, stop it," Dreya warned.

"Get out of my face. All of you! Shower and change for dinner."

"As you wish," Riven said as he stepped around him, but the sarcasm in his voice was palpable.

The vein in Orin's forehead looked like it was going to burst as I went to walk past him. "Not you, Lyra."

The others left me alone in the hallway, the door closing behind them. The silence was suffocating as he stared down at me. I was certain they'd only seen me strangling Hadley. But what if he knew I was trying to drown her?

"Hadley will be fine," he said finally. "If you care."

"I don't," I snapped, lifting my chin. But I did. I didn't want another person's death on my hands.

He let out a long, tired sigh and rested his head against the stone. "Lyra, you can't do that here. Your actions reflect on me. If I can't control a squad of initiates, they won't let me be lieutenant in the field."

I stepped closer, splaying my hands against his chest.

He stiffened beneath my touch, eyes dropping to meet mine. "I'm warning you. You can't do that again." Something in his voice softened; he swallowed, then curled his arms around my shoulders and drew me in. The scent of steel and leather steadied me.

"I'm upset with you," he murmured into my hair.

"I could fix that," I whispered, slipping fingers beneath his belt.

His hands caught my wrists, pinning them to his chest. "And where do you suppose we reminisce, Princess? In our shared room?" He pressed me back a step. "If you disobey me or attack a squadmate again, it will be twenty-four hours in a cell, and we both know you don't like dungeons. After that, the third strike is death."

My spine went rigid. His eyes softened in a blink of vulnerability before he bent and pressed a brief, longing kiss to my forehead, an apology and a warning wrapped together. "Stay in line, remember? Now go. Get ready for dinner with the squad."

The tall stone walls of the dining hall opened into vaulted ceilings that made the sound of hundreds of Iron Guards chatting amplify as they ate.

I gathered a premade tray from a large bench. Bread, grains, fruit and some sort of meat. I was hungry enough that it made my mouth water. I followed Dreya to a table near double doors that looked as though they opened to a balcony, where the rest of our squad sat.

"Can you tell us more about the war games?" Roman asked Bohdi as we sat down.

"They weed out the weak, prepare you for real war, and build squad camaraderie. But they also help initiates develop Sanctums."

"Yes, but when do they start?" he asked, aligning his cutlery in a perfect row.

"We don't know," Orin cut in with a frustrated sigh. "All we have been told is to expect a higher death toll this year. They want to force out strong Sanctums."

"Hmm games and death, two of my favourite things. Add fucking in there and you'd have a trifecta," Riven said with an arrogant smirk. Roman chuckled under his breathe despite himself. Whatever rivalry that had existed between them apparently gone. Probably worn down slowly by Riven's charm. He was a difficult person to dislike, unlike me. I had caught Dreya watching me out of the corner of her eye on more than one occasion since I had choked Hadley. I didn't blame her.

After eating, I returned to our room, leaving the others to chat and drink. Exhaustion pressed heavily on me as I lay on the small bed, the rough blankets scratching against my skin.

My entire body ached. Muscles I didn't realise I had ached with every breath I took. But I had survived my first day as an Iron Guard initiate. Even if it was short lived and unwanted, I felt a small flicker of pride. The only thing that stopped me from antagonising Orin into killing me was my curiosity. Water Sanctums were forbidden, linked to a prophecy that could kill the Gods. Was I, their villain? An evil worth killing?

Dreya had become paranoid around me after I asked about drowning. I needed to know why. Perhaps there was a purpose to this. To me surviving. Exhaustion dragged me with prying claws into the nightmares that waited for me each night.

A bell tolled, high and shrill, ripping me from the depths of sleep with a jolt. I sat up, squinting against the darkness. The embers in the hearth had died to a dull glow.

A woman in dark grey leathers and a thick winter cloak stood in our room, a lantern glowing in one hand and a bell in the other.

"Follow me," the woman said, watching us strip our blankets off. Roman reached for his neatly folded clothes. "No," the woman said. His fingers paused and he looked up.

"No boots. No cloaks."

"Sounds fucking freezing," Riven muttered as he threw his blanket off and stood, stretching with a yawn.

"If you do not comply, you will forfeit this round of war games."

"That won't be necessary, Lucy. We will follow you," Orin quickly rushed out. He gestured for her to walk and she nodded and turned, walking out the door. Nerves fluttered through my stomach. Everyone looked uptight and nervous, except for Riven. He looked the way he always did. Confident and unbothered.

We wound down the stairs to the common floor, passing the dining hall doors and turning right down a small corridor. An arched door was carved into the stone, two Iron Guards standing in front of it. They nodded at the woman leading us and parted, opening the door for her. I rubbed the goose bumps pebbling over my arms as we wound down a dark staircase. Mildew grew along the stones like veins, and I inhaled a shaky breath. The smell of damp earth and metal flooded my senses. Pure panic shot through me.

A dungeon. My feet faltered, not wanting to continue forward. Someone ran into my back and I stumbled forwards.

"Ugh! Watch it," Hadley sneered.

I swallowed the lump growing in my throat and forced my feet to take the next step down.

At the bottom of the stairs, the dungeon opened like a maw waiting to swallow us. The other squads were gathered here already, shivering and confused in their night clothes.

Commander Kragthorne stood in the centre of the gathering. An unwelcoming smile spread across his scarred face. "Welcome to the first war game."

NINE
A GAME OF TRUTHS

"War is harsh." Commander Kragthorne's voice rung with steel as he addressed us. "When in enemy territory, trust among your fellow squad mates is crucial." He paced in a circle, boots stomping with each movement, gaze piercing through the crowd.

"This game is one of trust. Each squad enters a dungeon and the first to escape wins. Simple right?" Murmurs broke out across the crowd. "Listen closely." He paused, running a hand over his greying beard. "Only truth can unmake what fear has chained. Answer wrong and beware the price. Answer right and be free tonight." He nodded, then the Iron Guards pressed in around us, pushing us into a small dark room.

A cell.

Breathe, I told myself. *The priest is dead. There are no knives. No chains.*

"Sit with your backs to the wall," Lucy said, blocking the exit to the small stone cell. I sat against the cold, damp stone, a shiver tearing through me. Orin crossed the room, choosing to sit next to me. His eyes gleamed with a hint of concern in the light of a single torch flickering next to the heavy door. I didn't want it too close, but I knew it would.

"Good luck," Lucy said, placing her hands against the stone wall. It rumbled beneath our backs as she closed her eyes in concentration. Coldness pressed around my wrists. I gasped, tugging against the restraints that now chained me to the wall. *No. No. No.* I struggled, thrashing against the stone binders. They tightened, gripping me painfully.

"Lyra! Stop fighting it!" Orin yelled at me. But it was too late, the memory drowning me.

"Stop fighting it, Princess." The priest ran his knife softly against my bare skin. The chains dug into my wrists. Into my ankles. My blood dripped on the floor. He always bled me first. He liked me weak. He shoved my nightdress above my thighs, unbuckling his belt—

"Lyra!" Orin's voice pulled me from the memory.

I stilled, glaring at him through a mess of silver hair that covered my face.

"Psycho," Hadley rasped. I bared my teeth at her.

"Why are they tighter now?" Roman asked, tapping his foot against the floor. He was right, the shackles were now bruising.

"They are enchanted. If you physically try to break them, they will tighten," Orin answered.

"And by the sounds of it, if we answer wrong, they are going to hurt us," Bohdi added.

"Kinky," Riven said, examining his wrists.

"I wish I could hit you right now," Dreya said, rolling her eyes at him.

"Could we be serious for a minute and get out of these damned chains?" Hadley glared daggers at them both, my finger marks still bruised across her throat.

I tried to steady my breathing, focusing on the coolness of the stone pressing into my back.

"Commander Kragthorne said, 'only truth can unmake what fear has chained'," Orin recited.

"So, we just need to say something that is true, and we will be free?" Roman asked.

Orin shrugged but looked hesitant. "It seems too easy."

"I'll go first," Riven said with a shrug. "I am devilishly handsome." He held up his wrists, staring at them, waiting for them to unclasp.

Riven's eyes rolled back. He slammed to the ground like a puppet, the chain protruding from the wall groaning with the effort. His muscles spasmed so violently I thought his bones would snap. Then he stilled, gasping like he'd been drowned. It stopped as suddenly as it began. Riven wheezed as he rolled into a half-seated position. "Oh. That fucking sucked."

"I told you you're not as handsome as you think," Dreya snorted. He placed a hand over his heart and frowned at her.

"Someone willing to try an actual truth?" Dreya asked.

"I didn't really want to be an Iron Guard," Roman mumbled, staring at the ground in front of him. He gritted his teeth as his head lolled against the stone, legs shaking violently. He gasped as it ended, looking at Riven. "You weren't wrong, that sucked." Sweat beaded against the bronzed skin despite the cold.

"Was that actually true?" Hadley whispered. Roman nodded once. "So perhaps the answer is not just any truth." Hadley moved to her knees, excitement flittering over her pixie-like features. Orin tilted his head, eyebrows drawn.

"What fear has chained..." he muttered.

"Our fears," she finished. "They want us to bare our weaknesses."

Bile rose in my throat.

"I fear that I'll keep failing the people I love." Orin braced, but nothing happened. His shackles groaned. My heart ached, a mere echo of the pain I had felt when he left me.

"They loosened!" He beamed.

"Wow, that was deep man." Riven raised an eyebrow at him and Orin glared.

Bohdi hung his head, blond strands that had been tucked behind his ears slipping in front of his face. "I'm fearful that someone else will die because of me." His shackles groaned and released. He said nothing as he rubbed at his wrists absently.

"You were just a kid, Bohdi. It wasn't your fault," Orin said. Bohdi gave him a tight-lipped smile and looked away. I didn't need to be an empath to feel his pain.

"I fear that I won't develop a Sanctum," Hadley said. Her shackles groaned.

"I fear I will fail as this squad's leader, that I'll mess up the first responsibility I've been given." Orin's shackles crumbled, he glanced around the room at each of us.

"Come on, guys," he said. "I know its uncomfortable. But the quicker you come out with your fears, the faster we win. Hurry up."

Roman sighed and tipped his head back against the stone. "I'm fearful that I'll die before I can avenge my brother. He died in the Fae realms at their hands. He was thrown back through the gate in pieces as a warning." Roman glared at his shackles. They groaned, loosening but not letting go. "Fine! I am fearful of the Fae," he whispered angrily.

The shackles exploded. He stood, brushing the stone debris off his pants. "This is a stupid game."

"Agreed," Riven said.

"I fear I will die, and my family will starve in the slums." Dreya spoke directly to the stone cuffs, ignoring us all. They groaned. She raised her eyebrows, surprised they hadn't released her. "I worry I'm not good enough to make it," they groaned again. "I fear the return of the Gods." Stone debris exploded over her, and she adjusted her dark brown braids, completely unbothered that she had just shared something vulnerable to a room of strangers.

"That is your only fear that makes sense," Riven said lazily. The orange torch light flickering over his smirk. "If they come back, they will be merciless."

Dreya's eyes cut to me, lingering for a moment too long and filling with weariness, as if she were seeing me differently in the torchlight. The look unsettled me more than it should have. I didn't know what she saw when she looked at me, only that her gaze carried the weight of suspicion I didn't understand.

"We need to hurry up," Orin said, pacing the small area like a trapped animal.

"I've always feared that people don't actually like me," Hadley rasped, her voice still croaky from my hands squishing her windpipe. Her shackles broke free.

"Your fear is also correct." Riven smiled sweetly at her. She raised her middle finger at him and crossed her arms. Riven looked at me, flashing his dimples in a challenging smirk. We were the last two. The most guarded.

"I fear nothing," he said. He gritted his teeth as his body contorted with pain. It lasted longer than before, as if punishing him for lying so freely.

"Why would you do that to yourself?" I whispered.

Riven laughed, the sound loose and reckless. He tipped his head back against the stone, dishevelled strands of hair falling over his brow as torchlight skimmed over the hard planes of his body. His eyes snapped to mine. Grey but with an underlying brightness, alight with something feral. His smile slowed, turning deliberate as his gaze held mine, unflinching. The air tightened between us. His chest rose with a slow breath, muscles rolling beneath skin as if he were savouring the effect he was having on me.

"Oh, darling. I like the pain," his voice had dropped an octave, and he ran his tongue along his teeth.

"Lyra?" Orin asked. I reluctantly dragged my eyes from Riven to Orin's tension filled face.

"If I don't answer, will the time run out eventually?"

Orin shook his head. "No, we will be trapped in this room for as long as it takes."

What was there to even say when I feared so many things?

"I fear my father," I whispered. The shackles loosened their relentless grip, and I sighed.

"Keep going Lyra," Dreya encouraged with a small smile. I took her encouragement and took a deep breath. "I fear that I will be killed."

For a moment nothing happened. Then pain invaded my senses in aggressive waves. White. Hot. Blinding. I gritted my teeth.

It left as quickly as it had started. I opened my eyes, panting. Riven was watching me closely, his eyes filled with curiosity.

"I fear I'm going to break everything I touch," he whispered, keeping his eyes trained on me. His shackles groaned.

"I'm scared of chains," I said back, pushing myself up

onto my knees. The shackles released a mere fraction. Out of the corner of my eye, I saw Hadley raise her eyebrow. Orin looked away.

"The dark frightens me," Riven said casually.

"Good Gods, why are you two so stubborn? It obviously needs something that is *deep* for you. Just get on with it," Roman groaned, pacing the cell like a caged animal.

"I fear I will never be free," I whispered, cheeks reddening with shame.

Crack.

"But most of all, I fear myself."

My shackles exploded, debris scattering over my scratchy cotton shift. I swiped a single tear away with a shaky hand. Dreya offered me her hand, helping me to stand.

"Thank you," I whispered, tilting my chin higher and avoiding eye contact with everyone.

"Just you now, Riven. Come on, get us out of this cell," Orin encouraged.

"Why?" Riven scoffed. "So, you can fool command into thinking you're fit for leadership?"

Orin closed the distance in two strides and drove his fist into Riven's face. The crack echoed off stone.

Riven's head snapped to the side. Riven's lip split as he grinned up at Orin, blood smearing against his white teeth and dripping down his chin. "That was cute," he said hoarsely. "But I honestly thought you'd hit harder."

Orin snarled and slammed his fist into Riven's stomach. The breath tore from him in a sharp, ugly sound, his body folding for half a second before he straightened again, laughter bubbling up dark and broken. "You can do better than that."

Orin's fist came down again. And again. Riven's head

rocked back against the wall, a dull crack as stone met bone. Bruising bloomed across his cheek, dark and fast, his lip split further, blood smearing along his jaw. But Orin's blows kept coming, relentless and furious.

"Stop," Dreya snapped, stepping forward, but Roman caught her arm, shaking his head hard.

"Bohdi?" I asked, my voice higher pitch with panic that had started to pump through my veins. What if Orin didn't stop?

Bohdi hovered at the edge of it, shooting me an apologetic grimace. His hands flexed uselessly, torn between intervening and knowing Orin wouldn't listen.

Riven sagged against the wall, chest heaving, a wet chuckle spilling from him even as Orin's knuckles drove into his ribs.

"Orin, stop!" I shouted, my voice cracking as I lunged forward. "You're going to kill him!"

Another punch landed. Riven coughed, blood flecking the stone, his cheek split now.

I grabbed Orin's arm, desperation burning through me. "Please!"

Orin hesitated, breath ragged. There was no anger in his eyes, just a quiet satisfaction as he looked down at the bloodied mess he had made.

Riven lifted his head slowly, a dark grin still spread across his gore-stricken face.

I crouched down in front of him, panic clawing up my throat. "Please, Riven," I begged. "Just say your fear."

For a heartbeat, the room went still as if everyone was waiting for Riven to give in.

Riven's gaze found mine through the haze, one eye nearly shut, the other sharp and lucid. His grin faltered, just barely, something dark flickering beneath it.

"...No," he rasped.

I placed my hand against his cheek. "Please," I whispered again.

He sighed, leaning into my touch and letting his eyes flicker shut.

"That I will never be worthy of love," he whispered into the dim light, voice cracking with emotion that made my heart squeeze.

The shackles exploded from around Riven's wrists and I stood back. Riven stood slowly, when he grunted in pain and stumbled, I tried to steady him. But he pushed me away. He gave a mock bow and the door flew open. We followed Orin out into the dungeon's walkway.

Commander Kragthorne sat on a chair in the centre of the room.

"You are thirteenth. Be smarter next time. A squad must work together and have each other's backs. Your squad has..." He paused, running a hand down his beard and looking at Riven's bloodied and bruised face. "Issues," he finished.

"Now get out of my sight and sleep while you can. Training begins in two hours."

Orin and Bohdi saluted our commander. He stared at us until we did the same, then gave us a dismissive nod.

We walked in silence back to our room, the sound of boots scuffing over stone filling the awkwardness.

I felt exposed, a part of me bared to these strangers that no one had seen before. Though judging by their downcast gazes, they all felt just as violated as I did. I knew their deepest fears. They knew mine. And somehow, that made them feel like more than strangers even though I had known them for three days.

TEN

A GHOST IN THE WOODS

My legs felt heavy as I ran through the snow. The first two laps had been torturous. My muscles ached with each movement, sore from yesterday's training. But I had found with each step, the pain faded into a bearable throb. I was surprised that the rest of the squad kept pace with me today. Even Hadley. Orin and Bohdi didn't have to run with us, but they chose to. A show of unity. Maybe our forced bonding had made us stronger, or maybe it was all for show.

The other squads seemed to run together as well, their lieutenant and corporal ran beside them too, boots crunching in time like a rhythm of survival. Two squads had still not made it out of the dungeons, and I wondered if they ever would.

We passed the grove of snow-capped trees behind the barracks. Each time we did, gooseflesh would rip across my skin, and a strange feeling would make my stomach uneasy.

But this time the feeling was stronger. Something in my chest pulled, a deep tugging sensation towards the grove that made me gasp.

My feet faltered. A familiar melody floated through the air, coiling itself deep within me.

"Keep moving, or they'll make us run extra," Hadley snapped, breathless. Her voice was still raspy, and her bruising had somehow become more vibrant overnight.

"Why are you singing?" Dreya asked from beside me, her bronzed skin glistening with sweat. I hadn't realised I was singing and my song died under the scrutiny of her gaze.

My eyes were locked on a ghost only I could see.

The figure wove between the oaks, but her feet left no trace in the snow. Her hair floated as if she were underwater, translucent strands shifting in slow, weightless waves.

I staggered towards the trees before realising I was moving.

"If your legs are tired, princess," Riven drawled, snapping me back to reality. "You could always rest them on my shoulders." He shot me a wink.

"Shut up, Riven," Orin ordered, shoving his shoulder and Riven stumbled back with an amused chuckle.

"Go, I will wait with Lyra while she catches her breath. When you lap us, we will stay together," Orin said.

Towards the ghost.

A warm hand on my shoulder startled me. I whirled, almost colliding into Orin's chest.

"Easy now," Orin said soothingly, running his hands gently over my shoulders. "Focus on where you are."

"I was..." I trailed off, looking back over my shoulder, searching for the ethereal woman.

"You were humming and walking after something no one else could see. You were having an episode. I know."

An episode. A bitter taste rose in my mouth, but I

nodded. The palace guards were trained to watch me for signs of my madness, to report me for bloodlettings.

"I worry about you being without your... treatments," he said in a hushed tone.

I stiffened under his touch.

"I know they were rough for you. But you did seem less... *troubled* for a few days after them."

"You've been gone for seven years, Orin. Trust me when I say I was more troubled *after* them," my voice trembled.

"What does *that* mean?" His eyebrows drew together, his hands stilling on my shoulder.

"Don't worry about it," I muttered, trying to peer around him.

Suspicion darkened his features. His hands gripped my shoulders tightly.

"Lyra?" He demanded. "How did it get worse?" But I couldn't tell him. I didn't want him to know how I had suffered through the priest's lust.

"Why did you leave me?" I asked instead, ignoring his question. It made me sick to my stomach even thinking about what the priest took from me. I couldn't tell him.

"Aldric caught me sneaking out of your room the night before the last Ascension. He gave me two options. It was either death by the king's hand or sacrificing myself." He sighed, leaning his forehead against mine. "It broke a part of me to disappear."

"It broke me too," I whispered.

"If you keep seeing things or hearing things that aren't there, promise me you will find somewhere private and..." He trailed off.

I gave him a stiff nod, but bile rose in my throat. He wanted me to slice a blade through my own flesh. *Gods, no.*

The idea made my skin crawl, like something vile had slithered under it. The thing growing inside me since my last bloodletting had begun to feel like a part of me. I could feel it, swirling in my chest behind the cage I had shoved it in. But it felt like it would protect me, which was more than anyone else had ever done for me. The sound of boots against snow made us jump apart. I turned to see our squad rounding the barracks, another squad closely behind them.

They grew closer and we started jogging again. The woman in the trees still watched me, beckoning me with her song.

"Are you alright?" Dreya panted beside me.

"Just not as fit as all of you," I puffed. It wasn't a lie.

"A life as pampered princess will do that," Hadley rasped, rolling her eyes.

"Yet here we are," Roman said, nodding towards the snow. "Running in the cold like we're all the same."

I kept my eyes forward, forcing my legs to move with the others. But as we passed the grove again, I couldn't help it. I glanced back.

The trees were still. Empty. But the air *hummed*.

And deep inside my chest, that tug was still there. *She* was there. Waiting.

THE DINING HALL BUZZED WITH LAUGHTER AND clinking plates. Our squad sat together, joking about drills and sore muscles. I tried to listen. Tried to eat.

But the song was still there, whispering beneath my thoughts.

Orin cleared his throat from besides me. "You're humming again, princess."

I cast my eyes down in shame, picking idly at the dried meat and dense bread made from potatoes on my plate.

"I like your singing, Lyra," Riven said lightly. Dark bruises bloomed over his jaw, his left eye purple and swollen shut. He grinned at me, the split in his lip re-opening and oozing blood. He had refused to go to the healers.

Hadley laughed. "I thought you were from Talloport?"

"I was only there for a month before Ascension. Why?" Riven asked curiously.

"She," Hadley snapped, pointing her fork in my direction, "is a lunatic. I was friends with a kitchen hand that worked at the castle. She said our princess here claimed to sing to ghosts. That if you listened closely, sometimes you could hear her screams —"

I gripped the edge of the table, knuckles turning white as my breathing laboured.

Claw her eyes out. Drown her.

The whispers slithered through my mind. Something inside me twisted. I wanted her to suffer. I reached for the water in her body and pulled. Hadley coughed, clutching her bruised throat. *No.* I dug my nails into my palm, grounding myself with the pain. *I need to stay in control.*

"Go and fuck yourself," I gritted out. Dreya spat her water across the table, eyes flashing with surprise.

"Lyra." Orin slammed his hands on the table as he stood. "You're dismissed from dinner." My nails split my skin; I focused on the sting. Riven grinned, as if he were watching the most amusing thing in the world.

"As you wish," I muttered, spinning on my heel and walking through the crowded dining hall. I kept my head high as I walked out, keeping my eyes trained on the door. I stormed out of the dining hall, stalking towards the main doors. At least I could go to the trees and see if the ghostly woman was still there. I could still hear her singing, like an undertone filtering through my body.

My boots scuffed across the dimly-lit foyer, and I pushed on the massive iron door. Its hinges squeaked, opening to the frigid winds that battered the island. Two Iron Guards turned towards me, metal helmets on as if going to battle, armour glistening in the faint light.

"Sorry, initiate, new curfew. No one leaves the barracks after dark." One of them stepped in front of me, eyeing the lighter grey colour of my uniform.

I let out a frustrated breath and spun on my heel. *I had freed myself from one cage to be locked in another.* With nowhere else to go but the room, I stomped up the stairs.

Orin's boots clipped the stone behind me, taking the stairs two at a time to catch up to me.

"Hey." He grabbed my hand, and I spun towards him. "Are you alright?"

"Just going to bed like I've been ordered." He stood below me on the stairs, and I enjoyed that I could speak down to him.

"You can't mouth off at your squad mates like that. It makes me look bad."

"She was the one speaking about things she doesn't know. Yet you—"

I stopped. My hands clenched at my sides and the words died behind my teeth: *You didn't save me. You did nothing. You let her mock me. You left me behind.* None of it left my mouth.

"Gods damn it, Lyra. You need control yourself. Especially around other Iron Guards. I am trying to protect you." He sighed and ran a hand through his red hair. He stared into my eyes and my breath caught, an unsteady sigh leaving me. I was no longer the broken princess he used to hold. I had saved myself and slayed my own monster. And worse, I enjoyed the darkness that he saw as a problem. He leant in, closing the distance between us.

"I'm sorry," I whispered. "I—"

He held his hand up to stop me. "I know I broke your heart when I left, princess. I know it will take time for me to heal that. But I won't stop trying. If you just stay in line, we could be happy again."

I softened. I *wanted* to be happy. "Come upstairs with me?" I asked, looking down at the hair I twirled between my fingers.

"I would like nothing more, but there has been an emergency meeting called. The Fae have gathered on the other side of the gate."

A shiver spread through my body. "Are they going to attack?" I asked, dropping my hair. Orin shrugged. "They haven't before, but things are different now that their Commander of Death is back."

He reached into his pocket and pulled out a pocketknife, pressing it into my palm and closing my fingers around it.

"For your..." He hesitated. "*Troubles.*"

He kissed me on my cheek before walking back down the stairs. I stared down at the knife, the thing inside me almost growling at the thought of spilling my own blood.

I won't, I assured it.

I didn't understand the darkness that lurked beneath my skin, but I knew it wanted to protect me. It had grown stronger every day I went without a bloodletting and I *liked* feeling strong. I climbed the stairs alone, and while a part of me was disappointed, the other part was grateful not to have to wear the mask of the princess he preferred.

ELEVEN
FIND THE PIECES

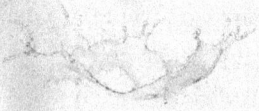

I wasn't sure what woke me. One moment I was tangled in dreams of chains and knives, the next I was blinking into the dark. The glow of the dying embers of the hearth was the only light as I looked around. Soft snores and the rustle of blankets were the only noise breaking the eerie silence. Something moved through the darkness. I whipped my head around, but nothing was there. A gentle ache blossomed behind my ribs, syncing to the now frantic beat of my heart. I pressed a hand to my sternum, feeling the faint raised edge of the silver birthmark. The ache deepened, sharp and insistent, until it was no longer just a feeling, but an instinct.

Come, a voice whispered from the darkness.

Cold air slid over my damp skin, raising gooseflesh. My breath bloomed in front of me as the air grew colder by the second. Around me, the others slept, but I knew something was wrong.

I froze.

Hollow eyes watched me from the corner of the room. Awareness crawled over my skin like cold, damp fingers.

Her long hair billowed around her like pale water as she drifted closer. I could see through her body as though she was stitched from moonlight and mist.

It was the woman from the woods.

My heart beat tripped. I knew that cold, voiceless pull. I had felt it all my life. I hadn't seen a ghost since my blood-lettings started. Until coming here.

I opened my mouth to sing, knowing that my voice would send her away. But the woman with the floating hair lifted a ghostly finger to her lips, shushing me silently. My voice froze in my throat as I watched her with curiosity.

She pointed towards the far wall, where I knew the woods behind the barracks laid. The same woods that had pulled me near every time I had run past. She floated towards the door, waiting for me to follow.

My heart fluttered violently against my ribcage as I swung my legs over the edge of the bunk.

A voice broke the hush as my feet touched the cold stone.

"Lyra?"

Dreya was sitting up on her cot, watching me with sleep-filled eyes, hair unbound in a wild tangle of black curls. "What are you doing?"

Before I could answer, Riven pushed himself up onto his elbows in the bunk across from mine, his hair falling in front of his eyes. "Why in the Seven Hells are you two talking at this ungodly hour?"

I swallowed, mouth ashen. "I...I have to go."

Dreya frowned. "We are on lockdown."

I gestured to the drifting woman before sighing heavily. Anyone who I had tried to explain this to in the past labelled me mad, had me punished and bled for being evil.

"I just need to check something, I won't be long."

Dreya sighed heavily then tore her blankets off, muttering as she pulled her boots on.

"Right, well, we'd better be careful. I don't want to know what happens if we're caught."

For a heartbeat, just one, I swore Riven's eyes fixed on the ghost as he flexed his jaw.

But then he blinked, and his mouth curved into that careless smirk. "I love a midnight stroll."

I didn't argue, not wanting to waste time. I pulled on my boots, laces fumbling in my numb fingers. We each pulled on our uniformed cloaks and creaked the door open.

Once we were out in the corridor, I watched with wonder as the translucent woman floated down the spiralling staircase. I trailed after her, Riven and Dreya following silently.

The ghost led us to the main foyer of the barracks, but instead of leading us to the front doors, where I knew guards were stationed, it took us down a hallway I hadn't walked before. Other corridors branched off in every direction, but the ghost glided steadily ahead, never hesitating. The orange flames of the oil lanterns guttered with each step we took, shadows dancing across the walls in shapes that looked almost human.

"Where are we going?" Dreya whispered.

"I don't know yet," I answered honestly. The ghost walked through the iron door at the end of the hallway, and I hesitated, before turning back to Riven and Dreya. Anytime I had followed ghosts, trouble had followed.

At twelve years old, before the bloodlettings began, it was this same ghost that had led me into the Dead Sea. Two guards had followed me into the waves to drag me out. Their blood boiled them alive while I watched. That was the last day my father ever allowed me outside the castle walls.

"I will meet you back in our room," I insisted.

Dreya shook her head. "No, I'm going to make sure you stay out of trouble."

I looked at Riven, determination shining through the bruises. He crossed his arms and raised his eyebrows at me. "Make me."

I sighed, turning and opening the door into the frigid night air.

With no stars able to shine through the thick, oppressive clouds, the nights were *dark*. If I squinted, I could barely make out the thick copse of trees behind the barracks. The pulling sensation inside my chest peaked, a painful ache that I rubbed absently as I stepped into the thick white snow.

"Wait," Riven murmured from behind me, disappearing back through the door. The sound of metal straining broke the silence of the night, and I gritted my teeth, worried someone would hear. Riven returned a moment later holding one of the lanterns that had lined the hallway, passing it to me with a proud grin. I turned back to the frozen night and held up the lantern in front of me.

The noncorporeal woman rushed towards me, stopping inches from my face.

I gasped, stumbling backwards. I tripped and landed with a wet thud into the snow.

"Are you okay?" Dreya's concerned face appeared in front of me, unknowingly going straight through the woman.

Riven gripped my arm and pulled me out of the cold snow that had begun to seep through my clothes. "You look like you've seen a ghost," he muttered, a playful glint in his eyes.

"I'm fine," I insisted. "I just tripped."

The ghost turned, moving towards the tree line. I sucked in a breath as I started to follow.

"I don't think that's a good idea. The gate stands in those trees," Dreya said. "There will be extra guards because of the lockdown."

"Then let's not get caught," Riven suggested, keeping pace next to me as we wound through dead trees.

The clearing was small yet seemed like a hollow gouged into the earth. As if some colossal beast had torn a crater in the forest and never returned to fill it.

Snowcapped pines ringed the perimeter, their branches motionless despite the sleet filled wind. Flurries of ice clung to our uniforms as we trudged through the thick snow. My thighs burnt with the effort to pull my boots free of the thick layer. The ghost floated above the ditch, watching me expectantly.

"Are you ready to go back now?" Dreya asked.

"I just need to see something," I muttered. If I told her why I was here, she would think I was crazy. The aching in my chest had almost become unbearable with every step deeper into the trees. Mist crawled across the ground, pale as old bone, making it hard to see the bottom of the ditch as I leant over it.

Find the pieces. Find yourself.

The whisper brushed my ear, cold breath trailing over my neck.

The hair on my arms stood on end, but I took a step, unable to stop myself. Riven's hand clamped around my wrist.

His fingers were warm, but his voice was low and tense. "Lyra, wait."

I turned, searching his face. In the hollow beneath his lashes, something dark flickered. Recognition. Or dread.

"I just need to see what's down there," I whispered, throat raw. Dreya's eyes darted nervously between us. "Something feels off. We should go back," she breathed.

"There is nothing but trees out here," I responded, gesturing around me.

She wrapped her arms around her body and eyed me suspiciously. At first, I had assumed she followed me out of loyalty. Now, I wondered if she was only here to confirm whatever superstition had taken root in her mind. Riven's gaze caught on something past my shoulder. For a heartbeat, his pupils dilated, before he swallowed and looked away.

I stepped forward and slid down the icy bank, vanishing into the mist. I landed hard, the impact knocking the air from my lungs.

The lantern lay next to me. I righted it, eyes adjusting to my surroundings.

"Lyra?" Dreya called, her voice panicked. I couldn't see her face above me through the unnatural mist.

"I'm okay!" I called back.

Something caught my eye in the tangle of roots in the snow, as if the tree itself had wrapped around the weapon. An axe. I couldn't tear my eyes away from it, the ache in my chest now pulsing. I needed that axe.

Silver and black metal twined together, etched in runes that seemed to squirm when I tried to read them. Power coiled off the weapon in invisible currents, prickling against my skin.

Dreya skidded down next to me, muttering a curse under her breath and flicking snow off her uniform.

"It feels even worse down here," Dreya grumbled as she stood beside me, looking down at the axe.

She bent down, her hand wrapping around its hilt. She tugged. The roots seemed to tighten around it. She grunted, tugging harder. Riven jumped down next to us, landing on his feet with a grace I longed to one day possess.

"It is like it's fused into the roots." She stood, panting from her attempts. I stepped towards the axe. Riven seemed to take a step at the same time, stumbling into me. His thumb grazed my palm, and a sharp sting bloomed. I gasped and yanked my hand back, fresh blood welling along a thin slice of skin.

"Ouch, how did you—"

Riven's mouth parted, but he didn't apologize. He only watched me, grey eyes unreadable.

"Whoops," he murmured, his tone too smooth. "You're bleeding."

I clamped my other hand around the cut, trying to stop the steady flow of blood as I bent in front of the weapon.

How could his nails cut into my skin so deeply?

The axe seemed to pulse in answer to my proximity. Drawn as if on a tether, I reached for it. The moment my bleeding hand closed around the shaft, the world lurched.

Voices erupted, ancient and layered. A thousand over-lapping murmurs poured into me like floodwater. The sigils flared white-hot, and warmth spilled through my veins, licking across my skin. My vision darkened.

A man held me in his arms in a field, thousands of dead bodies spread across the ground, fires burning in the distance. My face against his chest. I couldn't see his face, but dread oozed through me. He held me with a tenderness that didn't match the dagger in his hand.

"I am so sorry," his deep voice rumbled against me. Pain

erupted in my chest. White hot agony. My hands shot to the source, wrapping around the dagger that he had plunged into my heart.

My eyes shot open, the dark trees looming above me and the ghost watched me from between them. My hearing slowly came back into focus. Someone was shouting my name. She levelled those unsettling familiar eyes on me, a smile stretching unnaturally against taut lips before she plummeted towards me. I tried to move. My hands slipped against the snow. The noncorporeal woman dove into my chest. A strange coldness spread across my limbs, turning into a vibrating warmth that pulsed through my veins. As if the thing inside me grew.

When I looked down, the axe was no longer cradled by tangled roots. It thrummed in my palm, alive and free. The ache in my chest dissipated almost instantly. I inhaled, gasping for breath as though I had drowned all over again.

"Lyra?" Riven hovered above me, his warm hand resting against my cheek. "Shh, you're alright."

"There is someone coming." Dreya crouched in the snow next to us, looking up into the mist and muttering under her breath.

"The scream came from over here!" a male yelled from somewhere above us. Had *I* screamed? Their steps grew closer.

Dreya looked between us with wide eyes. And then she disappeared. One moment Dreya was sitting there, the next, she was gone.

"Holy shit," she whispered from thin air. She flickered back into existence, a wide grin on her face.

She clasped a hand on each of our shoulders; a light tingling sensation spread over me. I looked down and saw nothing but snow.

"Well, that's pretty fucking cool," Riven said.

"Shut up, I don't think it hides our voices, idiot," Dreya scolded in a whisper.

"Do you see anything?" a voice said from above us.

"No, nothing here. Clear out to the next section." The voice that responded was Orin's.

I held my breath, heart pounding in my ears. How many times could I disappoint him before he had to kill me?

The sound of their steps faded, and Dreya let go of us, her Sanctum disappearing. "Oh," she said, pressing a hand to her abdomen before emptying her stomach into the snow.

I gripped the axe in my hands, breathing through the strange feeling of magic swimming through my veins. Something had happened to me. Something had changed. I just didn't understand *what*.

Twelve
Maze of Death

My muscles burned with every step, my lungs aching as my boots slogged through knee-deep snow. I'd lost count of how many laps we had run.

Orin had been waiting for us when we returned from the woods, pacing the corridor outside our room like a storm about to break. He'd lectured us about our stupidity with barely leashed anger. I'd had enough time to hide my axe in my cloak and shove it under my bed before he forced us to the training yards. Eventually, the other initiates had joined us. But that was no break. We launched straight into hand-to-hand combat, which surprisingly, I was good at.

Bohdi had been running us through striking forms with swords while Orin stood silently. He kept his arms folded against his chest, watching us with an unreadable expression.

Bohdi raised his sword in a series of manoeuvres that we mimicked. Sword drills were worse today, but I gritted my teeth and endured it. At least no one was dragging me to a dungeon to slice my skin open. *Small mercies.*

"Lyra and Riven," Orin snapped from the sideline. I startled, nearly losing my grip on my sword.

"Spar," was all he said. Bohdi shot him an odd expression before sighing and stepping back.

I tried to meet Orin's eyes, hoping for a hint of reassurance, but he didn't look at me. Just like this morning, he gave me nothing but cold indifference.

I've pushed him too far.

Riven twirled his blade in a graceful arc around his body before settling into a loose attack stance, a grin tugging at his lips. He was infuriatingly casual, as though he knew exactly how this would end.

I had never held a *sword* against another person before, but I knew what it felt like to drive steel through flesh.

A smile ghosted my lips at the only fond memory I had of him. Perhaps I was more dangerous than I'd given myself credit for. Ever since I'd touched that axe, something else coiled beneath my skin. Restless and alive. I struck first, a clumsy jab that Riven deflected with ease. Effortlessly.

But he didn't counter. He just watched me, grey eyes bright with some unreadable glimmer. I gritted my teeth and swung again, putting all my desperation behind the blow. Metal met metal in a scraping clash that rattled all the way up my arms.

I tried to steady my breathing and swung again, a wide arc meant to drive him back.

He blocked it with a flick of his wrist, the movement so casual it felt like mockery.

"Come on, Princess," he said encouragingly.

I lunged once more, aiming low. He stepped aside, turning just enough that my blade met nothing but air. I grunted with frustration.

He swept his sword down towards my shoulder, slow

enough that I could scramble to parry. When the blades met, a sharp pain laced through my wrist, the weapon almost slipping from my grip from the force.

"Block with two hands, Lyra!" Bohdi yelled from the sideline.

The cut Riven had accidentally given me throbbed as I gripped the pommel, taking Bohdi's advice. I kept blocking.

He didn't relent. Another strike, then another, each one harder, each one precise and almost lazy, as though he were testing how many blows it would take to wear me down.

Gritting my teeth, I lifted my sword to block a high cut. Too slow.

His blade smacked against mine with a jarring crack. The force wrenched the sword from my grasp, sending it skidding across the snow.

"Give up, Princess?" His grin widened, splitting the cut in his lip.

"Never," I said, lunging for my discarded sword in the snow. I gripped it, rolling onto my back in time to block Riven's sword. I kicked my leg out, connecting with his thigh, and he stumbled.

Seeing an opening, I dropped my sword and threw myself at him, pulling Orin's dagger from my belt. His eyes widened as he crashed into the snow, his body underneath mine. My legs straddled his hips.

His pulse beat against the blade I pressed to his throat, steady and sure, and I hated how it drew my gaze to his mouth. The heat flooding through me felt nothing like victory. His eyes flicked to my mouth, before those storm-cloud eyes crashed into mine.

"Give up?" I asked breathlessly, though I wasn't entirely sure if it was from the fight.

His hips bucked up, throwing me off balance. In a swirl

of movement, I was suddenly on my back in the snow, my hands pinned over my head. Riven's body pressed against me, pinning me against the ground.

"Never," he said, his breath mingling with mine. He gave me a grin before pushing off me, standing and extending a hand towards me. My fingers clasped his, and he helped me stand.

Orin avoided looking at me, lips pressed into a hard line. "Back into formation," he grunted. His coldness hit harder than the wind. I'd thought his anger last night was punishment enough, but this was worse. I didn't know whether I wanted to scream at him or force him to look at me. I swallowed the feeling, forcing a mask of indifference to slip over my face.

After watching the others spar and eating dried meat around the fire barrels, Commander Kragthorne marched into the training yard.

"Good luck," Bohdi said as he walked with Orin to the viewing platform. My mouth went dry as I noticed the other Iron Guards leaving their initiates behind, and the growing crowd gathering in the viewing platform.

"Welcome to the second war game!" Commander Kragthorne announced, the crowd cheering. My stomach sunk. Orin would have known, but he didn't warn me. He hadn't so much as looked at me since his lecture this morning. And after my fight with Riven, the frown line on his forehead hadn't quite gone away. If I thought he was capable of caring about anything more than his role, I'd say he was jealous.

"Today, you will fight," Commander Kragthorne boomed. "Each squad will be issued a single medallion. Your objective is simple: protect your own and steal from the other squads. When the game ends, the squad holding the most medallions wins. The winning squad will earn an exemption from the next game."

Round golden medallions strung on a strip of worn leather were handed out to all fifteen squads. Dreya held ours and it gleamed in the dull light with the number one in its centre. The other initiates were either picking up extra weapons or making sure theirs were secured. Orin's dagger was still in my belt, but that wasn't the weapon I wanted. I wished I had the axe, but Riven had insisted on it staying hidden under my bed. Dreya had used her Sanctum to make it invisible while Orin had lectured us last night.

"May the Gods have mercy on your souls or find joy in feasting on your blood." Behind Commander Kragthorne, five Iron Guards walked towards us. Their hands moved in sync with one another, causing threads of power to twirl in a delicate shimmer. The ground shuddered beneath our boots. I stumbled backwards and Riven grabbed me under my arm to stop me from falling. Stone exploded from the ground in front of us, cutting us off from the other squads. The fighting pit had been transformed into a maze of jagged stone around us.

I stared at the towering walls, fear settling deep in my bones. The dull winter light vanished behind a curling mist, swallowing everything in suffocating silence. A scream pierced the fog, the clash of steel close behind it.

The mist slithered across the stone, thick enough to hide a body. My fingers found the end of my braid, twisting it until it bit into my skin. "It's a little barbaric, isn't it?" I said, eyeing the narrow walkway ahead. "Making us kill each other and calling it a game."

"Says the psycho who tried to strangle me." Hadley glared at me, as though she were trying to burn holes through me.

I smiled sweetly and looked down my nose at Hadley. The bruising around her neck had faded to an ugly yellow. Pity. It had suited her, like a collar on a dog that barked too much.

Roman quirked an eyebrow, boots crunching against the iced over stone. "Focus on the game. You may not care if you die, Lyra. But the rest of us want to live."

"We need to move," Dreya snapped in a hushed voice. She levelled us with a warning look before walking further into the maze. The darkness was so complete I could only glimpse the outline of Riven following her. A crack echoed through the mist, too close.

Dreya signalled for us to halt from the front of the line, her hand a swift, urgent motion.

I pressed myself against the rough stone, its jagged edges biting through my clothes as we crouched. The silence pressed in, thick and suffocating. I pulled the dagger from my belt as Dreya peered around the corner, gesturing for us to follow.

Two bodies lay on the ground, fresh blood oozing across the snow-flecked stone.

My stomach churned as I forced myself to look away while Dreya and Riven searched the dead, their hands moving with grim efficiency. I knew the dangers of Ascension. Of standing on the front line in the war against the Fae. I had accepted all the ways I might die when I chose this. Welcomed them, even. But I didn't think I could be killed in some stupid game.

"No medallion," Dreya murmured.

"Obviously." Riven chuckled. "The squad who killed them would have taken it."

The others kept walking. But I hesitated, watching

blood run between the grooves in the ground, a gentle caress marking the wasted lives of those the Gods had chosen.

Another scream cut through the fog. I jumped, hurrying to catch up to my squad. We had made so many sharp turns that I was beginning to feel disorientated. We came to a slight opening and the maze branched off in four directions from where we stood. The perfect place for someone to be hiding—

A large form lunged out of the shadows, slamming into Riven. He hit the ground with a grunt. An initiate loomed over him, the tip of his sword pressing against his throat so hard, a drop of blood began to ooze.

"Give me your medallion or I'll slit his throat!" Riven's attacker pressed the blade harder against him. Riven chuckled despite being in obvious danger and the steel scraped against his stubble.

I stared in disbelief as Riven's face warped. Morphing into the same features as the man pinning him to the ground. His hair shortened and changed, mirroring the male that pinned him to the ground. They looked identical. It was as if he had made himself into an exact replica. Taking advantage of the distraction, Riven grabbed a fistful of snow and threw it into his face. He pushed his hips up, throwing the initiate off balance. In a tangle of limbs, somehow Riven now straddled him, spinning his knife away from his body and squeezing his throat with his other hand.

His face returned to his own as he squeezed the life out of his attacker. The initiate struggled, legs thrashing against the ground, but Riven's grip only tightened. The initiate's eyes were glassy. He stilled, arm dropping limply to the side. Riven rose slowly, the lifeless body sprawled beneath him, its neck twisted at an unnatural angle.

"I think you just received your Sanctum!" Dreya said excitedly.

Riven grinned at her before searching the dead body. "No medallion," he said as he came up empty handed.

"But where is the rest of his squad?" Roman crossed his arms, looking around the small clearing.

Hadley was facing a dark alleyway. She exhaled sharply, flexing her hands. The air shifted around us.

I pivoted, my hair whipping me with the sudden movement. Two initiates were running towards us, swords raised. Hadley threw out her arms and wind roared. An invisible blast of air sent the initiates flying, slamming into the stone wall. The bodies crumpled against the ground, eyes fixed and unmoving.

Hadley laughed, staring down at her hands with open delight. "I did that—"

Her words cut off mid-breath.

A dagger tore through the dark and sliced into her throat, blood spraying as the blade sunk to the hilt. Her eyes went wide with shock, mouth opening in a soundless, wet gasp. She staggered, hands flying to her neck as blood spilled through her fingers and splashed against the snow-dusted cobblestone.

I hadn't realised I'd moved until I was there, catching Hadley as she crumpled forward. Her weight collapsed into me, slick and heavy, her breath gurgling against my ear.

Panic crawled up my spine as I looked past her into the darkness.

"You're okay. It's okay," I whispered, feeling the weight of the lie on my tongue.

Where had it come from?

The shadows stretched deep and unmoving. Too thick to see through. But I could *feel* them.

"Dreya," I whispered, my voice breaking as I tightened my grip on Hadley. She didn't hear me. No one did. Her attention was fixed on Riven as he rifled through a fallen initiate's pockets. "Riven—"

"Got one!" Riven yelled, his voice slicing through the eerie quiet as he yanked free a medallion and held it up with a triumphant grin.

Roman returned his smile from where he was crouched over the other body, searching for anything useful.

"Riven!" I shouted, panic tore through me as Hadley gasped violently.

Their heads snapped towards me.

Dreya's hands flew to her mouth.

Roman grimaced, turning away as if he couldn't bear to look.

"It came from that way," I whispered, my gaze locked on the darkness. "They are there. I can feel it."

The mist pressed close, swallowing the scent of blood sharp in the air.

Hadley's fear-filled eyes stared up at me, her breath slowing as she gurgled and choked on her own blood.

"You're free now," I whispered as I wrapped my hand around the dagger protruding from her throat.

A sound slipped from me before I knew what I was doing. Low and soft. A melody drawn up from somewhere deep within me, vibrating through my chest and into my bones.

I pulled the blade free with a wet squelch. Blood flooded down her neck and spread across my leg. Hadley's body shuddered once and went still. My song threaded through the rush of blood, through the roar of my pulse pounding in my ears, steady and consuming.

I did not recognise the tune, but it belonged here.

I hadn't liked her. But she didn't deserve to die in a game for Gods who had turned their backs on us.

Somewhere behind me, steel clashed, and more screams followed. My song died in my throat, the sound of steel clashing jarring me from the haze.

Dreya's voice snapped me back. "Move, Lyra!"

For us, the game had only just begun.

THIRTEEN
LOSS OF CONTROL

We wound between the stone walls in the dark, the mist growing thicker with every step.

No one dared to speak. The silence was thicker now, pressing down on us like a physical weight.

Dreya's gaze lingered on the blood coating my hands, accusing and uncertain, as though I were the one who had killed Hadley. I couldn't blame her. The horror on her face as Hadley bled out in my arms while I sang clung to me. It was the same look I had learned to expect from people my entire life.

Time would have to be running out by now, and with only two medallions and a dead squad mate, I doubted Orin would be impressed. We followed Dreya around a sharp corner into an open square. The centre of the maze. I froze. Five initiates snapped their heads towards us. A blood-spattered initiate with four medallions clinking against his broad chest swung his sword in a wide arc in front of his body.

"Hand them over," he snarled at Riven. But his eyes drew to me. A dark smile curled his lips. "The Kingdom's most protected cunt, playing soldier. You should've stayed locked in your tower." Bile burnt the back of my throat. His eyes burnt with the same heat as the priest's. The same hunger of a predator who cared nothing for consent. His squad spread out, circling us like wolves.

"Don't look at her. Look at me," Riven said darkly, a wild grin splitting his face. "I'm the pretty one in the group, and I like to play."

Before he could respond, Dreya vanished. Swallowed by the air itself.

"What the fuck—"

She grinned, appearing in front of him for a split of a second. Clutching the medallions and disappearing with them. She reappeared a few paces away, triumphantly clutching the bundle of medallions she'd stolen.

"Dreya! Move!" Riven shouted. Too late. Another initiate seized her by the hair, yanking her backward. Her head struck the stone with a sickening crack. Her attacker, a female cadet with a cruel smile and blood-flecked face, snapped her fingers. Fire bloomed in her palm, the heat licking up her arm as she stepped towards Dreya.

My world narrowed to Dreya, the first person to show me kindness. The image of her crumpling in the snow detonated something raw and hot behind my ribs. I couldn't let her die. Panic flooded me, jagged and dangerous. A new power hummed beneath my skin like a second heartbeat, begging to be let loose. I wanted to tear the sky open and rip the flame from that cadet's palm.

Kill them all. The voice slithered into my head. Louder than before, sharper, until it sounded identical to my own.

I moved without thinking, pure instinct guiding me. Everyone burst into action, Riven the first to raise his weapon. Swords clashed. Grunts of pain echoed off the stone wall. An arm wrenched around my throat, cutting off my air and halting my steps. I watched as Dreya and the redheaded woman grappled in the snow.

My vision blurred, but I kicked and scratched at the forearm pressing against my throat.

My attacker moaned, breathing heavily into my ear, "I've heard rumours, you know. Heard you like a soldier's cock." He squeezed harder against my throat, his other hand slipping into the waist of my pants. "Why don't I give you one last taste, before I slit your throat?"

Panic gripped. I began to thrash. Through the blood roaring in my ears, music grew. The melody crawled seductively beneath my skin, cold as death. It curled around my ribs like a vice. An eerie calm settled over me as a strange vibration pulsed beneath my skin. Every drop of water in his body called to me. I allowed my body to go limp against his and closed my eyes.

I ripped the water from his body and forced it to his lungs.

His grip faltered. A wet gasp. Then another. I felt his lungs fill. His body convulsed against me, gurgling against my ear.

He dropped me as he fell to his knees, and air whooshed back into my deprived lungs. His skin turned a deep shade of red, a vein bulging in his forehead. My eyes never left his, watching as red marks bloomed over his throat from his own fingers clawing in desperation.

I kept singing as I crawled over him, straddling him and pressing my hands against his chest. The water pooled beneath my hands. His body spasmed beneath me, a final, desperate fight against the inevitable. His fear seeped into me, unfurling through my veins, curling tight around something dark and primal. I covered his mouth, silencing the wet gasps, stopping the water from spilling. I watched him drown. And I *liked* it. The satisfaction hit like a drug, terrifying in its sweetness.

I stood from the dead body, and a scream sent chills through my blood. The redheaded woman held Dreya down and pressed flames to her skin. It licked up her neck and fuelled her screams. The moment Dreya's screams stopped—her body turned limp and her eyes fluttered shut.

The darkness inside me didn't rise. It erupted, tearing through the last scraps of my restraint. A haunting note left my tongue as I reached out, forcing the water inside her attacker's body to invade her lungs.

She began to splutter, confusion and terror making her eyes bulge as she drowned. My skin felt feverish, and a dizziness swept through me, threatening to pull me under like a tide, but I ran to Dreya's side. Her head lolled to the side, red angry burns licking up her neck. Relief hit me like a wave when I saw her chest rise and fall.

Riven was holding his own against the two initiates to my left. While they slashed at him with swords, he dodged with fluid precision and drove his fists into their ribs and jaws. His grin, bright and feral, gleamed through the blood smearing his face. I reached for the water coursing through their blood and was met with a burning feeling inside my chest.

The frustrated cry that left my lips was a mistake. One of the men fighting Riven charged at me, sword poised to strike.

A single note slipped past my lips, lyrical and winding.

I didn't know why, only that something primal inside me demanded I sing.

Weakness pulled at my limbs, threatening to drag me into darkness as sweat beaded on my skin.

His steps faltered. Slowed. He lowered his sword, head tilting, mouth slack with wonder. His eyes shone with a strange sheen. A wet gargle sounded as blood spewed from his mouth, breaking whatever enchantment I held over him. The point of a blade burst through his chest, spraying me with warm liquid.

Riven put his boot on his back and pushed, the initiate's body falling with a wet thump into the snow. Roman slit the last attacker's throat. I barely registered the medallions clenched in his fist. Riven wiped the blade on the initiates back before glancing up at me.

Each breath burnt my lungs. The power thrumming in my veins threatened to consume me. Something inside me cracked.

Riven's face had drained of colour. Still, he inched closer, like I was some wild beast that might turn on him.

I dropped to my hands and knees, gasping for air as my fingernails scraped against the pebbles. I clenched my jaw against the scream rising in my throat. The darkness was consuming, breaking through every wall I had put in place to keep it at bay. This was what the priest had bled from me not sin. Darkness and pure evil ran through my veins, tearing to the surface. I had blamed the priest, blamed the Gods, blamed the world. But the horror clawing its way out of me felt too familiar to deny.

I am evil. I had been all along.

Riven's water called to me. A pulse, a whisper. A promise of power.

I grunted, trying to resist. I wanted to drown him. I looked up at him. Riven stumbled backwards. His breath hitched, sharp and uneven.

"Run!" I screamed. I didn't know what was happening. But I didn't want to hurt him.

For the first time, his eyes held no humour, only something raw. Something dangerously close to fear. He opened his mouth, but no words came.

Orin's dagger laid on the ground next to me. I seized the blade and stabbed it into my wrist, dragging it upwards towards my elbow, leaving a gaping gash in its wake.

Blood poured from me, dulling the urge to *kill* as the pain grounded me.

It wasn't enough. I sliced open my other forearm, my blood spilling black across the snow, and with each drop, the monster inside me shrank back. My breath hitched. My head swam. I would *not* hurt Riven.

Riven screamed my name but he sounded far away. The heat consumed me, and everything went black.

FOURTEEN
LIAR

My head throbbed viciously, each pulse of pain syncing with the sluggish thump of my heart.

I pried my eyes open and winced. The dim flicker of dying torchlight seemed to make the pounding worse. The air felt thick, stagnant, laced with the sharp tang of medicinal herbs and something far more metallic beneath it. Blood.

My limbs felt heavy, my mind struggling to find a thought to grip onto.

Shadows slithered across the stone walls. Too thick. Too alive. They stretched towards the corners of the room where the darkness bled into itself. The faint glint of metal caught my eye: a wooden trolley, scattered with healer's tools. The hairs on my arms stood on end, sweat beading on my skin despite the cool air. The dying torchlight flickered lazily, as if warning me that something unnatural was happening. The shadows rippled and coiled, slow and oozing, holding me captive. My muscles locked in fear as they bled into an inky form. The torches guttered weakly, trembling back to life. And in the brief second the shadows recoiled, a large figure was watching me. The darkness hid his features, but I could make out a muscular form that stood well over six feet tall. The shadow man took slow, predatory step towards me. Darkness crawled along the stone, creeping towards me in an unnatural slither. That was all the warning I got before the figure lunged at me. Terror locked me in place. The thing lurched forward.

I screamed, sitting up and clutching my chest. My hair clung to my sweat sleeked skin as I frantically searched the room like a trapped animal. I was in the same room. The infirmary.

"Hey. Hey, you're safe." Riven leant forward in the chair beside my bed. Dark circles bruised the skin beneath his eyes, and his unruly brown waves looked as though he'd dragged his hands through them repetitively.

I looked past Riven, searching for *him*. But there was no darkness. The moving shadows didn't exist.

"I—There was..." I trailed off, trying to catch my breath.

"You had a nightmare," Riven reassured me, wrapping his hand around mine.

I startled, not moving for a moment before I wrapped my hand back around his. I needed a tether right now.

Logically, I believed him—yet it had felt real. The hairs on my arms stood on end, every nerve taut with the certainty that something unseen was still watching me.

"Just a dream," I mumbled, staring at our interlocked hands sitting on top of the blanket.

In a chair next to Riven, Orin's long legs stretched out with his head tilted to the side, his mouth parted in the depth of sleep.

Then it hit me.

Memories invaded my head like the dead clawing their way out of a shallow grave, unwilling to stay buried. The sound of choking. Initiates drowning on dry land at *my* hands. Did someone see me wield water? If they had, why was I not dead?

A merciless shudder tore through my body. I grabbed my aching head with my free hand.

Shame crawled up my throat, thick and bitter. *I'm a monster.*

But before I could drown in it, Riven cut through my internal panic. "It's alright, Lyra." His voice was soft, soothing.

My gaze remained ensnared on his fingers intertwined with mine, a strange feeling of familiarity settling into my stomach. If I met Riven's gaze, I was certain disgust would meet me.

"It's our little secret, okay?" he said in a hushed tone, sensing where my thoughts had gone.

"Why?" I asked cautiously. Why would he protect me? We had all been told the same thing. Anyone who wields water was too dangerous to be kept alive. I needed to be killed for the greater good. Because the estranged Gods deemed me a threat.

"I'm not going to let them kill you, Lyra." His voice had turned darker, not one drop of amusement laced his tone. My eyes shot to him. His dark grey eyes were already watching me with an intensity I didn't realise he was capable of. Those strange amber flecks seemed almost alive, like rays of sunshine tearing through storm clouds. He leant forward, his voice a soft whisper that sent a strange warmth through my stomach. "I can get you out of here, take you somewhere you can be safe."

Did such a place even exist? We were on an island surrounded by cursed seas filled with vicious beasts. Running away was impossible.

"Aren't we bound by the Ascension to be Iron Guards until we die?" I asked. The magic that had torn its way through me on that altar was binding.

He gave me a knowing half smirk. "I have a way around that."

I considered it for a moment. They would kill me the moment they realised I could yield water, a fate I would have embraced a few days ago.

But a small, stubborn part of me wanted to live simply because the Gods had decided I should die, just to spite them.

I almost agreed. The words hovered on my tongue, heavy and tempting.

My gaze drifted to Orin. His red hair had fallen across his brow, his face unguarded in sleep, stripped of command and fury.

I wanted to believe that if it came to it, he would protect me. He would help me hide.

"I can't," I whispered. Riven gave me a mischievous smirk and squeezed my hand softly. "Tell lover boy over there that it was Roman and watch what happens. My guess is you will want to run away with me after that."

The power inside me withered beneath my skin, threatening to spill free. I couldn't tell if the uneasiness curling in my stomach wanted me to take Riven's hand and run or stay.

Honestly, I didn't know which fate frightened me more.

"Why try to help me? Riven, I'm a monster."

He didn't flinch at my words. Didn't recoil. Instead, his

face softened, a breathy chuckle escaped him as his usual amusement settled back into his eyes.

"You're not a monster, Lyra." He shook his head, eyelashes brushing his cheek as he looked down at me. "People have a nasty habit of fearing what they don't understand."

My breath stalled in my throat. He wasn't afraid of me. My eyes flicked to his lips, inches from my face. Gods, all I had to do was lean forwards. One small movement and his lips would be against mine. He was offering to save me, even though I had almost killed him.

"Riven, I... I nearly... I wanted to..."

"Whatever it is you were going to do, you didn't." His expression shifted, darkening. "And even if you did..." He trailed off, eyes dipping to my lips and his voice dipped lower, huskier. "I was completely under your spell. You could have shoved a blade into my gut, and I would have thanked you for it and then kissed the ground you walked on." His throat bobbed as he swallowed hard. His fingers flexed in my hand as if fighting the urge to close the distance between us.

"I'm sorry," I whispered. He chuckled under his breath, letting go of my hand and sitting back in his chair.

Before I could protest, Orin stirred and sat up. His sleep blurred eyes scanned me for injuries. His gaze softened for a moment, reminding me of the guard I once loved before the hard lines of anger returned to his face. "I thought you were dead!"

Riven clapped his hand on Orin's shoulder. "We won boss man. Get your panties out of a knot."

"We won?" I asked cautiously as Orin glared daggers at Riven.

"I would love to know *how*," Orin said in a clipped tone. The vein on his forehead looked like it was going to burst.

"I don't know," I said honestly. "I remember fighting and getting attacked. I must have been unconscious."

I twirled the end of my silver braid between my fingers, making my eyes go wide with fear. Surely, he wouldn't expect the unskilled princess to have killed multiple initiates. Lying and acting weak were skills I had mastered long ago.

"See? I told you my skills are unparalleled," Riven smirked, puffing up his chest with arrogance.

"Riven and Dreya have shown me their Sanctums. So, who wielded water in the maze?" His attention made me squirm. I still didn't know what Orin's Sanctum was. *Did he know I was lying?*

"I don't have my Sanctum yet," I muttered, dropping my braid and settling my hands in my lap.

Riven glared at Orin with open hostility despite the amused smirk plastered on his face. "Leave. I need to speak to Lyra alone," Orin seethed towards him, crossing his arms.

"Maybe she doesn't want to be alone with you," Riven shot back, his arrogant smirk taunting.

Orin laughed without humour, standing to loom over Riven. "She has wanted to be alone with me *plenty* of times. Now leave."

Riven shoved the chair back with force as he stood, its legs screeching against the stone floor. Riven stood an inch taller than Orin, the two of them stared each other down.

The door swung open, Bohdi storming in with a concerned look on his face.

"What's going on? The emotions I can feel from down the hall are *intense*."

He eyed Riven, whose entire body was rigid as if he was trying to hold himself back.

"You need to calm down. I'm going to help you. Okay?" Bohdi's voice was calm, slow, laced with the kind of warmth that could settle a raging storm.

But his stance told a different story. His weight was evenly braced, and his muscles were coiled like a predator ready to strike.

"Don't fucking touch me," Riven warned, but there was a crack beneath it.

Bohdi ignored him, lashing out quickly and seizing Riven's face between his hands. His fingers pressed firmly against Riven's temples, thumbs locking over his strong jaw.

Bohdi's brows drew together in concentration, strands of honey-blond hair clung to his forehead. Riven's eyes were wild and my heart ached. He looked how I felt. Hopeless. Caged. Like there was something below the surface begging to break free.

"Let him go." My voice was louder than usual, demanding in a way I wasn't used to.

Orin shot me a look of warning that made me writhe with defiance.

Riven's hands latched onto Bohdi's wrists with bruising force, his fingers white-knuckled as he pried Bohdi's hands off. Riven swung his fist. Bohdi's head snapped to the side with sickening force. Orin moved to grab Riven, but Bohdi raised one hand to stop him, the other clutching his bleeding nose. "Leave him."

Riven started to leave, pausing at the door and turning to look at me over his shoulder. "Remember what we talked about."

I wrapped my arms around myself as I watched the door close.

"What in the Hells was that?" Orin asked Bohdi. "That's the second time your Sanctum has failed."

Bohdi exhaled, still holding his nose as blood dripped onto his dark grey uniform.

"All I could sense was darkness," his voice was hoarse and filled with confusion.

"What do you know, Lyra?" Orin directed his attention back to me.

Bohdi hesitated, glancing at me again. Not just *at* me, but *inside* me.

I knew he could feel my guilt, my shame, my fear.

But he said nothing to me, instead he turned to Orin. "I'm going to check back in with Dreya, she is about to get released." He left, closing the door behind him and leaving me alone with Orin.

"I need to know if you saw who drowned the initiates, Lyra," he muttered, dragging a hand down his face.

I studied him instead of answering. The tension in his jaw. The way his fingers flexed, restless. He wanted the truth.

Riven's warning echoed in my mind. Seven years was a long time for loyalty to rot, and trust was something I would not give easily. If I chose wrong... If Orin wasn't who I needed him to be, then Roman would be dead by morning and I would leave with Riven.

"Roman," I said quietly, letting his name hang between us like a blade. I met Orin's eyes and didn't look away. "Roman drowned them."

The lie slid out smoothly. I let my voice tremble just enough to sound scared.

"Thank you," Orin said gently, leaning forward and running the back of his finger against my cheek, slow and familiar, as though he were rewarding me. "Get some rest and I will see you at dinner."

Orin pulled a small metal cylinder out of his pocket and threw it onto my bed with a dull thud. "A royal hawk dropped that off for you while you were out. I kept it from leadership." He shook his head and ran a hand through his red hair, as if he couldn't believe he'd broken a rule for me. He turned and pushed open the door, his silhouette outlined in the dying torchlight. Leaving me alone with a deep unease that had settled beneath my skin.

FIFTEEN
ENTHRALLED

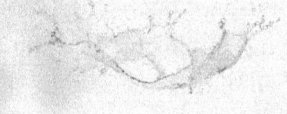

Lyra

I failed you as a brother. And I will not fail you again.

Father may not be able to drag you back to Stonebriar yet, but I fear he is working on a way to make that possible. He has become obsessed with your return.

The Southerners are furious and have been rebelling in the streets because your union did not happen, a civil war is nearing. Between that and the reports of entire townships being slaughtered overnight, nowhere is safe.

Please do not leave the barracks. You are safest there.

Stay alive, little sister. I am trying to find a way to help you. Stay safe. Stay alive.

Your brother, Aldric.

I refolded the missive with unsteady hands, tucking it firmly in the pocket of my leggings. I had read it enough that it was burnt to my memory at this stage, but I couldn't help staring at my brother's familiar writing. His words hollowed out my heart. He loved me, yet he had failed to protect me.

The infirmary door squeaked open, the flames of the torches flickering from the draft. A warm smile spread across Dreya's face as she sat on the edge of my bed. She wrapped her arms around me in an embrace. I stilled beneath her touch before slowly lifting my arms and resting my hands on her back. I was not used to being hugged.

"Thank you," she whispered into my shoulder. "Riven told me you saved my life."

"Consider us even," I replied, hating that a small amount of emotion leached into my voice. Caring for people was a task I was not used to. It felt warm yet cold at the same time, as if I were waiting for it to be taken away.

She pulled back, and her smile was as bright as the excitement in her eyes. "And we won!"

I studied her a moment longer, there was no fear. No suspicion. Just warmth.

My gaze drifted to the puckered skin along her neck. The healers had nearly erased the burns, but she would wear those scars for the rest of her life.

If she noticed me looking at her scar, she didn't move to hide it. I envied her. She almost wore it with pride. My scars cut too deep emotionally to ever feel like anything other than an open wound.

"Someone developed a water Sanctum, Lyra." Her face twisted with hatred. "I hope I am there to see them hang."

My chest ached at Dreya's words, as though someone had shoved a knife into me and twisted. It didn't matter that we were friends. It didn't matter that I had saved her life. If she found out it was me, she wouldn't hesitate to stab me in the back to appease the Gods. Even if Orin didn't kill Roman, I would still have to run away. Again.

"Is everything okay?" she asked me curiously, noticing my silence.

Do not leave the barracks. Aldric's warning echoed like a drumbeat in my skull. *I'm sorry, brother*, I thought to myself. *I'm not good at being told what to do.*

A healer broke our uncomfortable silence, a petite girl in dark grey leathers with strawberry-blonde hair. "You are both free to leave. Dinner should still be on in the dining hall. I can show you the way if you'd like?"

Dreya accepted her offer and we followed her through the dimly lit corridors until we stood in front of the familiar doors of the dining hall. She handed Dreya a small bag, giving her instructions to apply the ointment on her scars twice a day. I assured her I knew how to care for sutures and would not let my wounds become infected. We both thanked her and walked into the warmth of the dining hall.

Dreya pointed to a far table where our squad sat. "There they are."

The fragrance of food made my stomach rumble, and my shoulders relaxed. Knowing I would be leaving forced me to absorb every detail, every moment I might miss wherever Riven planned to take me.

We took our trays of food before taking the empty seats at our squad's table. I couldn't help but glance at the empty seat where Hadley had sat. Riven barked a laugh, legs stretched up on the edge of the table as he joked with Bohdi, their fight from earlier obviously behind them.

His mischievous grin spread across his face as he placed a hand over his heart. "As much as I liked seeing you in bed, princess, it's good to have you join us."

I rolled my eyes as I sat down, but I felt my cheeks warm despite myself. Dreya threw a piece of bread at Riven; it bounced of his chest and fell to the ground. "So, I get marked up and you're not going to ask me if I am okay?"

Riven tilted his head, eyes glinting as he leant a little closer. "Where? I hadn't even noticed."

She leant over and smacked his arm with the back of her hand. "Jerk" she said, lips twitching into a grin.

"Where is Roman?" I asked, realising he was missing.

"What a good question," Riven said loudly before shoving a piece of stale bread in his mouth.

Orin shifted in his seat but didn't say a word. Was Riven right? Had he been taken? Killed?

I ate my dried food as the conversation drifted around me, letting it go despite the sinking feeling in my stomach.

I accidentally bumped one of my bandaged forearms against the table and hissed. I wasn't used to having visible cuts. Father had instructed the priest to cut my back, where it was easily hidden by my dresses.

Orin caught my eye from across the table, inclining his head to the double doors that led to the balcony. I stood, my chair scraping against the floor as I followed him.

Riven's eyes watched every step I took.

The cold wind clawed at us as we stepped onto the balcony, the scent of salt and snow thick in the air. Below us, the Dead Sea churned, black and endless. Far beyond, the faint flicker of lights marked Stonebriar, the cage I had fled only to fly straight into another. At least this one wasn't as oppressing.

"Were you lying to me about Roman?" His knuckles gripped the railing so tightly they turned white.

"No," I said cautiously. "I saw—"

"Lie better, Lyra. I do not want to kill you!" He cut me off, green eyes boring into me with desperation. His voice cracked, and for a heartbeat, the mask of the dutiful soldier slipped. Heartbreak stared back at me, and I knew there and then that he wouldn't spare me if I told him the truth. My eyes stung, but I refused to let a single tear fall.

His hands found mine, guiding them to his chest. The steady rhythm of his heart thudded against my sweaty palms.

"If I see you wield water, Lyra, it's my duty to kill you." His forehead fell to mine, breath trembling. "I have a feeling that it's you. That you are the cursed one. But I love you. Gods help me, I love you. Even knowing you are evil."

The words struck my heart like a blade. The first time anyone had ever told me they loved me, and it came wrapped in rejection and threat. I stepped back, but he caught me, his thumb brushing my cheek as if to erase the hurt he'd just caused—and I let him. Because I wanted to believe him. Because I was so tired of feeling like a monster.

"What did you do to Roman?" I asked softly.

His sigh washed over my face as his body caged me against the railing. His closeness used to feel intimate. Now? I felt like I was in danger.

"I tortured him until his Sanctum came out," he said darkly. "It wasn't water."

My vision swam, my heartbeat roaring in my ears. He tortured him. Because of me. Because I lied.

Something cold and sharp suddenly pressed against my

collarbone. I didn't need to look to know it was a dagger. I was used to the feeling of a blade pushing against my skin. I ignored the aching I felt in my chest that made tears want to spill down my cheeks.

"Tell me I'm wrong," he pleaded. "Tell me that you didn't drown the other initiates." A tear slid down his cheek. His other hand cupped my face, the blade pressing harder.

"Orin, I—"

"Tell me!" he yelled over me, eyes wild. I stared at him helplessly, unable to lie to him. But he *knew*. A broken sob cracked through his chest as his blade pushed into my skin, blood dripped down my uniform. The power beneath my skin surfaced and instinct took over.

I sang. A soft melody that wove through the air and into Orin's skin. Into his very soul. His eyes glazed over. The knife slipped from his fingers and clanged against the stone.

"You are wrong, Orin. It was not me," I said. My voice layered in unearthly tones, and I placed my hand over his. His mouth parted and his face relaxed completely. He looked younger without the constant scowl that had been plastered on his face since I washed ashore.

"You would do anything to protect me," I told him, willing him to believe me.

He nodded, murmuring the sentence under his breath.

"Because you love me," I added softly.

"I love you," he repeated in a soft whisper. He leant in slowly, vacant eyes reflecting nothing but my power. His lips pressed against mine, moving them tentatively as though he needed to savour every touch. I couldn't tell where my power ended, and I began. It was wrong. He wasn't in his right mind, but Gods, I needed this. I wanted this to be real so desperately.

I looped my arms around his neck, pulling him closer

until the world narrowed and only we existed. His hands slid low over my back, drawing me flush against his hard body as though something had possessed him. My skin tingled, hot and soothing all at once. Power sunk into my pores. My hands gripped his waist. His movements became urgent, breath rough as his hand tangled in my hair. Heat pooled low in my stomach, need over taking all logical thoughts. Gods, I had missed him.

The sensation built, too much, too bright as he pressed me against the rail. My skin prickled as if it might burst into flames. No. Something was wrong. This wasn't right.

I shoved at his chest, tearing my mouth from his with a sharp, gasping snap.

Orin stared down at me, and a translucent gleam clung to his green eyes, shimmering at me unnaturally. It was almost like he wasn't him anymore.

The balcony door slammed open. Bohdi bursting through them with his sword in his hands. "The gate's been breached!"

Sixteen
The Commander of Death

An alarm split the air, high and shrill, the kind that made my ears want to bleed.

"Orin! Let's go," Bohdi snapped. But he just stared at me with that unsettling iridescent sheen. Not blinking. Not reacting. The dining hall roared behind him, but he didn't hear it. It was like he couldn't hear Bohdi. I waved a hand before his face. Nothing. Like an empty shell waiting for purpose.

Bohdi reached out and placed his hand on Orin's shoulder— and he jerked back as if he had touched hot coals. "What's wrong with him?"

"I...don't know." But I did know. The knowledge sank like a stone. I did this to him, broke him in some way.

Bohdi's voice thinned. "I can't read him anymore. I can only feel you."

Screams and shouting filled the air, the sounds of weapons clashing growing closer. The Fae hadn't just breached the gate. They had breached the barracks.

"They're here." My head snapped back towards the

dining hall. How was I supposed to fight the enemy after a week of training and a Sanctum that would get me killed?

"Orin, we need to fight." The shimmering in his eyes glistened, as if responding to my words.

"I will protect you at all costs," Orin said, gripping the hilt of his sword and unsheathing it with a metal rasp. He squared his shoulders and walked towards the chaos.

Bohdi looked at me with suspicion. Like he had never really looked at me before. Could he see the monster that lurked beneath the surface? Would he try to kill me too?

Bohdi unstrapped a dagger from his waist and carefully passed it to me, pressing the handle into my palm. "Try to hide. Or to run. The other initiates have been given the same instructions."

I nodded at him, my heart racing with anticipation.

Pure chaos greeted me as we stepped into the dining hall. My limbs froze. Tables were overturned. There was a flurry of movement and noise. Blood. Blood splattered the floor, oozing from bodies of the fallen. But it was the enormous shirtless, warriors with pointed ears that made my stomach churn. Their sharpened canines glistened as they smiled through the bloodshed. They looked barbaric. They looked like the bringers of death.

"Move, Lyra!" Orin's yell cut through my haze. A Fae warrior stepped into my path, grinning down at me with a blood-splattered face. Moving seemed like a good idea if I wanted to live.

I raised my dagger feebly, eyeing the blade with disgust. I doubted that it would do anything against the gigantic warrior. He took two steps towards me, my heart racing.

Orin dove in front of me. Their swords met with a sharp whack of metal against metal.

"Lyra!" Riven ducked to my side, covered in blood. He

took the dagger from my hands and pressed my axe into my palms. I wasn't sure how he had gotten it for me, but Gods, I was grateful to see it.

My eyes flashed to his, a storm raging in their depths. He winked, curling my fingers around its hilt before turning to stab a Fae in the ribs with my dagger.

I looked down at the axe buzzing against my skin. The silver etchings in the onyx handle began to illuminate with a dull, shimmering light. It was strange, but I felt connected to it.

I levelled my eyes on a Fae that had his back to me, locked in combat with Bohdi. He raised his large sword, swinging it down with force. Bohdi's sword was quick to meet it, and he moved with a lethal strength that I envied. My vision darkened around the edges, making everything seem a little bit clearer. I drew the axe behind me, its silver edge humming with heat. My stitches pulled uncomfortably, but I was going to do this even if they tore open. I sent a silent prayer to Gods I knew wouldn't listen.

Every ounce of fear and anger I had propelled the axe through the air. It was going to miss. But the axe veered, like it had a will of its own. It slammed into the Fae's back with a wet, meaty thud, blood spraying in an arc like gory rain. Perhaps the Gods weren't so estranged after all. A satisfied smirk slid across my face. The Fae warrior fell in a heap at Bohdi's feet who looked up at me with raised eyebrows.

"Bohdi, behind you!" I yelled, and he spun just in time, sword raised to block an attacking hit. The axe pulsed, darker lines appearing like veins on its hilt. It looked like it was feeding from the dead. I tugged the axe, struggling to pull it free. I put my foot on his back and pulled until it gave way with a wet squelch.

Wasn't I supposed to be running? I was never good at doing what I was told.

There were bodies everywhere. The remaining Iron Guards locked in combat with the Fae. I found Riven amongst the chaos, a sword held to his neck. The metal blade pressed in, drawing blood. The fool was still grinning as if he were in no danger at all.

Drown them. The voice echoed through my head. It was getting harder to resist the pull.

My vision darkened as the voices surged, and I let it pull me under. The metallic scent of blood suddenly felt electrifying, every detail at my discretion.

The song curled through my throat before I could stop it, like it had been waiting. I could feel the power swimming in my veins. I walked slowly through the chaos, hips swaying with every purposeful step. Weapons paused. Those who could hear my song watched with unwavering attention.

But I was singing to the Fae drawing Riven's blood. His head whipped in my direction, and he instantly dropped to his knees. His eyes were wide as he stared at me with parted lips, his breathing uneven. Riven had already moved on, locked in a brutal clash with another Fae as I stepped in front of my kill. I leant down, cradling his rugged face between my hands. He swallowed hard, eyes dilated unnaturally. That same iridescent sheen reflected at me that shone in Orin's eyes.

My movements were slow. Deliberate. Testing a theory, I leant into his face. Our breaths mingled and our lips almost touched. He dropped back onto his heels, and I followed, straddling his hips. He hardened beneath me and the tingling intensified over my skin. As though I was taking his power. *His desire,* I realised. It made me feel stronger. I leant in further, brushing my lips against his in a soft kiss. A kiss of death.

"Drown," I whispered against him. I pulled back, just enough to watch. He gasped soundlessly, convulsing beneath me and still I held him there. My fingers dug into his cheeks, forcing his panic-filled gaze to mine. I wanted to watch his life slowly fade away.

My own breath came fast, almost matching his struggle, until it stopped altogether. Water trickled from his lips, shimmering as it caught the light, and then—nothing.

His body stilled, his mouth frozen open in a soundless plea. I stood, watching with predatory fascination as his body slumped to the ground, heavy and still, like a marionette with its strings cut—

Pain burst through my thigh. The black tip of a spear jutting from my flesh, slick with my own blood. The scream clawing up my throat died before it could escape, breaking into a strangled whimper. The world tilted. Heat seared through my leg, every heartbeat a pulse of fire. I stumbled, breath catching on the agony. Then I saw my attacker and froze, heart aching.

Dreya stood several paces away, arm still outstretched from the throw, her expression frozen between horror and disgust. My stomach dropped. She had seen me yield water and didn't hesitate to sacrifice me for her Gods.

"Monster," she yelled, the word hurtling across the distance between us. Somehow, I heard it over the chaos. And just like that, my heart cracked.

I spun, barely taking a step before pain detonated in my leg and sent me crashing to my knees.

But it was the darkness pulsing at the edge of the room, as if it were alive that made me falter. It was hauntingly familiar. *Just like my dream.*

A monstrous Fae tore free from the shadows, darkness crawling over his muscular form as though it wanted to claim him again.

His onyx eyes met mine through the chaos, gleaming with the promise of death as he brought his sword over his head. His muscles strained as he launched it through the air. Towards *me*.

Something hard slammed into my side, pushing me forward. My hands slapped against the blood-splattered ground with a force that stole my breath. The spear jarring against the ground with sickening force, and I screamed through gritted teeth.

The world blurred.

This was it.

Death.

There was a wet thud. A grunt of pain.

Orin's body was suddenly in front of me. He dropped to his knees, looking at the Fae sword protruding through his chest with disbelief.

"No!" I screamed.

A chill of dread ran up my spine. I tried to stand, stumbling under the pain that throbbed angrily through my leg. I fell to my knees, and a sob escaped my lips. Orin slumped to his side, blood dripping from his mouth.

My very soul darkened. I threw my head back. My scream shattered into layered tones, as if something inside me had awakened, a creature with a hundred voices crying out through my bones. I focused on as many Fae as I could. I could feel the essence of their souls, cursing them to drown.

Thud. Thud. Thud. Dead bodies dropped around us. My eyes cracked open. At least ten Fae had fallen, the sounds of their wet gasps echoing above the bloodshed.

Heaviness washed over me, burning as though my nerves had been set on fire. I fought the grip of unconsciousness and crawled to Orin.

"No," I managed to whisper, voice breaking along with my heart.

His head hung weakly to the side, tears slipping from his eyes. His eyes that were wrong.

"Why did you do that?" I whispered, voice broken by a sob.

"I protected you." His words choked off in a wet splutter, gaze turning vacant. Unseeing.

"No!" I sobbed. Numbness spread over my body. A heaviness dragged at my limbs, as though grief itself was trying to burn me alive. The world around me erupted into chaos. This was my fault. Orin was dead because I did something to him.

"Kill the cursed one!" someone shouted in the distance. The yelling blended, a melody of hate that damned me in their eyes. But I couldn't run. I couldn't fight. My power felt empty.

The world tilted as my body slumped onto the blood-soaked floor next to Orin.

"Lyra, we have to go." A rough hand shook me. I pried my heavy eyes open. Riven was yelling at me, but I couldn't quite hear him. As if I had floated away from myself. As if I no longer existed.

Bohdi knelt over Orin's dead body, pressing his fingers to his neck to check for life as tears slipped over his cheeks.

"Shit." Riven's eyes widened, looking at something past me. "I will come for you, Lyra." Riven's words sounded muffled. My eyes trailed back to his blurry form hovering over me. His face was panicked as he let go of my shoulders, and I slumped back to the ground. I reached out, clutching Orin's lifeless hand.

The shadows seemed to move, crawling up Bohdi's arms. His mouth opened as if to scream, but the darkness plunged into his mouth, cutting off any noise. His skin sunk in on itself, withering and turning grey. Bohdi's corpse fell backwards, hitting the ground and exploding into a pile of dust.

Numb. I was numb. I couldn't move. Couldn't feel my body beyond the heated throbbing in my thigh or the unnatural stiffness of Orin's hand. He was dead. Bohdi was dead. Maybe I was too. Maybe this is what dying felt like. Weightless. Forgotten. Empty.

Then I saw *him*.

Death stepped from the darkness as if it birthed him, shadows clawing at his tattooed skin. He towered over the other Fae, taller and impossibly muscular. Black curls hung over his brow above eyes that weren't just black, but endless voids where souls went to die. *Death. The Commander of Death.*

He crouched beside me, those black eyes drinking me in hungrily. He studied me like I was prey. His teeth flashed, canines sharp and deadly.

My sluggish mind told me to flee. But I couldn't. He tilted his head to the side, like a wolf about to pounce on a rabbit.

"Hello, Little Drownling." His voice was low and gravelly, thick with a foreign accent. I wished Dreya's aim was better. That her spear had pierced my heart. It might have been a kinder death.

Seventeen
Kidnapped

The Commander of Death's voice raked through me, speeding up my sluggish heart. His hand reached for me. I wanted to run.

His fingers wrapped around the blackened shaft of the spear piercing my thigh. His other hand reached for the mutilated flesh where it had exploded through my skin. My muscles tensed, and I braced for pain. Instead, a strange warmth tingled across my skin at his touch. He drew his hand back, frowning down at my blood coating his fingers. I held my breath as he brought it to his mouth and slid it between his lips. His eyelids shuttered closed. A mix between a moan and a growl rumbled from his chest. My fear mixed with a strange warmth that pulsed in my stomach. I knew this is where I would die. Bleeding out next to my first love was one thing, but having my lifeblood drained by the Commander of Death?

No, that will not be my ending.

With the last bit of strength my body possessed, I lashed out, smacking my hand across the Commander's face. His head snapped to the side; predatory eyes springing open.

My breath hitched in my throat. Darkness spilled through his eyes, devouring the whites until only voids remained. But it was the dangerous smirk that slid across his blood-stained lips as he looked back at me that lit my body on fire. Without warning, he snapped the spear still embedded in my thigh. Pain tore through my body. I screamed. Or maybe I only thought I did. Blood poured from the jagged wound. Warm, endless blood. Darkness swept over me and carried me into unconsciousness.

WARMTH WRAPPED AROUND ME LIKE A FORGOTTEN dream. I nestled deeper into the soft furs that cocooned my body, the texture feather-light against my skin. I sank into them, lulled by a strange peace. The scent of pine trees and something sweeter that didn't belong, like caramel, enveloped my senses. I breathed in deeply.

Wait, where am I?

My eyes snapped open, the spell shattering. Canvas walls loomed around me in the dim amber glow of a lantern perched on a table. A soft rustle of wind made the tent fabric breathe around me. Furs covered me on a large makeshift bed laying directly on the floor, but it was surprisingly comfortable. Pain flared through my thigh when I tried to move.

And then it hit me. The battle. The blood. My own people turning on me. "Orin," I whispered, the name breaking in my throat. My heart caused me far more pain than my leg in that moment.

A single tear slid down my cheek, tracing the path so many had taken before it. I tore the furs off my body only to gasp. My initiate uniform was gone; black cotton shorts and a long-sleeved camisole replaced them. My thigh had been bandaged; black ooze stained the white material that wrapped tightly around it. Someone had undressed me and tended to me. But why? Why was I alive?

I braced myself to stand, pushing my unbound silver waves out of my face. *Maybe Riven had somehow gotten me out of there.* I tried to put pressure on my leg and a whimper spilled from me involuntarily. The tent flap burst open, and I stilled. An impossibly large form stepped inside, making the space feel claustrophobic. Shadows that seemed alive enveloped half of him, as though they were trying to drag him into their depths. The shadows dissipated as he walked inside the tent. He studied me with a predatory gaze, dark eyebrows drawn together slightly as the muscles in his strong jaw feathered. My eyes darted to the open tent flap behind him. A way out. His pointed ears stuck through his black curls, multiple metal rings protruding through the flesh. He tilted his head to one side as he took a slow step towards me.

The powerful muscles of his exposed abdomen seemed to ripple with every movement. I hated this monster with every part of my being. He had killed Orin, killed Bohdi, and abducted me.

"Did you get your name from staring people to death? Or are you going to get on with it?" I spat towards the warrior, limping a step closer. If I could get a better angle to the exit, maybe I could run past him. He held a wooden bowl in his large, tattooed hand. He extended it towards me, those dark, soulless eyes never leaving me. When I didn't take it, he sighed in frustration.

"Eat," his deep voice rumbled almost like a growl, thick with his accent.

I snatched the bowl from him without breaking eye

contact. The aromas that wafted towards me were mouth-watering. My stomach grumbled but I couldn't eat. Not now.

"Where am I?" I demanded, hating the way my voice broke.

"Eat," the warrior growled again. I hated being ignored. Blackness bled into the corners of my vision, my power pressing against my skin, begging to be let free. I was no longer something to be ignored.

"Tell me where I am!" I yelled; my voice layered eerily with multiple tones. My power flickered out like a candle dropped in water. I felt... empty. My vision returned to normal, and the Fae's lips tilted in an arrogant smirk.

"Lumireth."

A single word uttered flipped my entire world upside down. I'd been taken through the gate. I was no longer in my realm. No one ever came back from Lumireth, unless it was in mutilated pieces.

"Ugh!" I threw the bowl at him, gritting my teeth against the pain. Gods, everything hurt. Before I could think about it, I ran for the opening in the tent. I gasped, stalling mid-step as shadows formed in front of me, withering and bending unnaturally. They spilt like ink and twisted into the shape of *him*. My senses screamed at me to flee.

He stepped from the darkness itself, sculpted muscle pulling into existence as if the void obeyed his will. Or maybe he was the void. Liquid coated his chest from the bowl I threw at him. His nostrils flared as the amusement drained from his face, and his dark lashes feathered shut as a predatory growl rumbled through his chest. I took a shaky step backwards, as warmth trickled down my leg, the pain throbbing with every rapid beat of my heart. Gods damn it,

I had opened my wound. I glanced back up at the Commander, fear engulfing my body as the onyx of his eyes bled into the whites, swallowing them whole. Small, black veins spread from around the pits of darkness that were now his eyes. He bared his teeth at me, and my eyes caught on the sharp canines that could rip me to shreds. *Run,* my instincts begged me. I staggered forward, trying desperately to get past his ridiculously large body.

A cry left my lips as large hands wrapped around my waist painfully tight. He threw me over his shoulder as if I were nothing, my hair flinging into my face with the force. I screamed, my fists slamming into his back as I thrashed my legs. "Stop!" I screamed. His steps caused my body to bounce on his broad shoulder while I kicked. He threw me down onto the furs, their softness cushioning my fall. My breath whooshed out of me as I landed on my back, my hair splayed out wildly around me.

I scootched up onto my elbows and gathered my feet underneath me, but they gave way. Pain shot from my thigh, blood gushing from the soaked bandage. A whimper left my lips. I knew better than to let my pain show and instantly regretted it. The Commander of Death stood above me and my breath caught in my throat. My blood was smeared over his chest, mixed with the food I had thrown at him. He looked more beast than male.

"Don't. Move," his deep voice demanded, making my heart pound rapidly.

He closed his eyes, his chest expanding with a deep breath. Moments past, but nothing happened. When he finally opened his eyes, the black veins dissipated, and his eyes returned to normal. He knelt beside me, and I flinched like prey cornered by a predator. Because I was. I couldn't run. My power was drained, and I had no idea where I was.

His large hands gripped my thigh and roughly unravelled my sodden bandage. I kicked my leg, desperately trying to get out of his grasp despite the pain that begged me to stop.

"Be still, insufferable little thing," he grunted as I tried and failed to twist away.

"What are you doing?" I gasped through the pain. Hot, angry pain that radiated into my bones. He paused, raising one eyebrow at me as if I were daft.

"Fixing," he grunted.

Good luck with that, I thought inwardly.

"You did this to me and then try to *fix* me?" I scoffed. "Just let me die."

"The Mortals did this to you, not me." He finished unwrapping the bandage and I tried to kick out of his grip, but his hand tightened with punishing force. "Be still, or I will chain you to this bed."

I straightened, breath hitching. *Not chains.* He watched my reaction closely and released me, clearly satisfied. Gooseflesh pebbled on my skin where his hand had been.

He waved his hand to the side, and I gasped as a bowl of water and medical supplies appeared from the shadows. He picked up a damp cloth from the bowl, the muscles in his arms flexed as he wrung out the excess water. He could break me so easily.

This close, he was even more intimidating, yet I couldn't help staring at the intricate markings that covered his tanned muscles. How could something so dangerous look so—

No. He is a vicious killer. A predator who needed to wear a shirt.

I hissed, pain ripping through every nerve in my leg as he wiped the cloth against my wound. Bile rose in my throat. I was used to seeing my skin torn or split, but they were precise, deliberate cuts. Not *this*. The wound in my thigh was a round mess of gore and black ooze. I whimpered in pain, but he kept the same unrelenting pace as if this task was boring him and not burning every single nerve ending in my body.

"Why keep me alive?" I hissed through ragged breaths. I stilled. What if he knew I was Stonebriar's Princess? What if they were going to torture me and use my life to bend the will of my father? How disappointed they would be when they realised the king did not care for his daughter.

"Your power," he said as if it were obvious and tossed the dirty rag to the side. His eyes flicked up to mine. So dark. So endless. "This is going to hurt."

Before I knew what was happening, he had grabbed gauze and shoved it into the mutilated hole in my leg. The scream that tore up my throat burnt, the pain so deep and consuming I couldn't breathe. I looked away from him, my hair forming a curtain in front of my face. I didn't want him to see the tears trickling down my face, but I couldn't hide the sound of my sobs. I squeezed my eyes shut, refusing to scream again. He pushed against my leg, the pain threatening to pull me under. My head was spinning, my heart racing. My leg felt like it was being torn off my body.

"Fuck," the Commander cursed, sounding far away. My body was shaking uncontrollably. Cold sweat dripping down my temple.

"Here," a woman said. I couldn't open my eyes even if I tired. Something pressed to my lips and a warm sweet liquid coated my tongue before darkness enveloped me.

Eighteen
Blood Bound

I laid on the furs for what felt like hours, maybe even days, fading in and out of consciousness.

When I was awake, the pain was relentless, all encompassing. Sleep gave me no reprieve, offering only nightmares of the Dead Sea, a blade tearing through my heart or dark eyes watching me from the shadows.

The tent entrance rustled, and I braced myself for *his* presence to return. I hadn't been conscious enough to see who was tending to me, any time the pain spiked, a warm liquid would be pressed to my lips and unconsciousness would embrace me.

A tall slender female with long dark waves cascading to her waist stepped into the dim light. My eyes focused on her pointed ears. Diamonds pierced through the tips and dangling jewels hung from the bottoms. She regarded me and grinned, canines on view. My heart sputtered as fear spread through my body.

"Oh, good. You are awake." She paid no attention to my obvious fear and continued walking closer to me, her black skirt swaying around her. These creatures were not very modest, but it seemed warmer here. She placed a tray down in front of me, the smells luring a rumble from my empty stomach.

"You must be absolutely starving, darling. I will tend to your wound after," her singsong voice held the same accent as the Commander. I eyed the food suspiciously. I spooned what looked like meat and grains into my mouth, but there were other things I didn't recognise. A moan tore through me as the flavour spread over my tongue. Spices I had never experienced exploded on my tongue as the fresh vegetables melted in my mouth.

The Fae female watched me with amusement as I ungraciously downed the entire bowl.

"Thank you," I mumbled and wiped my mouth with the back of my hand despite the warm blush that had crept up my cheeks over my lack of decorum.

She nodded, her waves softly bouncing. "You are welcome, now come, let me look at this wound." She moved towards me, and I flinched instinctively.

"Oh, please, darling. Whose clothes do you think you are wearing?" Her plump lips formed a soft frown. "I have looked after you for the past three moons and you fear me?"

My body relaxed slightly. If that were true, she wouldn't hurt me. Would she? "Wait, are you saying I was asleep for three days?"

She smiled softly as she began grabbing supplies off a nearby shelf and laying them out on the table. "Yes. You had lost a lot of blood and depleted your magic, and the spear had torn through your bone. It was difficult for me to heal and more comfortable for you if I kept you unconscious. I hope you understand."

"Who are you?" I asked, curiosity prickling my skin. If my wound was that bad, I should have died or lost my leg.

"My name is Cerilla."

"Lyra," I returned. Withholding my last name felt like the right thing to do and I noticed that she had as well.

"Well, Lyra, you are lucky I happened to be here amongst all these brutes when you... arrived. Or you may very well be dead." She finished preparing what looked like some sort of paste in a stone bowl before kneeling next to the bed.

"I was merely visiting, you see." Her slender fingers paused over my bandage and her dark eyes lifted to mine. "May I?" she asked. I nodded reluctantly, and she began unwrapping my bandage. I braced for pain, but she was patient and gentle in her movements.

"Have you taken control of Stonebriar?" I blurted, my voice shrill.

Her giggle grated against my patience.

"Goodness no. We have far greater threats than Mortals darling, the Commander got what he wanted and got out." She finished unravelling my bandage and I took a quick intake of breath. It was nothing but a pink puckered line against my pale skin.

"What threats?" I murmured, unable to tear my gaze away from my healed leg.

She sighed, "I have said too much already. My dear brother will already be enraged." She began cleaning my wound with cold gauze. A dull ache pulled at healed skin, but nothing more. *How is this possible?*

"Your brother?" I asked carefully. I needed her to keep talking, any information could help me.

"The Commander," she said with a soft smile.

I clenched the furs in my fists, my knuckles turning white. Now that she'd said it, the resemblance was obvious. They were both beautiful, like a blade drawn in moonlight.

Hypnotic, dangerous, and captivating in the most primal way. They had the kind of beauty that lured you in, only to slit your throat. I said nothing, clenching my jaw so hard I thought my teeth would snap. Cerilla assessed me and sighed heavily, throwing dirty gauze to the side.

"Some advice, darling?" she said, mixing a salve in a small stone bowl. "Because I've decided I like you." She didn't look up as she added more ingredients to the small stone bowl before crushing them. "He needs you. But the Commander is the most powerful being this realm has seen since the Gods fell. The darkness he wields... isn't always in his control." She paused, meeting my gaze. "Mercy is not one of his virtues. Do not test the limits of his restraint."

I swallowed hard, looking anywhere but at her. I had known I was in danger, but her words weighed heavily on my chest. "Thank you for the warning," I whispered softly. She nodded, pleased with herself and gathered the salve in her hand, smearing it on my wound. I flinched automatically, expecting pain. A relieving coolness spread through my body like waves lapping at the shore. Her hands hovered over my wound, black mist gathered around her fingers. She began quietly chanting in a language I didn't know. I watched in horror as the black mist enveloped my thigh, but no pain came. A strange pulling sensation nestled against my skin, as if the tissue itself was knitting back together. *Healing*. The black mist slowly swirled through the air, sinking back into her fingers.

"Thank you," I whispered, my eyelids feeling heavy.

She gently began wrapping my wound. "Your body will demand rest now, to aid the healing process. I will check on you at sunrise." My body relaxed back onto the soft furs, my eyes closing against my will.

I walked around the small tent, without limping. A tolerable ache spread through my thigh with every step, but I could walk.

"Try to run again, Little Drownling," a deep voice came from behind me. *His* voice. My captor. "And you will regret it."

I whipped around to face him, almost tripping on my feet. When had he come in? I hadn't heard the rustle of the tent door or the sound of footsteps.

This monster has killed thousands of my kind. He killed Orin. He killed Bohdi. He could easily kill me. He pulled a small dagger from his belt.

"Imbue this," he grunted as he dropped it onto the furs at my feet with a soft thud. Clearly, he did not see me as a threat if he was giving me a blade.

"Excuse me?" Maybe it was a language barrier, or perhaps I had misheard him.

His head tilted, eyes darkening. "Imbue. The. Dagger," he repeated slowly, his accent drawing out the words in the rich timber of his voice. My eyebrows drew together and my fists balled at my sides. "Take me back or kill me. Just get on with it," I demanded, raising my chin slightly. I wasn't sure I wanted to go back. It was Dreya's spear that had struck me. Did everyone at the barracks know I was a monster now? Perhaps he *should* kill me, it would save everyone a lot of trouble. His eyebrows raised as he stepped closer to me. Too close. But I refused to step back.

"Oh, but Drownling, I have plans for you this time."

This time? I swallowed hard, hating the way my pulse quickened at his closeness. His muscles shifted as he took another step towards me. So close that I could feel the heat rolling off his body. My power stirred in the darkness of my soul. *Kill him,* it purred. My powers had been healing over the past few days, and I could feel it simmering beneath my skin. Not that it mattered, the male in front of me could snap my neck without lifting a finger.

I took a retreating step back. His eyes tracked the movement, and a smirk tugged at his mouth. I was nothing but prey to him.

"Let me go. I am useless to you," I whispered.

"No. You will imbue for me."

"I told you already, I don't know what that means!" I raised my voice; he merely studied me.

"Let's make a blood deal then, Little Drownling," he growled, clearly out of patience. The primal part of my brain told me to run from this predator, not make a deal with it.

"You will find the Soul Relics and imbue my weapons *then* I will give you a chance to run." His voice had dropped an octave.

"Will you chase me?" I asked, eyeing his predatory smirk.

"Clever girl," he chuckled, the sound a deep vibration through his chest that made my toes curl in fear.

"After you do as I ask, I will give you a head start." He leant back, pleased with himself. He obviously didn't know I was royal blood and had no plans to try to leverage me. Every bone in my body screamed at me not to make a deal with the Commander of Death. But what if I could get something in return?

"I want something else," I said, squaring my shoulders.

"You're not in a position to make demands." His eyes darkened, the whites growing smaller.

"Do you know anything about the Sea Goddess?" I shouldn't have asked. I was used to dealing with powerful men and I knew what happened to women who did more than aimlessly agree. But I couldn't help it. Not then. Not now. I was never good at doing what I was meant to do, a fatal flaw I was sure would end my life one day. The Commander was unnaturally still, shadows crawling across his skin as if they wanted to drag him into the darkness.

"Do you?" he countered.

Somehow, I was connected to her. It was what deemed me a monster and I needed to know *why*.

"No." The lie was partly convincing, but the way his mouth tugged into an arrogant smirk, I wondered if he had heard my pulse speed up.

He raised his hand to his mouth, dragging a canine against his skin, blood pooling inside his palm.

"I possess the journal of the goddess's killer, make a blood bargain with me and it is yours."

My pulse quickened, and I raised my palm towards him, offering for him to do the same to mine. If books existed on the Relics, I needed them.

He looked at my hand and then back up at my face, amusement flashing in those endless eyes.

"Do not tempt me." His voice had deepened slightly, and I drew my hand back instinctively. How naïve was I? I had just offered a blood-sucking Fae to sink his teeth into me. He picked up the dagger from the blanket with his large, callused hand. He flipped it and caught it by the blade, extending the hilt towards me.

My fingers wrapped around the handle, accidently brushing over his fingers and a shock of heat sparked where our skin met.

His nostrils flared almost imperceptibly, a quick

flicker of something dark flashing in his eyes. He dropped the dagger into my palm as if my touch had repulsed him. I stared into his onyx eyes as I ran his blade across my hand, slowly and deliberately not flinching from its sharp bite.

His strong jaw flexed, his gaze darkening as he watched me intently. A small gasp escaped me as his large hand grasped mine, our blood mingling between our palms. He murmured something in a language I did not understand before opening his eyes. They were completely black again. This close, it was terrifying.

"I will give you the journal," he murmured darkly. "*Once* you earn it, it's yours and until you imbue enough weapons for me, we cannot kill each other."

His eyes bore into me so heavily that they felt like a physical force. Drowning me all over again.

"Now you repeat your end of the bargain," he grunted, as if I were daft.

"I will *imbue* your weapons, or whatever it is you ask of me."

He gave me an unsettling smile as heat radiated through my palm and into my very soul. Searing. Alive. It felt as though I'd pressed my skin against a brand, and it had set every nerve on fire. I flinched, staring in shock as intricate lines bloomed over the skin of my left hand.

Delicate, deliberate lines that formed a symbol, pulsing with latent power. It was a wave, mid-crash, curled fiercely towards the stars inked above it. Sharp, celestial points arranged in a constellation I didn't recognize, yet something inside me *ached* with familiarity. The crashing tide mirrored the very shores of home... and the stars above felt like a map etched into my soul.

"Interesting," the Commander ground out, voice

lowered. I looked up and noticed he was studying an identical mark on the back of his own left hand.

"What does it mean?" I whispered.

His starless eyes shimmered with something unreadable. "A physical reminder of our bargain. If one of us breaks it, we both die." My heart stuttered. The large male stood, and without sparing me another glance, stormed from the tent. *What have I done?*

NINETEEN
BEHIND ENEMY LINES

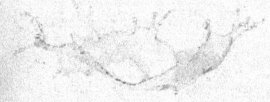

Another night passed, and sleep offered no mercy. I had dreamt of death—*my* death.

Countless times, and yet, each death was in a different place with a different dress clinging to my skin. But in the end, it was the same sword through my heart, wielded by the same man I could not see.

I burrowed further into the soft furs of the bed. The delicious scent of caramel and fresh night air was long gone, replaced by the sour stench of shame and grief that clung to my skin.

The monster lurking beneath my skin had replenished, and it felt as though it was its own sentient being. I could feel it, curling tightly around the cracked pieces of my heart, willing it not to shatter.

My only reprieve from my thoughts and nightmares was Cerilla. She brought me food, fresh clothes, and tended to my wounds. Despite her being a creature that I had been raised to fear, she was nicer to me than most of my own kind had ever been. I found myself almost looking forward to seeing her. She felt like a small candle flickering in the depths of night, not enough to illuminate, but enough to stop me from being blind.

I was trapped here. Bound to the formidable Commander of Death for a task I did not understand because of a power I couldn't control that was connected to a goddess killed a thousand years ago.

I didn't know what I was, only that the moment anyone saw the *real* me, they either tried to kill me or use me. I should have accepted that I was unlovable by now, but the hollow feeling growing in my chest felt like it would consume me.

I hadn't let myself think about Dreya. Not really. Her warmth had curdled into hatred the moment she saw me yield water. She had been the first person I thought might be a friend. Instead, she had been the first to try to kill me without hesitation.

Is that how Orin would have looked at me as he shoved his blade through my heart?

I buried my face in the pillow and screamed until my lungs burned dry, until my body convulsed and the sound ripped itself out of me, jagged and broken, leaving nothing behind but pain and breathless silence.

Grief swelled in my chest, sharp and suffocating. I shoved it down before it could drown me. I could not afford to mourn people who would gladly watch me die.

"Why do you scream?"

I startled and glared up at the hulking form entering the tent. Sunlight spilled in around him, making him appear to be a monstrous shadow.

A gasp escaped me, not in fear, but at the warm golden beams streaming into the dark tent. *Sunlight.* I had been too caught up in myself to even think about that. Lumireth was not cursed in the same way the Mortal Kingdom was.

The Commander's fists clenched at his sides, gaze raking over my body. What a weak, pathetic mess I must look like.

He was still shirtless, his powerful form on full display. Leather caps covered his broad shoulders, and a sword handle stuck up over his back, as if he needed a weapon to be deadly.

"Where are the Soul Relics located?" he demanded.

"Kill me already," I muttered, rolling onto my side, refusing to give him the satisfaction of a response. "Or go find a shirt."

"I do not typically get complaints," he almost growled as his boots thudded closer, unhurried, as though he expected me to flinch. But I wouldn't. I glanced up as he crossed his bouldering arms over his chest.

"Nor am I used to women crying in my bed."

His bed? *That* caused me to flinch. His gaze dragged over me, sharp and assessing as he smirked with satisfaction.

The words had slid under my skin like a blade, and every instinct I had went taut.

"Your wallowing makes you useless to me, get up," the Commander demanded.

My spine prickled with anger. *Useless.* "No," my voice rang with steel. "You promised me information," I asked, sitting up and pushing *his* blankets off me with disgust.

"Do as you are told, Little Drownling, and you will get what you want." He nodded towards the door, black curls falling across his forehead with the motion.

"Come," he growled. I didn't want to listen to him. But the thought of knowing how sunlight felt against my skin made me follow him. I stepped into the blinding sunlight, squinting against the brightness. Its warmth folded over my skin like the embrace of a long-lost lover I had forgotten.

163

Instinctively, I tilted my chin to the sky and inhaled deeply, letting the warmth sink into my frozen bones. The air here was crisp and sweet, flooding my lungs with something that made my blood sing in welcome. I had never known what warmth had felt like. A soft moan escaped my lips as I closed my eyes, drinking in the golden heat like nectar as though I was starved. I felt the heaviness of his gaze and opened my eyes.

The muscles along his shoulders bunched with tension as he turned around, expecting me to follow.

We walked a worn path between a labyrinth of tan-coloured tents, the sun casting long shadows against the soft grass that I longed to touch. It was so green. Lighter than Orin's eyes, but my heart pinched all the same.

We came into a clearing that seemed to be in the heart of the camp. I felt so small surrounded by Fae warriors. Some sparred with steel, blades clashing in a violent rhythm, sweat covering their war hardened bodies. Others shot arrows into straw-draped targets with precise, deadly focus.

Strong aromas wafted towards me, rising from a large iron pot that simmered over an open flame. I inhaled deeply, and my stomach grumbled.

Many Fae noticed us, unfortunately. Admiration, respect, and fear followed in my captor's wake before their gazes sharpened with disgust when they landed on me. But the Commander didn't stop walking, leading me past the hostile creatures to the edge of the camp.

THE FAE CAMP LOOMED BEHIND US AS THE Commander led me to the edge of the lush forest. Maybe he was going to feed me to a beast. Maybe the blood deal was a trick, and he was going to kill me after all.

"About time!" A Fae warrior stepped out of the canopy of trees, his large strides consuming the distance between us. Even from this far away I could feel that he exuded power, but the grin on his handsome face oozed charisma. His muscular form was covered in tattoos as well, and he seemed to prefer the same shirtless armour as the other warriors. The breeze teased his auburn hair that was tied in a high, messy bun that almost hid his pointed ears. Pointed ears that had holes in his earlobes stretched by black bands. I had never seen anything like it. He extended his hand towards the Commander of Death, who returned the gesture. Their hands clasped around each other's forearms in a greeting that looked as though they had done for a lifetime.

"Everything is prepared, except there was a complication," the warrior said with a grimace. "One you may not be happy about."

The Commander growled, a deep rumble of warning rolling through his chest that sent a shiver up my spine.

"It's just me, dear brother." Cerilla strolled into the clearing radiating grace and beauty, slapping the back of her hand against the warrior's shoulder. She wore dark, slim-fitting pants that hugged every curve and a matching slim piece of fabric that barely contained her breasts. I had never seen people display so much skin in front of others so casually. But given the heat, I didn't blame them.

"You wouldn't expect me to let a fellow lady ride with two *gruesome* warriors by herself now, would you? What kind of hosts would we be?"

"We are not hosts, Cerilla. That," he grunted, gesturing

over his shoulder at me, "is my prisoner. *Not* your plaything."

The warrior glanced behind the Commander, grinning down at me with glistening canines on display. "I'm Solas."

I took a reluctant step back and his eyebrows drew together. "No need to fear me, sweetheart, I won't bite unless you ask me to." He winked a heavily lashed hazel eye at me.

"She may look small and breakable, but she is a volatile little thing. Drowned twelve of our brethren on dry land."

Shame slithered into the pit of my stomach, and I cast my eyes down to my feet. I did what I needed to do to protect my people, but it still wasn't enough. They still turned on me.

Cerilla cut through the palpable silence as she pushed past the Fae males. "You were truly going to have her ride in this, brother? She will swelter!" She gestured towards my long cotton pants and tunic. "We will meet you at the horses when Lyra is properly dressed for riding in mid-summer."

The Commander glanced skyward and shook his head before following a chuckling Solas into the forest. Clearly the Commander held patience for only his sister.

Cerilla waved her hand, and a pile of black material landed on her open hand, making me jump. She glanced at me. "Oh, darling, it's just basic magic."

I wanted to ask so many questions, but she held up a top like hers and my voice died in my throat.

"I cannot wear that," I whispered. She looked confused as she held up the thin strap of material that would show every brutal scar that puckered the skin of my abdomen, back, and chest. Scars I did not want the world to see.

She sighed, the material disappearing before being

replaced with a dark blouse with elbow-length sleeves that would billow and band at my elbows. I nodded in acceptance and changed behind a nearby tree into the buttery-soft clothes she had given me. The breeze seemed to glide straight through it, teasing my skin with its refreshing embrace against the growing warmth of the sun.

We walked further into the forest, the sun filtering lazily through the thick canopy, casting shadows against the textured bark of the large, lush trees. They seemed to pulse with life, and the vibrant flowers that scattered the ground seemed to bend towards us. I had never seen anything like it.

"Where are we going?" I asked Cerilla.

"The Commander wants you far away from the gate. I cannot tell you much," she smiled apologetically. "But we will be travelling for five moons."

A small thrill shot through me. Five days of travelling. Of seeing. I was a prisoner, but the mercy of getting to explore felt *almost* like a taste of freedom. Before I could ask any more questions, three large horses came into view. The largest one was as black as midnight, large bags strapped to its sides. The Commander of Death leaned against the tree next to the large beast, shadows withering around him, crawling to him from the forest like they were bringing him secrets. Solas mounted his honey-coloured steed in one smooth motion; she kicked her front leg impatiently as he adjusted his weight in his saddle. That left only one grey-and-white flecked mare with a braided mane. Cerilla ran to her, patting her along the bridge of her nose.

I was probably going to be dragged along next to one of their horses like the prisoner I was.

"There are only three horses," I said out loud.

"Congratulations, you can count." The Commander pushed off the tree and readied his horse's saddle.

I glared daggers at him, wishing I had my axe so I could throw it at his face.

I was not allowed at the stables at Stonebriar. Father used to tolerate me brushing the horses in the early mornings, until I tried to ride one to escape. Fracturing my arm when I had fallen off that mare had been the least painful injury of the day. Maybe walking wouldn't be so bad.

"Get on the horse," he growled.

"No," I said before I realised.

The Commander held his hand and gestured, my blood bargain tattoo tingling with an uncomfortable heat. I took an involuntary step forward. *What was happening?* I tried to stop walking. Pain tore through my tattoo and up my arm, stealing my breath.

"You made a mistake, Little Drownling." The Commander paused, his amusement palpable. *"Whatever you ask of me,"* he mocked. "One little slip of tongue and your will is mine to bend."

Dread flooded through me, my naivety costing me once again. I opened my mouth to protest, but he held up his hand.

"Do not speak," he murmured darkly, causing my words to get caught in my throat until only a strangled gasp of pain could escape.

Bastard! I yelled at him in my head as I glowered at him.

His hands wrapped around my waist, and I hit them uselessly. He continued to lift me as though I were nothing.

The nightmarish horse moved beneath me, and my thighs clenched to keep balance. The horse reared in protest, tossing its head side to side. I slipped sideways, gripping the saddle with white knuckles. The seat jostled, warmth enveloping my back before a solid form melted against me. I sat rigidly, trying to break contact with his impossibly large form.

I glanced over my shoulder, his face much too close. My protest died in a strange, strangled sound.

He chuckled darkly, the sound vibrating straight through me, leaving my hands shaking.

Take his blood, the voice whispered to me on the breeze and I stilled. I hadn't heard it since I had almost died. *Take his blood, give him yours.*

He reached around me to grab the reins, his arms encircling me. His scent enveloped me, sandalwood and caramel overpowering my senses. His powerful thighs shifted around me as he nudged the beast into momentum. I jostled forwards violently, before slamming backwards into the smooth bulk of his muscle.

A growl of warning ripped from his throat as his hips ground against me from behind, matching the rhythmic movements of the horse. A large hand wrapped around my waist, and I stiffened beneath the touch, warmth tingling across my skin.

"Engage here." He slid his hand across my abdomen, his warm breath tickling my ear. His hand slid back to my waist sliding lower to rest at the top of my hip, strong fingers squeezing me painfully. "Soften here."

I looked at him over my shoulder, my silver waves jostling with every bounce of the horse, making him see just how pissed off I was.

Go to Hells, I mouthed at him.

He lent down, lips roughly pressing against my ear.

"Behave, or I will tie you up and *drag* you behind my horse." He breathed against me and disgust curled through my stomach. "Your screams would be fucking beautiful."

TWENTY
VOICELESS

Three days had passed. Three long, miserable days. I'd been dragged through dense forests and two bustling villages, their streets filled with colour, laughter, and life so vibrant it made the dark tales I'd heard about the Fae seem like cruel lies. But I knew better. I'd seen how they slaughtered my people. *Innocent* people.

The Commander hadn't said a word to me. Hadn't so much as looked in my direction unless it was to drag me up onto that cursed horse like I was some burden to be carted around.

I burned with fury, but I had no way to scream it since the Commander refused to loosen his hold over my will through my poorly worded bargain. I had no voice to spit my rage into his face. No words to demand answers. And that made it worse, the silence. *My* silence. It crawled under my skin like an ever-present reminder that I wasn't in control. Though it seemed, the power thrumming through my veins had plenty of commentary to make. *Plenty* of vivid daydreams of how to kill the Commander the moment I fulfilled my end of the blood deal.

Every night was the same. Solas, ever the charming cook, would hunt and roast some unfortunate woodland creature. He would hum to himself as if this were normal. I hated that I found comfort in the rhythm of it. The way his awkward jokes tried to fill the silence I wasn't allowed to break almost made him feel less dangerous. But I wasn't fooled.

Each horse carried a small tent strapped to its side, and by now I'd grown efficient at setting them up. I remembered the first night, watching Cerilla begin to unroll one like it was second nature. I'd stood there useless, a ghost in someone else's life, while they all moved like they belonged. I hated that feeling... Uselessness. Although it clung to me like a second skin. I'd worn it my entire life. A prized possession, seen but never heard. I had been trained to smile and obey while men played games of power and blood. And now, after everything I'd risked escaping that life, after *choosing* to leap into training, to fight, to matter... I was right back where I started. Muzzled, ignorant and *silent*. I was being dragged around like some fragile decoration, for reasons I still did not understand, fumbling after answers everyone else seemed to hold. My ignorance burned brighter than any shame, and I hated it most of all.

So that first night, I'd shooed Cerilla away, jaw clenched and hands trembling. I needed *something* to claim as mine, even if it was just pitching a damn tent. Because if I was going to be hauled through their war like baggage, I'd at least plant my feet and *do something*.

Solas talked at me constantly, telling me lazy stories of their world undeterred by the fact that I couldn't respond. It was almost comforting—his voice filling the silence my own had left behind. I had learnt that the Commander of Death was a legend in Lumireth.

A *monster hunter*. Solas told me stories of him fighting legendary beasts to save their realm. I believed none of his stories, but I still enjoyed them.

At night, I slept in a tent alone, the Commander sitting guard at its entrance. Strange noises jarred me from nightmares of the sea. It was always the sea.

I had, at least, found some rhythm in the saddle. I was proud of that, of learning to stay upright without gripping the reins like a terrified child.

I flinched as the fire cracked sharply, dragging me from my thoughts. Embers leapt into the air, swirling upward in an intimate dance with the smoke. I followed their path, amazed by the night sky that hung above us. An unimaginable number of twinkling lights shone down upon us in the clearing where we had made camp. Seeing the night sky was almost worth all of this. *Almost.*

Cerilla returned from the horse with three small bags filled with a dark liquid. She passed one to the Commander and he snatched it. His shadows consumed half of his body, withering uncontrollably. He stood suddenly and stalked away, his body disappearing into the shadows themselves.

Cerilla watched her brother disappear into the shadows, her lips pressed into a thin line. Solas sank his teeth into his bag without hesitation, drinking with a hunger that made my stomach twist. I grimaced, something inside me whispering to run. They were drinking blood. Solas threw the empty bag into the fire, wiping the dark liquid that smeared around his mouth onto his forearm. He caught me watching him.

"It's a blood bag," he said casually, as if it was nothing more than soup. But he stared at the flames, lost in thought.

"There were Mortals here when the realms were sealed," he said finally, voice light but hollow at the edges.

"There are many that live in Lumireth in their own communities and blood donations are paid handsomely." He paused. His next words were quieter. "In *this* court, anyway." His gaze drifted, not at me but through me, to some memory I wasn't privy to. The corners of his mouth twitched, not in a smile, but in the strain of holding something back. Then he blinked it away, flashing a grin and tilting his head with feigned ease. "Let's just say you do not want to know what the other courts prefer."

I gritted my teeth. I had so many questions. *What court were we in? How many courts were there?*

"Will you let the girl speak?" Solas said, looking past me. "It would make the trip far more entertaining."

"You'll regret that request," the Commander rumbled from behind me. He waved his hand in my direction, and the blood mark on my skin tingled in response.

I shot to my feet and spun towards his impossibly large form, shadows snaking around his body like they were alive.

"I hate you," I growled, eyes blazing. "The moment our blood bargain is over, I will kill you. I will slit your throat and watch you bleed shadows and send you to the *deepest* pit in the Seven Hells." I closed the distance between us until I was glaring up into his void-like eyes. Power thrummed beneath my skin, and my vision pulsed with flickers of darkness.

"As long as you find the Soul Relics and imbue for me, I will hand you the fucking blade myself."

"I don't know where they are!" I shoved at his chest, open palms striking warm skin that refused to give.

He didn't move. Not an inch. The realization snapped something sharp inside me, rage surging as I struck him again.

His eyes changed, thin inky veins bloomed outward

from his irises and consumed the whites. The eyes of a monster. He leaned in, closing the space between us until I could feel his warm breath wash over my face. My heart hammered in my throat, but I held my ground.

"You *are mine* to command. *My* prisoner."

I ground my teeth together. My hand lashed out before I could stop it, aiming to slap him across the face. His calloused hand caught my wrist effortlessly.

"You are impossibly mouthy, and violent," he murmured, almost amused. His calloused hand squeezed my wrist until I gasped, and I struggled against his hold uselessly.

"For something so—" His gaze dragged over me with cruel deliberation as he twisted his hand with brute force, and a sickening crack echoed louder than my scream.

"—breakable."

Agony ripped through my arm, white-hot and blinding. My knees buckled as I cried out, the sound tearing from my throat before I could swallow it. My fingers spasmed, and the world tilted violently as my bone protruded through my skin.

The word struck something raw inside me, a fault line I'd tried relentlessly to bury under my defiance.

He stepped closer, my chest flush against his abdomen. He was so tall. His fingers tightened painfully around my wrist, and cold tendrils crept across my skin. Painfully cold shadows. They moved like liquid frost, crawling and coiling against my skin.

"Is that what you want?" My chin lifted despite the tremble in my voice. "To break me? Many men have tried before you, Commander."

He clenched his jaw, a dark chuckle vibrating through his chest. "Do not compare me to those Mortal excuses you call men," he replied, voice low and lethal. He stepped forward, and I instinctively shifted back a pace. His eyes caught the movement, glinting with predatory hunger. "I am your Kingdom's nightmare, Little Drownling." His breath was suddenly hot against my ear. I retreated another step, bark scraping against my back. His body caged me against the tree. Too close. I couldn't move.

"And you are my prisoner. If I want to break you..." His lips brushed the shell of my ear. Anger mingled with the fear rising in my stomach. "Nothing can stop me."

But he was wrong. I would fight him *every* Gods-dammed moment. The world wavered. I hummed a haunting melody, and his form twisted in my sight like I was seeing him through dark, churning water. Power rippled over my skin almost like a living, breathing entity. Without shame, I pushed my breasts against his bare chest, using the distance he'd tried to weaponize. He blinked, a crack in his composed, deadly front. I smirked up at him through thick eyelashes and bit down softly on my bottom lip. I could feel the water within him—humming beneath his skin like a tide waiting for command. The moisture in his blood. His breath. The sheen of sweat. Every droplet was a thread I could tug.

Boil, I demanded it. I whispered power into the water that pulsed through his fingers, coaxing it to heat.

"What the fuck are you doing to me?" the Commander growled. He tried to step back, but I refused to let him, pulling him closer instead. If I kissed him, could I control him? Would his eyes have that iridescent sheen that waited for my command?

"I thought you wanted to play monster?" I asked innocently, my voice a melody of layered tones. His jaw flexed, his neck muscles straining against the pain I was causing, and he dropped my broken arm, falling useless at my side.

I tilted my head at him, drinking in his muscular form. I grinned. "I thought I'd show you mine."

I should've feared this power. It was a pull that threatened to drown me and kill anyone in my way. But I needed it. I lifted my good hand, skimming it over the tattoo on his chest. Gooseflesh broke out across his skin under my almost touch. He felt different to the others I had drowned, more powerful. *Older*.

"This will hurt, Commander. But I want you to watch me break you." I reached for the water in his cells, drawing on an instinct I didn't understand, forcing the molecules to vibrate—fast, faster—until heat built beneath his skin. His knees crashed into the forest floor. His head was just shorter than my standing height. My fingertips buried in his dark hair. His anger felt as lethal as his shadows burrowed into my skin. I hovered mere inches from his sweat-covered face.

My lips tingled as they brushed his, a whisper of contact that sent a violent shudder through his body. My lips moved, slow and intentional, sliding against his with reckless precision. The space between us disappeared, and the air became thick with something sharp and volatile.

He went utterly still beneath me, and I felt the way his control strained, as if he were one moment away from exploding. Steam curled from his skin, mixing with his seething shadows as they clawed across my skin with searing pain.

The growl that rumbled through his chest would make anyone cower as he pulled against my hold, not to escape, but to *test*.

The moment stretched until he broke free with unsettling ease, my spell unravelling as if it had never truly taken root.

His power rolled over me, and my body betrayed me as my magic bled away, each molecule slipping from my command like water released by an opened hand.

"No!" I shouted as my power collapsed in on itself.

"Lyra!" Cerilla yelled, suddenly beside me. I whipped my head towards her fear-filled eyes, my heart constricting with each beat under the weight of her stare. She was scared for her brother's life. Scared of the monster I had let surface. Scared of *me*.

His boot slammed against my shin and the world tilted in a sudden blur. I thrashed, trying to find balance, but it was too late. Air whooshed from my lungs, jarring reality back into place as my back slammed into the ground. Darkness swallowed me. Shadows coiled and crashed, devouring everything. Every nerve ending screamed, like I had been plunged into acid so cold I feared I would turn into ice itself. I thought I had known pain. I was *wrong*. Screams lodged in my throat, unable to break free as the shadows relentlessly pressed down on me. *Into* me. I couldn't move. I couldn't scream. I was dissolving, undone by the very darkness I had tried to control.

A sudden warmth spread over me like honey. Thick and slow, oozing over the coiling shadows that wreaked havoc on my body. It was *his* warmth. The Commander's face was inches away from mine, twisted in a snarl that would frighten the bravest Iron Guard. His massive form pressed down on me, anchoring me to the world. My fingers gripped his skin, desperate to pull him closer, to steal whatever heat I could to survive his volatile shadows. A whimper escaped my lips, my back arching against his chest. I was going to shatter. He convulsed above me, his form writhing, contorting. Flesh and shadow warped in a struggle I didn't understand. He was darkness itself. And yet, I clung to him as though he were the only light I could find. He roared so loud my ears throbbed, his hot breath washing over my face. "I cannot," he ground out breathlessly, "kill you, yet."

The shadows reluctantly began to crawl back into his body as he fought its control. He was the pure definition of volatile. How could all that power reside in one male without tearing him apart?

The glow of the campfire broke through the shadows as they receded, the light dancing against the sharpness of his face. The Commander hovered above me for a heartbeat longer, the stars reappearing behind him as my eyes struggled to focus. His jaw tensed before he finally pushed off me, and a strange coolness swept over my skin, not from the night air, but from the loss of contact of his body. That or, I was freezing from his shadows. He shot me a final, unreadable look over his shoulder before turning and vanishing into the night.

Cerilla appeared at my side in an instant, her hand wrapping gently around mine as she pulled me to my feet. I gritted my teeth against the pain and my legs trembled beneath me.

"Oh, darling, you are freezing." She gestured to Solas to grab a blanket from one of the tents. I could only focus on my breath misting in front of my face like it did in the depths of winter at Stonebriar. My muscles were rigid as I tried to take a step. A light-headedness swept over my body, threatening to pull me back to the ground.

"I think..." I stopped and cleared my tender throat that felt like I had been screaming for hours. "I need to lay down," I finished weakly.

"Of course. I will make you some tea for the pain before I heal your arm," Cerilla said.

Solas wrapped a warm blanket around my shivering form. I took a step and faltered, my legs quivering relentlessly. Solas caught me before I could fall and I glared at his hand steading my arm.

"Easy now," he said with a weary smile.

It must have been the near-death exhaustion, but I decided to lean on his arm. Trusting him, just this once, to help me. He took my shift in weight as permission and gently swooped one arm under my knees and gathered me against his chest. "Breathe," he said soothingly as he carried me to my tent.

Cerilla paced behind him, eyeing me as if I were going to disappear. I groaned as Solas laid me down on the bedroll.

"You are strong, Lyra. No one survives the Commander's shadows and lives."

I couldn't answer, too busy dragging air in and out of my frigid lungs through clenched teeth. Cerilla knelt beside me, pressing a small steaming cup into my uninjured hand.

"Drink," she instructed gently. "Slowly."

Solas helped me sit up, and I brought the cup to my mouth. The herbal liquid burned going down, not unpleasantly, but with purpose. Heat bloomed through my chest, dulling the jagged edge of the pain. My shaking eased by degrees, breath coming a little steadier.

"Good," Cerilla murmured. "Now, this will hurt."

She settled beside me, her hands hovering just above the bone protruding through my forearm. Small wisps of darkness slithered from her fingers, humming softly as it spread through my arm.

Pain flared, sharp and blinding. I cried out, fingers curling uselessly as white-hot agony lanced through me.

Solas held my other hand, squeezing reassuringly.

"Almost," Cerilla soothed, voice firm but kind. "Stay with me."

Her magic pressed deeper, deliberate and precise. I sobbed, gripping onto Solas's hand as if he could pull me away from the pain. My bones cracked, sliding back into place with a sickening sensation that made my stomach churn. The pain ebbed slowly, replaced by a deep, aching throb.

Cerilla exhaled and leaned back, the glow fading from her hands.

"There," she said softly. "It will be tender for a few days, but it is set."

She wrapped my arm carefully, movements practiced and reverent, before brushing damp hair from my face.

"You should rest," she added, eyes searching mine. "You've been through more than most survive."

But I was drifting. The tea weighed warm and heavy in my stomach, warping my sense of reality as they both left.

The silence was so thick I could almost hear the soft crackle of the fire.

I had nearly died. But, for a moment I had controlled the Commander of Death. Pride filled my chest like a brief flicker of a candle before being snuffed out by pure exhaustion.

I drifted off, falling into the depths of sleep.

TWENTY-ONE
MONSTERS

A sharp *click* shattered the silence outside my tent. Every hair on my arms rose. Another *click*... closer this time. My eyes shot open. A shadow swept across the canvas. I sat up, clutching the blanket to my chest and staring at the canvas wall.

I let out an unsteady breath, squinting in the dark. An outline loomed over my tent. Tall, thin spider-like legs jerked at unnatural angles as it moved.

The sound came again, faster. A high-pitched sound that sent my nerves on edge. It was so close, nothing more than a thin piece of material separated me from Gods knew what.

Its head tipped back, sharp pinchers at its mouth moving back and forwards.

Click. Click. Click.

My breath hitched. And in that one moment, the thing stilled. As if sensing my rapid heartbeat. As if hearing me.

It lurched towards my tent—and the scream tore free before I could stop it.

I threw myself out of the tent, crashing onto the cool grass. Air burst from my lungs. Fabric tore behind me.

The thing screeched, a sound that bled fear into my bones. I scrambled upright, my legs shaking beneath me. The thing's two front legs tore my tent apart. It looked like it had walked straight from a nightmare. Straight from the deepest parts of the Seven Hells.

The crisp air was laced with a pungent, rotting smell. My eyes watered. I couldn't move. Its head jerked towards me, six soulless eyes catching the firelight. It stood over ten feet tall on eight, insect-like legs. The sharp pincers of its mouth gaped opened, and a series of clicks echoed through the night, like bones clicking underwater. Every hair on my body stood on end.

MOVE, the voice in my head screamed. I turned and ran, pumping my shaky legs as fast as they could carry me. My power was drained. I'd used every drop on the Commander. I had no weapon. I was *prey*.

The thing screeched, scuttling after me unnaturally. Solas intercepted the beast, broadsword gripped in his hand. He swung it in a wide arc, bringing it down towards the insect-like monster. It dodged, slashing at Solas with its forward legs. They looked sharper than any sword. I hid behind a tree, pressing my back against its rough bark to stay upright. I placed a hand over my rapid heartbeat and tried to steady my breath. Cerilla caught my eye from where she was hidden behind a tree near mine. Her eyes were wide as she pressed her finger to her lips, gesturing for me to stay quiet.

I peered around the tree. Solas was splattered in blood; whether it was his blood or the creature's, I wasn't sure. The thing attacked him and Solas's sword collided with the creature's leg. Its screech sent a chill to my bones as one of its legs dropped to the ground, dark liquid spraying from the stump. The monster stood on its back four legs, lashing out in blind rage with the others. The blow caught Solas and sent him crashing through the undergrowth. Bright red blood sprayed in an arc as he crashed into the ground.

"No," I whispered, staggering forward. I had nothing left. No magic. No weapon. But I couldn't watch another person die because of me. Power trembled uselessly beneath my skin, thin and spent. I picked up a rock at my feet, flinging it at the monster. It spun towards me so quickly my breath hitched. Who cared if I died? I'd been willing to drown in the Dead Sea instead of being caged. I'd lived, but I still wasn't free. And now, with my death, I could take out the Commander at the same time.

"That's it, come and set me free, you ugly beast." The only warning I had was a few unnatural clicks. It lunged. I held my arms open, squeezing my eyes shut. Perhaps it ripping into my flesh would distract it for long enough for Solas and Cerilla to escape.

The air vibrated with power. Something—*someone*—snatched my arm, yanking me sideways with bruising strength. I hit the ground hard, stars bursting across my vision. When I looked up, *he* was there. The Commander of Death.

His eyes were pure darkness swirling with an anger so palpable, it felt suffocating. The sword he gripped made my skin crawl, dark flames licking up the glinting metal.

"Stay down," he snarled, voice more animal than person. His body evaporated into shadows, disappearing.

The creature dived towards me. I froze. Its pincers opened inches from my face, breath foul and hot. It emitted a single, rattling click, then a shriek.

A blade tore through its skull, silencing it mid-scream.

Blue-black blood sprayed across me. Its eight eyes clouded to milk, body collapsing into the dirt.

The Commander yanked his sword free with a moist squelch before jumping off its back and landing in front of me.

"Do you have a fucking death wish?" he growled, fury bleeding through every word.

"The thought of taking you down with me was too good to ignore," I said with a glare.

He laughed—a sharp, startled sound that made him look unhinged. "Clever girl. Though, I had not realised I would have to stop you from killing *yourself*."

He didn't wait for me to reply, gripping my bicep and pulling me to my feet. I gritted my teeth against the bruising grip of his hand against my tender arm.

"What is that?" I asked, staring at the dead creature. He ignored me, shoving me towards his nightmarish horse instead.

"We need to move. Now," he snapped towards the others. Cerilla was wrapping a bandage around Solas's chest where a gashed oozed.

"That was brave of you Lyra, thank you," Solas said, catching my eyes over the fire.

"No, it was fucking stupid." The Commander glared over his shoulder at me, squeezing my arm tighter.

"I will start packing up—"

"Leave the tents," the Commander interrupted Cerilla. "Get on your fucking horses."

As if to punctuate his urgency, a series of clicks echoed in the distance. A shiver ran up my spine. There were more of those things out there in the dark. Cerilla's hands stilled for a moment. She hurried to tie the bandage before jogging to Sugar, her grey and white mare.

The Commanders' hands circled my waist, throwing me up on the horse as if I were nothing. The horse broke into a gallop the moment his body shifted into the saddle behind me. The others followed close behind. The forest blurred around us. The horse's gallop was a living thunder beneath us. I could still smell the creature's blood on my skin. Acidic, metallic, wrong.

"Next time," the Commander growled near my ear, his voice a blade against the dark, "I'll keep you fucking chained to this saddle."

"You should have let it eat me," I muttered. "Would've saved you the trouble."

His arm tightened around my waist. "Don't tempt me, Drownling." His hand hadn't strayed from my body since he killed the beast. As if he thought I would throw myself into the darkness. The only sound was the pounding of hooves and the chilling clicking sounds bleeding from the darkness. I gripped the pommel of the saddle with white knuckles, looking up at the stars blurring above us through the treetops, begging for this night to end.

Twenty-Two
Waterfall

Morning brought no comfort, only the memory of shadows, monsters, and the weight of survival. The sun shone bright in the sky, almost mockingly. Golden light filtered through the towering trees, warming my skin in a way that felt almost sinful after the night of terror I had endured. I didn't think I'd ever grow used to that warmth. It almost made the dangers of Lumireth worth enduring.

The night had felt endless and terrifying. The Commander had driven us through the forest, galloping hard while those creatures hunted our trail. Only when the first blush of dawn spread across the horizon did we slow to a canter and he had stopped holding onto me. Apparently, the monsters only came out at night. My hips ached more than my arm, and I both longed for and dreaded getting off this damn horse. I had never heard of a creature like the one from last night. It felt like something the Iron Guard would have included in their lessons, but maybe I hadn't been in training long enough to learn about such monsters.

Winston came to an abrupt stop, and I tipped forwards

in the saddle before slamming backwards against the Commander. He growled in reaction to the contact, but his large hand gripped my waist to steady me.

We were in a small clearing of pink and purple wildflowers; the shade of the surrounding trees allowed the soft breeze to cool the sweat from my skin. I felt disgusting. I had never gone this long without bathing. I was covered in blackish-blue blood and smelled as horrid as the monster who had bled over me. The saddle shifted as the Commander leapt from the horse. Solas stood next to his, stretching his arms above his head as Cerilla sat down amongst the flowers.

I slung my numb legs over the saddle, sliding off the horse in the most ungraceful way possible. Instead of my legs catching me, they crumbled beneath me and I fell to the ground. The Commander chuckled at me before walking towards his sister.

Asshole. I glared at the darkness crawling up his body from the forest, as if bringing him secrets. I could almost still feel their icy tendrils clawing at my skin. Solas sat in the grass next to me, handing me a piece of bread and a canteen of water.

"Thank you," I mumbled.

Solas rubbed the back of his neck, grimacing at the smear of dried blood. He was covered in the same dark blue blood as me, mixed with his own. I picked at the bread, chewing it and chasing it down with a gulp of water.

"What does a Skathari call a Fae?"

I didn't answer, raising an eyebrow at him and taking another bite of the bread.

"A Fae-vourite snack." His grin didn't falter when I didn't laugh, his own chuckle filling the silence.

"Is that what that thing was? A Skathari?" I stumbled

over the word. The Fae accent had a way of making words sound beautiful. I had completely butchered it.

He nodded, stealing a glance over his shoulder at the Commander and Cerilla before lowering his voice. "Come on, I know you are curious."

"I didn't know such beasts existed."

"There are many monsters plaguing our lands." He leant forwards, leveling his eyes on me. "But you are going to help fix that."

"Me?" My voice turned high-pitched. What was *I* going to do to help? If anything, last night should have showed them I would be useless at fighting their monsters. I couldn't even fight my own.

"The weapons—"

"Solas!" The Commander was suddenly there, cutting off Solas's words. Solas gave him an easy smile, unflinching against his glare.

"Cerilla will fix your wound now." Solas chuckled softly before standing and walking towards Cerilla.

"Get up," the Commander growled, crossing his tattooed arms over his broad chest and glaring down at me. He had saved my life last night, yet somehow that made me hate him more.

"Do I need to use the bargain?" One corner of his mouth twitched into a lopsided smirk, but the threat in his voice was clear.

Venom pooled in my gaze as I stood, imagining what it would feel like to make him bleed. He turned, walking through the field of flowers, clearly expecting me to follow. I imagined my axe sinking into the shifting muscles of his back. If I ever saw my axe again, that's the first thing I would be doing.

We left the clearing, the trees above us whispering in a

warm breeze that scattered sunlight across the forest floor. I tilted my head back, marvelling at the serenity of the lush greenery. Through the branches, I caught glimpses of the endless blue above. Lumireth's sky stretched far and wide. Though, it wasn't entirely clear today; grey clouds gathered in the direction we were heading, bruising the horizon.

I lowered my gaze just in time to avoid colliding into the Commander. I stopped short, my hands shooting out as I nearly faceplanted into the wall of muscle that was his back. He exhaled sharply, the sound halfway between a sigh and a growl. My hands had only touched him for a moment, but it was a moment too long.

"If you got your head out of the clouds, you might not be so clumsy."

"Your sky is clear and your sun shines. It's beautiful." I said, my voice hollow and distant as I stared above me. I felt his glare on my face, yet I refused to let him darken this for me.

"I do not like the sun," he muttered.

Why would he appreciate the sun when he was pure darkness?

"Why do they call you the Commander of Death?"

"You don't know?" he asked, an eyebrow quirking. But my eyes darted past him and my words died. Sparkling water gushed down a sheer wall of stone, tumbling into a basin below. I stepped past the Commander, surprised that he didn't follow me to the water's edge. Mist hung in the air, kissing my skin and scattering sunlight into fractured rainbows that danced across the surface. The soft grass gave way to smooth pebbles as I grew closer, crouching by the edge. The water was so clear I could see smooth stones beneath the surface. It glittered with impossible colours, faint blues and silvers that rippled when I reached out. My fingertips brushed the surface, and it hummed.

"Bathe. You reek of death."

The commander didn't even look at me. He'd turned his back, sitting near the bank with his gaze fixed on the path we'd come from. I crinkled my nose. Unfortunately, he wasn't wrong. The stench of Skathari blood clung to my skin like rot. After checking he wasn't looking at me, I peeled my clothes off. They stuck to me uncomfortably, crusted with dried blood and dirt. The water was cool against my skin, the pebbles beneath my feet as smooth and soft as they looked. I scrubbed at my skin before submerging myself under the water. For the first time in days, I felt clean. Energised despite the sleepless night.

The Commander was a monster in his own right, but he was different to the evil I was used to. I was naked less than two meters away from him and he hadn't so much as looked my way. It was strange. Most men couldn't help themselves.

I had sung to him last night and brushed my lips against his. It was the same thing I had done to Orin and the Fae warrior, but I'd been able to twist something inside their minds until all they saw was me.

Why didn't it work on him?

My power had slid off him like water over stone. It was clear he wasn't like most men, maybe that was what made him *more* dangerous.

He sat there amongst the grass with his back turned to me, either keeping guard or making sure I didn't run. Either way, his silence brought a strange sense of safety after last night.

A towel and a folded set of clothes materialised from the darkness on the bank like a gift I wouldn't thank him for.

I waded out quickly, drying myself before slipping into

dark blue riding pants and a simple black blouse with loose sleeves. Fresh socks and boots followed, and for the first time in days, I felt almost human again.

"Are you... alright?" The Commander's back was still to me, his voice clear and sure but, he seemed to shift uncomfortably.

My laughter rang through the air like a cracked mirror catching the light. Jagged and broken.

"I need you to be cooperative. So, I apologise. For taking away your voice, and for the pain my shadows caused."

His words hung between us like a branch waiting for me to grasp it. Thin, fragile, and possibly a trap. I stared at him, dumbfounded; no man had ever apologised to me before. Maybe my kiss had affected him after all. But when his eyes turned to me, there was no iridescent sheen shining back at me. Just those soulless, dark pits.

"You killed the only man who had ever loved me, and you killed my friend. Fuck your apologies." I clenched my fists at my sides, nails digging into my palms.

He scoffed and the corners of his mouth returned to that arrogant smirk. "That man was under your spell; he did not love *you*. And your *friend* was about to shove his sword through your chest for being what you are."

The sheen in Orin's eyes flashed in my mind. He had looked at me like he was waiting for my command. It's because he *was*.

Something splintered in my chest because *I* had threaded those words into him with my magic. He didn't love me. Orin *and* Bohdi died because of me. I unclasped my shaky fists and wrapped my arms around myself to hold the frayed edges together.

"That's right, Little Drownling." His words grated over

me, pulling every bit of self-loathing to the surface. "It was your fault."

"You should have let them kill me." My voice cracked with tears that burnt behind my eyes, but I refused to let them fall. Not in front of him.

"No." His voice was low and steady. "I need you alive."

My chest tightened. *He* was the reason I was still breathing, the reason the monster inside me hadn't been silenced.

The edges of my vision darkened and that was the only warning I got. I moved before I knew what I was doing. My hand lashed out, nails sharpening mid-motion as I aimed to claw the smirk from his face.

His hand caught my wrist in a bruising grip. His other hand reached up to tuck the damp strands of my hair behind my ear. His touch sent a shiver through my body. My fingernails had darkened, pointing into lethal tips. My eyes widened, and as quickly as they had come, they shrunk to my normal, blunted tips. The Commander studied me, his jaw clenching and unclenching. He released my arm, fingers loosening.

"You don't know what you are, do you?" He asked, gaze searching me for answers I didn't possess.

"Do you?" I shot back, glaring up at him as the silence stretched between us. His knowing smirk was infuriating. My fingers twitched, itching to claw at him again. "What am I? Why do you need my power? Where did the Skathari come from? Are there other monsters? How am I meant to—"

"Stop," the Commander growled. He grasped my chin with his thumb and pointer finger, roughly tilting my face towards his.

The questions had poured from me like a flood through

broken gates. I needed to know. If he was going to refuse to let me die, I needed to know what I was living for.

"You want answers, Little Drownling?" he mused, fingers squeezing harder. "Earn them. Every time you obey me, I'll indulge you in a truth."

The Commander of Death *knew* what I was. He knew why the Iron Guard wanted me dead. Why I could drown men and sing them to their knees. He knew about my connection to the Soul Relics. And *I* knew nothing. What choice did I have?

"Fine," I gritted through clenched teeth.

"Good girl, now go back to the clearing and get on my horse." His hand dropped from my face, and I pushed past him towards the clearing. His low chuckle followed me, dark and amused. My arms wrapped tighter around my body, as if I could hold the pieces of myself together.

Twenty-Three

The Storm

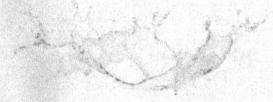

I stomped over the wildflowers, leaving a path of destruction to the damn horse. I gripped the saddle and hauled myself up the side of the enormous beast. It reared beneath me, but I clung on and pulled myself onto its back.

"Good girl," the Commander praised, mounting the horse behind me. I hated the small thrill that coiled in my stomach from his praise. His powerful thighs gripped the horse with commanding strength, pressing in tightly against me. Cerilla and Solas were already on their horses, locked in a heated discussion that had stopped the moment I had entered the clearing. The Commander kicked the beast's side as he took off. Every surge of the animal beneath us rocked my sore hips forward, forcing my body to move in time with his. The saddle bit into tender muscles already aching, and I could feel every breath he took, every shift of muscle, as if I were an extension of him. I was trapped between the beast's pounding stride and the iron heat of his body. The forest blurred around us in a rush of green and gold. Sunlight filtered through the trees, scattering patterns across wildflowers and moss below, as if nature itself refused to stay still. But the growing clouds looked like they would drown out the sun's heat any moment.

"You get one question," he said suddenly, his voice low and close. But I had a thousand questions. I stayed quiet for a moment, thinking what to ask. I felt like he wouldn't tell me what I was even if I asked.

"Why do you need me?" I asked, but the underlying question bled through. *Why not just let me die?*

"What a waste of a question," he scoffed, hand clenching around the reins until his knuckles turned white.

"Your power imbued into weapons can kill my enemy," he answered.

I hadn't expected him to tell me the truth, and it only fuelled my fire for answers.

"What does it mean to imbue a weapon? And who is your enemy?"

A soft, mocking sound escaped him, almost a chuckle. "Greedy little thing," he murmured, leaning close enough for his breath to tickle the shell of my ear. "You are reaching for answers you haven't earned."

I ground my teeth together. Of course he wouldn't keep answering my questions.

We rode in silence for hours, my muscles straining from trying to keep from pressing against his body.

The sky was dimming, not from nightfall but from storm clouds. Thick, heavy clouds churned above us, laced with veins of silver lightning that flickered like a warning from the estranged Gods.

"Gods, what is that?" The clouds above rumbled, a sound so deep I felt it in my bones.

"It's strange that *you* say, 'Gods' all of the time." Another question shut down.

Solas cantered up beside us on his speckled horse. "What is your plan?" Solas gestured up to the swirling clouds that reminded me of Riven.

"Scout ahead for coverage," the Commander ordered.

Solas gave a curt nod, squeezing his heels against the horse and flicking the reins. He sped off through the trees, towards the mountain ranges at our side. The Commander pulled back on the horse's reins, Winston. In my hours of boredom on his back, I had decided that was his name. Winston slowed to keep pace next to Cerilla, who stared at the sky with wild eyes.

"It's going to be alright, Ceri," The Commander grumbled towards his sister.

She gave him a tight-lipped smile, but the fear didn't budge from her eyes. The sky lit up with a white blinding light followed by a loud crack that echoed through the trees. I gasped in shock, our horses rearing beneath us.

Solas galloped towards us. "Follow me!" he yelled over the rumbling. We launched forwards, the gallop of the horses' hooves not loud enough to drown out the rumbling above us. A drop of water landed on my hand, and I glanced up at the clouds. Another bright flash of lightning flared, branching off in several directions before a deafening boom made me jump. The sky opened, heavy drops of water pelting down over us. My clothes were instantly drenched. I gripped the saddle, squeezing my legs for extra grip. We raced through the forest, towards the mountains. Solas slowed as we got closer, leading us to a gap in the rockface.

The Commander swung out of the saddle behind me, gathering the reins of the horses to lead them out of the storm.

I wiped a hand down my face to clear the water from my eyes while the Commander helped Cerilla from her horse. She didn't just look frightened anymore; she looked almost sick.

I gritted my teeth as he left me sitting in the saddle helplessly. Instead of getting me off the horse, he guided his sister into the darkness of the cave.

I threw myself over the saddle, slipping awkwardly, but catching myself before I fell.

I stood at the entrance of the cave, watching the trees bend against the wind and the sky flash violently with branches of white light that made me flinch.

"Come away from there, it isn't safe," Solas said from behind me.

I was almost mesmerised in its destructive beauty. Lumireth was beautiful one moment and trying to kill us the next. I took a small step back from the storm, but kept my eyes trained on the angry sky.

"Earlier, you said I am to help with the monster problem. How?"

"You're going to get me in trouble," Solas sighed from beside me. I expected him to say nothing, the sound of the rain pounding into the ground stretching between us.

"I do not know what history Mortals are taught but there is a prophecy about—"

"The Sea Goddess rising again. I know. But what does that have to do with me?"

"The Commander is the only one who can kill the monsters. But once you absorb the Soul Relics, imbuing your power into weapons will let us all stand a chance. You could save so many of my people's lives."

"Why can the Commander kill them?" A loud rumble of thunder followed by bright streaks of light made me startle.

Solas gently placed his hand around my arm and pulled

me backwards into the cave. "Come on, it is dangerous and will last *hours*." He led me further into the cave, past the nervous horses and into the narrow entrance where the Commander and Cerilla had disappeared.

THE FIRE THREW RESTLESS SHADOWS ACROSS THE CAVE walls, their shapes flickering in and out of the dark. We were sheltered, but the storm still raged outside. The thunder wasn't softened by the stone. It rolled through the mountain like the growl of something ancient.

Cerilla paced near the back of the cave, fingers twisting nervously in her dark hair. Solas lounged against a rock, a blood bag in hand, the picture of calm in contrast to her restlessness. "Thank you, brother," Cerilla said, taking a metal travel cup from the Commander's hands before frowning.

"I'm sorry it's cold," he murmured as he guided her to a blanket that he had laid out for her.

"It's fine." She took a small sip, forcing a smile to mask the grimace that flickered across her face. "The ingredients will still work."

My chest tightened in a way I didn't recognise, and I turned away before I could see more of it. Before I could watch him soften, before I could watch the Commander of Death become something other than my captor. What would it feel like to have someone care for you?

I glanced back, curiosity betraying me. The Commander was helping her get comfortable when Solas caught me watching them.

"Cerilla's powers are blocked during storms," he explained quietly, voice barely above a whisper.

"Solas," the Commander growled in warning, shooting a glare at the warrior that then settled on me. A shiver shot through me; did he see me as a threat to his sister?

"May I?" I asked, stepping closer. Cerilla hesitated before passing me the cup. The bitter scent of herbs hit me like a wall. "What is it?"

"A sleeping brew," she said softly. "Not having access to my power makes me... anxious. It's easier to rest through them."

I nodded, closing my eyes. Power thrummed through my veins, wild and familiar. The water in the cup whispered to me, waiting for my command. I drew in a breath and began to hum, the melody soft and haunting, the kind that made the air itself listen.

Heat, I told it. Within moments, the surface of the brew rippled and steamed. The tin cup seared against my palms. Cerilla took the cup from me slowly, staring down at it as if it might bite her.

"Thanks," she said quietly before sitting next to Solas to drink her tea. Perhaps she was just on edge from the storm. But the way she avoided my eyes made me wonder if it wasn't just the storm that made her nervous.

Hours passed. Hours of endless rumbling from the sky. The rain had eased, enough for the distinctive clicking of a Skanthi to echo through the trees outside between booms of thunder. A sound I had never heard before, an eerie rattle had also joined the chorus of horrifying noises. I didn't know what it was, but I knew in my bones it was another monster. At this stage, I wished I could go to sleep. My nightmares would feel like a reprieve. The others had long been asleep, the fire embers barely glowing. As soon as night had fallen, Solas had extinguished it. He said it would attract more unwanted friends.

I sat up with a frustrated sigh, running my hands through my damp hair.

"Can't sleep?" The Commander's voice came from the darkness. It was low and rough, but softer than I'd ever heard it. The fire had burned down to embers, painting him in faint orange light. No shadows withered over his skin, and it made him look almost normal.

"Not with that noise," I murmured, nodding towards the mouth of the cave. If I closed my eyes and a monster attacked, would I even wake before it ripped me limb from limb?

"I have a question for you," he mused, muscles flexing as he rested one arm behind his head.

I said nothing, hoping he would leave me alone. But he asked anyway.

"When I took you, Cerilla said the wounds on your arms were older," he stated simply. "*Self-inflicted,* perhaps."

My jaw tightened. I wasn't going to tell him I'd done them to myself, that I was so ashamed of what I was that I had tried to bleed it from myself to save Riven. "You're asking questions you haven't earnt." I threw his words back at him. Gods, I hoped Cerilla hadn't seen the scars on my back.

He chuckled, not the mocking sound I was used to, but a genuine laugh. Its rich timbre tones made my toes curl and made me shift uncomfortably.

"Do you have a question?" he asked after a moment.

The silence stretched between us. It was thick and uneasy, but not hostile. For once, he didn't look like the Commander of Death. He just looked... haunted. I could ask so many questions. But I was beyond exhausted, and I couldn't handle the weight of answers right now.

"Do you ever sleep?" I asked quietly.

Another chuckle. Gods damn it, why did I like that sound?

"That's what you're asking me?"

I glared at him through the dim orange light, and his grin told me he could see it.

"Not when I can help it," he answered. I wasn't expecting him to answer, or to overly care about his response. But I sat up and brought my knees to my chest.

"Nightmares?" I wondered, almost curiously.

"Memories," he corrected. His eyes flicked to the mouth of the cave, where rain still dripped from the stone. "Sometimes the two are the same."

I hesitated before speaking again, my voice barely a whisper against the rainfall. "I get nightmares too."

His eyes found mine once more. "I know."

The words hung there, cold and sharp, until he added, "I can tell. You exist like a shadow of yourself." He said the words so gentle that gooseflesh pebbled on my skin. "You hesitate before speaking, then flinch for speaking your mind. You move like someone waiting to be struck, and you keep throwing yourself at death as if you're begging it to take you. Yesterday, when I pulled you back, you didn't *want* saving. You wanted to die. Whatever made you that way, I'm not surprised you have nightmares."

I should have looked away. I didn't. His words settled under my skin, heavy and invasive, like fingers pressing against an old bruise to see how much it still hurt.

No one had ever said those things out loud before. They had seen the obedience. The silence. The broken girl who learned when not to speak. But he had named the rest of it — the waiting, the flinching, the wanting it to end. And that terrified me more than his threats ever had. There was something behind his voice that made me stare at him in a new light. It wasn't a threat, not mockery, not sarcasm. It sounded like empathy spoken by someone who had struggled and saw the same demons staring back at him.

"You don't know what you're talking about," I snapped, though the bite in my voice dulled as soon as it left me. His gaze didn't harden. It didn't soften either. It simply *waited*.

I tore my eyes away first, fixing them on the dying embers. On anything that wasn't the quiet understanding in his expression.

"You don't get to look at me like that," I said, lower now. "You know nothing about me."

Because if he did... If anyone ever truly did, then I wouldn't be able to pretend I was okay. And I had built my entire existence on pretending.

He stared at me for a long moment, contemplating. As though he were going to say something else, but instead, he leaned back against the rock, settling in. "Go to sleep, Drownling," he murmured, though it didn't sound like an order this time. "I'll keep you safe from the monsters."

I laid back down and turned away from him, but a faint smile ghosted my lips. The storm roared outside, but inside the cave, something between us changed. I still hated him. Still wanted to sink my axe into his neck and watch the blood spray like rain. Because hatred was easier than admitting that, for one unguarded moment, he was the one person in this world who had truly seen me.

TWENTY-FOUR

NIGHTMARES

The sea was on fire. Smoke bled into the sky, and blood-stained waves clawed at a crumbling cliff. A woman stood at its edge, wearing black battle armour with her silver hair braided beneath a crown of shells that shimmered like moonlight on glass. Her eyes were the most vibrant blue I had ever seen, brighter than mine. Unnatural.

"Hello, my love," she whispered, tears swimming in her eyes.

"No. I am your death."

A blade struck through her chest, a black flash of steel. It was so fast I didn't see who wielded it, only the spray of blood and the woman fall to the ground.

Blood poured into the ocean like spilled ink, staining the waves. Her crown tumbled from her head, falling. Vanishing beneath the water's surface. Blood, dark and oily, spilled from her mouth as her face began to change. Shift. Twist. Until it was my own. I was the one gasping for air, sinking to my knees.

"Find the pieces!" I screamed, my voice breaking into

layered echoes. Mine, hers, something older. The sword left my chest with a wet rasp, blood spilling from the open wound as I slumped onto the ground. My lifeless eyes snapped open.

I jolted awake, hands clasping my chest. I was in the cave. There was no gaping hole in my chest. It was a nightmare. The fire had burned down to ash. I knew before looking that the Commander was gone, and somehow that made me feel more alone. Cerilla laid at the back of the cave, still fast asleep. Solas was nowhere to be seen either.

I pushed to my feet, rubbing the sleep from my eyes and telling my heart to stop pounding. The air smelled clean, and there was no more rumbling thunder or pounding of rain. The storm had passed. Dawn's sunlight bled into the mouth of the cave, painting the rocks in a soft glow.

I walked to the cave's entrance, drawn to the light like something starved. The three horses were resting. Wherever Solas and the Commander were, they couldn't be far.

The sky was shifting from bruised purple to soft oranges and pinks. The sheer beauty of it made my nightmare seem almost distant. Almost.

It was rather arrogant of them to leave me behind with the opportunity to run, but where would I go?

I sat against the rocks, leaning my head back to watch the sky, mesmerised by its colours. The woman from my dream was the same ghost that led me to my axe. Was she trying to show me who had killed her?

"Are you hurt?" The Commander's voice startled me, and I jolted upright. My breath hitched. He walked through the trees, muscles covered in dark blue blood, black curls plastered to his forehead. Solas walked next to him, covered in the same gore.

"You were killing Skathari?" I asked, my voice raw.

He ignored me, kneeling in front of me. His black eyes roamed my body as if checking for injuries. Solas gave me a small nod before walking into the cave.

"You do not look injured," the Commander mused as he pursed his lips, and drew his eyebrows together in thought.

"What are you talking about?" I asked, crossing my arms over my chest and staring back up at the rising sun.

"You screamed," he murmured, voice roughened by exhaustion.

Had I screamed in my sleep? My cheeks heated, unable to look in his eyes.

"Ah, you were asleep," he murmured, voice rough with exhaustion. When I didn't answer, he turned away, rummaging through Winston's saddlebag until he found a towel. The muscles in his back flexed beneath drying streaks of blood as he wiped himself clean, movements steady, unhurried. I cursed inwardly when he looked up, catching me watching him with rapt attention.

"Get on the horse," he said suddenly and I groaned inwardly.

"I would rather choke."

"I could arrange that." His smirk turned into a dark chuckle as I glared at him. I should have been thankful for the rest the storm had allowed. I ran my hand along Winston's mane before placing my foot in the stirrup before swinging my leg over the beast and scrambling up onto his back.

I looked at the Commander expectantly. He quirked an eyebrow at me and crossed his arms across his broad chest, muscles bunching under the strain. I swallowed hard, looking away, almost disappointed that he hadn't praised me for doing what I was told.

"Go on then, ask your question."

I lit up, sitting a little straighter in the saddle.

"What do you know about the Soul Relics?"

He glared at me for a moment before tilting his head to the side, assessing me. "Not specific enough."

"Are they connected to me?" I asked wearily.

He gave me a stiff nod, jaw clenching, eyes turning black for a moment before he blinked it away. My stomach twisted into knots, and I knew without doubt that my axe was a Soul Relic.

"Are you trying to find them?"

He gave another stiff nod before swinging himself up onto the horse behind me. The smell of night air and caramel mingled with the crisp morning breeze, enveloping my senses, and I hated myself for breathing deeper.

Cerilla's light-hearted laugh echoed over the rocks as she walked out. Solas followed her with a large grin across his face that dissipated under the Commander's glare.

"We are ready," Solas said before swinging up onto the saddle. The Commander waited for his sister to mount her horse before whipping Winston's reins, taking off into the damp forest.

HOURS OF RIDING HAD PASSED, AND THE FOREST HAD begun to change. Slowly but subtly. The overgrown path wound through ancient trees, their limbs arching overhead like brittle bones. The once-lively sounds of the woods had drowned into a quiet so complete, it felt like its own presence, dense and oppressive. We trailed behind Solas and Cerilla, their usual banter replaced by stiff postures and unspoken tension. The air grew colder, heavier. The forest pressed down on us, almost insufferably close. Unseen eyes lingered in the shadows that leached between dying trees, watching. The silence clung to my skin like the stench of rot that drifted faintly in the stale air. My knuckles whitened on the edge of the saddle. A branch cracked to the left of us. I whipped towards the sound, my silver hair flying around my shoulders.

"Just a branch," the Commander murmured from behind me.

"Something feels wrong," I whispered. It felt like spiders were crawling over my skin.

"We are in the Mourning Woods. It feels *wrong* because it *is*." His voice sent an unnatural shudder through me. "This is where the veil is the thinnest. The Seven Hells and the six heavens bleed into our world here," he whispered back almost mockingly. "Things slip through, like monsters." Fear coiled deep within my core. The Commander pulled on Winston's reins, bringing the beast to a halt, though it chortled restlessly, as if being here startled it as much as me.

"We are stopping here?" I shrilled. His chuckle reverberated from behind me, radiating into my body.

"You are. I will be going the rest of the way alone."

I felt the subtle shift of his body as he dismounted behind me, the warmth of him vanishing only to return in the press of large hands encircling my waist. He lifted me from the saddle with unsettling ease, as if I weighed nothing at all. His touch lingered just a moment too long as he sat me down. His fingers brushed my ribs before slipping away, slow, deliberate. When I looked up, his eyes were already on mine. Dark, unreadable, and far too close.

"You are safe for now, Little Drownling," he murmured. His voice was low, rough with something unspoken, and I could feel it settle into my bones like a promise... or a threat.

But it was the unexpected ease that seeped into my body that surprised me. He had muttered a word I had never felt before: safe. I had never known safety, never been allowed the luxury of it. How was it that, in the presence of the Commander of Death, standing in a forest filled with monsters, I believed him?

I swallowed and took a step back from him, the stale air rushing between us. One side of his mouth twitched into a predatory smirk.

"Clever little thing," he mused before walking towards Solas and Cerilla. "Patrol the perimeter the moment night falls and do not let anything happen to my prisoner." My lip sneered at the word. It was another reminder that I wasn't free.

"You are *not* going alone," Cerilla interjected, crossing her arms over her chest.

"You both cannot come with me. I need her," he said with a gesture over his shoulder towards me, "alive and far away from the Fates."

"Solas will stay, and I will accompany you, brother." She began gathering weapons from the satchel attached to Sugar.

"No, I will not risk you like that. You stay here with Solas."

"No," she said, voice tight with emotion. "You protect everyone, all the time. Just this once, let me protect you."

The Commander sighed, running his hand through his dark curls.

"Fine," he muttered. His shadows curled tighter around him, thickening like armour, as if they could smother the flicker of emotion in his sister's voice.

They left Solas and me standing beneath the decaying husks of trees to set up camp. With every step the

Commander took into the gloom, questions unfurled through my chest. I needed answers. I busied myself watering the horses, but the silence pressed in, heavy and unnatural. Solas crouched by the fire, stirring grains in a metal pot over the open flame. He hummed to himself like we weren't surrounded by rot and the crawling sensation of eyes watching from the depths of the woods. Apparently, nothing lived here, not even woodland animals for Solas to cook. The Mourning Woods were utterly dead. His nonchalance grated against the eerie stillness. Every step I took sounded too loud, and every crackle of the fire made me flinch.

We ate in the eerie silence. Solas didn't seem to mind, and I was too scared the sound of my voice would alert whatever lingered in the depth of the woods to our location. The late afternoon sun shone lazily through the jagged branches, refusing to grace my skin with its warmth as if the Mourning Woods repelled even that.

Solas sat beside me on the log, the fire crackling between us.

"What are they looking for out there?" I whispered.

He gave me a sidelong glance. "Ah, you *can* speak. Thank the heavens, I thought the Commander stole your voice again." He laughed at his own comment before shovelling another spoonful of grains into his mouth. "The Commander is seeking the Fire Fates. They are dangerous creatures who know *everything*. If they don't burn you to a crisp and you can understand their riddles, that is."

I tucked that information away. A being that held every answer to every unanswered question I had was more than alluring. A part of me worried for Cerilla, the other hoped the Commander would come back with scorch marks on his stupidly handsome face. A monster should have the face of a monster, not one carved by the Gods.

"And he left me here with you? What if I run? What if I kill you?" I asked seriously.

"I am not worried. You risked your life to save mine already." He huffed a quiet laugh and gave me a knowing smile. "You do not want to admit it, but you like us."

A scoff escaped me. "Oh, how could I not like you all? I've been dragged into foreign lands as a prisoner to play a part in a war no one's explained against an unknown enemy."

He sighed before lowering his voice. "The enemy is the Seven Hells and the Gods themselves."

A shiver tore up my spine and I lowered my voice. "How is that possible? The realms were sealed when the Sea Goddess died."

He studied me, jaw tight. "Yeah, one thousand years ago. Her magic has faded, and her Relics are impossible to find to see if we can reinforce them."

I blinked, caught off guard. I opened my mouth, but the words caught in my throat. Had I weakened the veil by taking the power from the axe?

"We are fighting the monsters made by the Gods. They spill from the Mourning Woods like rot during the dark hours. That's where the Skathari come from. There are other monsters, too. Some from the Hells. But they aren't just hunting the Soul Relics. They are hunting *you*."

I couldn't breathe. "You're lying."

"I wish I were."

The fire snapped between us. The trees loomed darker now, as if they, too, were listening.

I stared at the coals, my heart pounding as the silence pressed in uncomfortably.

"Were you allowed to tell me any of this?" I asked softly.

Solas chuckled. "Absolutely not. But you saved my life and I take debts very seriously."

I stared into the fire as fear settled like ash in my lungs. It was the same reason my own people wanted me dead. The same reason the sea had sung to me. The same reason I didn't die as a girl when I'd walked into the Dead Sea.

My father and the priest, did they know? Rage twisted hot in my gut as I realised, they would have known I was connected to the Gods somehow. But beneath the hurt, something fiercer stirred. A heat I hadn't felt since Ascension when I plunged a knife through the priest's heart. I needed revenge.

My *treatments*. The endless blood lettings. Someone was using my blood. Just like they had bled the Sirens. Except, I wasn't sure I was a Siren.

The dream flashed inside my mind, the woman's face morphing and turning into mine. What did it mean? I stood, hands shaking as the anger flooding my veins had nowhere to go.

I lifted my chin, voice steady. "I want to spar."

His brow lifted and a grin tugged at his lips.

"Sure, that's my favourite way to pass the time." He stood, drawing the sword from his back and passing me the hilt.

THE LAST TRACES OF SUNLIGHT BLED THROUGH THE skeletal branches like veins of dying gold. Our breaths misted in the cooling air as we circled each other in our bare campsite. It seemed summer didn't touch the Mourning

Woods. And with our tents left behind, if it weren't for the flickering fire in the small clearing and Solas's cooking gear, it would look empty.

"Keep your stance wide," he said with lazy confidence. "I'd hate to see you fall before you've even managed to lift my blade."

I exhaled through my nose and lunged. His sword was larger and heavier than the Iron Guard's, but I managed to swing it. He dodged easily, stepping back to avoid his own blade. The steel met the ground with a hard thud, vibrating up my arms. I gritted my teeth, turning to strike him again.

"Again," he said. "But breathe before you strike."

I struck harder. Faster. Each blow sharper than the last. Anger lent me speed, and for a moment, I caught the flicker of surprise in his eyes before he twisted, grabbing my forearm and disarming me. The sword clattered to the ground.

I kicked him in the shin. He laughed, the sound loud in the silence. "Dirty move."

I snatched his sword from the ground, jaw tight. "Why did you tell me about the Relics and the monsters when it could get you in trouble?" I asked, each word bitten out between gritted teeth as I swung again.

He stepped back, missing the strike before he pressed forwards, his strikes quick and testing. "I would follow the Commander anywhere, but that doesn't mean I agree with him keeping you in the dark. You should know the danger you're in. Why we're asking for your help."

I ducked and spun and shoved the blade towards him. "I'm not being *asked*." I thrust my hand between us, the blood-bargain mark gleamed faintly in the dying light and his eyebrows rose in surprise. "I'm being *forced*."

"You chose to enter into that," he said, gesturing for me to swing the sword again.

"Before I knew what it meant!" My voice cracked, raw and trembling. But I didn't stop. The next swing of my sword was clumsy, desperate. He caught my wrist mid-strike, and the pain throbbed like an old bruise from the healed break. He held it still, his grip firm but not cruel.

His gaze softened, the humour gone. "Then learn what it means now," he said quietly. "Before it kills you, or him. Or both."

I dropped the sword, breath coming hard. Why was he trying to help me?

"That'll do for the night. The sun is setting," he said, nodding towards the deepening shadows.

I eyed the woods, my mouth drying. What sort of horrific monsters lurked nearby?

"Do not worry, I will be patrolling and using my magic to keep the monsters out."

I looked at him questioningly, and he shrugged.

"I can create a magical barrier, as long as I am patrolling, monsters cannot get through," he said confidently as he walked away.

And I'd be left alone. Either to drown in my thoughts, or—

I watched the darkness creep through the gnarled branches of the Mourning Woods and felt something inside me settle. I would find the Fire Fates, and learn the truth, whatever it cost me.

TWENTY-FIVE
FIRE FATES

I counted under my breath, matching each number to the ghost-soft fall of my feet across the dry leaves that littered the Mourning Woods. The darkness here wasn't just an absence of light—it was *alive*. It curled around me like breath, coiling between the trees, whispering things I couldn't quite hear. My power stirred beneath my skin, a restless tide responding to the primal terror prickling along my spine. I wished I had my axe, or any weapon, for that matter. I had nothing but the wild pulse of my heartbeat and the brittle resolve in my bones. I pressed myself against a tree, counting the seconds it would take Solas to get to the other side of his perimeter.

One... Two... Three... I slipped past the path Solas had been patrolling and walked straight into his magic. The barrier shimmered at the point of contact, invisible but solid, resisting me like a living thing. It clung to my skin as I pushed through, thick and warm as honey. Power thrummed through me, sharp and electric, raising the hair on my arms as the ward yielded and snapped closed behind me. I ran into the dark woods, praying to the Gods that

Solas hadn't felt me move through his barrier. The woods swallowed me whole. Leaves crunched like brittle bones beneath my boots, and I slowed, reaching out blindly, skimming the bark of the trees to stay upright. I didn't even know where to look. The Fire Fates would be close to our camp. But where? The sky was starless, a yawning void above me like even the heavens refused this place. Like the Commander's eyes.

A twig snapped behind me, and the woods held their breath. I froze, and the hair on my arms lifted ominously, as if I were being watched. Slowly, I turned, eyes straining against the black. Nothing. But the silence that followed was suffocating. *Laughter* echoed. Warped and inhuman.

Run. The voice whispered through the stillness, and instinct took over before thought could follow. Branches clawed at me. My feet pounded against the ground. The laughter followed. I ran through the suffocating darkness for what felt like forever, stumbling, colliding with tree trunks, skin burning where bark tore at me.

I came to a stop, leaning on my knees and panting as nausea clawed up my throat. Perhaps I would find nothing but my death in these woods, after all. But a small part of me didn't want to die anymore. I just wanted answers.

Cold breath brushed the back of my neck like a whisper from the grave. I stilled. I turned, tears pricking my eyes. Nothing but darkness and dead trees. My heart thundered against the deadly quiet, eyes scanning the dark for monsters.

"Lyra..." a soft whisper slithered through the silence. I spun, and my heart lurched into my throat.

She hovered over me with hollow eyes and translucent hair drifting as if underwater.

The ghost from my dreams. The same unearthly

woman who had led me to the axe. She lifted a hand and turned, gliding between dead trunks. If she meant to kill me, she would have done it already. Last time, she'd led me to power. She turned and wove through the dead trees.

Her unearthly glow illuminated the trees around us, and I was grateful to be able to see. My feet moved forwards, following her. To a horrible death? I wasn't sure. But I wanted to know who she was.

She led me towards a mountain that loomed, jagged and foreboding against the void-slick sky. Muted light leaked through the trees like a dying star from the base of the mountain, flickering through the dense trees. The light spilling from the cave wasn't warmth, not really. But it was the only light I'd seen in this forsaken place.

My boots slammed through the dead leaves as I followed the ghost—every step sounded like a gunshot in the silence. My legs burned with each frantic step, but still, I ran. I stumbled, hands out for balance—

Only to feel something wet and sleek beneath my fingers, a scream lodging in my throat. I snatched my hand back and ran as fast as I could. An unearthly snapping sound echoed against the darkness, right behind me. Then another followed—warped, and wrong.

The unearthly woman disappeared into the cave's entrance and I dove after her. I skidded on my stomach and my breath whooshed out of my lungs before I rolled onto my back, panting, bracing for—

Nothing. No monsters loomed behind me. No teeth. No claws. Only eerie stillness. I sat up, scrambling backwards. Each ragged breath filled my nose with the sharp scent of sulphur.

"Who are you?" I panted, turning to the woman. But she was gone. Nothing remained but rocks and an unnatural orange light flickering from deeper in the cave. I glanced back towards the woods, quiet. Watching. The trees leaned like mourners frozen in grief, their twisted limbs silhouetted against the starless sky. No footsteps marked the path behind me. Only mine. Was I imagining it all? My chest heaved as silence rushed back in, heavier than before. No laughter. No whispers. Maybe I was alone all along. I let out an uneasy sigh before pushing to my feet and walking deeper into the cave.

Lava dripped lazily from cracks lining the caves, like blood dripping from an open wound. It hissed where it met the stone floor. The molten liquid cast the cave in a flickering, hellish glow that pulled sweat from my skin. I walked slowly towards a bubbling pool of molten lava as steam coiled from the hissing liquid. The heat rolled off it in waves, blistering my skin. The glowing liquid rippled unnaturally, and my steps faltered.

The liquid seemed to bend, two heads breaking the surface. Their skin was cracked and glowing like smouldering embers, hair slick and clinging to their lithe, feminine forms. Their eyes opened, twin infernos that locked onto me with an intensity that made my spine arch. The lava lapped at their rocklike skin just beneath their breasts as they watched me. It felt like they were looking into me. The dark-haired one tilted its head. Her lips did not move, but her whisper slid across the cave like silk soaked in poison. "Maraveth."

The blonde echoed it, and the words layered over the first, like two instruments playing different melodies in the same key.

"You seek truth..."

Goosebumps prickled down my arms. I stumbled back a step, rubbing sweaty palms against my shirt. The lava clung to their skin like silk, glowing veins of flame pulsing beneath their cracked flesh.

"Are you... Are you the Fates?" My voice barely made it past the heat-stifled air.

"Obviously," they said in perfect, chilling unison. "We see all," one hissed, while the other rasped, "We see what was... What could be..."

I forced myself to swallow, though my throat felt carved from ash.

"What am I?" I asked, hating how my voice cracked.

"Not what, *who*," whispered the dark-haired one, head tilting slowly.

"*Who* am I?" I whispered the question.

"Maraveth." A bone-chilling smile spread across the cracked stone lips of the blonde one.

"The last. The first. The Soul Relics are yours," the other whispered, layered over the other. The cave spun. My stomach dropped.

"She could be the saviour of realms," the dark-haired one murmured, voice strangely soft.

"Or the destroyer, if she does not save her Fated Mate," the other cooed, overlapping and sickly sweet.

Their voices laced like venomous vines, one always curling around the other, never truly separate. My knees buckled. I swayed, sweat dripping down my neck. One of them laughed gleefully. "Maraveth, your fate is a tangled web."

"That's not my name," I whispered, the words shaking. "I'm Lyra Meridian. Daughter of King Vaylor. Princess of the Mortal Kingdom."

Their laughter crawled across my skin like insects. "You are none of those things, Maraveth." My nails dug into my palms, deep enough to sting. I understood now what Solas meant about their riddles. They were not giving me answers.

"The Mortals need to join the Fae. The Hells are rising. *You* are Maraveth. But you are also Lyra. Unite the fractured Kingdoms with vows, or all will be lost to the heat of the sun," hissed the other from behind, leaning in as if to scent me. Her words bled from the empty cave. I spun, but there was no one there. They hadn't moved from the lava, and yet they were *everywhere*.

"These are not answers!" I cried out. I had come here for information, yet all I had were more questions.

"Listen closely, Maraveth. Time is running out and you are depleted of water," the blonde taunted. "And our heat makes you weaker," the other hissed. They joined hands, glowing brighter than before. The heat pressed unbearably against my skin, my mouth as dry as sand.

"Three Relics of fractured soul..."

"...forced by a lover scorned."

"Scattered to guard... to hide... to stall..."

Their arms rose in unison and fingers tipped in fire. Their heads snapped backwards, their voices rising, screeching.

"One to wield..."

"...One to wear."

"One that bridges two broken hearts."

Their eyes burned brighter, and small rocks skittered down from the roof of the cave as the stone beneath my feet trembled.

"Only you can stop the sun, because you broke it."

A tear traced down my cheek before I could stop it. I didn't understand, but something in me did.

One laughed, a gleeful shrill that made my ears sting while the other seethed.

My hands were shaking and my mouth turned dry. I couldn't tell if I was frozen by fear... or by fate itself. Their words echoed long after their voices stopped. A large crack split open in front of me on the ground, molten liquid bubbling up from it as though it were reaching for me. I spun on my heel, running through the shaking cave as debris rained from the roof. I ran from the suffocating heat and into the cold embrace of the Mourning Woods.

The Fire Fates' laughter haunted me with every step.

Outside the cave's entrance, coolness enveloped my body like an odd comfort. My steps faltered, and bile rose in my throat. My hands grasped my knees, my stomach tensing. A heave tore up my throat, but nothing came out of my soured stomach. Absently I wiped at the tears trailing down my overheated cheeks as uncertainty threatened to burn me alive.

I took a deep breath to steady myself and almost gagged again as the smell of decay hit the back of my throat. Rot clung heavily to the cold, stagnant air as I glanced around me at the dead trees, covering my mouth and nose with my forearm. I stilled instantly. Creatures from nightmares stalked through the shadows, twisted mockeries of what once might've been men. Their black cloaks swayed with each movement as they walked without sparing me a glance. Fear brought me to a sudden stop as one passed through the flickering light of the cave. Bone jutted through torn skin, their flesh sagging in loose folds, rotting and half-melted against splintered ribs. Their eyes glowed with unnatural hunger, blazing like coals in hollow sockets. Some crawled, dragging their mutilated bodies behind them with clawed fingers slick with old blood. Others stalked upright, skeletal frames wrapped in the remains of human skin, their teeth exposed in lipless, eternal grins. In their hands, they carried swords forged not of steel, but of sharpened bone, stained dark with ancient gore. The air reeked of decay, of death left too long in the sun. And still, they kept coming... a legion of the damned, pulled from the veil's thinning grip.

A soft whimper left my lips, and I took a small step backwards. A snap broke through the heavy silence, my foot breaking a dry twig.

Unearthly glowing eyes snapped towards me. Jittered noises bounced between them, raking my nerves raw—some warped form of communication I wasn't meant to understand. They moved towards me, weaving through the dead trees with steady strides.

I was trapped. The rockface of the mountain loomed behind me and the decaying warriors in front.

Skeletal fingers grabbed my upper arm from the side, squeezing the already marred skin from the woods. A half-melted face loomed above me and maggots crawled through the liquified skin that clung to his skeletal form. I lashed out, struggling against his grip.

"No!" I screamed. Everywhere I pushed against him, my hand sank into soft, wet flesh with a cold squelch. Hands wrapped around my ankle, pulling my weight out from underneath me. A cry of terror left my lips. Dirt scraped against my body as they dragged me by my wrist, pain blooming in my shoulder from the weight of my own body struggling against the creatures' relentless pulling.

I screamed as my joint popped from its socket.

"Fight," the Commander's roar reverberated through my mind with a violent jolt,

and something deep inside me answered.

TWENTY-SIX

POISON

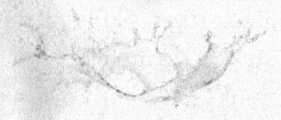

I felt a tugging in my chest, almost like a tether being drawn taut.

"Fucking fight!" the Commander roared, and I couldn't tell if I had heard it in my head.

Yes. I had to fight. *I won't let these vile creatures drag me away without a fight.* The sharp pain radiating into my shoulder was blinding. I pulled against the skeletal grip of the creature, screaming at the tearing sensation through my shoulder. I begged for my power to surface but nothing came. I couldn't control it.

I rolled, my dislocated shoulder turning at an unnatural angle, throwing the dead warrior off balance. It crashed to the side with my weight. Dragging my useless arm, I pulled myself on top of the decaying creature.

I lunged for the bone sword, fingers grazing its blood-stained hilt, only for skeletal hands to seize me, claws raking down my arms, and splitting skin with jagged bone. Fire lanced through me. Decaying fingers sank deeper, peeling flesh from bone. A raw cry tore from my throat. Beneath me, the corpse made a sickening gurgled laugh as we struggled for the weapon. It wrenched the sword from my grasp, bringing the hilt down on my head. Pain exploded across my temple, sharp and dizzying. I crumpled to the ground, clutching my head as the world tilted sideways, the trees spinning in and out of focus.

Darkness hit them first.

The Commander of Death tore from the shadows, eyes like starless pits, black veins spidering from their edges. A growl rolled out of his chest, more animal than male. An obsidian broadsword gleamed in his grip, black flames licking the blade. Steel met bone with a shriek. Bones snapped and rot peeled like wet parchment. Ash and rot burst into the air, the thing collapsing in a heap of filth. The Commander spun, disappearing into shadow and reappearing in front of another decaying monster. Their swords clashed, bone against steel. His shadows swarmed, tearing through its glowing eyes and pouring into its mouth. It slowed the creature down momentarily, enough for the Commander to swing his sword. Its head landed with a wet thump on the ground. He moved with lethal grace, cutting down the monsters. Hope flickered through my chest like a dying candle, briefly, before sputtering out as skeletal claws gripped my hair and pulled so hard, I thought my scalp would peel off. I screamed.

The Commander's lethal gaze snapped to me and he growled, baring his canines. My scalp burned, body dragging against the rough ground by nothing but my hair. I thrashed, kicking and reaching for the dead hands that gripped my hair. I couldn't reach.

The Commander ripped into the air in front of me, bursting from the darkness. His blade sunk into the creature's flesh with a sickening crunch. Dark blue gore splattered me as the creature slumped, and a whimper of relief left me as it let go of my hair.

The Commander crouched in front of me. "You are okay," he rumbled, more to himself then me.

Before I could yell at him, his eyes flared. He began to spin but, it was too late. The tip of a white, jagged sword protruded through his bare abdomen. He dropped to his knees, shadows angrily lashing out around him.

"Run," he whispered. "Get Cerilla." Dark veins spread from the sword against his skin. *Poison*.

The dead warrior grinned, half its face sloughing from exposed skull, as it planted a foot on the Commander's back. It tore the sword free with a nauseating, tearing squelch. The rest of the dead army swarmed towards us.

I gritted my teeth, digging past the pain and fear to the small thrumming of power within me. I pulled the power from my very soul. It was depleted, weak. But I took from it anyway.

My head snapped back as the sound tore from my throat, eerie and layered, an unearthly harmony of rage, grief, and something far more ancient than me. It wasn't just a scream. It was a *summoning*.

The air shivered. The dead paused, just for a heartbeat. And in the next, they exploded. Rupturing like overripe fruit beneath pressure, bones cracking outward as blue ichor sprayed in arcs through the dead trees. Skulls shattered. Ribs split. Spines twisted backward as if the scream physically repelled them. Ash spewed from their mouths. Eyes exploded in sockets. Until all that was left were heaps of bone and rot collapsing.

The forest went still. Ash drifted down around me like snow, but all I could taste was blood and the echo of my own voice. The Commander's large form was slumped and unconscious. I pushed against him, rolling him onto his back despite exhaustion trying to drag me into unconsciousness.

"Commander?" My voice shook as I put my hand against his neck, checking for a heartbeat. A sigh of relief left my lips when I found it, though it was too fast and thready.

I slammed my hands over his wound, trying to hold him together—but the blood that soaked my fingers wasn't red. It was a deep, dark blue.

I froze, then dragged my hands back, staring at them as if they no longer belonged to me.

Why the hell does he bleed blue? Did all Fae bleed this way? No, I had seen Solas bleed and his blood had been red.

I ripped my shirt off and pressed it against his bleeding wound.

"No. No. No," I murmured angrily as black veins spread rapidly over his body. I finally didn't want to die, and with my life tethered to *his,* finding answers did not look like it would be in my fate. I couldn't leave him here to bleed out while I looked for help, but I knew I couldn't carry him either.

"Gods curse my stupidity," I muttered to myself as I took his dagger from his waist belt. I didn't know if it would help, but it was worth trying. The familiar cold sting of the knife bit across the wrist of my injured arm. I clenched my teeth through the pain in my shoulder as I used my other arm to lift it to his mouth. I pressed my wrist against his lips. My blood trickled into the mouth of my captor. Of my enemy. And a small part inside me begged it to save him.

"Come on," I whispered, pressing my bleeding wrist to his mouth. His throat worked. Then his hands locked around my arm, his canines piercing my skin.

Warmth flooded through my veins as his wound knitted

together under my palm. The black lines eased from his skin. His eyes sprung open, gulping my blood down like a someone starved. The warmth spread low into my stomach, flooding my senses. The pain ebbed. All I could feel was *him*.

Before I could stop myself, a moan fell from my lips. He drank deeper, and wetness pooled between my thighs. I climbed on his lap, straddling his waist. I wanted him. I needed him to touch me. I needed *more*. My skin tingled, drinking in his lust. Fuelling the power thrumming in my veins. His hardness pressed against me, straining against his pants as though it were going to burst. A growl rumbled through his chest, making my core throb. I rocked my hips, grinding myself against his large length, desperate for friction. I wanted to touch him. To taste him. To feel him inside of me. I gripped his dark curls, pulling him closer. It wasn't enough. My head snapped back, a strangled sound tearing from my throat. Pure need surged through me, bright and blinding. His hunger bled into me, a heat that seeped into my bones, my veins, a tide that filled every hollow space until I felt impossibly, dangerously alive.

"More," I begged. My hand reached down between us, trailing downwards over the large divots of muscle. Shadows teased my skin, pressing against my breasts, my nipples tightening to painful points. My hand slid into his pants and his hips jerked against me.

My mouth found the side of his neck, leaving wet kisses there as I wrapped my hand around his cock, giving it one long stroke. Butterflies filled my stomach. Gods, he felt huge.

"Fuck," he breathed against my wrist, cock twitching in my hand. But he pulled away, gripping my forearm. "Stop," he demanded, voice strained.

I tilted my head at him, long silver waves trickling over my shoulder with the movement of my hand stroking his hardness again. "I want you," I whispered.

The Commander dissipated into shadows, disappearing from underneath me.

Shadows coiled violently, then reformed. Two feet away, he knelt on the forest floor, gripping his dark hair. His breathing was ragged.

I shifted back onto my knees, my injured arm dropping awkwardly, but I didn't feel the pain. The only thing I felt was pure need.

"No," he growled. The word trembled with restraint, almost broken sounding. "It's my venom. You do not actually want this." He ground the words out, each word clipped.

I pouted at him, my good hand trailing down my exposed abdomen before sliding into the front of my pants.

"It certainly feels like I want this," I challenged, pulling my hand free, sparkling in the dull light with my arousal.

He stared at me with his lips parted, breath coming hard and fast.

I didn't break eye contact as I brought my glistening finger to my lips, licking it from the base to the tip before pushing it into my mouth and sucking it with a wet pop.

"You are a fucking dangerous little thing," he muttered, nostrils flaring. "Get up before I make you," he threatened.

I stood, pouting up at him. My arm dragged unnaturally, and large wounds tore through the skin of my biceps. But I felt no pain. *How strange.* I wobbled on my feet.

"I can take you." I promised him. "I'm not innocent, Commander, I've taken men before—"

A deep growl cut me off and the darkness bled in front of me. The Commander suddenly towered over me, and I strained to look up at him. He stared down at me with murder written across his gore-splattered features.

"Stop." His warm breath washed over my face as he leant down. I pressed my hands against his waist, unable to stop myself from touching him. Gods, I wanted him to touch me.

"You think you can take me, Little Drownling?" he mused. "You can hardly even stand."

I bared my teeth at him, glaring through my eyelashes.

"There's my vicious little prisoner," he murmured. His eyes lingered on my lips for a moment. "It is just the venom from my bite making you pliable and willing. You will want to fuck me desperately for a few hours, but it will wear off and you will return to wanting to kill me."

I swallowed hard, my hands lingering as they traced the hard lines of his abdomen, memorising him despite myself. "I hate you," I murmured, forcing the words past my lips. "You're repulsive."

His chuckle rolled through me, leaving a shiver in its wake. "You are a liar, Little Drownling." He leant in, lips brushing my ear as if to tell me a secret. "Fae can smell strong emotions. And even when you first saw me, lust mingled with your fear."

Before I could respond, his hands wrapped around my waist and the other collided with the back of my knees. He cradled me against his chest and began walking, despite my sounds of protest.

"I can see it, you know" I whispered, voice breaking on purpose. "That you want to fuck me."

"Stop." He spat the command. The rejection should have hurt, should have made me feel embarrassed. But I pushed anyway. "I could feel it. Your cock got so hard for me."

His grip tightened on me with bruising force as his eyes darkened. "Shut the fuck up, before I make you." My stomach fluttered at the thought, the warm thrum of his venom pulsing through my veins made me want *everything* he would give me.

I BARELY REGISTERED THE TREES AROUND US ANYMORE. My head lolled against his shoulder, the motion of his stride rocking me. The venom pulsed in my veins like heat in dying embers. I felt drunk on him. On his scent. On the strength of his arms wrapped under my thighs, holding me as if I weighed nothing. One of his hands gripped my thigh, calloused and warm, while the other gripped my waist. Gods, he smelled divine. Like caramel and sandalwood and something I didn't have words for, something I'd only ever smelled on him. It curled in my lungs and made my skin tingle. The throbbing ache between my thighs returned with a vengeance, raw and unrelenting. I wanted him. Desperately. Shamefully. My fingers tightened against the back of his neck, urging him to lean into me. To taste me. I wanted to taste every part of his body, to feel him pulse against me, inside me—

"Stop." His voice was a growl. Deep. Commanding.

I blinked, dazed, and looked up to find his jaw clenched tight and his nostrils flaring. He could scent it. Scent me.

"I didn't say anything," I said, trailing my fingers against his chest.

"You didn't have to." He adjusted his grip on me, trying to break contact. "Think about something else."

I pouted and let my head fall against his shoulder again. "But you smell delicious."

He exhaled sharply through his nose, a sound that might've been a laugh, or a curse. "Tell me what the Fire Fates told you," he suggested, voice rougher than before.

"They spoke in riddles," I muttered, and a frustrated sigh escaped me. "I don't understand half the things they told me."

"Try." The command sat heavy between us. I scowled. My mind was fuzzy. But I tried to focus.

The words felt strange in my mouth. "They said I'm the key. The Soul Relics, I think only I can find them." His stride didn't falter, as if this information was not new to him.

"And they said..." I frowned, my memory piecing together their words. "They said I could save or destroy everything, and something about a Fated Mate." He stiffened beneath me, just slightly, but enough that I noticed.

"But," I added, trying to wave it off, "they called me the wrong name."

"What name?" he asked, voice unreadable.

"Maraveth." I waved my hand lazily, unable to focus through the haze and laughed bitterly. His jaw ticked, still silent. I shifted in his hold, leaning closer to his neck, drawing in another inhale of his maddening scent. Fresh night air with an underlying sweetness that made my mouth water.

"Do not speak that name again," he demanded.

Curiosity nagged from somewhere deep within me, but it couldn't surface through the heavy feeling that pulsed over me. I gently pressed my mouth against his collarbone, sliding my tongue against his warm skin.

"Why do you taste so good?" I whispered against him. His muscles coiled beneath me as he tried to readjust me in his grip.

"Stop it," he ground out. "My restraint has limits, Drownling, and in your current state, you would not survive the things I want to do to you."

My grip tightened around him and heat pulsed through me at his words.

"I don't care about surviving," I whispered against his skin.

He tugged me against his body roughly, my injured arm jarring against him, and sharp pain split through the haze. I groaned. Suddenly each step the Commander took caused a jolt of pain through my head.

"I care," he grumbled. Before I could dwell on his response, the agony surged, taking my breath away and pulling at my very soul.

"My shoulder..." I paused, trying to think through the fog. "Everything hurts," I whispered. He grunted in acknowledgment. A few moments passed in silence, and I stared at his chest, focusing on deep breaths and idly tracing the intricate lines of his tattoos.

"What does this one mean?" I asked.

He arched one thick eyebrow at me and clenched his jaw. "You do not ask questions about me."

"Commander, seeing that I had my hand around your cock—"

He cut me off with a growl so deep, it sounded more animal than male. With his next step my arm lolled off my body, dropping against my will and I cried out in pain.

The Commander stopped walking, frowning down at me. "I wanted to walk to give my venom time to wear off. But your pain is worsening."

"It's fine, pain and I are well acquainted," I said idly and stared through the treetops into the oppressive darkness.

"And how exactly are you so familiar with pain?" he

asked cautiously and I chuckled softly. "You do not ask questions about me," I mocked, and he glared at me for a moment. But I feared he could see straight through me. To every scar that marked my soul.

"Hold on to me." His voice vibrated through me, and I tightened my grip. I barely had time to inhale before the world unravelled. The air around us collapsed. It wasn't like falling or even moving. It was like being unstitched, each thread of my body pulled into darkness and reformed somewhere else, somewhere in between. Cold rushed over me like water. I couldn't breathe. I couldn't think. The world turned inside out. I could see nothing, but I felt everything. Wind that didn't blow. Screams that didn't sound. A thousand shadows brushing against my skin like fingers. It was cold and burning and nothing at all. And then, impact.

We landed hard enough to knock the breath from my lungs. Shadows tore from around us, from within me. My stomach flipped. My vision spun. I clutched him tighter, trembling. I blinked and the trees were no longer skeletal and looming, the air no longer thick with rot and whispers. Instead, the firelight from camp flickered just ahead, warm and familiar.

"You are okay," he murmured, his voice rough and oddly soothing. I wanted to believe him.

TWENTY-SEVEN
SURRENDER

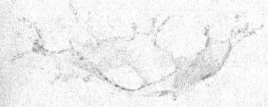

I clung to the Commander. My head spun and my stomach churned viciously. His hand was still splayed across my thigh, holding me as if he wasn't quite ready to let go. But suddenly, I needed him to. Desperately. The spinning, the pressure, the taste of my own blood still thick in my mouth was too much. My stomach twisted, bile lurching up my throat.

"Put me down," I rasped, squirming against him.

He looked at me sharply, dark curls falling just above his strong eyebrows that drew together. "Lyra—"

"Put me down!" I snapped, pushing at his chest with what little strength I had. The moment my boots hit the dirt, my knees buckled. I stumbled away from him with my hands pressed against my stomach. I heaved violently and the world spun. My body bent in half as everything inside my stomach tumbled onto the ground. It splattered against the dirt in hot, acidic waves. My hair fell forward, clinging to the sweat on my face. I was painfully aware of the Commander standing mere feet away from the mess that I was.

When the retching finally stopped, I wiped my mouth with the back of my trembling hand and staggered a few steps away from the mess. My entire body felt scraped raw.

"Don't say anything," I warned without looking at him.

He didn't, but I could still feel him watching me. I turned just enough to glance back at him. Shadows flickered at the edges of his form like they were tethered to him by emotion alone. His eyes were unreadable. But he looked... tense. Coiled. But not from disgust. From restraint. I wondered if feeding from me had affected him as well. I wrapped my good arm around my torso, trying to hold myself together through the unbearable pull of his venom and the dizziness.

"Sorry, that was... disgusting," I muttered.

The Commander chuckled, low and dark. "A normal reaction after shadow jumping for the first time." I looked up, but before I could speak, my knees gave out. The world tilted. He vanished into a rush of shadow and reappeared just in time to catch me. His arms wrapped around me, solid and sure and I let my fingers trail along the edge of his jaw, feeling the scratch of stubble. My hand slid into the dark curls at the nape of his neck, tangling softly. I imagined tugging them. Arching beneath him. Pulling him closer—

"Please, stop." His voice was husky and strained as his eyes darkened.

Voices cut through the trees, reminding me that the world existed outside of *him*.

"Try to behave, Little Drownling," he murmured under his breath. "I'm not the only one who can scent you."

I blinked up at him, dazed and confused.

"Well, what do we have here?" Solas's voice was all drawl and amusement as he walked towards us. Cerilla followed behind him, her eyes narrowing immediately.

The Commander lowered me slowly to the ground, gently setting me on my feet. A sound of protest slipped from my lips, my fingers clinging to his skin. I didn't want to let go. My legs barely held. Cerilla crossed her arms, her sharp gaze flicking from me to her brother, then to the way I leant into him, flushed and trembling.

"Well," she said dryly. "That explains the scent." She stepped closer, eyes dropping to my wrist. Her lips thinned. Cerilla sighed, rubbing her temple. But then her gaze dropped, to the puckered mark across his abdomen. Her breath caught. She tilted her head, her dark eyes assessing. Then her attention shifted back to me. "You used your blood to save my brother, didn't you?" Her voice was different now, no longer sharp. As though she couldn't quite believe what I had done.

I nodded, wrapping my hands back around the Commander. The only thing grounding me in the haze of his venom was the throb of his heartbeat beneath my hand.

Cerilla was suddenly in front of me, throwing her arms around me. No hesitation. No revulsion at the gore slicking my skin, or the blood soaking the small amount of clothing I wore. She simply held me, as if I were something fragile and fading, and she wasn't willing to let me slip away.

"Thank you for not letting him die," she whispered. I felt the words against my temple more than I heard them.

She pulled back, her face shadowed but no longer distant. Carefully, like I might break, she reached up and tucked a strand of silver hair behind my ear. The tenderness of the gesture and the rawness in her voice undid something deep inside me. I blinked, tears threatening.

"See?" Solas grinned at me from behind Cerilla. "I knew that you liked us."

"Come, darling, let's get you healed," Cerilla murmured, reaching out her hand to me.

I stared at it for a moment, then lifted my gaze to the Commander. My hand trembled as I reached for him instead, silently pleading. With a quiet sigh of exasperation, he slid his arms beneath me and lifted me effortlessly against his chest.

"I'd almost forgotten how strong the post-feeding lust can be," Solas muttered from in front of us, his voice tinged with amusement. "But that scent is *strong.*"

A deep rumble vibrated through the Commander's chest, darkness pulsing off him and digging into his own skin. I wondered if it hurt. Solas quirked an eyebrow at him, the amusement wavering from his face.

Before he could say anything, we came to an abrupt halt, as if the air itself repulsed me. The air ahead shimmered, a faint blue ripple stretching upward into the night like a glass dome over the trees. A frown furrowed his brow. Solas turned, confusion flashing across his face as he caught sight of the barrier.

The Commander lowered me gently to my feet. My legs wobbled beneath me, but he kept one hand at my back as he gestured for me to step through without him.

I took an unsteady step forward and slammed into something solid. The air pulsed where I touched it, a wall of shimmering blue energy radiating outward from the point of contact. It pulsed skyward like a living barrier, surrounding the camp in a protective dome. A laugh escaped me, bubbling up hysterically and uncontrollably.

"Well, that explains why I didn't feel her leave..." Solas muttered, rubbing the back of his neck. The Commander shot him a silent glare.

Solas gestured to the space in front of me, closing his

eyes in concentration, a gap large enough for me to pass through shimmered a light blue.

"Why do you laugh?" the Commander asked, pulling me back into his arms to carry me across Solas' ward.

"The barrier is to keep the monsters out," I gasped between jagged bursts of laughter that felt too sharp to be sane. "*I'm* a monster." The admission scraped from my throat, raw and cracked. He didn't look at me, his jaw locking hard as his grip sank into my flesh, cruel and merciless, a command for silence.

Then he let me fall. His warmth vanished in a breath, replaced by hard ground and pain that jolted into my dislocated shoulder and shredded skin on my arms. I glared at the inked lines across his back as he walked away, each step a dismissal that stung worse than the injury. He paused, looking at me from over his shoulder.

"From one *monster* to another," he said softly, his voice raw. He held my gaze, and I felt trapped in their abyss. "It is not what you *are* that makes you evil, but your intentions."

The words struck harder than the fall. For one fractured heartbeat, I couldn't look away from him. He was my Kingdom's nightmare. My captor. He was *evil*. Yet in his eyes, my pain was mirrored back at me. I tore my gaze away, wiping away tears with a trembling hand.

"Heal her," he commanded towards Cerilla. He didn't spare me a glance; his shadows had turned lethal. Sinking into his skin as though they were trying to tear him apart. Solas followed him, cursing under his breath. I watched him walk away, my body begging for him to come back. *It's just the venom,* I reminded myself. Did I still hate him? Did I still want to kill him?

"Lyra." A sharp snap of fingers cut through my daze. Cerilla stood in front of me, brows raised.

"Hmm?" I mumbled, blinking slowly.

"Drink, darling," she said softly as she pressed a steaming herbal cup of tea to my lips. The floral taste filled my mouth, spreading through me until the pain numbed.

"This will hurt," she said gently as I finished the last mouthful. Before I could brace myself, her hands moved, quick and precise. Pain sparked like lightning through my shoulder as she gripped and twisted. There was a sickening pop as the joint slid back into place. I gasped, the world spinning, but it dulled almost instantly. A warm haze rolled in, numbing the agony. I could still feel it, but distantly, like I was observing someone else's pain. The venom still swam through my veins, softening the pain that should have been agonising. Cerilla murmured softly in the Fae language, soft tendrils of darkness knitting the skin on my biceps back together as I stared at the tree line where the Commander had disappeared. I hoped it would scar, finally I would have a mark on my skin I was proud of.

Solas returned first, kneeling beside me with a worn blanket in his hands. Without a word, he draped it around my shoulders. Only then did I realize how exposed I was. My fingers clutched the fabric tightly. Beneath it, I wore only the thin, lacy scrap Cerilla considered a binder, and my pants were torn and dirty. Dried blood clung to my exposed skin. Between the gore covering my skin and my long hair, I hoped my scars were hidden. Worry coiled somewhere deep in my consciousness but my unnatural hunger for the Commander overshadowed my insecurities.

Cerilla and Solas sat next to me around the fire,

speaking in low voices beside me, but their words drifted like the smoke, weightlessly floating away from me.

My head snapped up, eyes following the Commander as he moved towards the fire, each flex of muscle dragging a pulse of heat through me. His venom hummed in my veins, blurring anger into want until my thighs tightened with the humiliating need to be closer. He was clean, and not one shadow was in sight. He said nothing as he approached, stopping on the opposite side of the fire, jaw flexing as though he were fighting the urge to look at me. He sat on the ground, stretching his long legs out towards the fire.

I made a sound, half frustration, half need, and rose unsteadily to my feet. Solas and Cerilla went quiet, but I didn't care. I crossed the space between us, the blanket dragging behind me like a train. He watched me grow closer, eyebrows pulled, dark curls damp with water. His jaw was clenched so tight I could see the vein twitch at his temple. Without hesitation, I lowered myself between his powerful thighs, leaning back against his abdomen and tucking my face against his chest. His body went stiff beneath mine, his breath catching as my weight pressed into him. He growled, but he didn't stop me.

"That," Solas said mildly, "is not something I expected to witness, ever."

"Exactly how much venom did you use, brother?" Cerilla's gaze flicked between us, her expression tightening.

"I did not think it was much. But it has been over five hundred years since I have fed from a living being, it was difficult to control," he said tightly.

Five hundred? Surely the venom was affecting my hearing. "How old are you?" I asked, surprised.

"Old," he replied instantly, avoiding my question. I

pouted up at him and his jaw clenched as he looked down at me.

"I'm over a thousand years old." His face looked like it was carved by the Gods themselves, not one ounce of ageing hung on his face. He didn't look older than twenty-five.

Before I could respond, Cerilla cut in. "Do explain what happened, brother. You suddenly got furious and disappeared into a heap of shadows, leaving me in the Mourning Woods *alone*."

"My little prisoner attracted a swarm of Nightbourne, after her visit to the Fire Fates."

Cerilla let out a small gasp.

I drew lazy circles on the Commander's thigh as they talked around me, wondering what it would feel like to trail my hand higher. To make him take me against the ground. What sounds would he make when he came undone? His hand pressed down over the top of mine, stilling it against his thigh. I looked up at his dark expression with a small smirk.

"Lyra? What did you find out?" Cerilla asked softly, leaning forwards on her elbows.

"Mostly just more unanswered questions." I closed my eyes, imagining the molten monsters that spoke in riddles. The memory felt hazy, like it was far away, and I couldn't quite grasp it. I sat up straight. My head spinning from the sudden movement.

"Something about Kingdoms. They said..." I pressed my fingers to my temples, rubbing the ache that was throbbing in my head. "It's up to *me* to unite them."

"We have been trying for years. What would you suggest?" the Commander said through clenched teeth.

What *could* I do? My stomach twisted and a fresh wave of nausea washed over me with the realisation. My hand in marriage would have united the Northern and Southern territories. Could marriage unite two warring Kingdoms? Perhaps I needed to do what I was bred to do all this time. Submit to a man.

"Do you have a king?" I asked breathlessly.

"Four courts rule the Fae lands—Ember, Frost, Dawn and Obsidian. Each governs their own territory." Solas tilted his head curiously at me as he answered. "But the Obsidian Court's high lord," he added slowly, "commands the others."

"Take me to him," I demanded, raising my chin and letting my voice carry across the small clearing. The Commander's body went still beneath me as the sound of wood crackling in the fire broke the silence.

"Why would I do that?" He asked.

The others watched me intently and I squared my shoulders, swallowing the bile that clawed its way up my throat. Slowly, I lifted my gaze—first to Cerilla, then to Solas, and finally to the male whose arms still circled me like he hadn't decided whether to hold or break me.

"I am Lyra Meridian." Solas stilled and Cerilla's eyes widened.

I lifted my chin, forcing the words past the ache in my chest. "Daughter of King Vaylor, and Princess to the Mortal Kingdom." Silence crashed down around us, and the Commander became unnaturally still.

"I will offer my hand in marriage to the Obsidian Court's ruler," I continued, voice raw but unwavering. "To bind our realms and fight the Seven Hells."

Twenty-Eight

Eavesdropping

The Commander tensed beneath me, his forefinger and thumb suddenly gripping my chin, tilting my head to look up at him. "You are the daughter of King Vaylor?" he growled, a low rumbling sound. I nodded, one sharp movement that would seal my fate.

"Well, this just got more complicated, didn't it?" Cerilla sighed deeply.

"Why the fuck were you with the Iron Guard?" There was a slight pull to his words through the heaviness lacing my veins, urging me to answer. I tried to resist, but words spilled against my will. He was using the blood bargain. *Asshole.*

"I... I ran away." The words clawed up my throat despite my best efforts to stop them. "They were going to make me marry viscount Barden. He was vile. I snuck into Asencion and sacrificed myself to the Gods. I thought I would die. I *wanted* to die." My voice grew thick as tears swam in my eyes. He looked down at me, and sadness reflected in his empty eyes.

"Please, I do not want to talk about my past," I begged,

hating the wetness that clung to my eyelashes and the heat that crawled over my face.

"Fine," he grumbled. "Tell me word for word what the Fire Fates said."

His shadows were pulling at his skin, sinking and tearing it repeatedly. It was mesmerising, watching his own power try to hurt him. The words slipped out, low, dream-like, pulled from the haze still thick in my mind as I repeated what they said. The blood bargain pulled the words from my memory for me.

"We are from the Obsidian Court, aren't we Commander?" Solas said enthusiastically after I had finished reciting the prophecy, breaking the silence.

"Enough," the Commander snapped, his jaw clenched so tightly I wondered if it would break. His volatile shadows plunged into his chest.

"Does that hurt?" I whispered, unable to stop myself.

"Yes, but I am also used to pain." He stared at the fire, and it reflected in the depths of his endless eyes. I wanted to ask what he meant by that. But by the look on his face, he wouldn't answer me. So, I asked one of the millions of other questions bouncing in my mind.

"What is a Fated Mate?" I asked, nestling further against the broad chest of my captor.

"The other half of your soul," he said softly, still gazing into the fire with a guarded look. I blinked at him, the venom still clouding my thoughts.

Solas continued from across the fire. "It's... alignment. The piece you didn't know you were missing until it stood before you. They are everything you will need, ever want." Solas paused, and I noticed he absently rubbed his left hand. The movement was slow and almost tender. "When the bond is accepted, the Mark of Anamryn appears. *Soul thread,* in our tongue. It forms on the left hand and binds you for eternity."

His voice cracked near the end, and I followed his gaze to his left hand. There, etched into his skin, half-faded by time but unmistakable, was more than a tattoo. It shimmered faintly in the firelight, a swirling script of silver and black lines, not drawn but *woven* into him. Not art. Not ink. Something sacred. Something permanent.

"It's beautiful," I whispered before I could stop myself.

"She was." His voice held a sadness I couldn't comprehend, and something felt heavy in my chest at seeing his small broken smile.

"I am so sorry for your loss," I whispered.

Solas nodded, his eyes glistening with something unsaid as they slipped down to the mark branded to the back of my hand from the blood bargain.

"So am I. One day I will avenge her. For now, I take comfort that she is amongst the stars, watching over me until I join her."

I wanted to ask him what happened, but the distant look that crossed over his face told me not to ask right now. Instead, the silence stretched comfortably as I watched the flames dance and crackle.

I looked up at the hulking Fae Commander, reaching up and flicking his nose gently. He raised his eyebrows at me in disbelief. "If I marry your king, I get to order you around," I mused, unable to hide my smirk.

"Unlikely," he growled down at me, barely tolerating my closeness.

"Shame, I had some very fun demands for you..." My words trailed off into a yawn, my eyelids heavy. "I am tired," I stated slowly.

Cerilla rose, her dark curls pooling around her. "I'll help you clean up," she said and offered me her hand.

I shooed it away, curling myself against my captor's chest, clinging to his body any way that I could. "I will sleep here," I responded, unbashful. Cerilla began to protest, but the Commander cut her off.

"It is fine, Cerilla, just leave her," he seethed. "She will go back to despising me in the morning," he muttered, and I thought I heard a hint of sadness in his voice.

THE FOREST STIRRED TO LIFE AROUND US, BATHED IN unearthly beauty that mocked the growing shame clawing at my chest. Winston, the enormous dark stallion, trotted along the narrow path. The sun trickled through the thick canopy above, illuminating the dense greenery and delicate flowers that surrounded us as I tried to clear my head. The venom had steadily trickled from my system. It leaked from me slowly, like fog lifting after a storm, leaving everything sharper. Harsher. Real.

My gore-splattered body sat rigid in the saddle, my spine pressed against the broad chest behind me. I longed to scrub my skin clean, of more than just the remnants of the Nightbourne, but from what I had done. The haze clinging to my thoughts had thinned enough for clarity to bite. Shame curled hot and merciless in my gut, my cheeks burning as fractured memories flickered like lightning. My hands on him. My mouth against his skin. I had begged. Moaned. Pleaded. I had fallen asleep against his chest, only to wake on the ground... Alone. I shifted, trying—and failing —to put space between us. The weight pressing down on my chest wasn't just humiliation. It was disappointment. I had been violated so many times in my life, and now I was upset that I wasn't?

Gods, how broken am I?

Something inside me cracked. My breath hitched, then stuttered. Air scraped into my lungs but didn't stay. Monsters were hunting me. A ghost was haunting me. I was supposed to save everyone from the Seven Hells. I was captured by my people's most feared enemy. I still had no idea what I was, *and* I had offered myself up for marriage for a war. My chest tightened, a crushing band pulling tighter with every shallow inhale. Too fast. Too shallow. I couldn't slow it down.

Why can't I breathe?

I leant forward in the saddle, clutching at air that refused to fill me, breath after breath tearing in against the frantic hammer of my heart, panic flooding my veins before I could stop it.

"Lyra?" The Commander's voice cut through the spiral, low and steady. "What is it?" he asked.

Instead of answering, a sob tore from my throat, hot tears spilling down my cheeks without permission. "Look at me," he murmured as he pulled on Winston's reins to slow our speed. Solas and Cerilla were in front, and they rode ahead, not realising we were falling behind.

"You are safe, Little Drownling. Breathe." His hand came to my waist, firm and anchoring, keeping me upright. The other hand splayed over my chest. I tried to shove him away, but he only held me tighter.

"Breathe with me. Slow. In through your nose." He drew a deliberate breath behind me, deep enough that I felt it expand against my back. "Out."

I tried. Failed. Tried again. But he kept filling his lungs with long, slow breaths behind me. And eventually, I managed to mimic one, my body obeying him before my mind could argue.

"That's it," he said quietly, as if every word was chosen with care. My lungs stuttered, then caught, dragging in a breath that burned but *stayed*. My chest ached, tight with something dangerously close to relief, and I hated myself for leaning into his steadiness.

"You did so well for me," he praised, sending a shock of heat through my system that I tried to run from. "I was worried you were going to spook Umbra," the Commander mused quietly.

"Who is Umbra?" I asked between measured breaths. I needed to take control—to anchor myself before everything slipped beyond my grasp again.

"My horse." He took his hand off my chest to pat its dark mane, keeping the other wrapped around my waist. I squirmed away, almost toppling to the ground. His gripped tightened and he pulled me against his body. "Easy now," he said low and smoothly.

"I had named him Winston," I muttered through the easing panic. His laugh rumbled through me. A genuine laugh. Gods help me, it was a noise that did something to my heart. I pushed that feeling down and locked it in a cage where it belonged.

"Do you think your High Lord will accept my proposal?"

A knot of tension worked its way in my shoulders. Gods, I wanted a bath. A long, hot bath was my only reprieve in the castle.

He seemed to consider for a moment. "If your father agrees to the terms, then yes."

A bloom of hope flared in my chest, swallowed by a wave of nausea. If Father accepted, I could unite the Kingdoms. Would I have to see him again? Would he somehow take me back to Stonebriar? I wouldn't leave it up to the Gods, if he tried to drag me back, I would plunge a knife into my own heart.

"Solas and I trained last night. I want to keep training while I am trapped with you," I said, trying to steady my voice.

He scoffed. "You want *me*," he said, "to train *you*?" His tone was smooth. Mocking. But there was heat beneath it. Interest.

I straightened, rising to the challenge in his voice. "I figured you would like a fair fight." I mused, and he hummed in response. "I want you dead, remember? As soon as this deal is finished, I want to pull your beating heart from your body and crush it under my boot." I poured sweetness into my voice, drenching it in innocence.

"Such pretty threats." He huffed a quiet laugh, breath brushing my ear. "Are you going to beg me to let you train?" His voice dipped, slow and deliberate as he rolled his hips against my ass. "I liked the sound of you begging."

Heat crept across my face and I cleared my throat. "No. I will never beg you for anything again. That wasn't *me*. I *don't* want you," I snapped, trying to wiggle away from him in the saddle.

"Ah, I see," he said, satisfaction dripping from his voice. "Pretend all you want, my little prisoner, but I can hear the way your heart quickens when I'm near you. *Smell* the way you react to my words." He inhaled deeply as if proving a point. "Even now, I can scent your arousal. When I touch you... You *like* it, even if it's laced with..." He paused, thinking. "Anger. Oh, you *hate* that you like it, don't you?"

"The only thing I hate is you," I muttered. It felt

violating that he could sense my feelings, even ones I didn't want to acknowledge myself.

"You are lying again," he chuckled darkly, and I threw my elbow into his hard abdomen. Pride swelled in my chest as a small amount of air whooshed out of him, and he went quiet. Truly quiet. No teasing. No provocation.

I folded in on myself and crossed my arms against my chest.

We had trailed through the woods for hours, and my hips ached with every rock of the saddle that slammed me against the heated wall of muscle that I still wanted to stab. My eyelids had grown heavy, and I had drifted to sleep against Winston's mane. I dreamt of a crown sinking in the ocean. Lost forever.

Find the pieces.

The voice made my eyes snap open. I quickly closed them when voices carried around me. "She is different to what I thought she would be," Solas said in a hushed voice. The sound of the horses' hooves almost drowning out their voices.

"She is exceptional." The Commander's voice was filled with a sadness so old it felt heavy on my heart. "It's different this time. She is different. I cannot bring myself to *hate* her. When I kill her, it might just kill me along with it."

My heart pounded rapidly in my chest. Had I misheard him? He was going to kill me.

I felt the Commander shift behind me. The sound of hooves drifted further away. I kept my eyes sealed shut. Did he know I was awake? Did he know I heard? Warm fingers brushed against my temple, pushing my hair off my face. I resisted the urge to press into the touch, or flinch.

"You are having a nightmare, Little Drownling." He sighed, hand lingering as if he didn't want to pull it away. I tried to keep my breath even and my eyes shut. Eventually his hand moved and I risked cracking open my eyes. The late afternoon sun-bathed us in an orange glow. No longer were we in the dense forest. The large, enchanted trees had given way to vast rolling hills in the distance. We were weaving through a town, neat buildings with flowerpots gathered at their doorsteps lined cobbled streets. Fae stopped what they were doing as we rode past. Some kneeled. Some bowed. But none of them seemed scared. If anything, they seemed delighted to see the Commander of Death darkening their streets. One thing was clear. I needed to get away from him and find their king myself.

Twenty-Nine
Manipulation

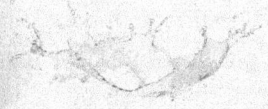

We came to a stop in front of a large building with a wooden sign hanging off its front. I couldn't read the writing but judging by the mouthwatering smells wafting from the building, there was food waiting inside.

I wasn't used to the bright colours of the buildings or laughter echoing through the streets and I found myself captivated by their culture. A culture I was taught was beastly.

Large hands encircled my waist, lifting me off the horse with ease. He pressed me against his chest, sliding me down his body until my toes touched the ground. My hands rested on his forearms to steady myself. He had told me I was safe and made a small light flicker back inside my icy chest. *It is all a lie.*

I looked up at him through my lashes. "Thank you," I said politely. I could lie too. "For keeping me safe. I..." I paused for effect, looking into his soulless eyes. "I am grateful for you."

A pained expression passed over his face and a familiar

tingling feeling pressed into my skin. His eyes squeezed shut and he stepped away from me, turning his back to me. "Follow," he grunted over his shoulder. Shadows coiled along his skin, burrowing into him as if they were trying to tear him apart.

Solas gave me an apologetic smile, holding the door open for us.

It was crowded inside. Cups were brimming with ale, servers topping them up from large jugs with even larger smiles. These Fae did not look intimidating. They looked *happy*. It was so far from the savages that had been painted in my mind since I was young. A path seemed to clear in front of the Commander. Wide-eyed patrons smiled and dipped their heads in awe, some even bowed. I thought it strange; Commanders did not get this respect in my Kingdom.

We sat a wooden table, and a bright-eyed Fae female walked up to our table with confidence, hips swaying. My eyes lingered on her exposed navel, a metal bar stuck through it, glinting with every step. My cheeks heated as my eyes wandered up. Her top crisscrossed over her breasts, so tightly that they bulged. Straight blue hair hung just above her shoulders, and she beamed at the Commander with a stunning smile.

Something ugly twisted in my stomach. *Hunger,* I told myself. My knuckles turned white as I gripped the edge of the table. I was hungry.

She said something in the Fae language and the Commander laughed, that genuine chuckle spilled from his full lips like music. The *hunger* twisted deeper, and I swallowed down bile. The Commander glanced at me from the corner of his eye, an arrogant smirk ghosting across his mouth. "Food and ale for everyone," he said.

He dragged his eyes away from me, settling them back on the server, "And Blue, it is *very* good to see you."

"Will you require anything else?" She leant over, enough for her breasts to bounce with the motion.

"Stop eye fucking my brother and get our food. We are starved." Cerilla sent Blue a tight-lipped smile. Blue's eyes widened before dipping her head and muttering in Fae under her breath as she walked away. If I didn't know any better, she seemed scared of Cerilla.

Solas chuckled under his breath, amusement dancing in his hazel eyes as the Commander turned to him. "You and Cerilla will head south to the castle. Prepare the court for a royal wedding and send invitation to the Mortal King."

"Sorry but, how do you know your king will say yes?" I asked, trying to sound polite.

"Because the Fire Fates told you to unite the Kingdoms this way. The *High Lord* would be a fool to refuse fate." The Commander said carefully, glaring at Cerilla as she scoffed.

My stomach sank. The thought of my father taking me made cold panic slither up my spine. But perhaps there was another way, where the Fae King would do as I wanted. My eyes darkened as I realised, I could sing to him until my magic curled around his mind, until his resistance softened and his eyes held that iridescent sheen. And once I held that power... nothing would ever be taken from me again.

"Can I go to the castle too?" I batted my eyelashes in a show. "I would like to meet the High Lord as soon as possible."

"No," the Commander said, not buying into my act. "You have a bargain to fulfil, Drownling. You will find the *remaining* Soul Relics."

Annoyance prickled along my spine. The way his voice

caressed the word, *remaining,* made it obvious he knew I had somehow absorbed one.

"Brother, please do not separate us—"

The Commander held up his hand, cutting his sister off.

"You will eat, then go with Solas. And hurry, I do not want you traveling in dark hours." Cerilla crossed her arms over her chest and sat back in her chair. There was no room for argument in the Commander's voice. Blue returned with three steaming plates of roast meat and vegetables smothered in a rich sauce. Another server set a glass of ale down in front of me, his hand brushing mine in a gentle caress. It was so fast I almost missed it. Almost. I looked up. A dark-haired Fae male flashed a mischievous grin at me, winking a storm-coloured eye at me before disappearing between patrons. I had never seen him before in my life. But there was something about that smirk that seemed so familiar.

We ate our meals in silence. The ale was bitter and strong. After downing the large glass, I felt light and warm. Cerilla and Solas left after we ate. Cerilla embraced the Commander, telling him to be careful. I embraced them both, surprised that I would miss them. Cerilla glanced over her shoulder one more time at her brother. It was obvious she loved him fiercely. I wondered what that felt like.

I followed the Commander through the crowded inn to the counter. He asked for a room. *One* room. I wanted to protest. But I knew it would land of deaf ears. And the more I protested, the less relaxed he would be. No. I needed to bide my time. Smile pleasantly and make him lower his guard.

I followed him up the stairs like a good little prisoner, my heartbeat pounding in my chest. He shoved a key into one of the many doors that lined the hallway and opened the door with a creak. I followed him inside. Willingly. Two lanterns bathed the room in a dull, flickering light. I ran my hand across the green satin sheets of the large bed, nearly sighing at their softness. But my feet stilled when my eyes landed on a large free-standing bathtub, rose-scented steam rolling off its surfaces.

"I asked Blue to prepare this for you." He watched me carefully, corded forearms crossing over his broad chest. Suddenly the room felt far too small. He inclined his head towards the bath and my breath caught in my throat. Did he expect me to bathe with him still in the room?

"May I have some privacy?" I asked sweetly, reining in the venom that wanted to leak into my voice.

His smirk sent a hot wave through my body. *Of anger,* I told myself.

"If the High Lord accepts your invitation, you will end a very long war. Your safety is now my responsibility. And you are far too self-destructive to leave alone."

I gave him a long, pointed look. If I turned around to undress, he would see my scars. Every mark of imperfection that made my soul bleed. *No.* He could see everything else, but not my scars.

I stared into the abyss of his eyes and kicked my boots off. My shaky hand unbuttoned the front of my shirt, undoing them one by one. A faint buzz sunk into my skin, one that I had felt before. Was he aroused? I dropped my shirt to the floor, my pants quickly following. Standing in nothing but my underwear, I slowly reached for the clasp in my binder.

"As you wish, Commander," I simpered, undoing the binder. My breasts sprang free and the lacy scrap fell to the floor.

The Commander no longer smirked. His muscles turned rigid, shadows digging into him without mercy. I ran my hands down my body over the buzzing feeling. Slowly, I slipped my underwear down and stepped out of them. His eyes weren't just on me now. They burnt into me. They were pure black, swallowing the whites. The eyes of a monster. A monster on a leash that could snap at any minute.

Gods, I wanted him to snap. The guards I slept with always fell asleep after spending themselves. The Commander was a monster, but he was still a male and I was willing to bet they were all the same.

I kept my eyes on him, taking slow steps backwards until the tub hit the back of my thighs. I glanced down at it and back up to him, biting my bottom lip.

"It's too high for me to step into with dignity. Could you…" I trailed off, batting my eyelashes.

He grunted and pushed off the wall, taking slow, controlled steps towards me. His nostrils flared with every fast breath he took. When he was close enough, I tipped forward, purposefully losing my balance. My breasts pushed against the bare muscles of his upper abdomen as I looped my arms around his neck. I hated how warm he felt. His hands gripped my waist, and I hated the thrill that shot through my stomach as his bare skin touched mine.

"Oh. I am so sorry Commander, I don't know what's come over me."

He didn't shove me away, but he also didn't drag me closer. He froze, as though one wrong breath would shatter the last of his restraint. His grip on my waist tightened, thumbs brushing the curve of my hip. His jaw clenched, like he hated himself for touching me. I hated myself just as much.

He was my Kingdom's enemy, and I was his prisoner. But the hardness pressing into my stomach and the needy pulse between my legs betrayed us both. I tilted my head, with wide innocent eyes. "Commander," I whispered, reaching up onto my tip toes to curl my fingers through the hair at the base of his neck. "Please help me."

Something inside him cracked. Not outwardly. Not visibly. But I felt it. The air changed between us, my skin prickling uncomfortably with his need. He swallowed, scooping an arm beneath my thighs and lifting me. For one tense heartbeat, my bare skin pressed fully against the heat of him. Against every wild, forbidden thing that lived under his hard body. His breath stuttered. Victory swirled in my chest.

But he exhaled slowly. Controlled. And gently—almost reverently—lowered me into the steaming bath. The water closed around my aching muscles. Despite the hot water, my skin felt cold where he had touched me. He remained kneeling beside the tub, shoulders rigid, the lantern light flickering across his sharp features. "I am not... him," he growled suddenly.

I blinked up at him, confused. "Who?"

"Whoever hurt you so deeply that you think your flesh is a weapon."

Shame surged up my throat. I resisted the urge to wrap my arms around myself, suddenly feeling exposed in a way that had nothing to do with nudity. "You can just say you do not want me." I raised my chin, ignoring the soft sting of rejection. *I didn't want this either,* I reminded myself. His voice dropped, dangerous and soft. "I do not have the energy to lie."

Something inside me melted, that stupid warmth in my chest growing brighter.

"But this show you are putting on, is not *you*." The shadows lashed up his throat, punishing him for the confession. He reached for a cloth and dipped it into the rose-scented water, wringing it out slowly. He held his hand out expectantly and hesitantly, I extended my arm out to him. He washed the dried blood from my shoulder like he feared hurting me. He smoothed the cloth down my arm like he had memorized the shape of me. When his fingers brushed the nape of my neck, I shivered, and his own breath fractured.

"What is your name?" I almost whispered into the quiet moment. This isn't what I wanted. *This* was intimate. Dangerous.

His eyes snapped to mine, dark veins pulsing around their edges. He shook his head once. "Ask a different question."

"No." I tugged at my arm, but his grip tightened.

"I don't have one anymore," he said, voice rough. "Ask a different question."

His finger grazed my neck as he brushed my hair over my shoulder. Just the smallest touch. But it lit every nerve ending on fire.

"Why are you being kind to me?" My voice broke and I cursed inwardly.

His answer was a blade that sunk into my skin. "Because one day soon, I'll be cruel. I want you to have one memory of me that does not end in blood." The water swayed between us, something unspoken sinking into my bones. I pushed it down.

"Lean forward," he said gently, reaching for me. Gods, he wanted to wash my back. Panic flared sharp and sudden.

"No." I straightened instantly, spine rigid, teeth clenched hard enough to ache.

For a suspended moment, his gaze held mine, heavy and searching.

"Why?" He asked slowly, as if worried he would spook me.

"Ask a different question," I whispered.

The weight of his gaze felt dangerous, like if he looked into my eyes a moment longer, he would see how broken I really was. I blew out the small flame flickering inside my chest. *He is my enemy*, I reminded myself. I was the one meant to be manipulating him.

I seized his hand in mine, holding onto it as if it were my salvation. He could sense my lies before, but perhaps if I took a more direct approach, he would break. He was so close to giving in.

"I've been afraid for a long time," I said. "And I have wanted to die for even longer." I reached out and cupped my hand against his face, trailing my thumb over his cheekbone.

"I'm hurting, Commander," I whispered. "And I think you are too." I leant in, just enough to feel his breath, my gaze slipping to his mouth. "Make me feel alive again," I murmured. "Please."

"Fuck," he growled.

He moved before I could breathe. One moment I was in the water, and the next, his arms were wrapped around my waist, pressing me against him. My bare skin was slick and trembling against the hard plane of his chest, my feet dangling off the ground. He moved us backwards; a wall pressed into my back. I couldn't breathe as he gripped my chin with his thumb and forefinger, tilting my head until I was forced to meet his gaze. His eyes burned, not only with lust, but with fury.

"Tell me to stop," he almost pleaded. "Tell me you don't want this." The timbre of his voice had gotten deeper. Huskier.

My chest ached with a longing I had never felt before. "You told me not to lie."

Before the words had even left my mouth, the air between us vanished. Replaced by *him*. Crisp night air, and caramel mixed with something dangerous. His mouth crashed into mine with feverish need. It wasn't soft. It was a collision. A war between hate and lust.

His tongue pushed into my mouth, warm and strong. His lips were so soft against the roughness that I felt like I was floating. The only tether I would ever need was him and his touch. I wrapped my legs around his waist, shoving my hands into his hair and pulling in closer. I slid my tongue against him, my hips moving, searching for friction. The growl that ripped through his throat sent a wave of heat to my core.

Every logical thought slipped away. Every reason I had for hating him vanished in one scary moment. There was only him. Only this. Us.

THIRTY
SCREECH

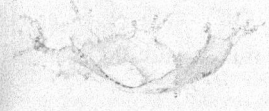

I was lost in the heat of the Commander's touch. "Please," I begged against his lips, reaching between us to unbutton his pants—

A high-pitched shriek pierced the night air, shattering the glass in the window frame. It exploded, showering the floor in glittering shards.

The Commander tore away from me, eyes snapping towards the sound. The unholy screech came again, a sound too sharp, too wrong. Gooseflesh rippled over my skin. *A monster.* "Fuck," he muttered, closing his eyes and taking a deep, steadying breath. He turned back to me, thumb grazing my cheekbone tenderly. "Stay here."

My legs were shaking and my head spun. All I could do was hold myself up against the wall and watch the Commander disappear into the shadows.

I pressed a hand to my chest; I could still feel him. Against my body. Against my lips. The heat of him felt burned into me.

Gods, what is wrong with me?

He was my enemy. A monster to my people. The Commander of Death.

And yet... the moment his mouth claimed mine, I had melted. I *had wanted it*. Craved it. I bit down on a trembling lip, disgusted by the ache that still lingered low in my stomach.

A broken laugh escaped me, a small, bitter sound. My plan had failed, but it had also worked. He hadn't used the blood bargain when he asked me to stay. He had *trusted* me to stay.

Just like every other stupid male who thinks with their cock.

Another screech ripped through the night below, jarring me into action. I pulled on my dirty clothes and shoved the door open, taking the stairs two at a time.

The inn was eerily quiet. The people who had been smiling and laughing were now huddled under tables, wide-eyed with fear. I stood frozen at the bottom of the stairs. The server, Blue, looked at me from under a table, tears glistening against her cheeks. She pressed a single finger to her lips, urging me to be quiet.

I rushed towards the door, ignoring the Fae gesturing for me to get down. As I pulled the heavy door open, a hand clasped around my wrist. Blue pulled at me, desperately trying to pull me away from the door.

"Let go—"

Her hand clamped down on my mouth, cutting off my words. I tugged my hand free, turning and running into the dimly lit street. The smell of rot lingered in the air, overpowering the floral scent of the town.

Blue's footsteps chased me through the dark, too close, too loud. But with every step I took, hers faded further away.

I skidded around a corner and kept running, heart hammering, waiting for her hand to close around my wrist. But she was too far away.

Relief hit first. Then something bitter rose underneath it, twisting in my gut. I swallowed it down hard. I couldn't afford to care about the Commander. About betraying him. About the way his voice had sounded when he told me to stay, or the way his lips felt.

I didn't question how I was still ahead, how a Mortal girl was outrunning a Fae. I slowed just long enough to glance back. The street was empty. Nothing but lantern light and strings of glassy bulbs swaying over the cobblestone.

I rounded a corner and screamed—

The Commander burst out of the shadows. Covered in blue gore, his jaw clenched, and for a moment, it looked like he was in pain.

A screech cut through the night, unearthly and high-pitched. I covered my ears, but they still throbbed. The Commander looked unaffected, grabbing my forearm with a bruising grip and pulling me into his shadows. My very being tore apart, dissolving into nothing. We burst back into existence in front of the inn, nausea swirling in my stomach. But it was the sight before me that made the blood drain from my skin. Blue's head lolled to the side, her scream curdled and weak. The thing over the top of her stood taller than a horse with hunched posture. Its skin was wet and translucent, stretched too tightly over sinew and bone. The sound of wet tearing made my stomach churn as it tore through Blue's stomach with grotesquely long claws. Red pooled against the cobblestone.

The Commander whistled and its head whipped towards the noise. It had no eyes, only slick, translucent flesh stretched where they should've been. Its mouth opened like a wound, circular and lined with teeth meant for tearing.

The Commander swung his sword, but the thing ignored him.

Its attention snapped to me, opening its mouth and screeching. Its muscles coiled before it lunged. I stumbled back, trying to pull my power to the surface. I didn't want to die, not anymore.

The Commander burst from the shadows in front of me, slicing his sword through the monster's skull. The horrible screech cut off. Its body twitched once before slumping to the ground. The Commander pulled his sword free with a wet squelch, boots stomping through blue gore towards me. His eyes were black pits filled with rage as dark veins pulsed through his skin. "You fucking distracted me and now they are dead!"

It wasn't just Blue. A dozen bodies littered the ground. Crimson oozed from the dead, entrails scattering the ground around them. "I could not protect them because *you* ran!"

I swallowed down tears. This town had seemed so peaceful, its people kind and filled with laughter. Now? The dead lined the streets and people hid in fear. Another screech split the air, this one longer, almost pained.

"Are there more of them?" I clenched my fists and squared my shoulders.

"Vaskra travel in mated pairs. It's coming to avenge its mate." The Commander didn't look at me. Black flames licked the metal of his sword as he swung it once and dropped into a fighting stance. The Vaskra crashed down the street, running on all fours with unnatural movements. Its claws scraped against the cobblestone, round maw opening impossibly wide to screech. The

Commander ran towards it. Two monsters charging at each other.

My hands shook at my sides. I needed to *do* something.

Kill, the voice whispered in my head as the melody carried to me on the breeze. With every whisper, the power in my veins surged. My vision darkened at the edges, yet I could see everything. I threw my hands out, head snapping back towards the stars. I could *feel* the Vaskra. Its heartbeat. The blood pumping through its veins. I held onto every particle of water in its body. A song scraped through my throat, urgent and haunting. I *tore*. There was a popping sound followed by a wet squelch. The Vaskra exploded in a spray of blue gore. My song cut off. My head flooded with exhaustion. I was floating and sinking all at once. My knees crashed into the cobblestones, as unconsciousness threatened to drag me into its embrace. Doors opened along the street and Fae emerged from their safety.

"Praise the Commander of Death!"

"The Commander keeps us safe!"

"Hail the Commander!"

"Get back inside! The threat might not be over! Do not come out until daylight breaks!" The Commander's voice thundered through the street.

I tried to stand, but my vision swirled, and I crashed into the ground again with a frustrated cry. I was so weak. So heavy.

Warm arms picked me up from the ground. My head lolled against the Commander's chest.

"I'm too weak to wield my power," I whispered.

He glared down at me with hatred, but there was a small crack in his expression. One moment of softness, before his lip snarled.

Find the pieces. Find the Pieces. Find the pieces.

"Find the pieces," I whispered along with the voice that was chanting in my head, losing my grip on reality.

"You've already absorbed one Soul Relic. I was suspicious, but the moment you couldn't cross Solas's barrier, I *knew*." His voice held a vicious bite to it. But he said what I had suspected. The axe. *One to wield.* I had stolen some of the Sea Goddess's power. But... How? My thoughts turned sluggish. Slow, like honey as my eyes closed, passing out in his arms.

My head pulsed with a sharp pain as my eyes opened against the soft golden glow radiating through the broken window. I was buried under the soft blankets; my skin had been cleaned from last night's gore. A black nightdress made of the softest silk slid across my skin when I sat up.

The Commander stood at the window, his back to me. I couldn't help tracing the rigid lines of his exposed muscles, remembering how they shifted beneath my palms.

"You ran," he said without turning around, fury simmering in his voice.

"I did." I swallowed the slimy feeling in my throat. Why did I feel guilty about running from this beast of a male? "You told Solas that you were going to kill me."

He scoffed as if I were the one who had offended him. "Why did you still kiss me?"

The silence stretched between us, and I shifted uncomfortably. He hung his head, a soft, humourless chuckle escaping his lips. My chest ached and I wrapped my arms around myself.

"It was nothing but a trick, wasn't it, Little Drownling?"

I couldn't answer. I couldn't bring myself to talk. Yes, it had started off as a trick. But I had gotten lost to it. To my want for *him*. When I didn't reply, he turned. Shadows swarmed him, burrowing under his skin. His face was pained as he walked towards the bed. He picked up a book from the bedside table and threw it on the bed in front of me.

"Stay here." His voice shot through me, our blood bargain tingling painfully against my skin. I glared at him as he left the room. I grabbed the pillow from behind me and shoved my face against it and screamed into the pillow until I had nothing left. I let out an unsteady breath and picked up the book, wanting to throw it. But the cover stopped me cold. Intricate silver lines gleamed against the black leather, an unsettling mirror of my blood bargain mark on my left hand.

My pulse throbbed in my temples as I turned the book over in my hands. The lines shimmered, bleeding like ink dropped into water. The first page unfurled in elegant, handwritten script, and I began to read. My lips moved silently as I followed the words.

> *Journal of Rythos Draven*
>
> *As the decades pass, my memories are harder to clutch onto. So, I will write them here. In case I forget.*
>
> *This story started when a goddess fell in love with a Mortal.*
>
> *The Sea Goddess loved the living. Fae, Mortal, even demons. She walked among them, defying the King of Gods, Helion. Her husband.*
>
> *Known for his trickery and cruelty, he ruled*

through fire and demanded sacrifices for favour, thriving off the wars and bloodshed of his subjects.

But Maraveth wanted peace. He hated her compassion, crushing her ideas and refusing to ease the suffering of his subjects.

So, my vicious little goddess created her own spies. Sirens, born of her blood and voice to rule the seas and keep peace between Mortal and Fae.

They were powerful sea-dwelling creatures that could control the will of human and Fae alike. They would often seek out evil souls, casting them under their spell with their song, and fucking them under-water until they drowned. They watched the realms for her, while Maraveth planned to overthrow the Sun God. But I ruined everything.

I had loved the sea as a Mortal and spent many hours on a boat that I crafted by hand. I had painted its sides with florals, waves and stars.

The day I met her, my boat capsized and I had prayed to the mother of the sea to save me.

I almost drowned that day, but when I opened my eyes, the most beautiful being I had ever seen held me in her arms. She visited me often after that. It was not long before I gave her my heart. But more surprisingly, she gave me hers.

I had distracted her, and the Sun God discov-ered her betrayal.

While they are the only beings capable of killing a god, it is the oldest rule that they are not allowed to. So, Helion created monsters to hunt her, forcing her to flee to the depths. So, he poisoned humankind—

Telling them that drinking Siren blood would make them stronger than any Mortal. The sea ran red. Maraveth wept for her slain children in my arms, and every tear broke my heart.

That is why I, a mere Mortal, tried to kill a god. But it was a trap. He changed me. Ripped out my very soul and shoved a curse so dark and twisted inside me that I became nothing but a weapon.

I killed her. I killed the love of my life. I couldn't help it. I had to, the curse demanded it. I shoved my blade through her heart on the Cliff of Souls; her crown of shells tumbled into the depths of the ocean as my heart shattered and broke beyond redemption.

Before her final breath, she split her soul into three Relics, hiding them across the realms. As long as they remain, she will reincarnate and I will be forced to hunt her.

I was forged by the Gods to kill her. But she was the only thing in this world I wanted. I would destroy everything to keep her. But I am bound to this curse, and I am not a hero.

I am her monster.

I am so sorry, Maraveth.

The words began to blur, the ink running like tears. My throat tightened. I could almost *hear* the ocean.

Find the pieces, a voice whispered. Not in the room, but inside me. The weight of the truth pressed down on me with such force I thought it would suffocate me. The Fire Fates had called me Maraveth.

Maraveth was the Sea Goddess.

"It's me," I whispered, voice cracking. All this time, I wasn't cursed. I was condemned. *Every* frantic breath collapsed in on itself. There was no room left for denial, or hope, or pretending I could survive this. I couldn't read anymore.

I slammed the book shut—like it could stop the truth from finishing what it had started.

Panic began to flood my senses, threatening to drag me into the depths of utter despair.

But a sound drifted from outside. Soft at first. A low hum of someone singing. Deep, resonant and threaded with an ache that pulled at the tenderest part of me. My chest ached and I rubbed at it as I hurried to the shattered window, brushing aside glass to lean over the sill. The town square stretched below, bathed in early morning light. Fae gathered in a loose circle, holding hands. At its centre were twelve crosses made from wood, beautiful, vibrant flowers surrounding them. My throat closed with unwanted emotion.

They were showing respect for their dead. I hadn't realised how many had died until I saw the crowd. The Commander stood with the crosses, his haunting voice carrying across the square and pouring into the most heart-wrenching song I had ever heard. A woman stepped into the circle with small, trembling steps. Her dress was torn at the sleeve, as though she had been pulled from the rubble too quickly to mend it. She carried a teddy bear pressed to her chest. Soft blue fur, one eye missing. She knelt before the line of flowers and laid the bear gently among them. A child's toy. *A child.*

My stomach hollowed. When the woman's knees buckled, the Commander moved without hesitation. He was beside her in a heartbeat, catching her under the arms. His dark head bowed close to hers, voice never wavering. The melody vibrated through the stone beneath my feet, low and raw, as though grief itself had found a tune. It wasn't gentle. It wasn't sweet. It was masculine, ancient, something born from mountains and storms and nightfall. A song carved for mourning. A song carved for the broken. I pressed a hand over my mouth.

He steadied the woman until she drew a breath, then he guided her back to the circle where others reached for her hands. His chest rose and fell with the song, powerful and solemn, each note soaked with pain. My chest ached so sharply I had to grip the windowsill to stay upright.

They died because of me. The thought slammed into me with such force that my knees weakened. Those monsters were hunting *me*. The Vaskra had followed *my* scent, my presence, my blood. Those people, the ones burying their dead, the ones clutching each other, suffered because of me. Because I existed. Because the Sea Goddess lived again in me.

Tears blurred the square below. They wouldn't stop until I was dead, or I killed every single one of them.

The Commander's voice grew rougher, like the melody itself was tearing him open. He lifted his head just enough that the sunlight caught his face. He looked older. Harder. But not cold. My breath shook out of me. A sob rose in my throat, sharp and humiliating. I clutched the windowsill tighter, trying to swallow it down, to force myself to be stone, to not feel the full weight of what I'd done. But his song wouldn't let me hide. Every note scraped against my ribs and settled deep, heavy as the sea.

"I'm sorry," I whispered to the empty room. To the broken town. To the people lighting candles. To the child who would never pick up their teddy bear again.

The song ended. The silence that followed was worse. It was thick, suffocating, full of everything words couldn't fix.

The Commander stood alone in the centre of the square, head bowed and hands at his sides. His shoulders rose and fell with a single steadying breath. And even from the distance between us, I felt it. His grief. His rage. His responsibility. Beneath all that, something dangerous pulsed, pulling at me as fiercely as the sea did.

I felt his grief, because I caused it and I wanted to drown whoever had caused so much death in my name.

THIRTY-ONE
RELIC

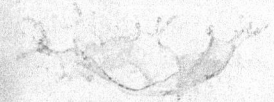

The mid-morning sun burnt my skin and made me slick with sweat as I squirmed away from the Commander in the saddle. He hadn't said a word the night before after returning from standing vigil in the courtyard. I had feigned sleep to avoid questions about the tear stains on my cheeks, and if he had realized it was a ruse, he said nothing.

He hadn't said much this morning either, aside from insisting that I find the next Relic. Never mind that I had no idea where they were.

"Like I have told you already, I don't know where they are!"

Winston shifted beneath us restlessly as the Commander shoved the reins back into my hands.

"You do know." He placed a large hand over my chest, and I stilled under his touch, hating the way heat washed over my skin.

"In here," he grumbled, "follow it."

I breathed out slowly, ignoring the heat tingling against my skin from his touch.

The ethereal woman had led me to the axe and perhaps she was still trying to lead me to another. Every night since the storm, the same dream of her death... *my* death had haunted me. The dream always ended the same way. With the crown tumbling off the cliff into the crashing waves, just like it was written in Rythos' journal.

What if the crown was the Relic? My chest ached at the thought, and I knew I was right. "It's in the Dead Sea. I think I have been dreaming of the first time I was killed. In it, I see a crown made of shells."

His hand still hadn't moved, as if he was frozen. A moment passed and everything was still. Too still. His hand still rested heavily against my beating heart.

"Do you ever see who killed you?" he asked quietly.

"No, I don't know what Rythos Draven looks like." The answer was disappointing. Not knowing the face of the monster designed to kill me was unsettling. It could be anyone.

"You have started reading the journal, I take it," he said, moving his hand away. My silence pressed down on him, stretching as Winston walked through the long swaying grass.

"Lead Umbra where your heart pulls you. Find your crown."

I dug my heels in and flicked the reins; Winston took off in a gallop. I refused to call him Umbra, but I had learnt a lot riding with the Commander. It felt exhilarating holding the reins. We galloped for what felt like hours, the sun following us across the sky. I couldn't help eyeing it, wondering if Helion watched us through the rays of sunlight. Something I had enjoyed so much when I had first gotten here now felt like a violation.

The smell of salt lingered on the breeze, making my skin tingle. We crested a small hill, and a gasp left me.

Blue. Endless blue devoured the horizon. The roar of waves crashing against the cliff sent a calming surge through my body.

I pulled on Winston's reins, slowing him to a trot. Ahead, the cliff expanded to a grassy outlet and my blood chilled. There. That was where I died. I didn't know how I knew. But I did.

The Commander slid off the saddle behind me, and I didn't wait for him to help. I slid off clumsily after him but caught myself before I fell. The wind pulled at my hair as I walked to the edge of the cliff. The waves crashed violently below, blue waves churning to white froth. A coldness washed over my skin, and I knew she was there. The unearthly woman stood next to me, tear-stained eyes trained on the water. She looked at me, full lips tilting into a sad smile.

"Find the pieces," she said before tipping over the edge. Her translucent dress fluttered in the breeze. I gasped, leaning over to watch her disappear into the waves. A thrill shot through me.

"Careful," the Commander warned as I moved closer to the edge. He watched me tentatively, his eyebrows pushed together when I gave him a small smile. His shadows tore at his skin, digging into him.

Before he could react, I leapt into the open air.

The Commander cursed behind me before the wind swallowed all noise. Whipping past me as I fell. My stomach dropped. The waves crashed over me. The cool embrace of the water tingled against my skin. I sank deeper into the depths, the saltwater pressing against me like a soothing balm. Unlike Ascension, I could see around me. Beams of sunlight pierced the sea. I tried to swim, but my boots dragged behind me. I kicked them off and kicked my legs.

The ghost of the Sea Goddess floated below me, leading me further into the deep. The current pulled me with every churn of the waves above. The aching feeling in my chest grew with every kick further into the deep. The Relic was close; I could sense it, but I was so far away from the surface now. My lungs clenched. The ache bloomed into a searing fire.

I couldn't tell if it was stupidity or instinct that pushed me forward, but I kept going.

My chest convulsed. Air. I needed air. The sunlight was nothing more than a distant flicker above me. Too far. I would never reach it in time. My arms grew heavy. My vision dimmed at the edges. I was going to drown. *Again.* Would I die this time?

Water pressed against my mouth, begging for entrance. I couldn't fight the instinct any longer. I inhaled. Water rushed into my lungs. I braced for the burning. For the insufferable feeling of being smothered from the inside. But it didn't come. I gasped again, but there was no panic. Only... strange clarity. My chest expanded easily. No burning. No choking.

A broken laugh shattered through me, turning the last of my air into a bubble that floated up towards the surface. Any doubt I had about being the Sea Goddess's reincarnation drifted away with it.

My vision sharpened, and suddenly, the water was no longer murky. The sunlight filtered through the water, casting rays of light that glittered over a crumbling castle below me. It was carved from stone and coral, towers half-devoured by barnacles and time. The windows were dark. Broken. It would have been beautiful once. Before the war.

Swimming along the ocean floor, my hand brushed through the glistening sand. I longed to explore the castle, to find its secrets. *My* secrets. But right now, I had to focus.

The Sea Goddess floated in front of me, tears flowing from her eyes into the ocean.

"Break his curse." Her words floated to me, crashing into me more strongly than any wave. "The light is in the dark, and the dark will see light again. Do not let him see the light again."

She rushed towards me, diving through my chest.

I gasped, frantically looking around. Glittering caught my eye amongst the coral growing from the sea floor. The pulling in my chest turned to an urgent ache. A crown lay half-buried in coral. My hand wrapped around the cold, ancient metal. But it didn't give. No matter how hard I tugged, the coral seemed to tighten. I slipped, the coral slicing through my palm. Black blood floated up like ribbons through the water. My blood seeped into the crown and the coral reacted, cracking beneath my fingers before breaking apart.

Black metal twisted into points that turned into vibrant blue coral at the tips, small shells nestled against it like jewels. I stared at it for a moment, enthralled by its beauty. Then power radiated up my arm. A sharp, vibrating pain flooded my veins and tore through me as the Soul Relic poured itself into me. My scream sent bubbles streaming to the surface.

Shapes rose from the depths in a frenzy. Ghostly figures flew past me, hair like liquid. Tails swishing through the water. Their bodies shimmered like fractured light. They were beautiful. *Sirens.*

"She is here..." one whispered, voice like a current in my mind. "The last one..."

"She has the crown..." They streamed through the water, circling me. I couldn't move. My heart raced in my chest. One dove forward. I tried to move back, but I wasn't quick enough. It was *her*. *Me*. The Sea Goddess.

She stopped an inch from my face. Gooseflesh broke out across my skin as her bright blue eyes bore into me. Her translucent hair floated like tendrils of ink, her dress gone and replaced by scales. She reached a translucent hand towards the crown, gesturing for me to place it on my head.

The Sirens paused to watch me.

I placed the crown on my head, the weight settling against my soul and the ghost of the Sea Goddess grinned.

Pain seared through my body. *Crack.*

I screamed, bubbles tearing from my mouth, hands reaching to cradle my leg, now jarred at the wrong angle. *Crack. Crack. Crack.*

My body contorted, pain overwhelmed my senses. I thrashed in the water. Was I being attacked? Was it the blood bargain? My bones snapped with a sickening crunch, twisting, tearing. Fire ripped through my veins, searing my flesh from the inside out.

My scream tore free— raw and animalistic.

A sob tore loose from my throat, raw and broken. Another crack splintered through my legs, white-hot pain cutting off my cry. I gasped through the torment, forcing water into my lungs. The pain ebbed, leaving me hollow, and shaking. I had sunk against the ocean floor, broken body heaped against the sand.

I looked down at my legs, expecting to see a mess of gore. A gasp escaped my lips. Where my legs should have been, a tail shimmered in their place. Turquoise, radiant, and impossibly alive. Scales overlapped like facets of gemstone, each one catching the light and breaking it into ripples of blue and green that danced across my skin.

I shifted, and the tail moved with me, powerful yet fluid, as though it had always been mine. The fin flared wide, translucent and veined with silver, delicate as silk but thrumming with strength. For a heartbeat I couldn't breathe. Not from the water in my lungs, but from the sheer wonder of it.

My body was no longer foreign. No longer broken. It felt... right.

I ripped off the remainder of my pants with sharpened claws. Scales shimmered over my hips, ending just before my navel. My breasts were uncovered, but fine scales traced across them like a glittering veil, offering only the illusion of modesty. Every grain of sand was suddenly distinct as if the sea itself had been carved from crystal. I could see farther than I ever had, shadows no longer hiding but gleaming with secret life. The water was no longer silent... It sang.

I heard the scrape of shells against stone, the deep thrumming call of something vast and ancient in the depths, even the faintest hiss of bubbles escaping my own lips. Every note layered into a melody sharper and more alive than air had ever carried. The current caressed my skin like a thousand fingertips. Something broke the surface above me with a violent splash. The Commander.

He plunged through the water like a stone, his sword still strapped to him. He swam frantically towards me. Eyes wild. The shadows that always moved with him bled away, thinning into the dark like ink bleeding away in water. Without them, he looked less dangerous, almost Mortal.

Panic seized my chest. *No.* The word tore through me without sound. The sea's curse would kill him. He was sinking fast, his dark hair streaming behind him. The sea wanted him. It wanted everything. I pushed towards him, the current slamming against me as though it meant to drag us apart. "No!" I screamed, bubbles shredding the word. My arms burned as I forced my body after him, my new tail slicing through the water with desperate power. The lines of his face softened, his mouth parted. The sight hit something deep and unfamiliar inside me. Fear, grief, maybe something older than either. I couldn't let the sea have him. I didn't know why. Only that it would break me if I did. I wrapped both arms around his waist and held on. His weight nearly tore me backward.

"Please," I begged, though he couldn't hear me.

The sea surged, angrily. The pull of it tried to wrench him away, to tear him back into the depths. I pressed my face against his chest and thrashed my tail, every stroke a fight. My body screamed, muscles trembling with the strain, but I would not let go. Couldn't.

The water around us brightened as I swam towards the surface, and the rays of golden light mocked my efforts. One last push and my head broke through the waves.

I gasped, hauling him with me. His body was heavy, dead weight in my arms, but I clung to him.

"No," I whispered against his jaw, salt lingering on my lips. "You don't get to die here." For a heartbeat, the waves stilled. I pushed him up on one of the large rocks, pulling myself up next to him with shaky arms. His head lolled to the side. I gripped his shoulders and shook him. "Come on!" I begged, my voice cracking with an emotion I refused to name. I pulled a knife from his belt, slicing a deep gash across my wrist.

Gripping his face with one hand, I shoved the cut against his mouth.

For a moment there was nothing. Just the frantic beat of my heart. The pull in my chest as though my heart was about to break and the dull crash of the waves.

Then he coughed. A ragged, broken sound. The air rushed out of me in relief so sharp it almost hurt. Water spilled from his mouth, and when it finally cleared, I pressed my wrist back to his mouth. His throat moved with every swallow, my blood pouring into his mouth. His eyes sprung open, endless darkness staring back at me. He sat up, blood smearing across his mouth and chin as he shoved my arm away.

"Why did you do that!" I yelled at him, "You know the waters are cursed—"

"You were in pain!" he shouted, his hands locking around my shoulders like restraints. "I *felt* your pain and nothing else fucking mattered." His eyes bored into me, holding me captive and threatening to devour me.

Darkness rose around us, tearing through me in a familiar, terrifying embrace as it tore me apart. Everything pitched into darkness for a moment until we burst into existence on the cliff that was above us. My scales prickled against the grass uncomfortably. That was the only warning I got before blinding pain gripped me.

Crack. Crack. Crack. The noise was more sickening outside of the water. A scream tore through me with each snap of my bones. Warm arms embraced me, holding me through each wave of pain. Just as I thought the pain was unescapable, it finally ebbed away. The only thing holding me together was *his* arms holding my now naked, trembling body.

"You absorbed the Relic, didn't you?" the Commander murmured, running hands through my hair. He looked at me with fascination, but his lack of shock unsettled me.

"Yes," I whispered into the quiet peace between us.

His arms tightened around me. "Hold on to me."

His shadows tore through me again. My stomach dropped as I pitched into the darkness, blinking a moment later against the dull light of the room at the inn.

THIRTY-TWO
SURRENDER

The Commander lit a candle on the bedside table, as I stood there holding the blanket he had draped around my shoulders and dripping water on the hardwood floor.

The muscles in his back bunched with every movement, and the aching in my chest made my breath hitch.

"I cannot be killed, you know. Not even by the cursed water." He paused and let out a heavy sigh. "Like you, I have tried to die many times."

I gripped the blanket tighter, knuckles turning white at the seriousness in his voice. He was comparing us. A monster and a princess, and as much as I didn't want to admit, we had more in common than we should.

"You thought I was going to die, didn't you?" he asked, turning to look at me.

"Yes."

"And you tried to save me?" he said slowly, mulling the words over in his accent as if he were worried that they would get lost in translation.

When I nodded and looked away from him, he took a step closer to me, and for the first time, I didn't retreat.

"Why?"

"I've never been good at doing what I'm supposed to do," I admitted softly. He grunted in thought, moving to light another candle.

"I was not soft enough to be a princess, nor was I strong enough to be a soldier."

"That is because you are neither of those things. You are a goddess."

My breath caught at the word.

He had known the whole time, hadn't he? I composed my features and pressed on. I did not want to talk about what I was. "I'm not good at being your prisoner, either." I took a slow step towards him, the blanket trailing on the floor.

He turned to watch me, dark eyes tracking the movement with open suspicion. "Because you tried to run?" His voice had deepened, taking on a hint of gravel.

"Because I want you."

His eyes closed for a moment, the muscle in his jaw clenching as he fought for his composure.

I dropped the blanket, the material pooling at my feet. My wet silver hair clung to my body, keeping my breasts mostly covered. His throat worked once, swallowing hard as his gaze slid over my body.

"I tried to save you, Commander. Because despite knowing better, I can't stop thinking about you."

"Fuck it," he growled, moving so fast towards me that I gasped. He towered over me, hands gripping my waist with bruising force. His eyes closed, jaw clenching as if he were struggling to regain control.

"If we cross this line, it will not be a one-time thing." He gripped my face roughly, forcing me to look up at him. "I am *possessive. Demanding. A monster.* You will be *mine.* Understood?"

I nodded. I shouldn't want this. But every part of my body ached to be his.

"Here's what's going to happen," he growled, caging me against the wall with his enormous form. He was a predator. But Gods help me, I wanted to be his prey. "You are going to crawl onto that bed, and I am going to ruin every fucking reason you had to run from me." His hand wrapped around my throat and tightened, forcing a breathless whimper from my lips as my body leant into him instead of away. "You will cum on my mouth. My hands. On my cock. Until you forget you fucking hate me. Until the only thing you remember is how fucking good I make you feel."

His arousal tingled against my skin like a living thing, sinking into my pores and feeding my power. Wrapping my arms around his neck, I rose onto the tips of my toes and dragged him towards me. His lips were so soft against mine at first. Just a small brush. Until he growled against me, gripped my thighs and lifted me until my legs wrapped around his waist.

"Never mind, I am too fucking impatient," he rasped against my lips before he threw me down onto the bed. His body suddenly pressed against me, muscles shifting beneath my roaming hands. His mouth was hot against my neck, my skin tingling where he touched me. His large hand splayed across my stomach, sliding down between my thighs, circling in a teasing motion. "So wet for your monster," he ground out against my flesh, biting down against my skin. A moan tore through me. "Fuck, make that noise again."

His fingers picked up speed, and I had no choice over the sounds escaping my mouth. His mouth brushed the swell of my breast teasingly before his lips closed around my nipple. I dug my fingernails into his back as he slid one finger inside me, my muscles flexing around him.

"You are too fucking tight for me." He pulled his finger out of me as he stood and I made a sound of protest.

His fingers dug into my thighs, dragging me to the edge of the bed before kneeling on the ground. He pulled my legs over his shoulders and his breath ghosted over the inside of my thigh, hot enough to burn.

The Commander of Death knelt before *me*, and I had never seen such a beautiful sight. He pushed two fingers inside of me, and my hips rocked against them, begging for friction he wouldn't give.

"Impatient little thing," he tsked before his tongue, warm and soft circled my clit. I cried out. Pure pleasure spread through me in pulses. He was merciless, sucking me into his mouth. The heat built. He added a third finger and slid his tongue against my clit. A broken cry left my throat as the orgasm consumed me, my body clamping around his fingers in desperate, involuntary waves.

"You came so fast for me," he praised. "You've got another one right there already, don't you?" His fingers thrust into me again, lips pressing against my throbbing flesh. Gods, he was going to destroy me. I fisted his hair, pulling his face harder against me as the pressure coiled tight and merciless inside my body. His fingers dug into my thighs, the hint of pain slicing through the pleasure and tipping it violently over the edge.

A helpless, broken sound tore from my throat as my thighs shook against his shoulders, my body locking around the sensation with no escape. Pleasure crashed through me in relentless spasms. Too sharp. Too consuming. Leaving me trembling and breathless as it tore me apart from the inside out.

The Commander dropped my legs, an arrogant smile tugging at his lips, like he knew exactly what he had just done to me.

I stood on trembling legs in front of him. He was still kneeling, and I tipped his face upward with my thumb against his chin, claiming his attention. "Stand," I demanded, my voice not entirely my own. A small thrill shot through me as he obeyed, standing to tower over me. It was my turn to smirk at him. I wanted to see him lose control, and Gods was he about to break.

His dark eyes devoured my every movement as I got on my knees and undid his belt, pushing his pants down. His cock sprang free and I paused. It was monstrous. Heavy. Thick and long. "This," I whispered, gripping his cock with both hands, "isn't going to fit."

A masculine rumble vibrated through his chest as I stroked him.

"I will *make* it fit," he vowed. I pushed at his legs, making him sit on the edge of the bed so I could reach him. He watched me hungrily as I brought the tip of his cock to my mouth, swirling my tongue around it. He cursed, cock twitching in my hands. My lips wrapped around him, and I shoved as much of him inside me as I could. My tongue ran along his shaft with each long movement as I took him.

"Look up at me with your mouth full," he rasped. Tears clung to my eyelashes, and his hand gripped my hair at the back of my neck, as he drove his cock in and out of my mouth.

I loved the way he tasted, even slamming against the back of my throat.

I may have been the one on my knees, but *I* was in

control. "That's it." His gasp turned into a growl of pleasure. "You look so fucking beautiful on your knees."

I moaned around him, his praise shooting straight to my core. He gripped my face, sliding his cock out of my mouth. He kissed me roughly, devouring me and pulling me onto his lap.

"This will help you relax." The sharp sting of his canines against my neck took my breath away, edging into pleasure. Warmth spread through me like honey. My hips rocked against his hard length eagerly, desperate for friction. I wrapped my hand around his length, feeling how he trembled. How tightly he fought himself. He was always so composed. So disciplined and deadly. But under my touch? He shook.

I lifted my hips, pushing his cock against my entrance. The Commander moaned against my neck, muscles coiling beneath me like he was scared to move. I pressed down, inch by inch. He stretched me, filling me to the point of pain. I stopped before he was fully seated in me, adjusting to his thickness. His breathing was laboured against my neck and his fingers dug into my flesh, anchoring me against him. Gods, he was so big.

"Fuck," he hissed against my neck before tipping his head back. My blood was smeared over his lips, dripping down his chin as he looked up at me.

"Lyra..." My name tore from him, raw, like he hadn't spoken it out loud before. Like it cost him something. His thumb brushed my skin with a tenderness that didn't match the heat in his eyes. And in that moment, I felt the truth he'd never say aloud. He wasn't worried about giving me his body, it was his heart he was protecting. *But I think I wanted to take that too.*

I pushed the rest of his cock inside of me, gasping and

digging my fingers into his back. So full. So thick. He was everywhere. He growled, struggling to stay still to give me time to adjust. I rolled my hips, giving him permission to move and he met me with every thrust.

"You take me so fucking well."

His hand reached between us, fingers circling my clit with every thrust. I was going to shatter. And Gods help me, I would not be the same again.

"Don't you dare cum yet," he commanded and my whole body trembled. "Look at me." He fisted my hair and pulled me into every thrust.

I was swallowed by the darkness in his eyes. I didn't know where I ended and he began. "Please," I begged between moans. I was right there—I needed—

"Gods!"

His hand slapped against the flesh of my ass, squeezing almost painfully. "That's it, scream to the Gods. I want them to know you are *mine.*"

Pleasure detonated low in my belly, a sudden, blinding rush that stole my breath. I clung to him helplessly as it tore through me.

"Good girl," he grunted, "cuming all over my cock." He thrust through every pulse before he groaned, cock twitching inside me as his warmth spread through me. We collapsed against each other, holding one another as if we were not enemies.

My chest ached uncomfortably as the world slowly settled around us, the room too quiet.

The Commander held me, his breath coming unsteadily as his shadows dug into his skin.

I wasn't ready to let him go. Not yet. Maybe not ever.

He reached out and brushed a loose strand of hair away from my cheek with shaking fingers. "We should not have done that," he whispered, voice breaking with emotion.

"Do you regret—"

"No," he cut me off. "That's the problem." He lifted his hand again but stopped before touching me, as if afraid his palm would burn. "What the fuck have you done to me?" he whispered, voice rough.

My heart squeezed painfully as my fingers skimmed his jawline. He closed his eyes like the touch undid him entirely. Leaning forward, his forehead rested against mine. It was something far more terrifying than letting him touch me. This felt like trust. Like intimacy.

I hesitated for a moment, then curled against his chest. His breath hitched as I placed a hand over his heart. After a long, shaking moment, he wrapped an arm around me and laid back, drawing me into the warm, solid line of his body. Bliss flooded my veins as butterflies swarmed my stomach. His hand trailed up my spine, slow and reverent—

"Stop!" I demanded, sitting upright. But it was too late.

He froze. Every muscle in his body turned to stone. His breath stopped completely. "Lyra…" My name left him in a tortured whisper. His fingers moved carefully, tracing one raised line… then another… then another.

My throat closed. Instinctively, I tried to pull away, but he caught my arm. Not forcefully, just firm enough to keep me from retreating. His touch shook as he brushed my hair aside, exposing the puckered scars marking my back.

"Who the fuck did this to you?"

A shiver ripped up my spine at the darkness in his voice. His eyes were pure black, his voice quiet and deadly. I shook my head, unable to look at him.

Gods, I wanted a hole to appear and swallow me. I didn't want him to see how broken I was.

"Lyra," he warned, voice almost pleading.

"Punishments," I ground out. His jaw clenched so hard I heard his teeth grind, but he sat patiently and waited for me to find the words.

"My father said I was cursed. The only cure was to bleed the evil from me..." My voice wavered. "The priest took over when I was eighteen. He left... other scars as well." I swallowed the rest. He didn't need the details. I couldn't survive seeing the disgust in his face.

He went unnervingly still. "*Other* scars?" he repeated, like each syllable repulsed him. Something dangerous lurked beneath the words.

My hands curled into the sheets as I struggled to find the right words. I was scared, but I wanted to tell him.

"He bled me..." I forced the words through numb lips. "Sometimes I would be chained in the dungeon for days, dripping blood into vials. But after, he would also *use* me."

The Commander closed his eyes—slowly, painfully. But before he did, I could see the devastation in his gaze. My eyes swam with tears that I would not let fall, my cheeks burning with shame. He lifted a trembling hand and touched the side of my face. "Look at me." His voice broke. "I will tie up every single person who hurt you and let you torture them until your heart heals, and when you are done, I will slit their throats." My breath hitched at his promise, something dangerous spreading through my heart.

"I vow it to you. Fuck the Gods. Fuck the Fates. Fuck any alliance. I will make you feel safe," he whispered into my hair. And for the first time in my life, wrapped in his arms. I believed it. His words hit me like a shockwave, sending heat spiralling through every inch of me.

"I stabbed the priest in the heart at Ascension." I

smirked up at him through tears. His large thumb brushed a tear away and his cock grew hard inside of me again.

"That's my vicious Little Drownling," he rolled his hips, moving against my sensitive flesh. I gasped and clung to him, rolling my hips against him.

The Commander's hand slid up my spine, tracing every scar, every wound, as if memorising them. He flipped us, hovering over me, bracing himself with strong arms. The candlelight painted his face in gold and darkness. Every thrust claimed me, anchoring me. It was possessive and gentle all at once. He saw every broken part of me, and somehow it felt like he was putting the pieces of my heart back together.

I let him, even though I knew it would shatter all over again the moment I had to give him up—to marry his king.

THIRTY-THREE
OBSIDIAN COURT

The afternoon sun had faded, and stars twinkled in the dark until dawn crawled across the sky. I had spent hours tangled in the bedsheets with my captor. Every inch of me was sore and warm with the memory of him. I had never felt so satisfied and confused at once.

I pressed my fingers into my temple, willing the dull ache to fade. I had offered my hand in marriage to the Fae ruler to unite the Kingdoms and then slept with his Commander. I couldn't deal with that.

Pale sunlight spilled through the broken window, refracting against shards of glass and casting scattered rainbows across the heavy book open before me. The Commander had left earlier to meet with the town's leader and help with the burials of their lost people. I hadn't gone. Their pain might have broken me completely. So, I hid. And I read.

My fingers trembled as I skimmed page after page, searching for anything useful. A way into the heavens, a weakness in the Gods, a description of the monster who wrote this journal. Nothing. Until something caught my eye.

> *No matter how hard I try, I cannot remember Helion's face. I know he created me, I know he cursed me. I must have seen his face.*
>
> *I found a mage; he looked through my memories and told me the god had stolen them to hide his identity. Fucking coward.*
>
> *I could not find him, but the other Gods could. I took it upon myself to tell the other Gods about what truly happened to Maraveth. Only a god is strong enough to kill another god, even though it is against their laws.*
>
> *They were not kind to my creator, but they were not cruel enough. The other Gods merely stripped of Helion his throne and broke his claim to the sun.*
>
> *The best torture was putting the god who craved light into the darkest pits of hell.*
>
> *That's how the Sun God fell into the dark.*

The Hells were rising. The beasts slipping through the Mourning Woods weren't just random horrors, they were *Helion's* creations, hunting *me*.

The Nightbourne flashed into my head. They had wounded me. But then they had dragged me as though they were taking me somewhere. My grip tightened on the book. The room felt suddenly smaller, the air colder. Were they trying to kill me? Or take me to Helion himself?

A soft creak cut through the silence, and I knew without looking that it was the Commander. My heartbeat stumbled, nerves fluttering in my stomach. I closed the book slowly, my palms damp against the worn cover.

Dirt smudged the edge of the Commander's sharp jaw, his eyes dark and weary. The burial rites had taken their toll. His chest rose in a sharp inhale, as though the sight of me in this bed was something he hadn't expected.

"You didn't run," he murmured, voice laced with exhaustion and something softer.

"I couldn't even if I tried," I admitted with a smirk.

His gaze dropped, lingering on the blanket pooled around my hips where bruises in the shape of his hands marked my skin beneath the thin slip he had given me. He took in the faint tremble in my fingers that held onto the book. His jaw flexed. "You're hurt—"

"I'm sore," I corrected, cutting him off as a blush crept up my face. "But in the most perfect way." His eyes darkened, shadows viciously pulling at his skin and burying inside of him.

"Your shadows—why do they hurt you when you are near me?" I wondered out loud.

"You are very observant, Little Drownling," he chuckled. "Do not worry, it is worth the pain."

My stomach fluttered, eyes roaming his body with open hunger. "When you drink my blood, it makes the shadows less... volatile, doesn't it?" His eyebrows raised. Perhaps he was surprised that I had noticed such a small detail. But the truth was, I noticed everything about him.

"Yes, it gives me relief," he admitted.

I hummed softly, pushing the journal aside. "You can drink from me whenever you want."

He crossed the room in three strides before catching

himself, stopping short of touching me. The muscles in his shoulders tightened, a visible effort not to reach out. To bite into my skin. "How has your reading been?" he asked quietly instead, controlling his urges.

My shoulder dropped and I tried not to frown at the question. "Horrible, actually. It is a tragic story," I said, unable to hide the disdain from my voice. "Helion's monsters are hunting me. But were they not designed to kill me? The Nightbourne acted like they were trying to *take* me." The Commander stared at the journal, his expression unreadable. Then his eyes lifted, locking on mine with terrifying intensity.

"He wants you because you are *powerful*. Whoever's side you pick will be the side that wins. But Helion is desperate, angry that his monsters are failing him. I have received word of another attack of Skanthi in Alton last night, a town north from here. Many were slaughtered."

A shaky breath escaped me as I twirled my hair with my fingers. "Will my marriage to your ruler make him angrier? Cause more death? Maybe you should give me to Helion and end it all."

The Commander stilled, muscles turning tense. "With you by his side, he will take the realms even faster. That's why he is hunting you this time."

The silence between us was too thick and a sinking feeling clawed into my stomach. "How do you know so much about this?"

"I've read the journal, and I have my hunches. That's why I want your power imbued into weapons. Only a god had the power to kill another god and their monsters."

"But you kill the monsters..." I trailed off, hands dropping into my lap.

"Because I am the Commander of Death. My darkness can kill *almost* anything."

My blood ran cold.

"Lyra—"

"Don't," I cut in sharply, though my voice trembled. "I can't... I shouldn't have. *We* shouldn't have. What if your ruler accepts my offer? Will you watch me marry another male to save the Kingdoms?" His expression crumpled for a heartbeat, just enough to reveal something raw beneath before the mask of the Commander slipped into place. "I cannot watch you marry another male," he said, stepping closer. "I want you by *my* side." His voice was low, even. But there was a vulnerability in his voice that I hadn't heard before and I stared at him for a long moment.

"I know you can feel it too," he said quietly, cutting through the silence. The shadows around him stilled, as if listening. "Stop lying to yourself."

I looked away, not wanting him to see *my* vulnerability.

"I'll stop lying if you tell me your name," I demanded, crossing my arms.

He chuckled, gripping my chin with his thumb and forefinger and forcing my gaze to his. "You are cute when you are demanding, but I cannot tell you that." Heat tingled against my skin, power sinking into my veins. *He wants me.*

I bared my teeth at him, smacking his hand away and reaching for his belt.

"I will torture it out of you then." Shoving his pants down, a thrill shot through my stomach to find his cock already hard, the thick veins pulsing with need.

"I might need that blood, Little Drownling," he gritted through clenched teeth, his shadows swarming him viciously.

I smirked up at him. "Tell me your name and you can."

"You touching me like that is worth any pain."

I glared up at him, shoving him deep into my mouth until his head tipped back and a masculine moan tore through his chest. Heat engulfed me, the power from his lust flooding through me. I squeezed his balls with one hand, and he cursed in the Fae language.

Shadows crawled from the corners of the room, circling around his body and striking him. I scraped my teeth along his shaft and bit.

"You fucking vicious little thing," he hissed. "Whatever you do to me I *will* return." The promise sent heat through my stomach that gathered between my legs—

A sharp knock on the door made me still.

"Go away," the Commander growled through the door. They knocked again, and I sat back on my heels, his cock popping out of my mouth. His eyes fluttered shut, his body dissipating into the shadows and reappearing, flickering like a spluttering candle. He shoved himself back into his pants and wiped a thumb across my mouth before stalking across the room. He gripped the door handle and pulled it open with such force I was surprised it did not break.

A blonde male stood in the doorway in black formal armour with an emblem of three-pointed silver stars over his heart. He bent at the waist in a formal greeting that seemed ill-fitting.

"What do you want?" the Commander ground out.

The guard handed him a scroll, and as the Commander unrolled it, the guard's grey eyes crashed into mine with such intensity the world threatened to fall away. Like storm clouds. His lip curled and heat crawled up my neck. I was still on my knees, wearing nothing but a slip.

"Keep looking at her and I will gouge your eyes from your skull and feed them to you,"

The Commander rumbled with deathly calm as he read.

The guard looked down at his feet. "My apologies, Commander."

He ignored him and turned to me with an unreadable expression. "Your father has accepted the alliance and is travelling here immediately. You will unite the Kingdoms by the end of this week." The Commander scrunched up the scroll, throwing it at the ground with a snarl. "Collect my horse from the stable and meet us in the square," he ordered the guard. My mind was spinning, the floor threatening to give way beneath me. Reality crashed into me with a sickening realisation. I was going to see my father. I was marrying someone I had never met. My time with the Commander was over.

Every gallop of Winston's hooves drove me forward like a blow. The jolt of each stride punched up my spine, rattling my teeth and turning my stomach sour. Nausea churned in my gut, low and stubborn. But it wasn't the riding... It was everything else. I hadn't spoken a single word since we left the inn. Not because I didn't have anything to say, but because I was terrified of what might come out if I tried. My thoughts were a knotted mess. Sharp and tangled. Every time I tried to grab one, three more slipped through my fingers. *His* hands on me, *his* voice in my ear, the tugging in my chest, the marriage, the book, Helion, the monsters, the Relics.

I had slept with my Kingdom's enemy. My captor. And

now he was taking me to the man I was meant to marry. To give the people the best chance of surviving the rise of the Seven Hells. *My* decision. But the man pressed up against me, the same man whose touch repulsed me mere weeks ago, was someone I wasn't ready to let go. The way he gripped my waist made me think he felt the same. If I refused to marry the Fae ruler, Helion could destroy everything. But I *wanted* the Commander. The shame. The confusion. The want. The dread. It all tangled in my lungs until breathing felt impossible.

The sun beat down without mercy, warm on my back, but inside I felt cold. Hollowed out. Like I'd left pieces of myself in that bed at the inn and wasn't sure which ones I needed to survive what came next. I swallowed hard, staring at Winston's dark mane whipping in the wind. If I opened my mouth, even for a moment, the truth would pour out of me in a broken, humiliating rush—

So, I stayed silent. Because silence was the only thing that would save everyone.

The guard galloped on a white horse in front of us, my eyes drawn to him. I could not shake the feeling of familiarity. Yet, the more I looked at him, the stranger that feeling sat. His hair stayed blonde, his posture too rigid, his build wrong. For a moment, his eyes had reminded me of Riven. Perhaps I was just missing him.

"There." The Commander's voice cut cleanly through my spiralling thoughts. He pointed as we crested a rolling hill. Wind swept across the tall grasses, brushing the blades in slow, rhythmic waves like the sea breathing on land. I followed his gesture, breath leaving me in surprise. Beyond the field, carved into the base of a sheer cliff, rose a fortress of pure obsidian. A castle of shadow. It had sharp edges, but it glittered in the sunlight captivatingly. I craned my neck as we approached, nerves fluttering through me. It didn't look built so much as grown from the mountain itself, as though the earth had birthed it. And I was riding straight into it. Straight into the arms of the king I had promised myself to, when every part of my being longed to stay with the monster dragging me there.

THIRTY-FOUR
SECRETS

We approached the castle walls. Towering slabs of impenetrable stone climbed so high that my neck ached to see the top. A cluster of Fae waited before the gates. They were shirtless warriors armed to the teeth. Solas stood at the front, huge and beaming, and relief pricked at my chest. A familiar face.

The male beside him, however, made my smile drop. Broad. Unmoving. Armoured in dark onyx scarred from battle. A jagged scar ran down the right side of his face. Harsh, but not hindering of his handsome features. His eyes swept over us once, sharp and calculating. A silent assessment. He didn't speak as we approached. Didn't even blink. And yet the warriors behind him shifted, the way prey reacts when the predator lifts its head.

The Commander brought Winston to a halt in front of who I assumed was my betrothed. The shift was near-silent, bodies straightening and gazes sharpening.

The male with the scar watched me curiously. I felt the weight of his attention as if it pressed against my skin, but I kept my chin lifted.

The Commander slid off the side of the horse, gripping my waist and lifting me off with ease. He let my body slide down his, the summer dress he had made me wear hitching as my feet found the ground. Heat blistered my cheeks at his inappropriateness. I straightened out the dark green dress; its material was thin and had two slits that went almost to my hips to allow me to ride on horseback.

Solas smiled warmly, already gripping the Commander's forearm in greeting. He turned to me, and before I could protest, wrapped his arms around me and lifted me into a hug. I gasped as he twirled me once before setting me down. A small laugh bubbled out of me despite myself. The Fae giant seemed more like an excited puppy than a warrior. His nostrils flared and his grin faltered, eyes shooting to the Commander with raised eyebrows. The redness in my cheeks deepened with understanding. He could smell the Commander on me. Oh Gods, I had ruined everything.

The Commander strode towards the waiting male and extended an arm. They clasped forearms, pulling each other into a solid shoulder-to-shoulder smack of a greeting.

"You're late," the male in armour said, voice low and stern.

"Or the old age is finally making you senile." The Commander smirked. The male looked barely of thirty. But then again, the Commander was also ageless.

There was a tense silence lasting a beat too long and I shifted from one foot to another until both men burst out laughing. It was the most informal greeting I had ever seen in court. "Caelum, this is Lyra Meridian," the Commander said as his laughter died off, gesturing towards where I stood, confused and lost.

"It is a pleasure to make your acquaintance, Caelum." I

dipped my head in formal greeting. The Commander laughed, that genuine sound that made my chest feel warm.

"And where were *those* manners when you met *me*, Little Drownling?" the Commander murmured from behind me. I tried not to smirk, remembering how ridiculous he looked with soup dripping off him.

I ignored him and tilted my chin higher. I needed this to go well.

"I am appreciative of you accepting my hand in marriage. May our vows bring unity against our shared enemy."

Caelum's eyebrows drew together, tilting his head in calculation. A few of the warriors snickered behind him and I cursed inwardly.

"What lies have you told this poor girl, My Lord?" Caelum asked the Commander without taking his eyes off me.

My Lord.

The world seemed to tilt, the words echoing like a crack through ice in my head. The Commander said something in the Fae language, his voice rough and punishing.

He turned, dark and unyielding eyes slamming into my widened stare. The truth slammed into me with brutal clarity. He had lied. Since the fire. Since he put his hands on my body. Since I shared my pain with him.

Something vicious and humiliated tore loose inside me. I was *not* his prisoner. Not his ally. Not his lover. I was his bride—and I'd been the last to know.

Before I registered what I was doing, I spun so fast that my head swam and I ran. My boots hit the earth in desperation. I could get to Winston. I could get away. There would be another way to unite the Kingdoms. A solid arm wrapped around my waist, and a frustrated cry left my lips.

"You *ran*, Little Drownling," he murmured into my hair, voice dripping with disappointment. He forced me to turn, trapping me against his chest and tilting my head up to look at him. "You have no reason to run."

I hit my fist against his chest, squirming in his arms and arching away. He lifted me easily, throwing me over his shoulder. I gripped the water in his body to bend to my will. I pulled as hard as I could. But his steps didn't falter.

"You cannot use your powers on me, love. I let you once, but it is in my control. Please, stop before you burn out." His words only fuelled the anger, the determination, the *need* to control him. To make him hurt.

My body began to tremble, the song in my throat spilling out with vicious intent. The warriors dropped to their knees, eyes wide and simmering with an iridescent gleam. If I couldn't hurt the Commander, maybe one of his own could.

Four of them rose, drawing their weapons with a symphony of steely rasps, pointing them at their High Lord. They lunged. Without putting me down, the Commander gripped his sword and pulled it from the sheath strapped to his back. He spun. The obsidian sword slashed across one of his warrior's throats. Hot blood sprayed against me, hitting my skin like a thousand knives. The song died in my throat. The spell I held over the warriors snapped like a rubber band. My vision wavered and a wave of nausea rolled through me. Exhaustion threatened to pull me into unconsciousness. The warrior crashed to his knees. Hands pressing against the gushing wound slashed across his throat, rivulets of blood spouting between his fingers. He spluttered, one wet gasp before crashing to the side. Dead.

The Commander said nothing, stepping over the warrior's body. He didn't look back at the warrior he'd slaughtered because of *me*. I went slack over his shoulder, watching Solas press his hand to his fallen comrade's throat to stop the bleeding. I was as lifeless as the warrior he was trying to save. The Commander stiffened beneath me, hand tightening on my thigh. "Lyra?" The raw edge in his voice barely pierced the buzzing in my ears. I couldn't answer. Couldn't even open my eyes. The world dimmed to nothing but the heat of his hands and the distant echo of my heart breaking. He only held me tighter and carried me into the darkness of his court.

PAIN EBBED THROUGH EVERY THOUGHT AS I BLINKED against the dull light. I lay amongst soft blankets that smelt like fresh night air and an underlying hint of something sweeter.

I flicked the blankets off me with a grimace. This was *his* bed.

Flames flickered in sconces, illuminating the most beautiful mural I had ever seen. It was so stunning that I almost forgot how *angry* I was.

It was painted with a swirling ocean. Dark flowers bloomed in random places across the wall, a familiar constellation of stars at the centre. The same stars that were tattooed on my left hand from the blood bargain. Movement caught my eye, and I startled, blinking so my eyes would adjust.

Cerilla sat at a small, round table in one of two velvet plush chairs, sipping tea from a delicate cup before it clinked back down onto the ceramic plate. Picking up the other cup, she walked over to the large bed that I laid in.

"Finally awake darling? How grand. Here." She

extended the cup towards me, and I sat up to take it, wincing at the throbbing in my head. "This will help with the pain."

"Thank you," I murmured and brought the tea to my lips. I wanted to be happy to see her, I had missed her. But her betrayal tasted as bitter as the tea she had made me.

"You lied to me," I said evenly, calmly placing the cup down on the bedside table.

Cerilla smiled and sat on the edge of the bed. "No. I told my dear brother to tell you *who* exactly you were offering your hand in marriage in hopes it would change your mind. But the sweet boy did not want to put that pressure on you while trying to find the Soul Relics." She reached out and tucked a strand of hair behind my ear, watching me carefully. "I am very protective and loyal to my brother, Lyra. But. I do not agree with him on this matter." She smiled sweetly, nose twitching as if she had smelled something rotten. Did the Commander's scent still linger on me? There was a strange undertone to her voice that almost sounded like a threat, but her smile stayed genuine, her eyes kind. Cerilla leant closer, lowering her voice as if the walls had ears. "No reincarnation of you has ever taken a Relic into themselves. Not once. Not in a thousand years." My heartbeat sharpened, each thud rising like a wave about to break over me. "Everything is different this time," she went on, eyes bright with something between fear and awe. "The war. The Gods. The balance of the realms. I can feel it shifting." She paused, studying me. "This feels like the end," she whispered. She clapped her hands with glee, "and we are the ones who claimed you."

The words struck like a cage slamming shut. *Claimed* me. Like a possession. A piece on a game board that could be owned. I had come so far since I escaped my father's hold, but here I was. In a castle. Trapped.

"So, how are you going to escape?" she asked lightly, as if we were discussing the tea I could no longer stomach.

"I'm not—"

"Oh, please. I can see it on your face. Look, I might be able to help you escape *after* you fulfill the bargain. It's dangerous, but you might be able to imbue weapons for us without all three Soul Relics in you." She sipped her tea as I stared at her blankly, unsure how to respond. I had reacted when I found out, yes. But I was hurt about being lied to. It felt humiliating. When my silence stretched, she shrugged one shoulder and stood, brushing out her skirts. "Think about it, it would be the best option for my brother. And for you." She walked to the double doors of the large room and disappeared through them, opening enough for me to see guards at the door before it creaked shut.

I laid back down, the smell of caramel and fresh night air flooding my mouth as I inhaled. Of course I was in *his* bed. Why would he have a mural of the Dead Sea in his bedchambers? The journal I'd earned through the blood bargain caught my eye, sitting on the bedside table. I sighed and pulled it into my lap, the spine groaning as I flipped to a random page. Monsters. The sketches were impossible to look away from. Detailed, haunting, each surrounded by lines of strengths and weaknesses like warnings left by someone. The Skanthi were the worst. Even the ink seemed jagged and frantic. If I closed my eyes, I could still see its claws sinking into Blue's flesh.

I swallowed and turned the page quickly, refusing to linger. My breath hitched. At the top of the next page read, *Rythos Draven.* The illustration was nothing like the others. No twisted limbs. No fanged maw. Just a man that I could not make out. Someone had scribbled over the top of the drawing, obscuring his face and body. Words circled the drawing in tight, almost hesitant script, as though the scribe hadn't known whether they were writing history or a confession. I read.

A soldier in the king's army. A noble man. A protector. I had loved Maraveth with all of my heart. I am not a monster.

My fingers froze on the page, feeling the pain in his writing, I turned to the next page.

When Helion stole me, he didn't just torture my body. He tried to rip apart my love for Maraveth. To tear love from bone, from soul. He wanted Maraveth to choose him, to love him. It hadn't worked. Instead, he was left with a creature forced to kill the woman he loved. Over and over again. A creature driven by curse and tormented by love.

I remember her. Every lifetime. Every touch. Every death. But she didn't. And each time I am forced to end her life, it destroys what little humanity I have left.

I stared at the page. It felt wrong to feel sympathy for a monster who was created to kill me. But here I was, heart aching from the story of a monster.

THIRTY-FIVE
VULNERABLE

Despite already being asleep for Gods knew how long, I had slipped back into unconsciousness while reading. Sleep had dragged me under like warm tidewater, pulling me into a dream I couldn't fight my way out of. Nothing more than flashes, but they were enough to unravel me. The curve of his smile. The rough scrape of his jaw against my throat. His hands large and steady spanning my waist, sliding lower. His breath on my lips the moment before he kissed me. The way he'd whispered my name like he'd been starved for it.

I reached for him in the dream, desperate, but every time my fingers brushed his skin, he dissolved into shadow. I chased him through the dark anyway. Always almost touching. Never reaching.

His voice echoed around me, broken and deep. "The last piece..." My heart clenched so hard it hurt. Everything slipped away at once, leaving only my aching heart lodged beneath my ribs—

"Lyra."

I startled, eyes springing open against the darkness. I

tore from the dream, breath shaking, sweat cooling on my skin. Moonlight streamed in through the large windows, and a tall figure stood beside my bed. I blinked, eyes adjusting. The guard from the inn. Panic gripped me. Power fluttered weakly under my skin, but I couldn't grasp it.

Jumping out of bed, I shifted into a fighting position.

"Good to see you missed me," he said, smirking down at me. I blinked. Confused. Disoriented. His face melted and morphed. Black hair shortened to brown waves that tussled across his forehead. His build changed to compact muscle and his dimples smiled down at me, using his Sanctum to shapeshift back into himself.

"Riven," I whispered, voice breaking. I threw my arms around his neck, burying my face into his neck.

"Hello, Princess," he sighed against my hair, arms wrapping around me.

"You came for me," I breathed, clutching his shirt. "How are you even here?"

"I told you I would come for you," he murmured, running a soothing hand up and down my spine. He grabbed my hand and tugged gently. "Come on. Time to go."

I took two steps, following him until something inside me stalled.

Riven frowned and quirked an eyebrow. "Want me to carry you? Come here."

"No." The word scraped out of me like a wound, and the truth followed on its heels. I didn't want to leave. Not because I doubted Riven—if there was anyone I trusted, it was him. But something inside me twisted at the thought of actually running from *him*. From the Commander.

My heart stuttered traitorously. He was my Kingdom's enemy. A monster. My captor. But he had become something more. And if I didn't fulfill the blood bargain... we would both die. "I..." my voice scraped out. "I can't."

Riven's expression softened as he grabbed both my hands in his. "I'm right here with you Princess, we will leave together—"

A deep, rage-filled voice cut over the top of him. "Take your fucking hands off her," the Commander growled, "before I cut them from your body."

My blood froze. The Commander stood in the open doorway, shadows twisting around him, poised and ready to attack. He took in the scene slowly as Riven let go of my hands.

The Commander's eyes roamed my body, every inch of exposed flesh that my silk slip left exposed. The flush of my cheeks. Something raw snapped across his face, something painful. But it was gone in an instant, primal rage replacing it.

Riven turned, blocking me from the Commander's gaze and drew his weapon with a sharp rasp. The Commander's growl vibrated through the room. Vicious. The noise of a predator.

"That weapon will not save you," he rumbled, walking towards him with clenched fists. Shadows lashed viciously around him, swarming towards Riven. I sucked in a breath and shoved myself in front of him. "Stop!" I yelled. The darkness stopped inches from my face. "Please, don't hurt him."

The shadows slowly retreated to the Commander, his eyes shooting to me, vicious and disbelieving. "Why the fuck shouldn't I?"

"He's a friend," I said quickly. "From Stonebriar barracks. We Ascended together."

"More reason to kill him," he ground out, taking a threatening step forward.

Riven laughed from behind me, stepping forward with that arrogant smirk that always got him in trouble. "You can try," Riven said with a grin, swinging his sword in a wide, graceful arc. "I came to save her and that's what I'll be doing."

The two males squared off, both lethal, both ready to kill.

Riven's words coiled around my fractured heart, pulling the pieces back together. But I wasn't sure I wanted to be saved. "Enough!" I shouted, chest heaving. They both turned to me like I was the only force in the world that mattered. "If he stays," I said breathlessly, "I'll begin imbuing tomorrow. I'll start before we search for the third Relic."

"No," the Commander growled. "It's too dangerous."

"Cerilla thinks it is possible. I'll start with one," I said. "I'll take it slow and stop before I burn out."

A long silence stretched, thick and suffocating.

Finally, the Commander exhaled sharply, and his jaw clenched so hard I thought it would break. "Fine." He stepped towards Riven, towering over him, voice low and venomous. "But hear me, Iron Guard. If you step foot in *our* bedchambers again..." His shadows bled around him, sharpening into deadly points, "...I will tear your spine out through your throat."

Riven didn't flinch, his dimples flashed in a dark grin. His grey eyes flashed to mine, softening at whatever he saw on my face. It broke him to leave me here.

"I will see you in the morning then, Princess."

Riven clapped a hand on the Commander's shoulder. "It was nice meeting you."

A low growl rolled from the Commander's chest in warning as a shadow lashed at his hand. Riven drew his hand back as if he had been burnt, chuckling softly.

"—or not."

The door clicked shut as Riven left and silence pressed in around us like a third presence. His shadows crawled up his feet, restless, tasting the air as though deciding whether to attack or retreat. The Commander didn't speak. He just stood there, chest rising and falling too fast, his eyes raking over me like he was trying to see if I hated him.

I wrapped my arms around myself, urging my broken pieces to stay together. "You lied to me," I whispered, hating how weak my voice sounded.

He sighed, running his hand through his dark hair. He seemed exhausted. He gripped the edge of one of the sitting chairs and dragged it out. He sat, elbows leaning on the arm rests, legs spread and relaxed. He looked purely masculine, and for a moment I forgot why I was angry.

"I did not lie," he murmured, tipping his head back to look at the high ceilings. He gestured for me to sit in the chair across from him, but I stayed standing, crossing my arms against my chest. His lips tilted in a small smile that didn't reach his eyes, and his shadows began crawling up his arms and burrowing against his skin. "You have been forced into every choice in your life. I wanted you to want *me*. Not be another person holding your leash."

His words broke open a piece of my heart that I wasn't ready to look at yet and I sat next to him.

"You cannot hide from these feelings anymore, Little Drownling."

I stared down at the bargain tattoo, tracing the lines that marked my left hand while he spoke. My finger stilled, my eyes shooting to his left hand where the mirror image etched into his skin. His words were pretty, but he had been lying about more than his identity.

I stood so abruptly that the chair skidded against the ground. The Commander's brow creased as he watched me pace in front of him. A broken laugh escaped me. Marrying him didn't matter. It wouldn't change anything. I was already his.

"This mark isn't just from the bargain. Is it? It's the Mark of Anamryn."

When he stared down at the matching mark on his left hand, the room tilted. Like something ancient inside me had been waiting for this truth, whispering it in every stolen glance. I felt the bond then, not fully, not completely, but like a heartbeat beneath my own. The ache deep in my chest. It was *him*. "You are my Fated Mate."

THIRTY-SIX

BONDED

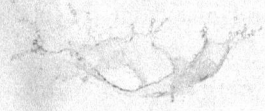

I continued to pace in front of the Commander, bare feet sinking into the soft carpet with each footfall.

"I did not know we were Fated and I did not mean to invoke it. But when our blood mingled during the bargain, it partially accepted the bond." His eyes opened, lashes fanning his cheek as he looked down at his hands. "Do not worry though, Little Drownling, you will not be stuck with me for long."

The pain in his voice melted a small part of my fury. "What is that supposed to mean?" I snapped.

His dark eyes lifted to mine, swimming with something dangerously close to grief. He had lied to me by omission. Twice. He wasn't perfect. He wasn't safe. But neither was I.

The realisation hollowed me out. I should have been terrified. I should have run. I should have done a thousand sane, logical things.

Instead, the earth shifted beneath my feet, pulling me towards him. Or maybe it was the bond, forcing me to want him.

Gods, I wanted him in a way that felt older than time.

Like remembering a story that I used to know. Like coming *home*. No. I stopped myself, turning away before he could see the choice tearing me apart. Before I could give in.

Without a word, I crossed the room and climbed into the bed, pulling the blankets around me like armour. I laid on my side with my back to him, curling in on myself.

"Yell at me. Be mad at me," the Commander whispered. "But please, do not shut me out."

I squeezed my eyes shut, fingers tightening in the blankets. His words seeped into the cracks I was trying to seal.

"Silence has always been safer for me," I whispered back.

"There are things I physically cannot tell you," he explained in a pained voice. "I am sorry."

His apology sat heavily on my chest, a weight I didn't know how to lift off my heavy heart.

I lay there in the quiet, staring at nothing, listening to the slow rhythm of his breathing and the distant hush of the sea beyond the windows.

I told myself that turning my back was strength. But the silence stretched, thick and aching, filled with all the words I wasn't ready to say and all the ones he hadn't dared to offer.

Eventually, exhaustion won. My grip on the blankets loosened, my thoughts blurring at the edges, and sleep crept in like a tide, gentle but relentless.

I woke to the quiet light of dawn seeping through the billowing sheer curtains, basking everything in a soft orange glow.

The Commander sat in the same chair he had been in

last night, slumped awkwardly. His long legs stretched out, one arm draped over the armrest. His head had fallen forward, dark hair shadowing his face as he slept.

He looked wrong like this. Unguarded, exhausted and almost human in a way I wasn't used to seeing. He chose to sleep there instead of his own bed, because I had claimed it.

I watched the slow rise and fall of his chest, the faint pull of shadows curled loosely around his boots, dormant in sleep. He had kept his distance. Given me space.

I sighed, climbing out of his bed and walking across the soft carpet.

I *had* to unite the Kingdoms. I *had* to marry him. And it was my lack of control in my fate that made me hate it.

He blinked wearily at me as I grew closer, waking from sleep as if sensing me.

"You are right," I told him softly as he stretched. "If you had told me about our bond when it appeared, I would have probably killed myself to take you down with me."

His lip quirked in a sleepy half smile. "Vicious little thing," he murmured.

I closed the distance between us before I realised what I was doing. I sat on his lap and curled myself against his chest. He let out a shuddering breath, a sound of disbelief. Like he couldn't trust that I was real. His heart raced beneath my cheek, wild and uneven.

"Do I have a choice in this?" I whispered.

He tensed. His fingers lifted to my chin, tilting my face up so I had no choice but to meet his eyes. "I do not want the Seven Hells to destroy Lumireth. But if winning means *forcing* you to choose me," he said as he ran the back of his forefinger over my face. "Then the whole world can fucking burn."

I leant into his touch and looked up into the endless depths of his eyes, where I could see nothing but devastating truth.

"What if..." I trailed off, trying to find the courage to be vulnerable. "I want to choose you."

Something in him broke, his expression softened and raw emotion shone in eyes. How did I once think them soulless? There was so much suffering in them, so much grief.

He cupped my face with both hands, thumbs brushing my cheekbones with a tenderness that stole the breath from my lungs. His forehead pressed to mine, and for a heartbeat, we simply existed.

Save him, the voice whispered, barely a breath that sent gooseflesh over my skin. Our breaths mingled, and our chests rose in the same rhythm. Then he kissed me. Softly. Carefully. Like he was memorising me. My hands curled around the back of his neck as warmth bloomed through me, magic unfurling like petals desperate for sun. His thumb stroked the corner of my mouth, coaxing me closer, deepening the kiss with tenderness. I sighed against his mouth, fingers curling into his shoulders. Our lips moved with aching reverence, slowly and deeply.

He made a pained noise, and I drew back. "Your shadows," I gasped, eyes widening. Darkness crawled across his skin, burrowing into him in aggressive strikes.

I tipped my head back, brushing my silver hair behind my shoulder to expose my neck. His hair was silky between my knuckles as I gripped the base of his neck and pulled him towards me. A shiver shot through me as his lips brushed my neck, his breath fanning against the sensitive skin.

His teeth grazed me teasingly. An excited flutter spread

through my stomach, warmth sinking between my thighs. His large warm hands wrapped around my waist, and he bit down. A sting of pain, then warmth and pure want flooded my system. But he didn't use his venom.

A moan left me, and I ground against his growing hardness.

His hands roamed, squeezing my breasts and rolling my nipples between his thumb and forefinger in a way that made me whimper. Slipping between my thighs, a growl vibrated against my neck as he slid his fingers over my panties. Mouth leaving my neck, he stood and lifted me until my legs wrapped around his waist. A metallic taste filled my mouth as his tongue slid against mine. But I didn't care.

My panties bit into my skin for moment before they were ripped from me. I gasped as his hands gripped my ass, squeezing the flesh and walking us backwards until my back hit a wall. "Please," I whimpered against his mouth. I was desperate. Desperate to be consumed by him.

A strange urge washed over me, and without thinking, I bit his bottom lip.

He paused, muscles tensing beneath me as if he had turned to stone. "Be very fucking careful, love," he ground out with his lip between my teeth.

I let go, a deep blush creeping up my neck. Consuming his blood would mean sealing the bond.

He slid his hand slowly down my chest, gripping the material of my slip. It tore from my body, the air washing over my over-heated skin. His teeth grazed my nipple before his tongue swirled around it, just once before his fingers dug into my hips to hold me against the wall.

He dropped to his knees. My legs trembled against his

shoulders, and I gasped as he dragged his tongue along my sensitive flesh. Suddenly, he was done being gentle. He sucked on my clit, letting his teeth graze me and my back arched.

"You taste so fucking good," he growled against me. Each stroke of his tongue brought me closer. Closer.

Release swept through me like a tide answering its moon. I was nothing but sensation and surrender, breaking apart in luminous fragments while he remained, steady and sure, holding me through every crest and collapse as the world dissolved until there was nothing but us.

He stood, hands on my ass to support me as he walked towards the bed.

"You can bite me," he said, throwing me on the bed and straightening to undo his belt. I held my breath, unable to look away. He was breathtaking, pure masculine beauty that made my mouth water.

He climbed onto the bed, body pressing down on me and pulling my leg around his waist, his cock pushing against my entrance. "But *do not* drink my blood," he warned as he inched himself inside me, stretching me until I squirmed. Gods, he was big.

"If you do," he snarled softly as he rolled his hips, teasing me with his tip. "You will be *mine* completely."

My gasps turned into frustrated moans, and I gripped on to his shoulders to try and pull him closer. More. I needed more.

"Fuck me already," I demanded.

"Say that again," he growled, voice rough and wrecked, "and I might break you."

I pushed up onto my elbows, until our noses touched.

"*Fuck. Me. Now.*" My voice came out in layered tones

and his eyes turned pure black. He slammed into me, the full length of him finally seated to the hilt with a sound that undid me.

I trailed my tongue up his neck as he drove his hips into me, moaning with each merciless thrust. Our lips met, his tongue claiming me. His hand reached between us, fingers stroking my clit in time with his cock.

Something primal flooded me, and suddenly, my teeth sunk into his lip. A sweet metallic taste flooded into my mouth. *His blood.* I was never good at doing what I was told.

Pleasure tore through me in wave after wave of pleasure.

The Commander roared, his cock twitching inside me as he crashed over the edge with me. My left hand burnt as though it had been drenched in flames. My chest felt like it was being torn open, my heart itself being *remade.* Something inside my very soul *snapped* into place, a tether. Like a puzzle piece clicking into place. A silver thread that wrapped around my very essence that connected me to *him.*

The Commander's breath whooshed out of him, as if he could feel it too.

"You bonded me," he whispered, voice dripping with both disbelief and panic. "Fuck, love. I warned you."

The silver thread vibrated, sending feelings that were not my own into my chest. I could *feel* his happiness radiating into me, his wonder, his adoration. His *fear.* Or perhaps that was mine. I couldn't tell anymore.

I clung to him like he was my lifeline as we stared at each other in shock.

His cock was still buried deep inside me, and his cock twitched. His mouth crashed against my lips, devouring me in a possessive kiss. "Mine," he ground out. Gods, he was so fucking deep.

"Yours," I moaned. My eyes rolled into the back of my head, the pleasure crushing me. The mix of his emotions. His sensations. All of it flooded into me from the bond, making my soul sing.

The Commander's arms tightened around me like a vice as he impaled me with desperation, and I met each one with my own feverish need.

I could *feel* his pleasure, and something beneath it that felt dangerously close to what I imagined *love* to feel like, and it made me clench around him. He fucked me harder. Faster. Moans blended with masculine rasps of pleasure cut through the sound of our flesh meeting. He was right, I was going to break—

The world exploded. The stars trembled in the sky. Pure, unadulterated ecstasy coursed through our veins like a wildfire that could never be tamed. He ripped his mouth from mine, and he roared. We held each other excruciatingly tight, like a tether to this plane of existence, through the waves of pleasure that threatened to push us into unconsciousness.

Our bodies trembled, and unlike mine, his emotions were clear. He rolled off me and curled his body around mine. My back was pressed against his chest and sighed into my hair, tightening his arm around my waist as if he thought I would disappear.

The bond pulsed between us—warm, alive and unmistakable. His emotions surged through me in a rush so fierce it almost stole my breath.

Love.

Gods, it was so raw, so overwhelming, tears prickled at the corner of my eyes. But beneath it—something bittersweet. Something that *hurt*.

"Am I... can I feel what you're feeling?" I whispered

into the moonlit dark, unsure if I was slipping back into madness.

"*Yes.*" His voice unfurled through my mind, and I stiffened in his arms. "*I can feel you as well.*"

I shuddered, his hand drawing circles on my hip. He could feel everything. My confusion. My fear. The soft, shameful truth that I felt safe in his arms.

"When the Nightbourne attacked me, your voice in my head was real wasn't it?" I had put it down to my own madness.

He nodded against my head.

"Please, never do that again," I whispered.

His body stiffened behind me, and I felt his rejection flood me.

"I've heard voices in my head since I was twelve, sometimes I can't tell what is real," I explained slowly, sharing the last of my broken soul with him.

"Then I will speak out loud," he murmured into my hair, punctuating it with a kiss. That overwhelming feeling of grief slammed into me from the bond and I gasped.

"Why are you sad?" I asked him.

For a moment he didn't answer, and I let my eyes fall shut, sinking into him. Letting myself enjoy this quiet, impossible moment—his warmth, his steady breath against my neck, the way our souls tangled like they had always known each other. His voice finally brushed the shell of my ear, barely a breath. "Because this is all I have ever wanted..." He paused, a surge of anguish pouring down the bond, "and it's going to be ripped away."

"I will drown anyone who tries," I promised him and he chuckled darkly, but I *felt* the affection beneath it.

Sleep dragged at me, pulling me under, but I thought—

just faintly—I heard him whisper one last thing: "Monsters do not deserve a happy ending."

As I drifted off, something unsettling slithered through the bond. Or perhaps it was a dream. There was a ripple, tremor of violence. The urge to *kill*.

The Commander exhaled against my neck, warm and gentle. "Sleep, my Little Drownling."

THIRTY-SEVEN

IMBUEMENT

The sun beat down without mercy, pulling beads of sweat from my skin. After spending the night tangled up with the Commander, my energy felt renewed. Waking up in the Commander's arms had felt like a gift I didn't deserve.

He'd kissed me lazily, lips soft and warm, pulling an orgasm from me with nothing but his fingers and a low murmur against my throat. But when I'd tried to reach for his hard length, he had chuckled. "As much as it pains me," he'd murmured against my ear, "I need to make preparations for the Mortals' and Fae lords' arrivals."

I'd pouted and made him promise not to stay away too long. We'd shared a quiet breakfast in his bed, knees brushing, his thumb stroking idle circles on my thigh. It had been... intimate. Comforting. Except for the intense heartbreak that oozed down the bond, dousing my quiet contentment with questions. What wasn't he telling me?

Now, not even an hour later, my chest ached. I could still feel him through the bond, a faint simmer of frustration on his end, like he was fighting the urge to come straight back to me.

I had been led through open hallways lined with floor-to-ceiling windows that revealed breathtaking views to a training field carved into the side of the mountain.

Bright green grass extended through the clearing despite warriors sparring, launching arrows, and using magic. Fae magic lit the air like sparks off steel. They called lightning, flame, and wind. Sanctums were *nothing* compared to this.

I was in awe, and suddenly I understood the need for the Iron Guard, without them, the Mortal Kingdom stood *no* chance against this.

Solas beamed down at me as I approached him, his smile almost as blinding as the sun. A kindness I didn't deserve after yesterday.

His nose crinkled once, and his eyebrows raised. His gaze crashed to my left hand. The mark had grown last night, during our bonding. Intricate lines wove just past my wrist and extended down over my fingers around the original wave and pointed stars.

"You bonded!" His arms wrapped around me in a tight hug. "Oh, I am so happy right now."

His voice sounded warm, genuine, but worry creased his brow and his smile slipped.

"Does Cerilla know?" he asked as he stepped away from me and passed me a sword.

I dropped into a fighting stance. "I don't know," I answered honestly. Considering she was offering to help me escape yesterday, I didn't think she would be thrilled about it.

Solas swung his sword, expertly twisting it and clashing it against mine.

"Aren't you upset with me?" I asked, drawing back and sidestepping his advance.

He pivoted, blade slashing so close to my neck it nicked my skin.

"Deron was a good male. He didn't deserve to die. But you were frightened. Cornered animals lash out."

Deron. The male who had died by the Commander's blade yesterday. It made it worse somehow, knowing his name.

Solas did not relent, his blade crashing against mine until my arms felt weak. But neither did I, because I was upset with him, too. He could have told me about the Commander, about the mating bond.

"Why didn't you tell me?" I yelled, lunging and swinging my sword. Steel flashed. In one smooth motion he caught my wrist, twisted, and my weapon was gone. His sword was suddenly at my throat, not touching me but close enough that I felt nervous.

It wouldn't be the first time someone I had thought was my friend tried to kill me. I stood there, unflinchingly staring into his warm hazel eyes.

"I gave you so many hints, Lyra," he said, throwing the sword against the grass.

He stepped towards me, arms open and I took a small step back. He advanced anyway and wrapped his arms around me in a gentle hug.

"I am your friend, Lyra. I tried my best without betraying the Commander."

The fury drained out of me all at once, leaving something hollow behind as he released me and stepped back.

He *had* tried to tell me. I saw it again in my mind—the way he'd traced his mark absentmindedly, before his gaze shifted to my own. The weight in his voice when he'd explained what it meant, what it cost.

"You tried to help me," I whispered, the realisation settling heavy in my chest, shame threading through the remnants of my anger.

"Always," he responded with an easy smile.

A throat cleared and Caelum walked towards us in the same black armour as yesterday, arms clasped behind his back. "You fight well for a princess, my lady." He bowed his head in greeting.

I wiped the sweat from my forehead with the back of my hand and leant against my sword.

"I am sorry for how our meeting went yesterday," he said. "I am the Commander's mage."

"I didn't realise mages still existed," I said carefully, trying to school the surprise on my face. I thought they only existed in books; in the tales I had read as a girl. They were always the villains.

"Do not look so shocked," he scoffed as he tilted his head at me. "I am not the first mage you have met."

I frowned, waiting for him to enlighten me.

"Cerilla was my apprentice."

The pieces clicked. The teas she brewed. Her healing abilities. Why her powers were blocked by the storms. The way she seemed to *know* things about me.

He smiled, watching me with intrigue. "My Lord has requested we start imbuement."

"CLOSE YOUR EYES," CAELUM INSTRUCTED, CIRCLING me with slow, steady steps.

Caelum had pulled a table made of stone from the

ground of the training yard with sheer magic and laid a sword on top of it.

My eyelashes fluttered closed despite my nerves.

"Mind if I watch?" Riven strolled through the training yard lazily, smirking as if he belonged amongst these warriors.

Before I could answer, Solas had blocked his path. "You must be Riven," he said, extending his hand. Riven eyed his hand for a moment too long but clasped his hand around his.

"I am Solas." He smiled down at Riven with warmth, dwarfing him with his height. "If I stab you, it won't be because you are Mortal. I love Mortals. It will be if *you* step out of line."

Riven chuckled, eyes lighting up with challenge. "That makes me *want* to step out of line just to see you *try*."

Solas laughed, ushering him over to a wooden bench at the edge of the cliff face.

Riven shot me a wink as he sat down, and I couldn't help but smile. I had missed him.

Caelum cleared his throat and I turned back to my stern teacher, closing my eyes.

"Focus on where your power comes from. It will feel like a well inside you. Find it." I focused inwards, feeling the pull in my chest. Power swirled there, a steady wave of energy.

"Pull at that power," Caelum said, voice steady as steel. "Tug on it. Gently. Take just a thread. Imagine it's something you can *see*. Something you can *feel*."

I drew in a slow breath, the training yard suddenly too quiet, too watchful. I reached inward, tugging. It seemed to be stuck. It looked like a pool of shimmering blue light in my mind, with darker threads that glittered almost mesmerizingly. I tugged at it. The cage around it groaned.

My eyes snapped open. My spine jolted straight. "I can't," I gasped, breath catching like barbed wire in my throat. *Let it free,* a voice carried to me on the breeze. *Her* voice. Maraveth. It slithered across the ground, skimming my skin like a thousand cold fingers. *You are complete now. Save him.*

I clutched my head, nails digging into my scalp as if that could claw the voice from my head. Something felt different, inside me. Something had changed and it wasn't just the bond tethered to my soul.

"No!" I cried.

"Refocus yourself," Caelum's voice wove through the chaos, low, grounding. *Real.*

"Let your power surface, or it will consume you."

I squeezed my eyes shut. The world pulsed around me. I reached towards that shimmering light within me again. Deeper. The cage groaned again, and I sucked in a sharp breath. I could feel its anticipation. That dark part of me I had suppressed begged to be free. It had grown stronger with each Soul Relic, and for some reason, after bonding the Commander it felt, *complete.*

My heart pounded, but I pulled harder. My veins blistered with magic, splitting me open from the inside as if it was poison. It felt like my very soul was tearing, reforming. Her whispered voice grew louder in a crescendo, mingling with the haunting melody that had plagued me for most of my life. My throat was raw; I wasn't sure if I was screaming or if she was screaming *for* me.

Agony tore through me like lightning in a storm. I dropped to my knees, the earth biting into my skin.

The cage shattered. The shimmering well of turquoise

burst from the cage like a dam wall breaking, flooding my system. Energy pulsed through me like it was a living thing, and every nerve ending in my body burned in response as though I had been set aflame. "Good, let it run through you." Caelum's voice grounded me again, reminding me that I wasn't being torn apart, I was in a clearing in the forest. The burning ebbed to a dull warmth with every frantic beat of my heart. "Now pull a piece of your magic."

I grasped at the raging waves of power surging through my body, pulling a thread of turquoise that rippled with that shimmering darkness.

"I have it," I yelled. My hands were tingling with a strange warmth, and I cupped them together as if I were holding something real.

"Yes, you do. Open your eyes."

My lashes parted to searing light. I gasped. The shimmering glow I'd imagined was *real,* pulsing between my palms like the tide.

"Hold it above the sword and push it into the blade. But slowly."

With trembling hands, I held the power above the sword and tried to push it down with my mind, willing it into the sword. It poured out of my hands into the metal, the sword glowing with an unnatural blue glow. It began to hum in harmony, and I mimicked the sound, weaving it into a melody. The light was so blinding, it almost burnt my eyes. But I was enthralled. Unable to look away. A loud crack echoed through the clearing. I flew backwards. The metal exploded. I shielded my face from the sharp debris raining over me. My ears throbbed from the noise, a high-pitched ringing ebbing through the pain.

"That," Caelum said, voice hushed, "was not what I expected." His eyes lingered, longer than before, studying me with his lips pursed. He turned without another word, selecting a new blade, and placing it on the stone. "Again. But be *gentle*. You have more power than you should for only absorbing two Soul Relics."

Six more swords exploded. One after another. I failed. Riven and Solas started betting, many of the Fae warriors joining in. It only fed my frustration. My hair clung to my sweaty skin. At some stage between attempts, Solas had given me the leather from his hair so I could braid it, but small strands escaped, just to pester me.

"Your anger is working *against* you. You need to let the tide of frustration wash around you."

I glared at the mage, pure venom oozing from my voice. "I could take it out on you, if you'd like?"

He said nothing, calmly placing yet another sword on the stone table for me to destroy. "Again. But ground yourself. Breathe. Be *gentle*."

I huffed in frustration and reluctantly did what he said. The magic *did* come easier this time. When I reached into the swirling pool within me, glowing turquoise threaded with glittering black, it responded like it was waiting for my command. I stood over the new blade, laying the glittering thread gently across the cold metal.

A song rose in my throat. I wasn't sure why I was singing, but it *felt* right. As the notes slipped free, the thread of light sank into the steel, spreading from the hilt to the sharpened tip of the blade. The sword began to hum. Pale blue light shimmered over its surface, flecked with specks of inky darkness that shimmered in the sunlight.

I held my breath, bracing for the explosion. But it didn't come.

Riven clapped loudly and a few of the surrounding warriors joined in.

Caelum appeared at my side, silent until his eyes caught the faint pulse of the blade. "It is imbued," he stated slowly. His brow furrowed as though trying to solve a puzzle he hadn't seen in centuries. He cocked his head to the side, narrowing his eyes as he slid a finger over the darker lines etched through my magic.

"Are you adamant that you have only absorbed two Soul Relics?"

"Yes," I said carefully. He hummed in thought, his gaze assessing me. I had absorbed the axe, *one to wield*. The crown, *one to wear*. I hadn't dreamt of the third, *one that bridges two broken hearts*. My eyes widened, flashing to the Mark of Anamryn on my left hand. The bond. The final piece, it was in the Commander the whole time.

"Again," Caelum said, oblivious to the questions flying through my head.

I LOST TRACK OF HOW MANY SWORDS I IMBUED. THEY stacked behind me like offerings, each one glowing faintly, humming with my power. My limbs dragged. My breath came rough and uneven. Still, I reached for another blade.

So much for just imbuing one. At some point, Solas had forced food into my hands and it sat like a stone in my stomach. The training yard was empty now, and the sunlight had dipped into late gold. Riven sat relaxed in the grass, his face tilted towards the sun as if it were an old friend. The sword dragged across the grass behind me. It felt heavier than the others, as if it carried my fatigue in its hilt.

"I advise that you stop," Caelum said, voice low with warning. "Imbuement is different from ordinary burnout. You are not merely using your power—you are giving it. If you exhaust yourself during imbuement, I am not certain even you would survive."

"I'm not done yet," The words came out hoarse. I wasn't done. I *couldn't* be done. Every sword imbued was one more chance to kill the monsters hunting me. One more chance to stop them tearing through villages. Through children. Sweat stung my eyes. I wiped it away with the back of my hand and curled my fingers tighter around the next blade. My magic barely stirred. I tried again, reaching deeper. It slipped through my grasp like wet sand.

"I hate myself for saying this," Riven muttered from where he lounged, arms draped over his knees, "but maybe you should listen to the mage."

Solas paced uneasily but stayed silent. He wanted as many weapons as possible for his people as well.

I swayed on my feet, the world tilting around me. Caelum had told me to stop three swords ago, but stubbornness dug in like claws. I licked my dry lips before hauling the sword onto the stone with a grunt. Nausea rolled through me. The slab of rock was mercifully cold beneath my fingers as I braced myself against it. I reached for the swirling power in my chest and found nothing but an empty ache. A frustrated sound tore from my throat.

"C'mon, Princess," Riven said, the edge of worry cutting through his usual drawl. "Come sit down."

I ignored him and reached again. The magic slipped away, like I was trying to catch the tide with my bare hands. The ground rushed up to meet me. Grass cushioned my cheek, the scent of dirt and sweat and steel flooding my senses. The wind punched out of my lungs.

"For heaven's sake," Caelum muttered somewhere above me, boots crunching across the clearing. He knelt at my side, cool fingers brushing my temple. "You are empty, aren't you?" Caelum said, somewhere above me. "The only thing that can restore her magic is the ocean... or lust."

His words drifted to me as if I were sinking underwater, despite my body being doused in scorching flames. It burnt through my veins, licking at my bones and chewing through whatever was left of me. My thoughts wouldn't hold. They melted as soon as I reached them. The only constant was the burning, growing hotter, hungrier, like something inside me had finally found an excuse to consume me whole. My eyes closed without my permission.

"What do you think you are doing?" Solas snarled. His voice sounded far away, like it was coming through water.

"Saving her," Riven said, voice low, breathless with determination. Warmth ghosted over my cheek. I barely had time to inhale before his lips pressed to mine.

THIRTY-EIGHT

THREATS

Warmth slammed into me like a wave as Riven's mouth met mine. Soft and wrong, yet unbearably right. A spark flared under my skin. No, *not* a spark. A light.

His lust bled through the kiss, molten light rushing into the empty well in my chest.

The agony dulled. The world steadied. My fingers twitched. I gasped into him. He groaned as if the sound dragged him under.

The haze loosened, just enough for the horrifying truth to register: I was kissing him back, matching his hunger. It was like I'd been smothered and he was the oxygen bringing me back to life. I fisted his shirt, dragging him closer and clinging to him with desperation—

Riven's body jerked and his groan became a sharp, ragged sound, breaking the kiss.

My vision snapped into painful clarity just in time to see the hilt of a dagger jutting from his thigh.

Solas stood behind him, chest heaving, quiet fury crackling in every line of his body. "Get. Off. Her."

He wrenched Riven backward by the collar. I slumped sideways into the grass, the world spinning again.

Black blood poured down Riven's leg, a dagger was embedded to the hilt in his thigh.

"Princess—"

"Don't you fucking move," Solas barked over the top of him, stepping between us like a wall of iron.

"I was saving her," Riven drawled, wiping his thumb across his bottom lip. "Not my fault if she liked it."

Solas grabbed the knife jutting from Riven's thigh and twisted with brutal, slow force.

Riven grunted, gritting his teeth, but his smirk didn't falter. "Still worth it."

"Your orders were *not* to kill him, yes?" Caelum asked calmly. "Keep twisting and you will sever his artery."

Solas grunted, turning and scooping me into his arms like I weighed nothing. My head lolled weakly against his shoulder. The movement jolted my raw nerves; a thin whimper escaped me.

"Easy, sweetheart," he murmured, voice gentler now. "I've got you." Riven limped after us, leaving a trail of black blood.

"Escort this fool to the infirmary before he bleeds all over the damned floor," Solas yelled to a warrior as he strode through the stone archway that led back into the castle. Solas carried me through corridors, but I couldn't appreciate the beauty over my racing thoughts.

I kissed Riven. It had felt so familiar, that it was almost right. Shame curled through me. Guilt. Fear that the Commander would *feel* this through the bond and it would hurt him.

I pressed my forehead weakly into Solas's chest, eyes burning.

"Where is he?" I whispered. The bond pulsed in my chest, tight and wounded, and I couldn't tell if the pain swirling there was mine or his.

"He had to travel to Someria, a town levelled by a swarm of Nightbourne last night. Just hold on."

While I was tangled up in bed, people were dying. Because of me.

Solas opened the large doors to the Commander's rooms by kicking them with his feet.

Riven pushed in behind him, a trail of black blood oozed across the floor in his wake. Cool silk blankets soothed my feverish skin as Solas lowered me onto the bed.

Shadows erupted in front of us, violent and choking the air with power. The Commander of Death stepped out of them, onyx eyes wild. He looked carved from darkness itself.

His gaze landed on me first, taking in my trembling hands, the feverish flush crawling up my throat before landing on my swollen lips. Something shattered across his face as his nostrils flared, breathing in deeply. The bond flooding me with his whirlwind of feelings. *Terror. Guilt. Realisation. Rage.*

His eyes cut to Riven and every candle guttered. Shadows surged like a tide, slamming against the walls hard enough to rattle them.

"She is not yours to touch," he said, voice low and lethal, "now, I will make you pay the price with your fucking pain."

"All I did was save her, and I would *gladly* do it again," Riven said, amusement dripping from his voice.

The Commander's snarl ripped through the chamber, raw and feral. "She is *mine.*" He closed the distance between them in three long strides and wrapped his hand around Riven's throat, lifting him off the floor and shoving him against the wall.

"She... Kissed... Me back," he gasped, an unhinged grin splitting his face as his head slammed against the stone. I flinched, worry rising through my exhaustion. Riven's sarcasm was going to get him killed.

The Commander leant in, voice a low growl. "She may have let you kiss her. But she *begs me* to fuck her."

Riven's grin faltered as shadows crawled up his body. The image of Bohdi being melted from the inside out flashed through my head.

"No," I said weakly. If the Commander heard me, he didn't show it. "Please, stop"

"I'm... more useful... to you alive," Riven choked out. Shadows crawled across his face, creeping into his ears. He squirmed. "The Mortals are setting you up!"

The Commander paused, loosening his grip enough for Riven to gasp.

"Speak," he demanded.

"They just want the princess back. The Iron Guard accompanying them have been tasked to take her. They want to sacrifice her. To gain back favour of the Gods."

"*You* are still more useful to me dead," the Commander seethed.

Riven's features morphed, ageing and transforming into the face of my father. I cringed, nausea swirling in my gut.

"I can be whoever you need me to be," my father's voice said.

The Commander dropped Riven, letting him crash to the floor as he shapeshifted back into himself.

"And what new display of testosterone is this?" Cerilla's voice drifted in like cold water as she stepped through the doorway, skirts whispering behind her. She raised an eyebrow at her brother and helped Riven stand, touching the wound on his leg. Her fingers came away covered in red blood. My brow creased. It was red. Not black.

"I follow the path of blood," she sighed, "and of course it leads to you, brother." She flicked her wrist. A steaming pot of floral tea appeared beside me. I managed the faintest smile of thanks and she returned it warmly.

"Come along, *Mortal boy*," she said, tugging Riven by the wrist. "Let me put you back together."

Riven shot me one last smirk. But something unreadable flickered in his eyes before the heavy doors closed behind them.

Solas lingered, his shoulders tensing as his eyes flicked between me and the Commander. It was like he expected violence to erupt at any second.

"Go," the Commander snarled without looking at him.

Solas didn't move. "I'm not leaving her alone with you," he said quietly, steel under every word. "Not when you look like *that*."

Shadows snapped like whips across the floor. The Commander lifted his head slowly, looking at him with pure black eyes.

"She is *bonded* to me," he said slowly, his voice rough. "She is safe."

Solas opened his mouth, ready to argue.

A pained sound escaped me, soft and broken as my body trembled against that insufferable heat surging violently through my veins.

Solas's expression crumpled as he took a step towards the door. "Stay the fuck in control," he pleaded, voice dripping with worry before he slammed the doors shut behind him.

The room fell silent. The Commander was suddenly in

front of me, hands cupping my face. "I am sorry," he said, voice breaking on the words as if they hurt him.

My eyebrows crinkled together. I had kissed another male merely *hours* after I bonded him, and he was apologising to me?

"I should have been here. I should have known you were too stubborn not to empty your power."

I leant into his touch, letting it cool my burning skin. "I didn't mean to kiss him," I whispered so softly that it was barely audible.

He gathered me into his lap, arms wrapping firmly around me even though it cost him, his shadows were attacking him.

"I can shadow jump you to the ocean," he muttered to himself, panicked and furious.

I shook my head weakly. I didn't think I could survive being torn apart and stitched back together.

"Or—" he hesitated.

My stomach fluttered in anticipation at the way his eyes heated and dropped to my lips.

"I will take care of you," he promised, voice dark and breaking.

I could already feel the familiar tingling seeping into my skin. Knowing how good he could make me feel turned the anticipation into its own quiet torment.

His lips brushed mine, a touch so tender it almost hurt. He became unnaturally still; nose twitching and anger surged down the bond. He could *scent* Riven.

I wanted him to smother any trace of it with his own. I lifted my head, closing the space between us and claimed his mouth. He stayed deathly still for a heartbeat, startled that I had made the first move. But he melted beneath my touch and his hands tangled in my hair.

I deepened the kiss, sliding my tongue into his mouth and my toes curled at the moan that rumbled through him.

The lust, the pure *power* oozing into me through the bond was enough to bring me back to life.

His hands gripped my blouse, tearing it from my body and I gasped against his mouth as his palm squeezed my breast.

"You are going to have to do better than that," he whispered when I moaned. His voice shook with restraint and something hungrier. I arched into his touch, warmth flooding into me, sinking into my skin. He pulled away, trailing his tongue down my neck, leaving a warm wet path in his wake. I cried out as he bit down on my nipple, pain ebbing into pleasure. This male would be my undoing. No one had ever made me feel the way he did. *Alive.* I plunged my fingers through his hair. I needed to kiss him. Needed him to fuck the life back into me—

"Your shadows," I whispered, eyes widening as the volatile things crawling over his skin. *Hurting* him. His eyes were pure black, dark veins spreading around his eyes.

I tilted my head, exposing my neck.

"No. You are too weak right now," he growled, pulling my pants from my body. "I can stay in control." I wasn't sure if he was reassuring me, or himself.

A whimper left my lips as he trailed a feather-light touch down my stomach, pausing between my thighs.

"I need to make you moan loud enough for that fucking Mortal to hear from the infirmary." His unhinged words sent a needy rush of heat between my thighs, and he slid his fingers against my overheated flesh. Excruciatingly light. He chuckled at the impatient noise I made.

"It is a matter of pride," he murmured, plunging two fingers inside me.

A low, involuntary moan escaped me, far louder than I meant it to be. My body jolted, inner walls twitching around his large fingers as they moved in and out of me without mercy.

"Just like that, love," he praised as his dark eyes devoured me. He loved this. Loved seeing me shaking under his touch. I could feel it through the bond. It tingled against my skin and overfilled the hole in my chest. He growled, the bond flaring hot and sharp between us. "I want to hear it," he grunted, adding a third finger into me, and I threw my head back from the stretch.

"Who. Do. You. Belong. To?"

His fingers drove into me, each word punctuated by his knuckles striking my flesh.

When I didn't answer, he pinched my clit between his thumb and forefinger, hard enough to steal my breath.

"I belong," I moaned, surrender curling through every word, "to the Commander of Death."

A sound more animal than male tore through him as he pulled out of me. He flickered like a wraith as he undid his belt and shoved his pants down to his knees.

Darkness tugged at his very existence, but those dark, endless eyes stayed on me. He gripped my ankles and pulled me to the edge of the bed.

He looked unhinged. Like a monster. It should have scared me, but the wetness coating my thighs showed us both just how much I liked it.

He gripped my legs behind my knees with brutalising force and I reached between us, wrapping my hand around his thick cock and pushing him against my entrance. He growled, shoving into me without mercy.

My back arched off the bed, stars shooting across my vision.

He was fully seated in me with one thrust. I struggled to adjust around him, pain and pleasure blurring as he slammed into me. He snarled, throwing his head back, half of his face consumed by shadows. He reached between my legs, thumb pushing against my clit and rubbing it in time with each merciless thrust.

"Fuck!" My back bowed off the mattress, the pleasure crushing the air from my lungs.

His need slammed into me through the bond, replacing every bit of magic I had lost.

"Please. I need—"

The words fractured apart with every claiming thrust.

"Tell me," the Commander panted, voice rough and uncontrolled.

"Harder," I moaned.

His control snapped. Shadows surged, wrapping around my wrists with a cold bite of pain to hold me in place. He slammed into me with brutal, devastating force, gripping my hips as if the world would end if he let go.

My vision went black at the edges and the world splintered into heat and light. "Commander!" My cry fractured, my fingers clawing into the sheets as my body tightened and then shattered beneath the wave of release. He fell over the edge with me, roaring with a deep, primal sound that shook the bedframe.

His body locked over mine, cock pulsing hard as warmth spilled inside me.

Pure bliss engulfed me, but it was short lived. The Commander pulled out of me, panting and baring his teeth. He dropped to his knees, fisting his hair and screaming as shadows tore through him.

Thirty-Nine
Veilstrider

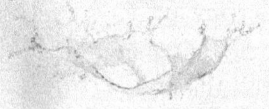

Something was wrong.

The Commander screamed. His agony tore through me like a heated knife tearing open my skin. It shredded every single piece of calm in me.

I jumped off the bed, rushing to where he knelt on the floor. The sun had dipped behind the horizon, casting the room into darkness that the Commander was bleeding into.

"Stay away!" he roared, flinching away from me as if *I* were the danger. But I couldn't. I couldn't leave him like that. His canines flashed in a vicious snarl as I knelt next to him.

A show meant to scare me, but it didn't work. A shadow lashed out and coiled around my hand, sinking in with brutal, icy agony. I choked on a gasp but splayed my hand against his chest anyway.

"What is happening?" I managed, voice cracking. I needed an answer. I needed him to look at me.

His shadows burned like ice as they tore at my skin, but I forced my wrist towards his mouth anyway. It was the only thing I could think to do, the only thing I had to offer.

If my blood could anchor him and soothe the darkness, I would give it. All of it, if I had to.

A guttural sound ripped from his chest, half-beast, half-man as he struggled with control.

He squeezed his eyes shut before his canines pierced my skin and cold agony dug into every nerve as his darkness crawled up my arm.

Warmth oozed through his bite as he drank from me. But his venom wasn't enough, I bit down on a cry. He had endured this pain just to be near me. I could endure it too, for him, even if his darkness consumed me.

His suffering crept into me, it was like a hole inside his chest I somehow knew I could fill. I closed my eyes and imagined my pool of shimmering blue magic pouring towards it.

The bond ignited, flooding between us in a searing rush.

His panic slammed into me, raw and suffocating as his *pain* coiled around my heart like a vice. My magic thrashed in response, filling the empty hole in his chest—

His mouth ripped away from my wrist. "Stop," he breathed, horror creeping into his voice.

I couldn't stop. Not when his shadows were tearing holes through him. Not when the bond pulsed like a second heartbeat between us. Not when I could feel how much he needed me.

"It's okay," I whispered, though my voice shook.

His eyes widened, broken and beautiful as my power seeped into the gaping cracks in his soul. I felt it leaving me, my own soul weakening.

"No," he rasped.

He tore himself away from me, breaking my touch. His shadows recoiled, slamming back into his body hard enough to send him flying. The connection snapped. My magic came rushing back all at once, violently rejected, flooding my chest like a dam wall exploding. I pitched forward onto my hands, gasping down ragged breaths.

"Don't ever do that again," he wheezed as he rolled onto his side, voice raw and filled with terror.

I lifted my head and the room spun. "You needed—"

"I need *nothing* worth losing you!" He yelled over me, hands fisting as if he were barely restraining himself. "Do you even know what you were doing?"

I shook my head, tears swimming in my eyes.

"Your magic was trying to *fix* me by sacrificing your-self." He gathered me into his lap, arms wrapping around me with a gentleness that broke me. The Fire Fates words echoed through my head, *"the destroyer, if she does not save her Fated Mate."*

I curled against him, fitting as if I were made for him. The room felt quiet. Heavy. The only sound disturbing the darkness was the uneven sounds of our breathing.

"I will not survive my darkness," he whispered. "But you will."

Realisation crashed into me with a heartbreaking squeeze, sharp enough to steal the air from my lungs. "It won't be for long," I whispered, repeating his words from yesterday. The words tasted like ash. That *feeling* in the bond. The quiet ache. That relentless, hollow sorrow that radiated through him. The way he held me like someone memorising a goodbye.

"You're dying."

He didn't say anything, just stroked my hair softly and letting his silence stretch too long.

"It's true, isn't it? That's why the bond feels like you're mourning something. That's why the shadows are getting worse—"

My voice broke, tears welling in my eyes. I had *just* found him.

His eyes fluttered shut and he held me close, brushing a kiss onto my forehead.

"My death..." He paused and opened his eyes, tears shimmering like starlight against the endless abyss of his gaze. "It is the cost of having you, Little Drownling. One I am willing to pay," he said, voice low and ragged.

I sat up straight, anger snapping through me, bright and vicious and I made sure he could feel every single drop of it.

He had said it so calmly, as though his death was already decided. As if I would allow it.

"Why is your darkness killing you?" I demanded. Maybe if I knew why, I could help him fix it.

A breathless chuckle escaped him. "I cannot tell you—"

An impatient knocking wrapped against the door, shattering our quiet moment.

It swung open with force and Solas held his forearm over his eyes as he barged into the room.

"I love you like a brother Solas, but if you look at her, I *will* rip the eyeballs from your skull," he snarled as he pushed me behind him to shield me with his body. Solas grimaced, turning his back to us completely. "I am *not* looking," Solas snapped urgently. His usual light-heartedness, gone.

"What is it?" The Commander asked carefully.

"Veilstriders."

That one word shot the Commander into action. He stood and grabbed his pants, pulling them on with speed. I knew without asking that it was more of Helion's creations and hurried to dress quickly. The Commander grabbed his onyx sword that rested against the wall.

"Stay here," he said as he followed Solas into the corridor.

I scoffed and followed him through the bedroom doors, two strides to their one. If he thought I would let him out of my sight from now on, he was *wrong*.

He stopped abruptly and turned, looking down at me wearily.

"Get back to the room," he said on a rough exhale.

"No," I challenged, squaring my shoulders and raising my chin. "People are dying because these monsters are hunting *me*. I will not cower and put more innocent blood on my hands."

"It is not safe, Lyra." He rested his hands on my shoulders and bent to kiss my forehead. "Please, do not make me use the bargain."

I stiffened, stepping back and glaring at him with venom.

"Do it," I hissed. "I will find a way to break it. And when I do, I will cut off your balls and *feed* them to the monsters."

"We are wasting time," Solas said, clearing his throat to stifle a small smile despite himself.

The Commander sighed heavily, shaking his head as he leaned down, took my hand, and pulled me down the hallway.

From now on, we would fight together.

WE JOGGED DOWN A SLOPED PATH CARVED INTO THE mountain, boots slamming against stone. I had been unconscious when the Commander carried me through the gates and seeing what was behind those walls was breathtaking.

Nestled safely within the semicircle outer wall that joined with the mountain—or what should have been safe—was a town. But it was unlike anything I had ever seen before.

Lanterns twinkled, and strings of golden lights crossed the cobblestone streets like a festival frozen in time. Flowers bloomed from vines that had grown over the cottages. It was beautiful. *Magical.* But the people were frantic.

People scattered. Running. *Hiding.* A shopkeeper dragged in his baskets of fruit, slamming his shutters. Women ushered children through doorways, bolting them shut. The entire town was sealing itself in.

A bell tolled, deep and thunderous. It rolled over the town in a warning that made my mouth turn dry.

"Fuck." The Commander's head snapped towards the sound.

"They are inside the wall!" Solas shouted, picking up speed.

A child darted in front of me, almost making me trip. A little boy, no more than four. Tears streaked his chubby cheeks as he ran to an abandoned toy he must have dropped on the street. A small wooden horse, laying on its side.

"Leo!" a woman screamed from a doorway; arms stretched for him helplessly.

The street suddenly went silent, as if something had stolen the sound.

The Commander pulled his sword from its scabbard. The energy pulsing off it made my stomach churn, and I took an involuntary step backwards. An eerie ringing sounded in my ears. The complete absence of noise.

Gooseflesh tore across my skin. The street was not empty. Not quite. It was *wrong.* Like the air itself was holding its breath.

Solas eyed the dark as if it might lunge for him, gripping his sword with two hands as the lights above us flickered.

I walked towards the child, but my steps faltered the moment I saw *it*. At the far end of the street, just past a flickering lantern stood a Veilstrider. Too thin to be human, too tall. Its charcoal skin stretched tautly across its body, making it hard to see in the dark. Its limbs stretched long enough to scrape against the cobblestones if it were walking. But it stood eerily still. The little boy scooped up his toy and ran for his mother—but the door slammed shut, locking him out as she sealed herself inside the safety of the cottage. He stood next to me with tears streaming down his face.

When I looked back up at the Veilstrider, it was gone. As though the world had blinked and misplaced it. The back of my neck prickled. I spun—

It was right there.

Where there should have been a scream, there was no sound. Just a suffocating pressure, like static crawling under the skin, prickling down the spine. Fear. Pure, distilled fear spread through me like an infection. I couldn't move, couldn't breathe.

But the Commander was already there, stalking the creature. Shadows erupted with violent force as he sprinted towards us.

The monsters head snapped towards the Commander as if it could sense him. It had no eyes to see, but it *knew* he was there.

I blinked and it was gone. Erased, as though someone had wiped it off the face of the world.

The air suddenly felt lighter and the pressure vanished from my skull. The street brightened by a single shade as noise bled back to my ears.

The boy's sobs echoed through the street, the sound no longer distorted by the strange magic.

The Commander stepped forward, shadows coiling violently around him like a storm that had not decided who to kill next. His eyes were still black, hunting, searching for the Veilstrider. "Cowardly things," Solas muttered. If *that thing* had feared the Commander, enough to blink out of existence... What did that make *him*?

I crouched in front of the small boy, his bottom lip trembling as he clutched his toy to his chest. His large hazel eyes shone up, glittering with tears.

"You're okay," I told him and scooped him into my arms. The poor boy trembled violently, his skin too cold for the summer night.

"What is wrong with him?" I asked, wiping an almost frozen tear from his chubby cheek.

The Commander placed his hand on the boy's forehead and bowed his head. The sorrow in his eyes as they crashed into mine took my breath away.

"He is dying." The Commander said solemnly. "Veilstriders induce a fear so intense that it *freezes* their victims." The little boy had stopped crying, his head resting against my chest weakly, his little breaths blooming against the night air.

"No. I will *not* let him die because of a monster made to hunt *me!*"

A scream echoed in the distance.

"More of my people are dying, Lyra." The Commander looked at me, willing me to understand.

"Go. Save them. But I am not leaving the boy." He nodded once. There was no time to argue.

"Keep her safe." He said to Solas as his shadows consumed him, pulling him into the darkness.

"We should let the boy's mother say goodbye to him," Solas said softly, gesturing to the cottage.

I ignored him, squeezing my eyes shut and placing the small boy on the ground in front of me. I was a fucking goddess; I would save this boy even if it killed me.

I imagined my well of power, the swirling pool of glittering turquoise in my chest. I pulled at it, urging it to my hands that pressed over the boy's weak heart. I did not know if this was going to work. But he was dying, and I was willing to try anything. My hand turned warm and tingly as my power thrummed along it, sinking into the small lifeless body.

Nothing happened. Just the silent weight of a child slipping away and the hysteric wails of his mother who had opened the door.

"No," I whispered, shaking. "No, no, no—come on." The turquoise glow deepened, pulsing with streaks of shadowed black as I poured more power into him.

"Lyra," Solas warned, voice soft and patient. "Goddess or not, if you force too much—"

"Stay back!" I snapped, tears burning hot trails down my face. "I *will* do this."

My power surged again, hard enough to make my teeth grit together in effort.

The boy gasped. A shallow, fragile sound. Then another. Then another. His little chest hitched under my palms, and colour seeped back into his cheeks. He blinked up at me, eyes no longer hazel, but a clear crystal blue.

A sob burst out of me, half laugh, half relief, as I gathered him back into my arms. "There you are," I whispered, "you're safe."

Solas knelt beside us, eyes wide with awe and something dangerously close to reverence. "Holy Gods," he breathed out as the boy's mother fell to her knees next to me. I tried to pass her the boy, but she stared down at him with fear filled eyes, muttering something in the Fae language.

"Take him," I said, but she snarled at me. Solas took the boy from my arms, speaking to the hysterical mother in their native tongue. I stood on shaky legs and began walking towards the feeling of *fear*.

"Where are you going?" Solas called after me. I lifted my chin, breath shaking, but resolve like steel hardening beneath my ribs.

"To kill some fucking monsters."

FORTY
GODDESS

The night air was too quiet. The town felt suspended, like a held breath waiting to be exhaled. Lanterns glowed above the narrow streets in golden strings, swaying gently as if the wind itself was trying not to be noticed. Their warm light flickered over shuttered windows, bolted doors, and abandoned baskets of half-sorted fruit left on stoops. A place built for joy, now suffocated by fear.

My power should have been empty, burnt out completely after forcing magic through my veins to pull the dying child back from the brink. But instead, magic thrummed quietly beneath my skin. Waiting and begging to be released. All because I *accepted* it. I *am* the goddess of the sea.

I stepped down the middle of the deserted street, my boots brushing over scattered petals that had fallen from the vines overhead. The vines themselves trembled as though sensing what lingered just beyond the veil of the visible.

The first note that left my mouth was soft and inviting.

The monsters wanted me, perhaps I could lure them in with my song.

A low, resonant melody left my lips, rippling through the street and weaving between the shuttered homes. My voice wasn't sweet or gentle; it was a *summoning*.

Power threaded through the song, coiling in the air like fine strands of shimmering water. The street widened as I moved deeper into the town square. Shop fronts crowned with flowers lined the perimeter, and the centre fountain shone like a bowl of liquid moonlight. My melody echoed across its still surface, making the water quiver.

The air changed. The first pulse of pressure rippled across my skin like a hand pressing softly against my spine. The lights darkened, dimming until a coldness pressed into my skin.

It was *here*.

The magic in my song sharpened, shifting to a minor key, each note rising with purpose. The world around me grew dense, heavy, as if invisible walls were drawing inward. The cobblestones at the far edge of the square darkened, the lantern light bending as if swallowed.

I blinked and it was there. Thin and impossibly tall with gangly limbs ending in sharpened claws that dragged across the ground. It had no eyes. No mouth. Yet its face tilted towards me, drawn to my song. The fear it radiated struck like a knife of ice stabbing into my spine.

The melody threaded into the night air, curling around its unnatural form. Its head snapped to the side, bones cracking wetly. I blinked—and it had moved closer, another wave of crushing terror slamming into me.

I forced my voice louder and my magic surged, swirling beneath my ribs. I reached inside the monster's body, pulling at its blood.

My hands lifted, palms trembling from the force rising inside me.

The Veilstrider thrashed in pain, pulling against my hold. But I pulled harder. The blood tore free from its body, seeping through its dark grey skin in a spiralling torrent. Its body shrivelled instantly, collapsing like a decaying corpse. Its chest caved inwards, and its body disintegrated into the ground. Blue blood spiralled upward in a glittering arc, suspended in the air. My arms shook under the weight. Its lifeblood trembled in the air like waves in the ocean, flowing and ebbing like the tide.

The Commander walked towards me, blue gore splattering his bare chest.

His jaw had slackened, eyes fixed on me as though the world beyond my song no longer existed. As if he couldn't look away. Something seemed off.

I dropped the blood, and it collapsed in a heavy crash, splattered over the cobblestone as my song died in my throat.

He stilled, blinking a few times as if waking from a strange dream.

"Commander?" I asked, taking slow steps towards him. Was he hurt?

Something dark crossed his face as I stood in front of him. A wave of dizziness curled through my vision, dark spots dancing in the streetlights but I wasn't burned out, not entirely.

"Are you okay?" I asked him as he blinked down at me.

"Lyra—" his voice cracked and I lifted my hand slowly. My fingers weakly brushed his jawline, warm and grounding beneath my touch.

"You used too much power," he chastised, voice hoarse with something deeper than worry. "You—"

I didn't let him finish. Reaching up, I brought my lips to his, desperately kissing him as if he was the very air I needed to live.

His mouth answered mine with a low, broken groan that shot heat through my entire body. My skin tingled against his want, sinking into my veins and feeding my power.

His hands slid to my waist, pulling me against him in a movement so instinctive, it tore a soft gasp from my lips. The kiss deepened, hard and consuming.

"What have you done to me?" he murmured against my lips and cradled the back of my neck with a shaking hand. I reached up, brushing my thumb along his cheekbone. He leant into it like he was starving for my touch.

"The same thing you have done to me," I whispered.

I swallowed hard as the truth burned through me like a fire I had no intention of extinguishing. "Before you, I only knew pain," I breathed, placing my hand on his chest.

His eyes snapped open, dark and endless as his fingers tightened at my waist.

"You brought me back to life and I *refuse* to let your darkness consume you."

He opened his mouth to speak, but I held up my hand to silence him.

"We have monsters to hunt," I stood on my tiptoes and pulled him into one last, soft kiss. "And a god to kill."

His eyes flared, at the mention of the fallen Sun God.

"You are fucking perfect," he whispered, voice fierce.

The word sank into me, threatening to tear open old wounds. *Perfect* was all I was ever meant to be.

I hated *perfect*—until it came from him. Someone who saw every jagged piece of me and still held on despite the risk of getting cut.

THE MID-MORNING SUN SHONE THROUGH THE WALL-TO-ceiling windows in beams of pale gold, making last night's horrors seem far away.

It wasn't though, the Commander was arranging burials and helping the grief-stricken families the dead had left behind.

I may have saved the little boy, Leo, but I couldn't save the fifteen other Fae who succumbed to the Veilstrider's fear.

The tea's floral steam washed over me, and I inhaled deeply before taking another sip. Cerilla sat across from me in the green plush chairs of our bedchamber.

"Thank you for the tea." I smiled at her. I knew she didn't think I was making the right decision by marrying her brother. But for some reason, I craved her approval. I had never had female figures in my life, and Cerilla was someone I wanted to like me.

"My pleasure, darling." She paused to take a sip of her tea. "Thank you for killing the monster that breached our walls."

"I will kill them all, someday," I told her, raising my chin.

Cerilla's cup clanked down a little to firmly. "That's what I am worried about," she murmured. "Anyway, this morning's visit is not about monsters and killing. It is about your wedding dress."

Nerves swam through my stomach, and suddenly my tea tasted sour.

"It is Obsidian Court tradition to wear black. But you are a goddess, so, I am thinking *silver*. Like a star shining in the night sky." Would it upset his Court to go against tradition, would it upset the Commander?

"I like silver but—"

"Good!" She clapped her hands together with a brilliant smile. "I have had the seamstress make your dress already. But if you want anything changed, we can make it happen." She beamed with genuine excitement and my heart warmed. I had started to love the idea of my life in the Obsidian Court. Never leaving the Commander's side, training with Solas, sharing tea and gossip with Cerilla, even Riven could stay.

He hadn't come to see me since he'd kissed me, but Cerilla assured me his leg was healed. It felt like he was avoiding me, though I wished he wouldn't. He was merely trying to help, and after not seeing him for so long, I found myself missing him.

Cerilla stood and walked to the double doors of the suite, flinging them open with both arms. Six maids walked into the room, a Fae male in a tailored suit and white hair leading them. He smiled widely. "Cerilla, darling, you were not exaggerating! She will look fabulous in my creation!"

An hour passed while I stood in the centre of the room, getting pinned into the most beautiful dress I had ever seen.

Ronaldo fluffed out the train and I stared in wonder. It was breathtaking. The material was like a waterfall of stars, shimmering with each tiny movement.

The strapless bodice formed to my curves and plunged between my breasts. The material gathered at my hips before flowing around my legs.

Some of my scars would be visible, but I didn't care anymore. If anything, they were physical proof that I was strong, a *survivor*.

The silver looked like it belonged against my pale skin,

making the vibrant clear blue of my eyes appear even brighter.

"Absolutely beautiful," Cerilla said with a dazzling smile. "You have out done yourself, Ronaldo." The seamster blushed, bowing his head at Cerilla. The way other Fae responded to her made it obvious they feared her. I should have noticed back at the inn that something was off.

The door began to open, and Cerilla cursed, extending her hand out. Magic pulsed against the door, a shimmering darkness that stopped whoever was on the other side from being able to enter.

"Cerilla, let me in my fucking room," the Commander yelled, radiating urgency.

"She is honestly fine without you for a few hours, brother. Go about your business."

His growl rattled the door, and I didn't bother hiding the smile curving my mouth. The truth was, I was *not* fine with being apart from him.

Cerilla pushed harder against the door, clearly struggling to hold her brother at bay.

"You better get her out of that dress before he breaks the door down," Cerilla gritted out towards the maids. They scurried towards me, helping me to undress.

Just as I got my silk dressing gown over my shoulders, the doors slammed open and Cerilla made a disgruntled noise.

The Commander's eyes were wild, the darkness consuming them completely. "Everyone out!" The maids scrambled out like frightened mice and Ronaldo followed them with his head bowed, my wedding dress clutched to his chest in its bag.

"What is it, brother?" Cerilla asked, taking a small step towards him.

"I said everyone, Cerilla, that means you as well."

Cerilla huffed, spinning on the heel of her slipper and walking out with her black skirts billowing behind her.

The Commander walked towards me and gripped my waist with his large hands urgently. It would have made me flustered if it weren't for the anger pulsing through the bond.

"You told me you killed the priest. The one who punished you for your father, yes?"

I froze under his touch, not understanding the urgency in his voice.

"I used his own blade to stab him in the heart," I said softly.

"And are there many priests in your kingdom?" he demanded.

"No," I said, shaking my head. "He was the only one."

"Then why has your father arrived with a priest at his side?"

My hand flattened against my stomach and nausea surged and flecks danced across my vision. The priest was alive. I had felt the knife plunge into his heart. That was not an injury any Mortal could survive.

"I need you to tell me *exactly* what he did to you."

My mind was spinning, and I was grateful for his hands around me. Without them, I may have fallen.

"The bloodlettings were my treatment. They said my condition was an imbalance in my blood. That if they didn't drain it out, the madness would swallow me." I hadn't meant for my voice to crack, but it did. Betraying me.

The Commander made a broken sound that radiated danger, a mix between a snarl and strangled gasp.

His shadows burst outward in an uncontrolled pulse, the nearby candles sputtering violently. "Those weren't treatments." His words were a snarl. A sick twist curled through my stomach. The commander cursed in the Fae language.

"They were *using* your blood Lyra. That's why the priest didn't fucking die."

FORTY-ONE
DOMINANCE

The Commander lifted me into his arms without hesitation, and I curled into his chest, breathing him in. He smelled like cool night air, sharp and clean, softened by the deep, molten sweetness of caramel that made my mouth water.

It was the smell of safety, of what had become *home*. The rising storm inside me slowed and panic melted away.

"Fuck the alliance," he murmured, voice raw. "I want to watch you drown every single one of them."

A small smile curved my mouth, not because he was right—we needed the alliance, but because he had accepted me. All of me. Even the darkest parts.

"I want to, but the Fates said to unite the Kingdoms to stand against the Seven Hells."

They had also said if I didn't save the Commander, I would become the destroyer of everything, but I kept that to myself.

A muscle ticked in the Commander's jaw, and he lowered me gently onto the edge of the bed. His hand cupped my cheek, his thumb brushing my lower lip.

He was the missing piece I had needed to feel whole, and somehow, he had been holding a part of my soul for a thousand years—*waiting* for me to claim it.

The Fates were right about one thing. If I couldn't save him from his darkness, I would drown the whole fucking world.

"I cannot face them just yet, Little Drownling," he said, voice low, frayed. "Not when you look at me like that."

"Like what?" I taunted, knowing full well I was staring at him like he was the moon that pulled my tides.

His eyes darkened, devouring me where I sat in my silk dressing gown, the thin fabric slipping down one shoulder.

"You know exactly what you are doing," he said with gravel in his voice, pushing up the sleeves of his black button-up shirt over his corded forearms. Gods, how did he look *more* devastating this way?

"Maybe I do," I said, leaning forward and gripping his belt buckle. His breath faltered. Just slightly. Just enough for truth to spill into the space between us. He needed me just as much as I needed him.

His forehead pressed to mine, breath shaking, lips barely brushing mine. "Lyra," he whispered, like a prayer and a threat rolled into one.

I closed the distance and kissed him, pouring every overwhelming feeling I couldn't voice down our bond.

I forced his lips apart and drove my tongue in without permission. He made a low broken sound beneath me, instinctively yielding as I set the pace and refused to let go.

My hands slipped up his chest, over the soft fabric of his shirt, the hard muscles shifting beneath. I ripped at his shirt and the buttons popped free as the fabric tore beneath my grip.

"Fuck," he muttered against my mouth, clearly struggling to let me stay in control.

"You are testing my restraint, love."

I broke the kiss and smiled wickedly up at him, teasingly trailing my hands up my body and letting the dressing gown slip down my shoulders.

He watched with rapt attention as my fingers dragged slowly over my aching breasts, mouth twisting in a snarl against the pain of his shadows attacking him.

"I respect you—remember that," he warned, his voice so deep it rumbled through me. "Because what I am about to do will make it seem like I don't."

"Show me," I breathed.

He groaned, a deep, devastated sound, and shoved me backwards onto the mattress. His body caged mine, held up only by the last thread of restraint he possessed. His lips trailed along my jaw, down my throat. His hand slid under the edge of my gown, fingers tracing the bare skin of my thigh. My hips tilted forward, eager for his touch.

His canines sank into my neck with two sharp stings. They disappeared instantly, replaced with the warmth of his mouth suckling against my skin. He pushed the silk dressing gown up my thighs, skimming a finger down my overheated flesh and I gasped.

"Already so fucking wet for me," he murmured against my neck before breaking contact.

He gripped my hips and I gasped as he flipped me onto my stomach with force.

I had always hated being controlled, yet something wild and unhinged in me answered to his dominance and made desire drip down my thighs.

He lifted me up onto my knees, forcing my back to arch and my face to press into the mattress.

"That's it, love, spread those legs for me."

A warm sting bloomed across my ass cheek as his hand struck bare skin. My lower stomach fluttered, need spiking sharp enough to tear a cry from my throat.

The bed shifted as he moved and the sound of his pants thudding against the carpet made my stomach flutter with anticipation. But I kept my head shoved against the mattress obediently.

His fingers pushed into me while his other hand gripped my ass.

"Commander!" I yelled into the blankets as pain melted into pleasure.

"You like that, don't you," he rasped in a voice like gravel. "Fuck, I can't wait anymore."

His fingers disappeared and his hard, pulsing cock pressed against my entrance. I moved forwards and he growled, gripping my hips to hold me in place.

"Grip the bedsheets, love."

He rolled his hips forwards, plunging his cock inside me and stretching me open. My fingers fisted the bedsheets, knuckles whitening as I tried to adjust around him. He was too big like this. I couldn't—

"You can take it," he encouraged when I gasped and tried to squirm away. He leant over me and fisted my hair, slowly pushing into me to the hilt—

A sharp knock split the air. I froze, but the Commander didn't stop moving in and out of me. Another knock, louder and more impatient.

"Commander," Solas called through the door. "The Mortal king demands an audience."

Dread swept through me, my panic threatening to creep up my throat and strangle me.

The Commander ignored it, ignored Solas, splaying his

hand against my lower back to deepen the arch. When he thrust, he hit something so deep inside me I cried out in pleasure. Heat bloomed against my face, bright with embarrassment.

"Let him wait," the Commander growled loudly as he made my eyes roll back into my head with pleasure.

"And when he asks why?" Riven drawled through the door, something dark undercutting his usually amused tone.

The Commander snarled, like an animal. I couldn't help the breathless laugh that escaped me, even as heat flushed across my skin. He thrust into me with force, making me cry out again. I twisted to glare up at him, but his dark smirk made my insides turn to liquid.

"Then tell him I'm fucking his daughter," the Commander yelled through the door.

His dark, beautiful eyes never left mine, and despite the harshness of his words, the warmth of love flooded the bond between us.

There was arguing behind the door, but I didn't care. I only cared about the Commander. My Fated Mate. His hand slipped around my waist, sinking between my legs to circle against my clit.

"Cum for me love, let me make you feel good."

His thrusts became merciless, his groans harmonising with my needy gasps. A sound tore from me, soft at first, then deepening into a trembling moan threaded with the faintest echo of my magic. My pleasure slammed into me and warmth spiralled outward, stealing every thought, every drop of humility. My fingers clenched and my body shook as another cry slipped free before I could stop it. Everything inside me tightened, then unravelled all at once, until I was a trembling mess beneath his deep, unravelling thrusts.

He roared with his own release, and his hands gripped me with bruising force as his cock spilled warmth inside me.

For a long moment, the room was nothing but breath. Mine was shaky, still trying to remember my own name. His was ragged and warm against the back of my neck as he held himself braced above me.

"Nice finish, Commander," Riven called out, his usual charm warped by something darker as it cut through our intimacy. "Can we secure an alliance now? Save the Kingdoms? Or do you have another round in you?"

I buried my face in my hands, a breathless laugh slipping out.

"I'm going to kill him," the Commander muttered darkly, pushing himself upright and slowly pulling out of me.

"Please don't," I said as I rolled over, though my voice shook with concealed amusement. "He was the first person to accept me for what I am."

He sighed, cupping my cheek with a gentleness utterly at odds with the name the world had given him.

"Fine," he said, voice low. "But only for you."

A pounding fist knocked on the door and the Commander closed his eyes like he was counting backward from ten. "But know it is *really* hard for me."

I laughed again and he helped me stand, steadying me as my legs remembered how to function.

"We need to go," he said, voice gravel-soft but threaded with iron.

"Father will be furious that you made him wait." A slow smile curved my lips at the thought of him feeling belittled.

His answering look was wicked as he crossed the room to the tall, carved wardrobe. I could not look away from the shifting muscles of his ass. No male had ever been so breathtaking in the history of the Kingdoms, it was like he was carved by the Gods themselves.

Silk whispered as he sifted through garments until he finally paused, deciding on something and turned towards me.

My breath caught. The dress he was holding was black, pure obsidian silk with long sleeves fitted closely to the wrist. Its bodice was fitted, cinched at the waist with delicate silver embroidery that resembled constellations. The skirt flowed like melted shadow with a slit high enough that would reveal my legs when I moved. The neckline was a deep, plunging V. Not like the modest, oppressing dresses of the Mortal Kingdom. This was powerful, weaponizing my femininity into something that could draw blood.

"Wear this," he murmured as he stepped towards me.

I let him help me into the dress, the silk whispering across my skin with a soothing coolness. His fingers lingered at the fastening, brushing the back of my neck with unexpected tenderness.

My wild hair spilled down my back in silver waves. I gathered it, trying to tame it into a braid, but his hands closed gently over mine, stopping me.

"Leave it," he urged, holding my gaze for a long, unreadable moment. "One more thing," he said quietly, crossing to the bedside table. He opened the top drawer on the side I slept on and pulled out the Soul Relic crown.

The iridescent shellwork shimmered as though alive. Pearlescent blues, greens, and silver threaded through the bone-white coral. When sunlight caught it, it glowed faintly, like moonlight trapped beneath the sea.

He stepped closer, eyes never leaving mine. He lowered the crown onto my head carefully. It settled against my hair as though it had been made for me.

I turned towards the mirror next to the wardrobe and gasped. The girl who stared back was not the broken princess my father had last seen. She looked like a goddess. Like the sea made flesh. Power curled beneath my skin, reflected in the silver-blue of my eyes.

Behind me, the Commander was still dressing. Black combat pants slung low on his hips, boots planted wide as he pulled on a black button-up and shoved the sleeves past his elbows, exposing the corded strength of his forearms.

My eyes traced the veins and ink as the hard muscle shifted beneath his skin. His black curls hung over his brows, dishevelled and wild from fucking me.

His darkness and shadows were thrown into stark contrast against my pale skin and silver hair. Light and dark. And yet beneath it all, we were broken in the same way.

A knock rattled against the door again and the Commander snarled.

"Are you ready?" he asked, grabbing my hand in his.

I nodded, not one part of me *wanted* to see them. But with the Commander at my side and my power thrumming in my veins, I knew they couldn't break me anymore.

When the door opened, Riven lounged against the opposite wall with his arms crossed. "Finally," he said darkly, raising his eyebrows and pushing off the wall.

Solas couldn't hide his smile as he took us in but said nothing, for which I was grateful.

The Commander ignored them both, pulling me gently but firmly forward.

The corridor stretched before us, sunlight streaming through the large floor-to-ceiling windows cut into the mountain.

"The Mortal King waits with six others," Solas briefed

us as we walked. "The prince, his priest, a viscount and three soldiers."

Aldric was here? My chest flooded with a strange mix of shame and hope. I hadn't thought of him much since I read his letter, his apology. Anger crawled over its place. Did he know they were using my blood for power?

"The Iron Guard soldiers," Riven added, keeping pace with us. "Are Commander Kragthorne, Captain Bronwyn and initiate Dreya."

My step faltered, a small misstep, but big enough for the Commander to notice.

"A friend," I said to him when he shot me a questioning look.

"If friends spear each other, then sure," Riven scoffed.

"This Dreya, she is the one who speared you?" the Commander asked, fury swirling through bond.

"She was protecting herself," I tried to explain, remembering the pure fear she had in her eyes when she had looked at me.

Riven walked with his hands in his pockets, a carefree smirk plastered on his face, but I didn't miss the way his gaze kept flicking to my hand in the Commanders.

Fae soldiers and nobles froze in our path, eyes widening before they sank to their knees as the Relic crown on my brow glittered beneath the lights.

"They bow to you even in your own halls?" I asked in wonderment, not even my father had this sort of respect.

The Commander chuckled darkly, mouth pulling into a dangerous half smirk.

"They are not bowing to *me*."

The words landed slowly. I had spent my life being arranged, displayed, and ignored. I was an ornament polished for other people's power.

Not anymore.

We wound through the open corridors, coming to a foyer where Cerilla and Caelum waited. Caelum looked bored, as if this were beneath him, whereas Cerilla paced restlessly like a caged animal.

The Commander leant down, his lips brushing the shell of my ear. "If you won't kill them," he whispered. "Humiliate them."

A thrill shot through my chest as a dark smile spread across my face.

The massive doors to the throne room loomed ahead, carved with swirling runes and the three-pointed star crest of the Obsidian Court.

I lifted my chin and let power ripple through my voice.

"Open the doors."

FORTY-TWO
ALLIANCE

The doors of the Obsidian Court throne room burst open under the Commander's shadows, the sound rolling through the vast chamber like distant thunder. The Commander looped my arm through his as he escorted me inside, and the moment we touched the onyx tiles, the room shifted. Silence cracked like ice. All eyes turned.

Solas, Caelum, Cerilla, and Riven walked in behind us like four shadows of power. Each of them radiated their own kind of danger.

Riven sauntered with a lazy arrogance, Cerilla seethed cold fury, Solas looked ready to tear out throats, and Caelum watched everyone like they were already dead.

The Mortals were already assembled, and Fae soldiers lined the walls like sentinels waiting to kill.

My father stood at the front with his arms crossed against his broad chest and an expression as hard as I remembered. The priest stood beside him, blond hair slicked back, handsome face disguising the brutality of a torturer. The moment his eyes flicked to me, my body betrayed me. Cold terror locked my muscles in place. My skin burned as if his hands were still crawling over me, as if I could still feel his blade sinking unforgivingly into the flesh of my back.

His presence crushed the air from my lungs, a bruise on the world that made it hard to breathe.

I wished I had stabbed his face, to make it as physically ugly as he was on the inside.

The Commander's arm tightened around mine, the hatred radiating through the bond matching mine in its depths. The priest would regret surviving me after I let the Commander have him.

Instead of cowering, a slow smile traced my lips. Not the practiced mask my father liked, no. A vicious smile that promised pain.

Aldric stood behind him, looking like a dishevelled version of the polished brother I had known. His face relaxed when he saw me, as if he were able to take his first full breath in weeks.

Next to him was viscount Barden and the Iron Guards.

Dreya's eyes stayed trained straight ahead, as though she was refusing to look at me. But the moment her eyes landed on Riven, her fists clenched at her side.

The throne room itself was vast and impossibly beautiful. Midnight stone had been polished to a mirror shine, and silver veins ran through the floor like frozen lightning. Above us, obsidian pillars spiralled upward, painted with stars and florals. Streams of sunlight poured through the high, arched windows and skylights. At the centre of it all stood the throne, a towering construct of black granite and carved shadow wood, rising like the spine of some ancient beast. Silver filigree wrapped its edges like constellations frozen mid-burst, and behind it, a star-shaped crest of polished obsidian fanned like a halo.

I went to take my place beside it. Unlike at Stonebriar, I would stand next to his throne with pride. The Commander placed a firm hand on my back, stopping me as he lowered his head towards my ear. "Take your seat, my love," he whispered on the ghost of a breath.

The entire Mortal delegation stiffened as I sat on the throne.

The cold granite bit into my skin with a delightful chill.

The Commander leant casually against the massive armrest, crossing his corded forearms over his chest, shadows coiling around his boots like restless smoke, still sated from my blood.

He looked down at the Mortals as though deciding which one to kill first.

"Speak," he growled, voice echoing through the chamber like a blade drawn from its sheath.

King Vaylor stepped forward, grey battle armour glinting beneath his red cloak, chin held high as if he wasn't standing in front of the most powerful male in existence and a goddess. His eyes cut to me. Then to the Commander. Then back to me. For a moment, he was speechless.

"The alliance," he finally said. "It must happen today."

The Commander didn't move, didn't react. "You do not make demands here, little king. Why the rush?" he asked flatly. Vaylor lifted his hands in a practiced gesture of urgency. "Because monsters are tearing through the Mortal Kingdom. My people are dying. Entire villages wiped out in a night. We need the alliance formed immediately. Even our castle is no longer safe. We need your protection." The Commander scoffed, a low, vicious sound.

"You need protection?" he echoed. "My people are

dying as well." A hush fell. He pushed away from the armrest, stepping forward slightly. "In fact," he continued, voice dripping poison, "the only chance *any* of us have for survival is weapons forged by your daughter's magic. It is her choice if you get any out of this deal, perhaps you should beg her."

Vaylor's nostrils flared. Aldric shifted his weight, looking between us with a tight jaw, a silent conflict burning behind his eyes.

"This is no time for games, High Lord," King Vaylor seethed, eyes as hard as steel.

The Commander's shadows rose instantly, ready to strangle my father where he stood.

"Let him finish," I murmured, laying a hand gently on the Commander's forearm.

The shadows withdrew and Vaylor watched them wearily as he continued, voice dripping with grim authority. "If we do not unite, *both* our Kingdoms will fall. The threat grows with every hour. I will not have my people slaughtered because of your temper."

The Commander barked out a laugh, a dangerous, unhinged sound.

"Then get on your knees and beg the goddess for her protection, or I will put you there permanently."

King Vaylor spluttered, his face reddening with rage but he didn't move.

The Commander leaned towards me, bowing his head to hide his lips. "Which one can I kill to prove a point?" he whispered, so only I could hear.

Down the bond came steady, controlled bloodlust begging to be set free. But I could feel him waiting for my approval.

The name spilled from my mouth before the thought had formed. "The viscount."

I should have felt bad, but the viscount's slimy words from the Ascension ball crawled through my head.

The Commander pushed off the edge of the throne and strode towards the Mortals. My father did well not to retreat, but a satisfied smirk tilted my lips when he flinched.

The Commander prowled straight to the viscount, his regal features twisting into fear as he raised his hands.

But the Commander didn't slow. He slammed his fist into the viscount's stomach so hard that he dropped to the floor and the air whooshed from his lungs. The Commander drove his knee into Barden's face, blood spraying from the impact. Barden wheezed, making pathetic whimpering sounds. The Commander drew a dagger from his belt and caught Barden's face in his grip, fingers crushing his cheeks together as he forced his head up.

He ran the blade down his face, not hard enough to cut his skin, but enough to threaten. "See, when I am not listened to..." He pressed the blade into his skin and Barden cried out in pain. "I get a little violent."

"You and the bitch can go to hell!" Barden spat, blood spraying with each word.

The Commander laughed, a dangerous chuckle that promised pain. "Haven't you heard? Hell is already here." He slammed the blade down, sinking it to the hilt through his eye with a wet, nauseating squelch. Barden's body crumpled against the ground as the Commander ripped his knife free.

He paused in front of my father, towering over him to wipe the blood from his blade on the king's cloak. I had never seen my father so angry, so humiliated and it was delicious.

"See, little king, I can unite the Kingdoms by force if I must. The only reason I do not take your throne with blood is because of Lyra. Because she wants to do it *peacefully*." He leant down to look my father in the eye. "Beg for her mercy. Or die."

Aldric was the first to drop to his knees. The others followed. Even Dreya knelt, obvious disdain oozing from her.

As if it were the most painful thing he had ever done, the King of the Mortal Kingdom knelt below me.

"The Mortal Kingdom begs you for your mercy and protection, Lyra."

"Please," Aldric said looking up at me first, then at the Commander. I wasn't sure if the circles under his eyes were bruises, or from exhaustion. "This isn't just politics. Not anymore. The creatures are multiplying; our Kingdom is infested."

Before I Ascended, there were no monsters in the Mortal Kingdom. I didn't understand why, and judging by the curiosity pulsing through the bond, neither did the Commander.

"Say plainly what you want," the Commander demanded at Vaylor.

"I want the marriage finalized today, the alliance in effect immediately, Fae warriors to travel to the Mortal Kingdom as protection, and access to fresh produce," he listed his demands. The throne room erupted in whispers and outrage, but through it all, the Commander did not look away from me. He was reading me through the bond, gauging my feelings while still respecting my wish to keep my mind untouched.

"You ask for much, little king," he said softly. "You are

fortunate I would give anything for your daughter. But she has the final say."

"Lyra Meridian," he said, dark and deliberate. "Will you marry me today?"

The room held its breath and the world narrowed to a single word humming beneath my skin.

Even now, he was offering me something I had never been given. Control.

"Yes."

A small, private smile tugged at the Commander's mouth as he looked at me in disbelief. Love and bittersweet joy surged down the bond in such a wave my breath hitched.

"Then it is done," the Commander said to Vaylor. "The alliance will be sealed with our vows when the moon rises." He walked back to where I sat on the throne and perched on the armrest, shadows crawling to him from the corners of the room. "Caelum, show the Mortals where they will be staying and ensure food is sent to their rooms."

Caelum walked towards the door deliberately stepping over the viscount's corpse.

My father stood, shooting one wary glance at me before looking down at my brother still kneeling against ground.

"Aldric—"

"No," my brother snapped over the top of him as he rose to his feet, boots planting against the marble as if daring him to pull his leash.

Our father dragged a hand through his beard, his gaze raking over Aldric with detached fury. "Fine," he spat, and left the room.

A trembling breath left my brother as he nodded once, a small, broken gesture that cracked something open inside me. My heart clenched painfully.

I moved before thought could catch up.

Aldric met me halfway, a choked sound breaking from him as he pulled me into his arms.

"You're alive," he whispered, squeezing me tighter as if to check. "Gods, you look so strong Lyra."

Strong. Not beautiful. Not an object. Not broken.

I could feel the Commander's curiosity pulsing through the bond, but he didn't interrupt. I let go of Aldric, smoothing the wrinkles I had made in his pressed white shirt. Leave it to him to be able to travel and still not have one golden hair out of place.

His warm brown eyes took me in, filling with grief. "Lyra—"

"It's okay, Al," I reassured him with a soft smile. None of it was his fault, and in some ways, he was trapped in the same gilded cage that I had been.

"Come, there are people I want you to meet." I grabbed his hand and turned towards the Commander. "This is my brother, Aldric." My brother smiled wearily at the Commander, extending his hand. I didn't miss the slight tremble in his movements as the Commander reached out to shake it.

"You did not protect her the way a brother should," the Commander said darkly.

"A mistake I have made myself bleed for every day since she ran away. Scar for scar." Aldric unbuttoned his shirt, turning his back to us and lowering it. I gasped, hand fluttering to my mouth. Large scars ran along his back. Some were puckered, and others were gashes that still oozed between fresh sutures.

"I paid the priest to carve my skin as he did yours." Aldric redressed silently, grief and guilt written in the lines of his shoulders.

"Your scars do not absolve you." The Commander's voice cut deeper than any wound in his flesh.

Aldric closed his eyes in a pained acceptance. "I know," he whispered. "But I would carve ten thousand more if it meant she hadn't felt a single blade."

Something inside me twisted sharply. I reached out, touching Aldric's arm. "Hurting yourself will not change the past." His gaze lifted, raw and vulnerable. "It's now that counts."

"They are going to try to steal you, Lyra. They think the monsters are the Gods punishing us for letting you live. They want to sacrifice you."

A shiver slid down my spine. It was almost exactly what Riven had told us, but hearing my brother defy my father to tell me made it real.

"We already know," Riven said in a singsong voice from where he leant against the wall.

"Well then, suppose I have just promised myself a death sentence for nothing."

"Stay in Lumireth with me," I said. The Commander nodded once in approval.

"I would love to," Aldric said hesitantly, warmth shining in his eyes.

"Solas," the Commander said, "get Prince Aldric settled in the southern wing and post a guard." He turned back to me, his voice softening. "Come, Little Drownling. We have a wedding to prepare for."

FORTY-THREE
PREPARATION

We have a wedding to prepare for...
The words rang in my ears as we walked through corridors bustling with staff and people of the court. The Commander's hand never left the small of my back as he guided me through the high-arched corridor. His touch was light, but the intent behind it was not. I could feel his possessiveness radiating down the bond, and judging by the heat in his eyes, he could feel mine pushing right back at him.

"You are going to be my husband..." I murmured, a flutter of nerves shooting through my stomach.

"I *love* weddings," Riven called from where he walked with Cerilla behind us. The Commander glared over his shoulder before wrapping his arm around my shoulders.

"My mark sits on your hand, tethering your *soul* to mine. But it is a ring that makes you nervous?" he said with amusement.

"Yes," I answered, my voice coming steadier than I felt.

He glanced down at me, the corner of his mouth ticking in something that wasn't quite a smile.

We rounded a corner into one of the inner courtyards, the air cooler here, scented with night flowers that Solas had pointed out on our travels. I knew coming through here would be stunning once the sun set and the moonlight made the flowers bloom.

Riven walked past us and sat on the low stone wall by a pond, picking up pebbles to flick into the water. Cerilla's skirts swishing angrily as she rounded her brother.

"That was a disaster!" she chastised.

"Oh, I thought it went well," Riven drawled, eyeing the crown on my head, then the blood still speckling the Commander's forearms.

"Quiet, *Mortal*," Cerilla hissed, though her eyes were soft when they landed on me. She hurried forward, gripping my hands. "Are you all right, darling?"

I exhaled slowly, my heart warming at her kindness. "I think so."

"She is getting *married*," Riven said, smirking. "I would say she is more than *fine*." He threw the next stone a little too hard, and it splashed over Cerilla's skirts. They started to bicker, but I blocked it out and turned towards the Commander.

"Do you regret capturing me?" I said, unable to push down the fear of this not being real.

The Commander brushed a kiss to my cheek, lips lingering a heartbeat longer than propriety allowed. "The only thing I regret is not taking you from that castle the moment I felt you."

My smile faltered. *Castle*. Not *barracks*. His shoulders locked tight, as though bracing for a blow. Fear surged from him, raw and unguarded.

Before I could correct him, Cerilla looped her arm

through mine and with graceful force, pushed the Commander away from me.

"Enough," she scolded, dragging me away from him. "You two are not to see each other until the ceremony. How you expect to pull off a royal wedding in *five* hours is infuriating beyond belief."

She dragged me down the corridor and Riven trailed after us with his hands in his pockets.

Behind him, the Commander stood rooted where we had left him, his gaze fastened to me as if tearing it away might kill him.

Ronaldo was already pacing when Cerilla dragged me back into my chambers, rings glittering on his hands with every frantic movement.

The maids from earlier, Leena, Seli, and Tamsin, stood tensely behind him, each holding jewels, pins, and shoes.

"There she is!" Ronaldo shrieked, clapping a hand to his chest like he'd just survived a battlefield. "Gods save us. We have *hours*, ladies. *Hours!* Move!"

The maids scattered instantly, swarming towards me.

"Wait!" Cerilla yelled and they all flinched. "Bathe first," she said, lowering her voice. "You reek of bloodshed, sex, and my brother." Her nose wrinkled in distaste and embarrassment flooded my cheeks. She lifted a hand, and a glittering stream of magic slipped from her fingers, wafting beneath the bathroom door.

Floral-scented steam curled into my face as I stepped into the bathroom and closed the door. The bath chamber was warm and dimly lit by lanterns that blazed to life. Steam curled lazily through the air. The tub itself, if one could call it that, was carved directly into the black stone floor, large enough to swim in, its edges lined with silver inlay that glowed faintly when touched. A waterfall of warm water spilled continuously from a carved serpent's mouth, filling the rippling pool of water. Pale blue and white tiles spiralled across the walls, reminding me of waves reflecting soft light. Along the far end, shelves held oils and soaps infused with moonflowers, obsidian petals, and some kind of sweet berry I couldn't name.

I undressed quickly, stepping out of the beautiful gown and lowering myself into the water with a sigh. The heat sank into my muscles, pulling at the tension as my hair floated like a silver halo around me.

My mind jumped back to the Commander's words. Surely, he had accidentally said castle instead of barracks. Mortal was not his first language, but why had he felt *frightened?*

Someone knocked, a single, soft rap.

"Come in," I called, assuming it was Cerilla.

Riven stepped inside the bathroom, closing the door with a quiet click. He stood side-on with his eyes fixed on the ground, shoulders slumped as if weighed down. His brown waves fell into his eyes, and for once, there was no easy smirk. His grey button-down was open at the collar, as if he had undone them to loosen whatever troubled him.

"You shouldn't be in here," I said, not bothering to cover my skin. The barracks had made us comfortable with each other's nudity.

"I know," he said, his voice low and gravelly. "But I needed to check on you."

"Are *you* okay?" I asked instead. The absence of his usual ease made something ache in my chest.

He let out a rough sigh and ran a hand through his hair. "Do you truly want to marry the Commander of Death?"

"Why are you asking me that?" I blinked up at my first true friend, taken aback.

His gaze roamed my face for hesitation.

"I offered to take you somewhere far away, where you will be safe. That offer still stands." His throat bobbed, voice serious.

My gaze lingered where I knew his birthmark lay beneath his shirt, my fingers drifting to my own at my sternum. Riven had never spoken of his mark, yet his quiet understanding of my darkness made me wonder what battles he fought alone.

I wanted to be upset, to feel offended or cornered—but all I could feel was how deeply he cared.

"My soul is *tied* to his." I held up my left hand, examining the intricate lines that connected us. "I don't want to run from him."

His lips twitched, a shadow of amusement returned. "You and your idiotic heart."

"Riven—"

"I want you to be happy, but I do not trust *him*."

"Would you trust anyone I wanted to be with?"

Riven huffed a laugh, a quiet, humourless sound. "Probably not. But I am worried about you." He turned then, slowly. Like he was afraid any sudden movement might shatter whatever fragile calm existed in the room. His gaze dragged over me only once, not in desire, but like someone memorizing the face of a person they feared they were going to lose.

"Do you know what happens to a soul that binds itself to darkness?" he asked quietly.

My stomach dropped and I pressed my lips into a thin line.

"It consumes it," he said softly. "Darkness swallows all." Before I could reply, he moved again, coming to sit at the very edge of the bath. Close enough that I could see the tiny flecks of golden light buried in the darker grey of his eyes. The air between us felt charged as he dipped his hand into the water, just his fingertips. The ripples carried across the surface, touching my skin like a whisper.

"You deserve someone *warm*," he said quietly. "Someone that doesn't consume and kill everything."

I blinked at him, heart beating too fast. "He isn't going to kill me, Riven."

"I'm not saying he *wants* to. But creatures like him can't deny their natural instincts for long." He stood abruptly, the moment snapping like a thread.

"I should check that Ronaldo hasn't thrown himself off the balcony."

I laughed weakly, tension breaking just enough for my heartbeat to settle.

Riven paused at the door, hand on the handle, shoulders tight. "I'll be here at every moment. If you change your mind, I can take you away."

The door clicked shut behind him and I pushed myself underwater. The water closed over my head, muting the world to a soft hum of blue and silver. But even beneath the surface, Riven's warning clung to me, repeating in my head. *Darkness swallows all.* I exhaled in a stream of bubbles and resurfaced slowly, air cool against my heated skin.

A sharp knock rattled the door.

"My Lady!" Ronaldo screeched. "Please! We do not have much time."

I sighed, dragging myself from the warm water and wrapping myself in one of the softest towels I had ever felt. The moment I stepped back into my chambers, chaos smothered every thought I had. Riven was nowhere to be seen.

"There you are!" Ronaldo gasped, hands flying dramatically to his chest. "One would think you want to marry him looking like a drowned rodent."

I laughed at his flourished words, his accent dragging over the syllables.

Cerilla gave me a knowing look, eyes softening as she patted one of the chairs where we often had tea.

"Sit, darling." I obeyed and one of the maids dragged the large dressing mirror in front of us. My reflection looked pale and wide-eyed, silver hair damp and curling over my shoulders. Cerilla stood behind me, fingers gentle as she began combing through the wet strands. "You don't have to be afraid."

"I'm not," I lied. The truth was, a small seed of doubt had been planted by Riven, and I wasn't sure if I should let it grow. He had planned to kill me, I still didn't know *why*.

She hummed, unconvinced. "You love him."

"Yes," I whispered.

"And you will always do what's best for him?"

I nodded.

"Then everything will be okay," she said as she smiled at me in the mirror.

Seli rushed forward with a dozen glass bottles. "Hair oils, my lady."

Leena had brushes in both hands. "We'll braid some of it up, let the rest spill over her shoulders. It's so long," she said to Seli.

Cerilla stepped back to let them take over and sat in the chair next to me, pouring us both a cup of tea.

Leena's fingers moved quickly, braiding thin sections of my hair with strands of woven silver thread. Seli massaged sweet-scented oils into the ends. Tamsin dusted shimmering powder along my collarbones.

They worked on me for what felt like forever, pinning

my hair, painting my lips, and pressing powder against my eyelids. The sky bathed in late afternoon gold through the large windows as they worked. My hair glowed like captured moonlight, braided intricately at the crown and falling in shimmering waves down my back. My skin held a soft sheen, my eerie blue eyes bright and sharp. And the Soul Relic crown lay nestled against the braids, making me look like something carved out of a myth.

The maids helped me step into my shimmering silver dress, pulling the boned bodice up into position and tying the ribbons at the back. I gasped at the new detailing Ronaldo had added. The neckline still plunged in a sharp, elegant V, but now it was edged with iridescent shellwork that matched the Soul Relic crown.

Cerilla's eyes met mine in the reflection, her voice soft, almost regretful.

"You look like Maraveth." A chill ran over my skin, and before I could ask how she knew what the goddess looked like, a gentle knock echoed through the room.

Solas cracked the door open only a fraction. His voice was low, reverent. "It's time."

Time. My heart stopped, then surged, beating like a bird trying to take flight. I smoothed my shaky hands over my dress, the material sparkling like spilled starlight as I stepped towards Solas. I knew the seed of doubt would die the moment I was in the Commander's arms again.

FORTY-FOUR
VOWS

My heels clicked against the granite tiles like a countdown I welcomed. Each step echoed like a declaration of love that only he could answer. After all, my broken pieces fit perfectly against his.

Cerilla had left Solas and I to walk to the ceremony alone. She had given me a soft smile that didn't quite reach her eyes and insisted that she needed a moment before meeting us there.

Solas escorted me through halls lined with flickering tea candles, looking far removed from the warrior I had travelled with. He wore a dark green button-down shirt that fitted against the breadth of his chest before tucking neatly into black trousers. His usually wild auburn hair had been scraped into an elegant bun, a single silver band keeping it in place. I had never imagined he could look so formal.

"You look stunning, sweetheart." Heat rose to my cheeks at his wide smile.

"Thank you, Solas. You look..." I trailed off.

"Unsettlingly handsome?" he offered.

"Sure." I shrugged a shoulder and grinned. "For a vicious Fae warrior."

Solas let out a low laugh, rich and unguarded, the sound warming the space between us and making my heart feel light.

"I am so proud of you for making a joke," he said, smiling down at me.

Obsidian Castle seemed endless, as though it took up the entire mountain it was built into. I didn't recognise the hallway we walked through, and it dawned on me that I was going to need a formal tour after all of this. Or perhaps a map. I knew so little about my new home, about Lumireth and its people.

"The ceremony," I blurted, voice thinner than I'd intended. "I assume it's different from Mortal weddings?"

Mortals had vows, rings and a kiss. Everything was simple. Predictable. I knew what was expected of me.

What if I make a fool of myself?

Solas looked down at me with a smile so gentle my worries frayed at the edges. It was like he understood every fear twisting inside me.

"You will love the ceremony," he assured. "The Commander will guide you through every step." He bumped his shoulder lightly against mine.

I tried to let his words settle the frantic storm in my chest. But doubt pricked at the edges of my thoughts like thorns.

The bond thrummed faintly, a distant calling, a pull towards where he waited. Nothing but hope and love bled through the thread that connected us.

We turned a corner, and the corridor opened into another—this one shorter and lined with tall arched windows that allowed moonlight to spill across the floor like liquid silver.

We walked through it and I marvelled at the sheer beauty that dared to exist in such a simple space.

The carved doors at the end of the hallway opened as if sensing our arrival and the sight stole the breath from my lungs.

The ballroom was a wonder of granite and starlight. Half the roof was open to the night air, an enormous carved frame that revealed the night sky in all its glory. Stars glittered overhead, reflected in the polished obsidian floor until it looked like we were suspended between two heavens.

On the far side of the room, floor-to-ceiling glass panels overlooked the sleeping town far below. Thousands of lights flickered across the dark landscape. Soft, distant, shimmering. They looked almost as far away and unreachable as the stars above. Candles hovered mid-air, drifting like glowing petals on the breeze and making silver runes shimmer across the walls. At the centre of the room stood the Commander with his back to me, a candle-lined aisle stretching towards him and opening into a circle of flames that held the crowd at bay.

I ignored the hundreds of onlookers, not wanting to find my father or the priest amongst them.

A string ensemble began to play a soft romantic song that weaved through the air as Solas led me to the beginning of the aisle. But it was the Commander's voice that brought tears to my eyes. He sang, the deep timbre of his voice weaving around the strings in an enchanting pull. It carried through the vast, starlit chamber like a secret the world itself leant in to hear. While I didn't understand the words, it felt like a song made for *me*. Like a melody for the damned.

"Go to him," Solas said as we stood at entrance to the aisle. But I was already moving.

The Commander stood tall in a fitted black suit that looked carved onto his body, the sharp lines of the jacket framing the brutal strength of him. He turned towards me and I lost all breath in my lungs. His black hair had been smoothed back except for a single curl falling loose over his forehead, as if even his appearance refused complete obedience. His clean-shaven jawline was devastatingly sharp without his stubble. But it was his expression, and the emotions flaring through the silver thread between us, that dissolved my last flicker of doubt. I may have agreed to marry him for the sake of Kingdoms, but Gods... my heart had never felt so impossibly full.

His shadows reacted, erupting outward in a ripple before crawling over his legs. Gasps rose from the Fae gathered along the edges of the ballroom. Even the candles flickered, as if his darkness threatened to extinguish all light.

I reached the end of the aisle as his song ended, and he took two slow, measured steps towards me, eyes never leaving mine.

"Lyra," he whispered. Just my name, but the way he said it made my knees weaken and my heart swell behind my ribs.

"You are the most beautiful thing I have ever seen," he said, voice thick with emotion. "It feels like I am drowning every time I look at you. I cannot breathe—and yet I will gladly give up every breath I have to be your husband."

The world swayed around me, narrowing to nothing but *him*. I gathered my shaking breath and took his outstretched hands like a lifeline.

"I won't let you drown," I whispered back to him.

The bond hummed between our touching marks, warm

and steady. His voice dropped to a low rumble meant only for me, "I have been waiting an eternity to see you walk towards me like this."

Shadows caressed his skin without burrowing in and I hoped he had taken enough blood from me earlier to sedate them.

The ceremony circle glowed beneath our feet, soft, silvery light that pulsed like a heartbeat.

Solas, Riven, Caelum and Aldric stepped over the threshold of candles, standing within the circle.

"It is Fae tradition to have those dearest to us in the circle of Amarta," the Commander explained quietly.

He had included Riven and Aldric for me, and my heart swelled with something tender and pure. I had never been surrounded by so much love.

The musicians drifted into silence and the candles stilled.

Cerilla glided down the aisle, her obsidian gown floating behind her, studded with tiny crystals that mirrored the night sky above. Her raven hair was loose around her in perfect curls that bounced as she walked towards us with a serene smile.

She nodded towards Riven as she stopped in front of our joined hands.

"Tonight, we join the Fae and Mortal Kingdoms through marriage to fight against the Seven Hells!" The crowd cheered around us, clapping and yelling out praise. The Commander held both my hands in his as we faced each other.

"A union between two souls requires many things, but as our tradition demands, that is decided by the individual." Cerilla's voice echoed through the hall with an eerie pulse. "Brother, state your vows to your bonded."

The Commander squeezed my hands gently as I stared into his gaze, candlelight fracturing there until it felt like an endless abyss of stars staring back at me.

"I vow to love you, to keep you safe, to give you freedom and to respect you. I give myself to you," the Commander vowed, voice growing thicker with each word. He reached up, brushing away a tear that had slipped down my cheek with his thumb as he leaned close. "You can choose your own," he murmured, "or repeat mine."

"Princess Lyra, give your vows to your bonded," Cerilla's said, voice echoing around us.

My heart lodged in my throat, the butterflies in my stomach making it hard not to move.

"I vow to love you. To trust you. To choose you. And I vow to save you. I give myself to you."

I gasped, eyes widening as a mixture of grief and anger drowned me through the bond.

"Take it back," the Commander hissed, eyes wide and panicked.

"No," I said softly.

"Turn your palms over," Cerilla instructed, moving on with the ceremony despite the Commander's distress.

Cerilla summoned a dagger from thin air and took the Commander's hand from mine. Without hesitation, she sliced her brother's palm open while chanting in the Fae language.

"This blood oath will bind your vows, if they are not upheld, you both will die."

My heart pulsed widely in my chest as I stared at the blue blood welling in his palm.

If I failed to save him, I would die alongside him. I held his gaze, refusing to look away as I raised my chin and let him feel my sheer determination through the bond.

I offered Cerilla my hand and she took it in her sweaty palm. The tip of the blade trembled against the soft skin of my palm before she slowly sliced open my skin. I gritted my teeth but refused to flinch. Instead of pressing my hand to his to seal the bargain, she let the knife linger against my hand for a moment too long, dark eyes shining with tears.

"I am sorry," Cerilla whispered, low enough that only I could hear.

"Cerilla—"

Her hand shot out. Magic slammed into the Commander, tearing him from my grasp as he flew backwards.

Pure panic tore up my spine as I reached for my power —only to find it gone. In its place was a familiar floral scent that overwhelmed my senses.

Forty-Five

Betrayal

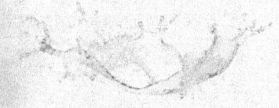

"**I**'m sorry."

Cerilla's words echoed through my head as time seemed to slow.

"Cerilla!" the Commander roared. "What the fuck are you doing?" He thrashed against a cage made of her shimmering magic.

Before I could register what was happening, Cerilla tipped my hand. My blood spilled onto the silver symbol at our feet, and it drank it in as if starved.

A symbol of the *sun*. How had I not noticed that before?

I tried to rip my hand from her grasp, but that overwhelming floral scent was making me weak.

She chanted in a language I didn't understand, the words ancient and bone-chilling.

Power exploded from the symbol in a rippling wave of wrongness.

The bystanders screamed, scattering away like frightened mice. The symbol glowed a deep, hellish red that crawled out across the granite like veins bursting beneath skin.

The Commander's roar shook the ground as shadows exploded outward with each animalistic thrash against the cage. *"No!"* he snarled, slamming himself against the barrier.

Skanthi crawled through the open roof as if summoned by the hellish glow.

Solas ducked and rolled across the ground as one dropped in front of him, rearing on its back spider-like legs.

Caelum threw balls of white power from his hands towards the monsters skittering down the glass walls into the chaos-filled ballroom.

And Riven—

Riven stood still, grinning as if the world wasn't ending in front of him.

Cerilla's magic wrapped around me, locking me in place with the same floral scent that blocked my power. It smelled the same as the bath she had drawn for me.

An ear-splitting scream tore from my throat as betrayal cleaved straight through my heart.

"I had to," she choked out, muscles trembling under the amount of magic she was using. Tears ran down her cheeks. "You were going to die for her!" She screamed at him with her teeth bared. "One day you will thank me."

A sob ripped from my chest as the ground cracked beneath us, splitting me from the Commander. The earth screamed, deep and hungry, as the fissure widened into a void.

The cage around the Commander flickered as he slammed into it, threatening to give way under the force.

Cerilla screamed and dropped the barrier—only to hurl the last of her magic at him, sending him flying backward.

The crack expanded, the ground falling away, crumbling like a stale piece of bread, swallowing everything that got in its way. Monsters and Fae alike fell into the chasm.

The sulphur infused heat that radiated from the cracked earth was unbearable, like a thousand hands clawing at my skin.

The Commander hit the floor, rolling into a fighting stance amidst the chaos.

Solas and Caelum were fighting their way towards him.

The ballroom, once filled with hundreds, was now a graveyard. Most had either fled or been slaughtered. Only warriors remained.

Warriors... or the terminally foolish. Like my brother who had no business fighting.

"Let her go!" the commander roared through the chaos, shaking the ground and my very soul.

Cerilla dropped to her knees with tears streaming down her face and her magic let me go.

Aldric lunged out of nowhere, dagger outstretched, aimed straight for Cerilla's heart. She barely turned, flicking her wrist and sending him flying into the horde of Skanthi that was attacking the Commander.

"Aldric!" I cried out, tears streaming down my face. He wasn't a fighter. But I was.

I clenched my fist, slamming it towards Cerilla's face. But, with one click of her fingers, heavy shackles bound around my wrists.

"I am so sorry, darling," she whispered as I fell to my knees with a broken noise scraping from me, half gasp, half sob.

"You have done well, Cerilla," Riven praised.

My head snapped to him, and I bared my teeth in an ear-piercing scream, thrashing against the shackles.

"Don't look at me like that, princess." Riven pouted down at me. "I gave you the chance to come with me willingly." He crouched in front of me, brushing a stray strand of hair behind my ear as if I were something he loved.

The priest strolled through the chaos, untouched by the monsters as if he were one of them. I stared between my torturer and Riven, trying to connect the pieces.

"Who are you?" My voice trembled.

"Come on, you already know the answer to that." He grinned down at me. "I saw the Commander's journal on your nightstand."

Pure agony tore through my heart, twisting through me and threatening to devour me.

The Commander's journal.

The truth slammed into me with vicious clarity—and fury followed, white-hot and blinding. *It was him.*

He had stood beside me, touched me, sworn himself to me, while knowing exactly what he was.

He was the monster created to kill me.

My chest burned as betrayal ripped through our bond, twisting every memory into something sharp and poisonous.

I wanted to scream. To reach inside my soul and destroy the bond that tethered me to my killer. To make him feel the same pain I was feeling.

And yet—

"Rythos!" I screeched his name like a curse.

"Do not say his name! You are supposed to be *mine!*" Riven yelled down at me, spittle flying from his mouth. "I made him into a *monster,* and you *still* chose him over me!" His fist slammed into the ground, those golden flecks in his eyes blazing with fury.

"Helion," I whispered, voice breaking on a sob.

"I've missed the way you say my name," he smirked at me in a flash of dimples.

My heart didn't break. It stopped. Shuddering like it didn't know which betrayal to die from first.

Cerilla had betrayed us and turned to the fallen Sun God.

Riven was a *lie*.

A trick.

A manipulation.

And the Commander—*Rythos* hadn't told me who he really was.

My breath shuddered out of me as though I had been winded. Riven closed his eyes, features morphing to reveal the real him. He filled out, becoming more muscular. Taller. The build of a god.

It broke my heart that he still looked like Riven.

"Edgar here has watched over you for me. Harvesting your blood for me to slowly resurrect the powers those other fuckers stripped from me. You were different, Lyra. The other versions had never dared to touch the Dead Sea. That's how I found you before my monster could kill you, pet. I kept you weak enough that he couldn't sense you."

My breathing was coming quicker, tears spilling down my cheeks.

He was the one taking my blood.

"Until you fucking Ascended, plunging into my own ritual." Riven chuckled.

I looked down at the symbol below my knees. The same mark worn by the Iron Guard. *His* mark. Ascension hadn't been a plea to estranged Gods. It had been *feeding* the one God who had fallen.

In that single, shattering moment—I understood. I

hadn't escaped my cage that night. I had run straight into the arms of the god who built it for me.

"Don't cry, there will still be a wedding tonight." His voice sounded far away over the roaring in my ears. "Ours. And together, we will take back the Throne of Gods."

Rythos roared from the other side of the ballroom, a primal heart-breaking sound that shook the heavens.

Helion lifted me into his arms, cradling my numb body against his chest. I was so numb. So *broken*.

My head lolled to the side, and through the swarm of monsters, I saw *him* fall to his knees—panic etched into his eyes as they locked on me.

Rythos. My cursed lover. My monster.

Tears spilled down my face as the realization finished its cruel descent. He was dying because he had chosen not to kill me—and that truth hurt almost as much as the lie.

Shadows exploded from him in a storm of pure agony as Rythos screamed my name.

"I love you and I will save you," he vowed to me through the bond, his overwhelming grief pouring into my chest as another Skanthi rushed him.

I shut him out. I slammed the bond closed, cutting him off mid-breath, mid-feeling, and pushed him away as I fought to breathe through the soundless fracture of my heart.

Helion jumped into the gaping hole in the earth with me cradled in his arms, and the world dropped away beneath us.

Wind tore past my ears as the ballroom vanished above, swallowed by suffocating heat as we fell toward the Seven Hells.

I didn't scream. I didn't fight. I simply fell—letting the

broken pieces of my heart sharpen into something dangerous.

I once believed the absence of love created evil.

I was wrong.

It was betrayal.

— THE END —

Dear reader,

Thank you for stepping into the dark with me. I loved every second of brining this story to life and I hope with all my heart that you enjoyed it as much as me.

As a debut author, I appreciate you trusting me with your time and your heart.

If you loved Melodies of the Damned, I have some exciting news for you...

Lyra and Rythos' journey does *not* end here.

This story was always meant to be told in two parts. Melodies of the Damned is the first half of a duology.

The next book will take them deeper into the darkness, expect a villain era for one heartbroken goddess and a lot of grovelling from a certain monster.

There are truths yet to be uncovered, choices yet to be made, and wounds that will either heal or tear everything apart.

If this book unsettled you, made you ache, or left you holding your breath, thank you for letting it. Stories like this ask something of the reader, and I do not take that lightly.

I cannot wait to return to the dark with you.

Yours Sincerely,
Nakita Kirwan

Follow me on Instagram for sneak peaks and behind the scenes content.

@nakita.writes.romantasy

Acknowledgments

I never believed writing a book was something I would actually achieve. This started as a quiet, almost impossible dream. One I was scared to say out loud. There were so many moments I doubted myself, questioned whether I was good enough, or wondered if this story would ever make it beyond my own head. I wanted to take a moment to thank the people who helped me get here.

To my husband, thank you for listening to my endless rambling about plot twists, characters, and scenes that refused to let me sleep. Thank you for giving me the time, space, and quiet belief I needed to bring this story to life, even when it meant sacrificing your own time.

To my beautiful children, thank you for your patience and your love. Thank you for understanding when Mum needed quiet moments, late nights, or time alone with her words. You are the reason I push myself to chase dreams I once thought were out of reach.

To my parents, thank you for your constant support and for stepping in whenever I needed help. Your belief in me made this possible, and I will never take that for granted.

To my work family, thank you for every kind word, every check in, and every moment of encouragement. You reminded me that this dream mattered, even on the days it felt too fragile to hold.

Thank you for helping me believe I could do this.

Love always,
Nakita Kirwan.